Daughter of Redwinter

Daughter of Redwinter

ED McDONALD

A TOM DOHERTY ASSOCIATES BOOK

NEW YORK

This is a work of fiction. All of the characters, organizations, and events portrayed in this novel are either products of the author's imagination or are used fictitiously.

DAUGHTER OF REDWINTER

A Tor Book
Published by Tom Doherty Associates
120 Broadway
New York, NY 10271

www.tor-forge.com

Tor® is a registered trademark of Macmillan Publishing Group, LLC.

Library of Congress Cataloging-in-Publication Data

Names: McDonald, Ed (Fantasy fiction author), author.
Title: Daughter of Redwinter / Ed McDonald.
Description: First Edition. | New York : Tor, a Tom Doherty Associates Book, 2022. |
Series: The Redwinter Chronicles ; 1
Identifiers: LCCN 2022008027 (print) | LCCN 2022008028 (ebook) |
ISBN 9781250811714 (hardcover) | ISBN 9781250811738 (ebook)
Classification: LCC PR6113.C3778 D38 2022 (print) | LCC PR6113.C3778 (ebook) |
DDC 823/.92—dc23
LC record available at https://lccn.loc.gov/2022008027
LC ebook record available at https://lccn.loc.gov/2022008028

Our books may be purchased in bulk for promotional, educational, or business use. Please contact your local bookseller or the Macmillan Corporate and Premium Sales Department at 1-800-221-7945, extension 5442, or by email at MacmillanSpecialMarkets@macmillan.com.

First Edition: 2022

Printed in the United States of America

0 9 8 7 6 5 4 3 2 1

This book is for Alfred Wolfe Thomas Morgan.

Daughter of Redwinter

The stories of this age begin and end with blood, and mine is no exception.

I went still when I saw it. Stark, bright spots of poppy-red trailed across the snow, leading upwards between the pines. Dark voids fell away through the pure white glare, where blood's heat had cut into the banks.

I saw her curled beneath a tree, the snow around her stained bright as summer flowers. A woman. She was young and ragged. Bloody. Unmoving.

I knelt and scanned between the trees. Checked the ground for churned snow. Bear tracks or bootprints. It all seemed quiet. Just a body, and the bloody trail.

Dead? It was hard to say. Maybe.

No sign of a lingering soul between the trees, no bitter ghost of the unhappy dead. They were often around us, silent, unknown. Silent to everyone else, at least. They passed by the living, their presence felt as little more than the rise of hairs on a neck, or the momentary, unplaceable feeling of something lost, or forgotten. Nothing but echoes of the past. If the woman in the snow had breathed her last, her ghost had already moved on.

She wasn't my concern, and time was not on my side. We'd fled to Dalnesse, once a proud fortification that had sheltered monks from the hardships of the world, now barely more than an echo of its former grandeur. We'd fled here because it had walls, and walls count for a lot when a lord takes it upon himself to slaughter you. But once our safe haven was surrounded, it had become a cage. Opening the doors would invite in malice, and blades, and the end. So when I found the river tunnel beneath the crypts, saw the light of day beyond the tunnel mouth, I had allowed myself a flicker of hope.

I had not expected to find friends out here in the snow.

Whoever this was, or had been, she was neither friend nor salvation to me. And yet seeing her fallen body set that little flame fluttering. She had climbed up here, which meant that, spirits willing, we could climb down. There was a way off this cursed rock. We might yet get out of this alive.

Someone—or something—had got her pretty good, judging by all that blood. Another reason to get us out of here. I should leave her and follow her trail. Track it down off the mountain.

That's what I ought to do.

Ah, damn it.

I crept towards her, snow crunching softly beneath my frozen, leaking boots. The cobbler had sworn they were winter-proof. You can never trust a cobbler. Anyone who spends that long thinking about feet has something wrong with them. I kept an arrow nocked on the string. If this was some kind of trap, then it was an elaborate one. No one should be up here, not even if they were just crawling up the mountain to die.

The slope was steep, the trees ahead sparse. Mountain pine, a scattering of stark-branched shrubs. I looked for plumes of steam, the breath of men hiding in the still morning. Nothing. Not a sound, save for the call of mountain blue-birds, the occasional rustle of snow dropping from a branch. I put no tension on the bowstring, moving fast, tree to tree. No point exposing myself here.

I crossed the last distance and knelt beside her. Not much older than me. Dark haired, her complexion too dark for the highlands. Her threadbare, tattered clothes were better suited to city living than a hike in the wild, and better than I'd ever worn, that's for sure. A few embossed buttons clung to the edge of her coat, the silver slicked red. No ghost lingered over her, or wandered the trees, but that didn't mean much. Only the unhappiest dead appeared to me. I'd seen ghosts bound by bitterness, chained with ropes of remorse, caught in nets of grief. But most of the time, dead was just dead.

'I'm sorry you're dead,' I said into the cold. Just a whisper of frosted breath in the stillness of the mountain's mantle.

She was probably dead. She looked dead. I felt a pang of guilt as I eyed her buttons. The coat was ruined, but the silver would sell. It was a sour thought, but Light Above, Braithe and I needed the money. We all would, if I could find a mountain trail to carry us from Dalnesse. Money to feed us, to hide us from a cold heart's fury. But before I went cutting off a dead woman's buttons, I had to make sure she was actually dead. I took my arrow from the string, jabbed it down into a foot of snow and reached to check for a pulse.

Her eyes flared open and her hands shot out, wrapping my throat. She stared without recognition, confused and angry as her lips curled back in a snarl. I jerked away but she was strong, cold fingers choking me. I thrashed backwards, once, twice, couldn't break her grip. There was no air. No air! I fumbled at my belt, and then my dirk was in my hand and I drew it across her forearm. The not-dead woman gasped and I snapped free. I kicked back, the light snow flying as I fell, rolled clumsily, head over heel.

She struggled to rise, the pain across her face mirroring the snow across mine.

'Hold it,' I panted, brandishing the blade in front of me. 'Just hold it there.'

Blood pounded through me, but relief fed my bones. I hadn't wanted her to be dead. I didn't have to cut off her buttons now.

The woman's eyes were unfocused as she pushed herself back against the tree trunk. Not much older than me, and just as frightened. I'd told myself that if I came across one of Clan LacCulloch's clan riders, I'd be able to do it. Able to put an arrow into an enemy. But this girl wasn't one of his men. She'd no clan colours on her at all, and her coat was made for summer days in summer towns. A southern girl lost in the northern fall. She blinked, tried to focus, appraising me as I had her.

'I have to keep going,' she said. Her voice was hoarse, weak, and she pressed her hand against the shallow slice in her arm. Red drips in the snow. But there was already a lot of blood on her coat, and none of it my doing.

'You don't look like you're going anywhere fast,' I said, still holding my knife. 'You aren't with LacCulloch.'

'No,' she said. Too much weight in that one word. 'I have to get to the monastery.'

The burst of panic had faded. In the moment, she'd seemed wild and terrible, but as my heart slowed and my breathing calmed, I saw how ragged she was, how thinly worn. Red-tinged eyes over gaunt cheeks. She was twenty, twenty-two at a push and she didn't belong here, up in the mountains where we were fighting to stay alive while others were fighting to kill us. None of us did. I gathered up my bow and arrow. I didn't trust her.

'Dalnesse is under siege,' I said. 'Niven LacCulloch's men have blocked the mountain road. Guess you know that already, seeing as you're trying to get in the back way.'

'I have to keep moving or he'll catch me,' the woman said. She shivered. Her fingers were bolts of white marble against the blood oozing from her forearm. 'Please. Which way is Dalnesse?'

Nobody in their right mind wanted to go to Dalnesse. Monastic absolution houses were literally the most miserable places in the world, and I never saw the appeal of a religion that tells you that you're inadequate all the time. But Dalnesse was even worse, since the monks had all buggered off years ago, and the people inside—my people—were beginning to starve.

'It's that way,' I said, jabbing a thumb over my shoulder at my footprints. 'Who hurt you?'

'Men who want to stop me,' she said. She was sweating despite the cold.

'Where are they now?'

'Think I lost them.' She spoke in a desperate, pleading whisper. 'I have to get to Dalnesse.'

Thrice-damned Dalnesse. We'd been stuck for over a week now. It wasn't Braithe's fault. He only had forty grown men and women, and fewer than half were capable fighters, while Niven LacCulloch had brought nearly one hundred mail-clad warriors. We were caught now, behind Dalnesse's walls, our backs to the mountain. If Braithe's cousins didn't show up soon with a whole lot of swords, then we were in trouble. All the walls in the world weren't going to feed us.

I'd reasoned that not even monks would pen themselves up against a mountain without a back way in, but I'd only found the underground stream, and the tunnel that had let me out onto the mountainside, by following the ghost of an old monk. He'd probably been dead for a few hundred years or more, but that's what the dead do: repeat, repeat, and endlessly repeat. Echoes of their lost lives.

'You need to get that arm wrapped up,' I said. 'You're not going to make it much further.'

'I don't have a choice,' she said. She forced herself up from the snow and began to stagger in the direction I'd pointed, boots even less suitable than mine sinking into the snow.

'Wait,' I said.

My plan had been a simple one. The iron grille that had blocked the stream tunnel had been rusted, easily kicked free. If I could find a safe path down the mountainside, maybe we could all slip away through the tunnel, onto the mountainside. We'd have a chance to get out of Dalnesse, avoid LacCulloch and his men in the night. Some of the sooth-sisters and their followers were probably a bit too old for a daring nighttime escape, but desperation was leading me now. I wasn't supposed to be out here, and Braithe would be angry when he couldn't find me. Strange that sometimes I feared his reaction as much as I feared LacCulloch's swords.

The woman stumbled in the snow, leaving a stark red handprint sunk below her as she pushed herself back up. If I followed my plan, I'd be leaving her here to die. My mother may have been a bitter old soul, but for all her spite, she'd not raised her girl to leave people to freeze to death in the snow. Shit. I couldn't take her with me down the mountain, and I couldn't abandon her to die here either.

I pulled her good arm up over my shoulders. She was made of sticks, like she hadn't eaten in weeks, weighed about as much as a rabbit.

'I'm Raine,' I said as I dragged her along. It was less than an hour back to Dalnesse. I could get her into the sooth-sisters' care and be back on my way before midday. Probably best to avoid any questions about where I'd been. If

Braithe knew what I was planning, he'd stop me. He loved me too much to let me go.

. . . . . .

The bloody young woman grimaced. Her strength was a shallow pool, drained by exhaustion and blood loss, and after an hour's struggle through the snow we'd managed less than half the distance I could have traversed alone. The cut on her arm had stopped bleeding, but there was fresh blood on her coat. Every step drew an animal grunt of pain from her cold-hardened lips.

'I'm Hazia,' she said. It seemed to cost her a lot. Somehow, she didn't sound certain.

'Why are you trying to get into Dalnesse, Hazia?' I asked. She didn't reply. 'It's one of the worst places I've ever been to, and I've seen some shitty places.' I didn't expect an answer.

'Have to take it back there,' she muttered.

'This is an awful lot of effort to make a delivery,' I said. 'Watch out for the log. Right in front of you. Big step over. That's it.'

'Nothing else matters,' she said. Pain cobwebbed through her voice.

'Maybe focus on staying alive first, and delivering things second,' I said, since she visibly had nothing of value on her. No bag, no purse, not even a knife on her belt. Not even a belt. Nothing to deliver. 'Not too far to the bridge now. We're going to have to take that slow and careful.'

'Need to hurry,' Hazia said. 'I can hear him. Like drums, through the hills. He's coming.'

'Drums?'

'Yes. Drums. He's coming.'

Delirium must have been setting in. Wounds and cold twined together into ropes of uncertainty in her mind . . . but someone other than me had put that blood on her coat. Only then, as I dragged her onwards, I heard them. Distant, to the east.

Dhum, dhum, dhum.

Dhum, dhum, dhum.

A soft, gentle sound, the rhythm perfect and steady. I felt it as much as I heard it, like a painless headache, a pulsing that rose gently at the edges of my mind. I shook my head to clear it, but the three beats replayed themselves, one-two-three, one-two-three, over and over. Hazia whimpered as I forced a harder pace, following my own trail of footprints.

A sound on the slope below us made me stop, pulling Hazia down behind the wide trunk of a pine before a man on a huge black horse rode slowly through the trees. He was the biggest man I'd ever seen. Not tall, but wide, filling his oxblood-red coat as though it were inflated with hot air. His hair was tawny, his face didn't need to see a razor very often, and he wore eyeglasses. Expensive ones, with brass rims. He wore mail beneath his coat, and there was a five-foot longsword on his saddle, but I knew a lot of tough men, and he didn't have their cast. That size spoke more of bread than brawn.

'He's the one that's after you?' I said.

Hazia nodded, her voice a whisper of wind. 'One of them. But not the one to be afraid of.'

I settled an arrow on the bowstring and kept sight of the young rider. He wasn't exactly scanning the trees, only half-focused on what he was doing, and he looked soft beneath his armour. Though I kept some rough company, I'd never killed a man, and I didn't think I would be able to start with this one. At seventeen, I was a woman grown, and men treated me like one when it suited them. But though he had to be around my age, the man on the black horse seemed more boy than man to me. I lessened the tension in the string.

'Wait here,' I whispered. 'Maybe he'll ride by. If he had your trail, he's clearly lost it. We can cut along the high ridge there. He shouldn't see us unless he turns north.'

Hazia winced, shifting against the tree as she put a hand beneath her coat. Her fingers came away licked with red.

'He's no threat,' she said. 'Listen for the drums.'

They were still there, off to the east. Faint, but steady. *Dhum, dhum, dhum. Dhum, dhum, dhum.* Repeating, over and over. I felt my eyes close and opened them again with a jerk, suddenly aware that time had passed. How long, I didn't know. Like I'd just woken from sleep. This, all of this, felt wrong to me. Hazia's eyes were closed, exhaustion taking her. I tapped her cheek twice and her eyes opened blearily. At least she didn't try to strangle me this time.

'Hey,' I said. 'Come on. Stay awake. Can't let you pass out and die out here, can I?'

I could have. My mother would have said that the weak deserve what they get, and then hated herself for saying it. She'd hated a lot of things, including me, which hardly seemed fair, but she'd seldom demanded fairness except for herself. What would Braithe have done? I supposed he would have helped Hazia too. I hoped he would. He was a hard man, but he did his best. That's why I loved him. If not for him, those poor soothsaying sisters would have been severed heads on LacCulloch's castle walls by now.

Hazia winced as she struggled to rise. I hadn't looked at the wound beneath her coat. I was no surgeon and couldn't have helped her out here even if I was. Sometimes it's better not to know how bad it is.

A sound made us both freeze. The fat young man was back, a good hundred yards away, retracing his steps, but that wasn't what had taken my attention. Another sound was emanating from him, like the distant drums, but instead of a steady, constant rhythm, it was more akin to a drunk child beating a spoon against a saucepan. Hazia grabbed my jaw and turned my face to hers as she pressed her finger to her lips. Her eyes were near rolling with fear and she held me until the young man and his clattering racket had gone on their way.

'What was that?' I asked.

'You heard it too?' Hazia said.

I nodded.

'That's not normal.'

'None of this is normal,' I said. 'But if I don't get you somewhere warm in the next hour, you probably aren't ever getting warm again.'

Hazia grunted with pain as I dragged her up.

'What do they want with you?' I asked.

'Trying to stop me,' she whispered. 'No talk. Just walk.'

Dragging a person is hard work, and dragging them through snow is worse. My feet were numb and heavy and I started dreaming up painful deaths for the cobbler who'd sold me my now entirely sodden, freezing boots. I hated snow. The monks who'd decided to live up here may have enjoyed plenty of clear mountain air and a big open sky, but snow is like springtime dancing: idiots think that it's fun, and everyone with any sense avoids it.

'Not far to the bridge now. Dalnesse is less than half a mile beyond it,' I said. Hazia walked with her eyes closed, trusting me to guide her feet. My teeth were gritted against the cold. Not so much further. There wasn't much to eat in Dalnesse, but there were warm fires and kettles of tea. And company. I should never have set out on my own. I'd thought I was being clever, thought I was going to impress everyone, maybe even save us.

A deep, male voice bellowed on the wind.

'Hazia!'

Another rider, his horse black and monstrous beneath him, emerged on our trail. He was thick and broad as the pines, his oxblood-red leather coat hanging over green-and-black breacan trousers. Iron rings protruded from the ends of his sleeves. A slate-grey beard framed a wide face, the morning sun shining from his scalp.

Dhum-dhum-dhum, dhum-dhum-dhum.

The vast black charger stalked through the trees, its rider's eyes filled with deadly intent. His sword was alive and gleaming in his hand, the steel silver-blue in the dappled light.

'Hazia!' he bellowed again. Snow dust shivered from the pines.

'Run,' she whispered. But it was too late for running. The warrior drove his heels into his mount's sides, and the glossy beast kicked forwards snow erupting around its hooves.

You can't outrun a horse. Panic cycloned in my gut as Hazia staggered ahead of me. Our options flitted through my mind, instinct pulling my thoughts one way, reason another, fear a third until they solidified into something that resembled a plan.

I put an arrow to the string.

When you learn to shoot, you become one with the bow. You reach out to make it an extension of you, drive your essence through the grain of the wood so that arm, stave and spirit are one. Woman and weapon together, a mystic dance of precision and poise.

Not really. You just pull the string back, point it and let go. The less you think, the more likely you are to send it where you want.

I loosed. The string slapped against my bracer as the arrow took flight. The horse screamed in pain as the shaft hammered into its chest, its pounding advance ending as its forelegs collapsed beneath it and the rider pitched headfirst into the snow. Poor horse. With luck, the rider had broken his neck in the fall. That would have been something.

No luck. He surged from the snow in a cloud of white, the drum-beat thundering louder in my mind.

'Kill him!' Hazia yelled back at me. 'Kill him before he takes your mind!'

There was a savage determination on the fallen rider's wide, round face. One cheek was grazed and bloody, but he still had a grip on his sword and he came on, ignoring the dying horse behind him. His murderous intent was clear, his shoulders working up and down. The drums grew louder, louder, *dhum-dhum-dhum, dhum-dhum-dhum*. I was taller, but I couldn't outrun him and help Hazia. She'd fallen down a short way on, staring back with terrified eyes.

'Drop the bow, girl,' the old man bellowed. He favoured one leg, the barest twitch of an eye and the clench of his teeth telling me he hadn't fallen well. 'You don't know what you're dealing with. I will kill you if I have to.'

'I'll only warn you once,' I shouted. 'I will shoot you.'

It was true. It had to be true. I could do it. I had to be able to do it.

'No,' he growled. 'You won't.'

He was stocky, built like an ox, and he made an easy target, floundering through the snow. I'd given a warning. Couldn't ask much more than that. My second arrow was for him.

Braithe would be proud of me. He always said I was too soft. That the world was hard and I needed to harden myself to match. Not all lives were precious. That's what he said.

Draw, settle, breathe out, release. Snap of string against bracer. The arrow flew.

The warrior struck out and caught it.

He caught it. My damn arrow.

And then he was limping towards me, tossing the cracked shaft aside, staggering as he blundered into a snow drift. I'd thought fast, I'd acted fast. Now I just stared at him.

He'd caught my damn arrow.

I turned and fled onwards, dragging Hazia's arm across my shoulder. Whoever or whatever he was, Hazia's enemy was now mine and I was damned if I was going to let him catch me. I got to see enough ghosts without becoming one myself. He sure as damnation shouldn't have been catching my arrows. The bow had an eighty-pound draw. It wasn't possible.

I dragged her, dodging beneath the pines where the snow was lightest, glancing back to see him struggling behind us, limping and getting bogged down like he'd never seen snow before in his life. Didn't know how to find the easy footing. Even dragging Hazia, half-blind and mumbling to herself, we began to pull ahead. I tried to look everywhere at once, vision roaming between the trees. Where was the second rider, the young one with the child-and-pan clatter about him? He couldn't be ahead of us. He couldn't. I pushed the girl to move faster. Hazia gasped in pain, but pain is fleeting and dying is forever. No resting now.

This way, a whisper seemed to ride on the breeze. Calling me on. Louder than the tapping of the drums. Desperate hope giving rise to imagination.

I dragged us up a bank, turned and looked back. He was a good way behind us now, foundering in deep snow. Maybe he'd got lucky with that catch? Maybe the part of me that was telling me to run and run and never stop running was wrong. I drew a shaft, knocked it. Another chance. This time it would—

He locked eyes with me and made an angry swipe of his hand. The snow around him evaporated in a cloud of steam, a boiling cloud obscuring him from view. I lost my target, I lost control of my jaw, and then the snow between us melted away, mud, stones and sheltering plants revealed as the air grew hot and wet, winter blossoming into summer. The warrior surged through the new-formed mist, splashing through wet mud as he closed the distance.

Run, that whisper ghosted into my mind. *You cannot fight him yet.*

Whoever or whatever he was, all thought of shooting him died at that moment. His sword gleamed with morning fire, reflected across his broad, mastiff face. He was a charging bull, and no arrow was going to stop him. I fled, felt him closing the gap behind us as snow hissed and boiled away to nothing, clearing his path.

The trees ended and we staggered to a halt, lungs heaving, drawing up on the edge of the canyon. The mountain river flowed below, a twenty-foot drop to fast-flowing water which frothed across blade-edged rocks. The bridge ahead was old, and rotten in parts, but the monks had made it to last.

A woman from another time stood on the far side of the river. Her form rippled like a mirage, trailing vapours in a wind I didn't feel. A heavy fur-lined cloak sat over a royal-blue dress, raven-dark hair falling to the small of her back. Feathers formed a wreath above her ears, and streaks of battle paint crossed her cheeks and eyes. A queen from a bygone age, a ghost. A useless ghost. She couldn't help us.

'Please,' Hazia breathed. 'Have to get to Dalnesse.'

'You will,' I said and pushed her forwards. 'You go first.' The bridge creaked beneath her, rotten planks groaning. It was only forty feet to the far bank, and her strength seemed to flow out of her as she got halfway. Planks creaked, and one cracked beneath me, but I slowly made it to Hazia and pulled her across.

The ghostly queen's eyes seemed to track me, though the dead did not see the living, the living did not see the dead. That was how it always was. Her face was narrow, her eyes deep-set and hard as the ice beneath feet that drifted off into mist. But she smiled, a feral curl of her lip.

The warrior was panting as he drew towards the far end of the bridge. Blood ran down his right leg.

'Keep back!' I yelled, but I didn't even have an arrow ready. My heart hammered in my chest.

'It's over,' he called in a deep voice that spoke of a life far from here. 'Hazia. Stay there. Let me end this.' He held out an open hand. Almost a gesture of friendship. 'Hazia. Please.'

'No,' she said from the far bank. 'Let me go. I have to finish it.'

'Run, Raine. They shall not catch you. Not today,' the feather-crowned queen said, and the last of my reserves blew away like dandelion breath with my sudden rush of fear. She was calm as snowfall; vapours rose from her shoulders, twisting on unmoving air. She had spoken my name. It was impossible. I sank to my knees. People didn't see the dead. The dead did not see people. They were only ever echoes of the past, blind and broken shadows of what had been.

Only she had called me by name . . .

The big warrior stepped onto the bridge, the wood groaning beneath his armoured weight, but he advanced anyway, one steady pace after another.

'Do not fear. This is not the end,' the ghost queen said. 'I will not let him hurt you, Raine. This is only our beginning.' She smiled. A warm, ghostly smile. And then she uttered a word. A word that was a tangle of three different equations, all identical and all giving different answers, an impossible word that was the things that only the glaciers know, a word that was never spoken but always heard, that was ancient and new and *powerful*. And for a moment, I thought I saw the shadow of raven-feathered wings spreading behind her.

Wood splintered. The bridge in front of the warrior groaned, and then the long beams shattered, as though a giant had grasped them in his hands and twisted. Supporting beams that had been laid long years ago buckled, and with a vast crash the whole bridge gave way. The mail-clad warrior and his oxblood coat disappeared into seething, vicious water below in a swirl of sharp debris, the current sweeping it all away to dash against the rocks.

The ghost queen was gone. She left no plumed breath on the wind, no tracks in the snow. It was as if she had never been there at all, and perhaps she hadn't been. Her stark white eyes amid the face paint, the flicker of corvid wings at her back, even her rich voice already seemed a distant memory. Though the twisted, broken spars of the bridge were very real.

It shouldn't have been possible to shiver more than I already was, but my body insisted. I shook it off. Blinked back the betrayal of my eyes. I had no time for wondering, no time to examine my own senses. I was needed.

Hazia was facedown in the snow. The man who'd been trying to kill us was nowhere to be seen.

I stared down into the foam-crested waters, expecting to see a hand burst from the wreckage as it was swept away, hoping to see a body. But there was nothing, no more sign that there had been a man there than there was evidence of a lady wreathed in feathers.

I looked around for her again. It seemed impossible that she had destroyed the bridge, that she had spoken to me. Called me *by name*. A ghost was nothing but an echo, a confused, misplaced portrait of the person that was. Her words were tangling in my head, in the pumping fire of the battle-rush. It was all wrong. Nothing made sense.

I looked down at the crumpled woman. I'd brought Hazia this far, and she still needed help. She was semi-lucid, speaking nonsense about books, and the darkness, and fire and a black well. Nonsense talk on the edge of consciousness. If we didn't hurry, her babbling was sure to end altogether. I didn't know this woman, didn't owe her anything, but she was hurt, and she was alone, and that's enough to make someone deserving of your help.

It wasn't all that far to the hidden back entrance to Dalnesse, but Hazia was barely able to stagger, tripping and falling constantly. Fresh blood wetted her coat as whatever wound lay beneath it tore open.

'Come on, just a little further,' I said. 'Haven't dragged you all this way for nothing. You might as well live until tomorrow, given all the trouble you've put me to.'

We were twenty feet from the stream that cut a tunnel into the rock face when she went down again and wouldn't get up. I rolled her over. Still breathing, just worn through. This time, slaps didn't get her moving, and my strength was spent. No choice but to leave her there. I'd left a cadanum lamp inside the tunnel when I left. A few flicks of the mechanism got the little chunk of blue-grey metal inside it glowing. As the tunnel lit up before me, I cast a glance back towards what had once been a bridge, and my hope of escape, and felt that last chance tumble down into the crevasse below to be swallowed with Hazia's pursuer. There was no way out now.

Light Above, had I saved one soul only to damn us all to LacCulloch's spears?

One thing at a time.

I splashed into the calf-deep stream, slipping on uneven stones, past the broken grille, and on into the crypts. The monks had buried their dead down here, but we'd been using it to keep our last few barrels of ale cold. The tunnels extended a fair way, further than anyone was interested in going, and some of them were flooded where springs and streams had forced their way through stone. Dalnesse was old, predating the Succession Age, raised and burrowed out in a time that predated the Hallenaen War, perhaps even the Yanni Dominion. There were many places like that across Dunan, our shoes falling in the tread of once-mighty empires. They all came to the same end, though: dark, faded and flooded. My feet were wet, my legs were wet, and my cheeks must have been rosy with the cold.

The monastery of Dalnesse must have been a busy place in its heyday. The large absolution house which held the sept and the crypts was one of only a dozen granite buildings set behind the defensive perimeter wall. For all that the monks believed the Light Above was going to come and save them all, provided they said enough bad things about themselves, they seemed to have placed a great deal of faith in erecting battlements too, to ensure that brigands or feckless highborn thails didn't decide the gold-loving monks would be better off living a life of pious poverty. That had worked out just as well for me, Braithe, the three sooth-sisters who formed the centre of the troop, and their forty or so followers, who were probably regretting their life choices right about now.

Braithe wasn't going to be pleased with me, and I feared that, but there was no helping it. I found Lochlan and told him what I needed. He went off to find it with an open mouth and overly bright eyes. Poor Lochlan. He was sixteen, a year younger than me, and he was a sweet boy. Everyone had a different reason for following the sisters, but I didn't know what had possessed him to leave what had seemed like a pretty good gig on the farm to travel with us misfits. I'd hated living under my mother's heels in a dank, wet scribing house, and I regretted not one of the four years I'd spent on the road with the sisters and their people. It seemed less important to me to be part of a friendly community than to believe in singing the colours. But Lochlan had shed tears as he bid his parents and at least a dozen siblings farewell, in a bright, sunny valley filled with golden corn. It hadn't really mattered to me whether what the sisters said was true or not. They'd offered me a way out, and I'd had a bag packed and was out the door before my mother even knew I was gone.

I pushed the memories away as I waited, trying to suppress them like the ghosts I ignored. She had fed me, clothed me, given me what passed for an education in the thaildom of Dornoch. Even if she hadn't loved me the way other mothers loved their daughters, I'd still thrown all of that back in her face the day I walked on out. Perhaps she was on my mind now, brittle, with her old-thatch-coloured hair, because I'd absconded again. Perhaps, all the time I'd been looking for a way down the mountain for my new family, a quiet voice at the back of my mind had been telling me: Run.

I had not run. I had come back, and I had helped a woman in need. I was none of the things my mother had bitterly said I was.

Lochlan returned with a wide plank of wood and one of the big dumb miners who'd joined us the year before. I took them to Hazia, and together they loaded her onto the plank and did the hard work of carrying her inside.

'Who is she?' Lochlan wanted to know.

'I don't know,' I said. 'She needed help.'

Lochlan winced as a splinter bit into his hand, but he didn't complain. He was a good kid, really. Like the brothers and sisters he'd left behind, his hair was yellow as the corn. Judging by where we'd all ended up, he should probably have stayed there. Hazia should probably have stayed wherever she'd run from too. There was a fairly high chance that we were all going to die, or find ourselves chained and indentured.

'No parley this morning?' I asked.

'There's nothing much to say,' Lochlan said. 'LacCulloch's still camped down there, and he's not going anywhere.'

'You'd think he'd be bored by now,' I said. Saying the words gave them solidity, as though they might be true.

The two men with the plank negotiated the bend in the stairs that led up, out of the catacombs and towards the light.

'LacCulloch thinks Sister Marthella is grave-touched,' Lochlan said sadly. 'So he's not going to stop until he has them. Or until he's made to go away.' For a moment his eyes shone with fervent zealotry. 'But we'll stand and fight. They showed us the way, didn't they?'

'Aye,' the big dumb man agreed. He, like Lochlan, wore one of the many-coloured tabards the sisters knitted. They'd abandoned their breacan, their clan colours, in favour of a riot of mismatched hues. They wore them in the morning when the sisters led them in meditation, when they danced the colour dance, and when the sisters were reading their futures in the ashes of a fire or the lines of their veins. It hadn't occurred to any of them that despite the three sisters' supposed power, they hadn't foreseen our being forced to flee from a town in the middle of a night, chased into the mountains and besieged in a monastery so on the verge of collapse that not even monks wanted to live in it.

It wasn't fair to blame the sisters. It was my words that had brought us here. Careless, ghost-ridden words. I thought that I'd been helping. Just once, I thought I'd offered something others could use.

There were barely fifty of us in total, hiding behind the monastery's stone walls. Half a dozen men and women were up on the wall, their hunting bows resting against the battlements. We didn't think LacCulloch would try to attack us directly. He had overestimated our fighting potential, but Braithe had us ready for it if he did. At least, that's what we told ourselves. If he did try to attack us, then some of his men would be hurt, and possibly killed. He had us like rats in a trap. The stream tunnel could have changed that, even if only for the young and the hardy. But the feather-mantled woman had torn the bridge asunder and taken even that chance from us.

It was my fault. Sister Marthella had shared my unwise words. And now the bridge was gone because I had tried to help Hazia, who was not one of us, not a burden our buckling backs should have had to bear. But what else was I to have done? A sob was brewing down in some deep, wet, crooked place inside me. I swallowed it down, just as I swallowed the rest. I had to be strong for Braithe. Had to be his right-hand woman. Had to make him proud.

Lochlan delivered Hazia to Sister Marthella. She was a wrinkled old thing, sunbaked and white haired, lodged in one of the old monkish cells. She had no teeth, but she once told me she'd pulled them out to aid in her augury casting, and they rattled on a string around her neck. She hustled the young men from the room.

'Cut away her clothes,' the sooth-sister said. 'Let's see how bad it is.'

'Will she live?' I asked.

'I'd have to cast some proper guts and bones to know that, dear child,' she said. 'And I think if I spend the time to do so, I might as well use hers. She's very weak. Where did she come from?'

'I don't know.'

'How did she get in?'

'Not sure of that either,' I said. Better to avoid those questions until I'd spoken to Braithe.

'If she can get in, we can get out,' Sister Marthella said slyly.

'Maybe. Let's make her better so she can tell us. Please.'

Marthella summoned her sisters as I laid Hazia out on a trestle table, one of the ones they usually set up at summer fairs. I drew a knife along the seams of her clothing, rags so torn and damaged that I hardly seemed to be cutting anything at all. I sliced through the last of the fabric and pulled her coat away. A yellowed piece of paper covered in rows of red-and-black script covered the wound. I lifted it carefully away, but it hadn't stuck to it, hadn't even soaked up her blood. I put it to one side, and though I'd seen a few gruesome injuries before, even I had to wince.

'This is very bad,' Sister Marthella said. Her sooth-sisters murmured their agreement. 'The wound was made with a blade. A knife, a sword, perhaps a glancing blow across the ribs from a spear. But it has torn open further.' She leaned in and sniffed at the red-and-black mess, wiped her brow with the back of a hand. 'Her colours are weak. I fear your efforts may have been in vain.'

'Just do what you can,' I said. I had no authority to command them, not truly, but I was Braithe's woman. That had started to count for more in recent days. I was not surprised when they nodded quiet agreement, but perhaps they were just nodding to themselves. I'd had my reasons to join up with these travelling fortune-tellers, and they'd welcomed me along though they had little need of me. They had been a way out from beneath my mother's skirts, an escape from a life she had always told me was beneath her, and there was something magical in the portents and omens they read in soup and bone. And of course, there had been Braithe. Strong, handsome, commanding, and his eyes had slipped on me the first time he saw me. I would have followed those eyes anywhere.

But what did I know back then, thirteen years old and pining for a man twice my age? He didn't touch me until this last year, and I was the one who had opened that door. The frustrations of my young teenage years had only blossomed into admiration that he had waited for me to grow up. He had made me promises, and he had kept them. I loved him all the more for that.

I picked up the odd sheet of paper. I'd learned my letters early, the one thing my mother had done for me. And yet, I had no idea what the writing was. It wasn't Harran. It wasn't Kwendish or Iska either. The letters were laid out on faint lines, but as I looked they seemed to be drifting off into the distance, and a wave of nausea hit me. I glanced away and they were back where they should have been.

The paper was old, yellowed, but surprisingly clean. Lying atop the dreadful mess of Hazia's ribs, it should have been soaked through with blood. Some kind of wax or oil that made it resistant to water? I tried dripping a couple of drops from a clay cup, and it ran right off, like it was made of glass.

'Hm!' I exclaimed, rather impressed by my discovery.

'Very bad, very bad indeed,' the sisters crowed together. One threw piles of fragrant herbs onto a brazier while another lit incense sticks, but one of them was mixing a salve. That wound was going to turn green with infection without toadbell, or the paste they made out of those slugs in the northern reaches. Rhinar horn was said to clean a wound too, but Braithe had laughed at that and told me it was a myth. Her injuries looked so hopeless I was glad I hadn't looked at them before I brought her here. Dragging Hazia through all that snow had left a stiff ache in my arms and thighs, and if I'd seen just what shape she was in, perhaps I would have been weak. Perhaps I would have left her there, to bleed and freeze and die alone.

If I had, we would still have the bridge. Would still have some hope. The world seemed washed with grey, little distortions eating away at the possibilities of the future, like beads of rain running down a clouded windowpane.

Lochlan was waiting for me outside.

'Where'd you find her?' he asked.

'Nearby,' I said. I didn't want to talk about it, not while so much needed sorting out in my mind. Half the things I'd seen had been too strange to believe. Snow bursting into clouds of steam, and a ghost who'd shattered the bridge. None of it made any sense. I kept walking, hoping that Lochlan would drop away, would find someone else to bother. People were at work around the compound, cutting wood, sawing planks, shoring up the doors as though we could just sit here forever. They'd started to follow the sisters because they believed they had a string reaching up to the Light Above, heard its whispers in the splashing of wine, saw its plans in the drifting of a cloud. If the sooth-sisters were touched by divine inspiration, surely they had a plan to get out of here?

I'd known it was all bollocks from the first day their travelling party had set up outside the scribing house that Mama so resented. She had been a child apprentice to the village scribe until the woman shuffled on to the next life, and Mama had found herself a woman of learning in a community of illiterate foresters. She left to live with others as educated and extraordinary as herself, only to find that outside the highlands, her knowledge of letters and numbers was considered mundane. Capable enough to record sales and write up deeds of ownership, and little more, she had to swallow her scorn and scribe for her bread. Then of course there was me, and I was no great joy to her, but the sooth-sisters had, for a moment, lightened her life. They talked godliness in a language the common ear could understand, opened up a path to spirituality that went beyond the droning priests in the churches. Morning meditations, using little bits of rock crystal to cleanse their auras, all of it was welcomed wherever the sisters dispensed it, but I'd seen from the first that all of it was nonsense.

I'd allowed myself to think it was a bit of harmless fun at first. Why shouldn't someone believe that a piece of rock crystal beneath their pillow will bring them good fortune? But then I saw Sister Anthra whisper to an old, dying woman that she could talk to the spirit of her husband, ten years in the grave. Saw her pretending to relay information back and forth, when there was no spirit there. If there had been, I would have seen it.

It was no easy thing to live with the dead. As a young child, sitting beneath my mother's desk in the scribing houses she so loathed, I hadn't known what they were, or that they were worthy of comment. The first time I mentioned one, my mother took a slipper to me so hard that I never dared breathe word of it again. It was a kindness, of a sort. Had I spoken freely of what I saw, I would not have lived. The sisters were careful. They stuck to their singing-colours, their rabbit's feet and dandelion prophecies for the living, and resorted to spirits only to comfort the dying. They meant no harm by any of it.

My only question on that score was whether they were under a collective delusion, or if they knew how full of horse shit their proclamations were. And all the same, despite their care, they had made a mistake. LacCulloch's wife had but hours left to her when Sister Marthella comforted her, using her long-gone mother's childhood pet name for her. Only 'Snowbell' hadn't faded. She had rallied at the last, and when she told her husband of the sooth-sister's secret, deathless knowledge, he turned his ire upon us. I'd heard that long-gone mother's soul talking around the keep. I'd told Sister Marthella. Joining in, like I was one of them. It had felt safe, and perhaps part of me desperately wanted to trust someone with this secret I'd kept hidden for so long. And perhaps I had been testing Sister Marthella. Perhaps I wanted reassurance that having the grave-sight didn't make me evil. Didn't make me a thing that needed killing.

Whatever my thoughts, whether or not the sisters had saved Lady LacCulloch's life, LacCulloch did not agree. He hated and feared the spirit-sight as much as anyone. And now he would kill us all, because I had given the sisters a name.

I needed to be alone. I needed air. I needed to be away from all of it.

I walked up the steep flight of stairs onto the walls in a bid to escape Lochlan's attention. He didn't like heights, or the wind up there, but apparently he was prepared to brave them for once. The mountain gusts blew hard, turning wet legs and frozen boots even colder. I gazed out at LacCulloch's encampment. A single road led up to Dalnesse, flanked by towering limestone rock faces. It must have been impressive, once, but yesterday's splendour was today's rat trap. They were camped out of bow shot. I knew because Braithe had made me try to get an arrow to them. They were safe in their tents, the smoke of their campfires quickly whipped away on the wind.

'More soldiers arrived today,' Lochlan said. 'How many do you think there are?'

'I counted a hundred, give or take,' I said. 'He can't attack, though.'

'He has enough men.'

'He does, but the gates are big, these old walls are still high, and we've enough bows to hurt a lot of his men on their way up here. Besides, how would they get through the gates?'

'A battering ram,' Lochlan said. 'I saw them felling trees yesterday.' He worried at his thick yellow curls.

'Look down there,' I said, pointing at the thick mud in front of the gate. 'Anyone trying to carry a ram through that is going to get themselves full of arrows. LacCulloch has his household warband, his sworn-swords, and a bunch of men from his clanhold who're feeling feisty. But there's nothing they can do here. With luck they'll start drifting back to make sure their farmers aren't fiddling the harvest.'

I spoke with a confidence I didn't feel. I was mimicking Braithe, I realised. He would have been proud.

'You think it'll all end peacefully?' Lochlan asked.

I wanted to give him some encouragement, but I didn't hold out much hope. The worst of it was, I couldn't really blame Niven LacCulloch for wanting to get his hands on the sisters. Everyone knew the grave-sight was forbidden, that it marked a person as drawn to the Night Below. Every great terror of the past—Hallenae the Riven Queen, Sanvael LacNimue, Grandmaster Unthayla, the Remnant Sul, the ancient Faded Lords—all of them had seen the dead and bound them to their will. And my selfish little whisper had broken the seal and cast the sisters onto my own pyre. LacCulloch's wife I could resent, but the thail himself was only doing his duty. I had never felt that I was a monster, never felt that what I saw hurt anybody. I would have cast off the ability if I could. But since the sooth-sisters' followers were true believers—in what wasn't exactly clear, but they were definitely believers—surrender had proven not to be an option. And that was why we were all going to die.

'It's okay, Raine,' Lochlan said. 'I'll keep you safe.' He made to put his arms around me, and I snorted a laugh and pushed him away.

'The only thing you're keeping safe is your virginity,' I told him, and Lochlan reddened, then drew a long dirk with a flourish, making me step back. He brandished the blade before me.

'I got this from Braithe,' he said. 'I'll fight if I have to.'

'You think you could kill a man, Loch?'

He shrugged, and maybe for the first time I saw how much he'd filled out over the last year. He had farmer's shoulders. But he sagged a little and lowered the knife.

'I don't know,' he said. 'If you were in danger, maybe I could.'

'I'm always in danger,' I said. 'Don't wish it, Loch. The sisters preach about inner peace, don't they? It'll be a sad day that they bring us to violence.'

Braithe had taught me to shoot, shown me how to stick a man whose hands wandered so he wouldn't die but would remember it. Until today I hadn't known if I could do it. Whatever I'd said, I hadn't really believed that I could.

Only I'd loosed an arrow straight at that warrior's chest. I'd not had a choice. I'd never wanted to kill a person—I'd seen too many ghosts to make one myself—but neither was I going to lie down and die. But he'd snatched my arrow out of the air like it was nothing. It didn't seem to matter now. He was dead in the river, and Hazia probably wasn't going to last much longer either. All that fear and panic had been for nothing, and I was right back where I'd started, looking out at a bunch of men who wanted to kill us.

I didn't want to look at them anymore. But when I turned to head down the stairs again, I saw Braithe staring up at me. He did not look happy. He stalked up onto the wall beside me, while Lochlan muttered an excuse and melted away like a shadow.

'Where did she come from?' he demanded. Braithe was tall, broad and thick in the chest without being muscular. Just naturally big. His hair was northern-red, his beard smartly brushed. He was wearing his mail shirt, and his sword, as he'd done ever since we'd been forced to run. I'd given him that sword to celebrate his thirtieth winter, and I think he fancied himself the leader of a warband now, rather than the unelected leader of a bunch of spiritualists. It suited him. Made him look dashing.

I told him everything, save for the painted queen with feathers for a crown.

All of our troubles had come because the sooth-sisters had played with fire when they whispered comforting lies to the dying. And I had only given them a name . . . I could never tell anybody I saw ghosts. Every clanhold had a different name for those that had the spirit-sight: nightcrafters, witches, dark-speakers. But the message behind the name was always clear. The lucky ones were banished. The unlucky met the end of a rope. I wasn't just a corrupted thing that saw the dead. I was poison to anyone around me.

I needed time to think. I wanted to go back, to live those moments again when the ghostly woman had spoken to me. If she had been speaking to me. My blood had been in my ears and a man had been trying to kill me. Maybe I misremembered. But then the bridge, twisting, buckling and tearing apart like that? None of it felt real to me, even as I told Braithe that it had collapsed beneath my pursuer's weight.

'You've let me down again, Raine,' Braithe said, leaning on the crenulation and staring out towards LacCulloch's men. 'Whoever Hazia is, she's bad news and she's not one of us. I don't want her here.'

'I couldn't just leave her out there to die.'

'She wasn't my problem,' he snapped. 'I've problems enough!'

'Hush, love,' I said, linking my arm through his and leaning my head on his shoulder. 'The man chasing us might well have been one of LacCulloch's men. So at least we got one of them?'

I meant it light-heartedly, but I suppose it wasn't funny. Braithe swung me around to look at him, all affection gone.

'Are you half-asleep in there, Raine?' he demanded, rapping the side of my head with his knuckles. 'More of LacCulloch's men are going to go up there looking for him. What if they find the tunnel?'

'The bridge is gone,' I said, knocking his hand away. 'And don't do that. You don't get to treat me like a child out here and a woman when it suits you.'

I didn't see the slap coming. One moment I was standing in front of him, and the next I was leaning against the battlements, my face stinging and red, unsure sure what had happened. My mind wasn't quite there for a few moments while Braithe stood over me, red-faced and furious. I trembled.

'Then be the woman I love, not a feckless girl!' he snapped. I was too shocked to move. I had no words. 'I'm sorry,' Braithe said, his anger fading as swiftly as it had risen, and his big arms enfolded me in his heather and wild-oat smell, in his warmth. The other followers on the walls stared out at LacCulloch's men as though they'd heard nothing, seen nothing. 'I'm sorry, Raine,' Braithe said. 'I was scared. I can't bear the thought of anything happening to you. How could you go out there alone?'

It was hard to account for what had just happened. It seemed as impossible as the ghost queen at the bridge. It always felt impossible. Like something from another world had risen up and shut out the sky.

'I'm sorry.' I don't know why I was apologising. My face hurt. He'd done me more harm than the warrior in the red coat, and still somehow I was apologising.

Braithe kissed the top of my head, twice, three times, and leaned it against his broad chest. We'd kept our relationship secret for a time, but there were few secrets once we were in Dalnesse. The others had treated me differently the first morning I walked out of his room. At first I'd thought it was respect. Then I'd realised that if it was, then it wasn't respect for me.

'We'll escape this place, don't you fear,' he said. 'My cousins will come. They'll go to the Brannish governors, and raise enough men to make LacCulloch back down. You don't have to be so scared.'

He spoke with such confidence, though I couldn't see the bottom of the trench from which he dredged it. The Brannish had sat upon the throat of our nation for over six hundred years, and Braithe's cousins held no lands of worth. I could not imagine the lord of a Brannish garrison riding to our aid with their banners fluttering in the wind. They took our tithes and left clanland bloodshed to the clans.

'What if they don't?'

'Then we're all going to be sick of pigeon and rat by the end of winter.'

He smiled, and he was strong and warm and sure and it was better to think on those things than the burning in my cheek.

There is always magic in an old woman's hands. Sister Marthella had done a good job with her needle and thread, and Hazia was still alive. For now. Breath eased in and out of the thin hollow of her chest in shallow, strained exertions, and perspiration slicked her skin. The fire was banked, although there was little dry wood left in Dalnesse. I didn't want to think about how we'd keep warm once that ran out. Niven LacCulloch didn't need to get in here to kill us all; he could sit back and let nature do the killing for him.

I found Lochlan wrapped in blankets in the cold of a monkish cell, huddled close to a fire that was running low on fuel as he sharpened his new dirk. He didn't meet my eye as I sat down beside him. Didn't say a word, just drove the edge along the whetstone. The light was starting to fade from the world.

Another day, gone. Nothing achieved. Just less food to go around tomorrow, less wood to keep us warm.

I was so tired of the despair. Tired of trying, and failing, and hurting and failing again. I wanted to cry, but I wanted to cry all the time, and tears had never brought me anything but more of the same.

'Want to see something interesting?' I said, dragging an edge of enthusiasm from the dry pit where I put the parts of me that weren't quite spent. Lochlan just shrugged. He wasn't one for sullen moods, but the days weighed heavily on even the most deluded of the sisters' followers. They still sang and prayed in the morning, still danced to the colours in their minds, but their voices had grown quieter.

I took out the page that I'd taken from Hazia. It had been torn from a book, ragged along one edge.

'See this?' I said. Lochlan nodded. I took my waterskin and poured water across it, let it run onto the floor. 'Doesn't get wet. That's pretty interesting, 'ht?' Lochlan glanced up at me, looked away quickly and resumed his knife-grinding.

'I guess,' he said.

'Now look at this. Stab it with your knife.'

'Why?'

'Just do it.'

I stretched the page out in front of him, and Lochlan gave it a short jab with the blade. Nothing happened. 'Come on,' I said, 'put some effort into it.' Lochlan's pride took the bait, and he tried harder. Still nothing. We stood up and took one side each and tried to force the blade through, but the paper—if it was paper at all, which I doubted—didn't show the slightest of nicks. We tried to score it, scratch it, but nothing. Lochlan forgot his sullen mood and started grinning.

'Doesn't make any sense at all,' he muttered as he tried to saw at the edge.

'You think that's impressive? Watch this.'

I took the page from him and fed it slowly into the fire.

'Don't burn it!' Lochlan said. He watched as the paper crumpled in on itself, a pained look on his face. 'What a waste. That must have been worth something.'

'Come on, I'm not an idiot,' I said. 'I tried it on a candle first. Look.'

I fished it from the fire with a stick. The paper had curled into a ball, and it was hot to the touch. The flames hadn't even singed it.

'This is really something, Raine,' Lochlan said. He beamed at me, happy to be sharing a secret.

'At first I thought it was treated with some kind of oil,' I said. 'Now I don't know. It's stronger than steel. I wonder if I could make it into a helmet?' I draped it across my head. It felt heavier than ordinary paper, like the meaningless words forced whatever weight they carried into the world.

'Don't think that'd work,' Lochlan said seriously. 'Your skull would still break, even if you didn't get cut through it.'

'I thought I'd find you here.'

Braithe loomed in the doorway to Lochlan's cell. I folded the paper and put it to one side. The skin on my cheek seemed to tingle. Flesh remembered, even if I didn't want to.

'How's everything out front?' I asked.

'Quiet, for now. Are you coming to bed?'

I nodded and rose.

'Good night, Lochlan,' I said.

'Good night, Raine. Good night, Captain.'

Captain. That was new. It had always paid for the sooth-sisters to travel with a group of strong young folk. In the north, children played at stick-and-shield as soon as they were big enough to hold them, although Mama had never allowed me to join in with those games, which was a shame, as a bit of skill with a sword would probably extend my life by a few moments in the near future. So even though they gathered carpenters, milkmaids, flower dancers and bored tavern maids, the sooth-sisters weren't short of a few strong arms when they needed them.

'Captain now, is it?' I asked, my arm linked through Braithe's as we walked the short way towards the rooms he'd found to make his quarters. 'It suits you.'

'It seems to make them happy to call me that,' he said. 'Come on. I have a real fire going. Some wine warming.'

He ushered me into his small domain, and I could see he'd made an effort to clean it up. Old bread crusts and bird-bones had been tidied away, the blankets on the floor had been smoothed out as if to make a bed. Little efforts, but they counted.

'I'm sorry about before,' he said. 'You just make me so worried.'

'Let's not talk about it,' I said. I didn't want to, and I could see he was trying. You don't blame a horse if you spook it and it kicks you. This was the same. Sister Marthella had explained it to me the first time Braithe hit me. She'd said his aura had been out of alignment and she'd work some rock crystal over it on the morrow, but what did I expect, embarrassing him by calling him drunk in front of his friends? Sister Marthella was about the oldest person I'd ever known, so there had to be something to what she said. It sounded wise. Didn't feel right to me, though.

'Have some wine,' Braithe said. He poured into wooden beakers for us both.

'We should probably save that,' I said. 'For when we get hungry.'

A big arm wound around my shoulders.

'Can't deny ourselves all the best things in life,' he said. 'I'm keeping optimistic. I want to hear more about this stream tunnel.'

'There's not much more to tell,' I said. 'It leads out onto the eastern slopes. They're not steep, but there's a river that cuts a gorge there. With the bridge collapsed, I don't know if anyone can cross it.'

'You think someone could swim across it?' he asked.

'I wouldn't want to try it.' My eyes would have narrowed suspiciously, but the bruise on my cheek was stiff and swollen and the expression came out more like a slow wink. 'What are you thinking?'

'I'm thinking that if worse comes to the worst, we've a back way out of here.'

'The sisters would never make it out that way,' I said. 'Or the older followers.'

'I'm doing all I can for the sisters, Raine,' Braithe sighed. 'And I'm a believer in their teachings. I do my singing and my colour dances with the rest of them. But I have to be the practical one here. I have to plan for the worst. Have to know what we'll do if the trumpet sounds on the walls.'

After we made love, Braithe stroked the hair from my face and kissed me on each eyebrow, as delicately as if I were the last autumn leaf clinging to a bough. Then he turned his back, lying on his left side as he always did, leaving me to curl around him. Other girls talked about falling asleep in a strong man's arms, but that had never been our way. By day, I clung to him: to his strength, to his worldliness. By night I clung to him in a different way, latched on to his back like a babe in its mother's basket. I held to his solidity, to his realness. To his need for me, in a world where no one else saw any need for me at all.

The torn, impervious page lay between us that night, tucked inside my winter coat. I felt my heart beating against it, the dull pulse bouncing back at me, not into him as I sometimes imagined it did. Out there, in the dark beyond our borrowed walls, men would be sitting around campfires, drinking ale and telling stories. Maybe they would sing a song. Mama had made me sing to her, when she was filled with whisky and her tongue was too slow in her mouth to find the lash. She was slow when she got deep in her cups, and for a time she'd forget what I'd done to her. Something had twisted inside her when she forced me out into the world, some bone had misaligned, and she had never walked easily after that. Had never been able to stand for more than a few minutes without the pain spreading from her pelvis, cutting down through her legs and up into her back. Her body had not wanted me to live, I sometimes thought. In retribution for breaking her, it had wrapped my cord around my throat and turned me purple before I had even entered the world. But when she was drunk, and when I sang the songs she had brought down from the highlands of Ardentathy, she sometimes forgot that I had taken her legs, and that she had killed me for it.

I died before I was even born. Before I even had a name.

The midwife had unwound my mother's garrotte and filled me with life again. But I wondered some nights whether all my mother's resentment and spite had somehow conspired to do it. It must have been a relief for her when I ran away with the sooth-sisters. Was it guilt that gave her venom so much fire? I had tried to turn my sorrow to anger, but it's hard to despise someone when you are the one who cut their wings away. It was safer to accept that her dislike of me was driven by resentment. I'd taken her legs, and trapped her forever in the scribe-house, in a life she hated, looked down on by the rest of the clerks for her clumsy northern script and lack of culture.

I felt her absence tonight as I had not, not even once, since the day I followed Braithe's bright eyes and the sisters' mumblings. A woman had appeared to me today, a woman I did not and would never know, and she had uttered words that I had never thought to hear.

'I will not let him hurt you, Raine. This is only our beginning.'

To speak of seeing the dead was to die. That was why we were all trapped here in the first place, wasn't it? I could explain away the collapse of a bridge. What remained of the rest of the monastery was practically falling apart. And perhaps there was part of me that couldn't quite admit, even to myself, the things that I'd seen. How could I explain what even I didn't understand? Those beams, twisting like wet cloth being wrung out, and the man who had pursued us, who had boiled snow from his path. Everybody within Dalnesse's walls believed in magic, except perhaps the sooth-sisters themselves, but reading a child's life line and proclaiming good health was a long, sobering mile away from seeing the dead tear the material world apart with a word. I lived in a realm of blame, of such fear of the unknown that even claiming to see such things marked one out as a witch; a nightcrafter; a dark-speaker. Confined in Dalnesse, with the noose-bringers at our gates, how long before a friend saw their way out through betrayal and revelation?

Whoever she had once been, that lady in her feathered glory was not of my time. Not of my world, perhaps. My education had been gathered piecemeal here and there, but many hundreds of years ago, wielders of great magic had levelled civilisations with their spells and workings. Maldouen had brought the Riven Queen and her Sarathi sorcerers to their final defeat. Fireside stories from passing troubadours talked of their great magic and said that even death could not contain the most powerful practitioners. But the one thing every story agreed upon was that no good came of such power. Darkness followed in the shadow of those that broke the laws of nature.

'If you are out there, watching over me,' I whispered into the slow rise and fall of Braithe's back, 'whoever, whatever you are, help us escape, without hurting anyone else. Please. It's not their fault. It was my fault. Don't hurt anyone else because of what I did.'

I lay quietly in the darkness, my fears keeping me from sleep as I listened to Braithe's low snoring. I thought that I'd been clever, that I would find a way to impress him. I'd been foolish, and now my cheek throbbed for it. I wouldn't anger him again tomorrow. Dawn began to rise, faint light beyond the shutters, and I clung to him as though he alone could protect me from the dead.

Three trumpet blasts sounded from the walls.

Braithe started alert, a rat-terrier's excitement bright in his eyes.

'Up,' he said. 'Help me with this.'

I dressed him in his coat of mail, secured his sword belt, fixed his cloak. He looked so grand, so much the man who could lead us out of the nightmare into which I had led us. I grabbed my bow, slung my quiver of arrows over my shoulder and followed him, already striding for the wall.

4

'They want to talk,' Braithe said as he came back down from the parapet. 'Got a parley branch up.'

'How many?'

'Just four,' Braithe said. He took a deep breath. Steeled himself, filling up as if he inhaled pride from the cold mountain air. 'I'm going to go meet them.'

'I'm coming too,' I said. I shouldered my bow.

'No,' Braithe said. 'You've had enough adventures. Stay here with the children. You know your place.' He called to his two best men, Farlan and Fergus, both sturdy highlanders with heavy beards.

The children. I was seventeen, and by highland law I'd been a woman for two years already, and Braithe's "men" counted a dozen women among their number, two of them barely a year or two older than me. I glared at his back, willing him to see that I was capable, but he was busy with his preparations. Was that how he saw me, beyond the fall of his sheets? No. He was just afraid for me, sheltering me. That's what yesterday had been about. Fear and anger are the head and thistle of a coin, and one cannot exist without the other.

I had to show him that he didn't need to fear for me. How could he protect us if worry for me filled his mind? I saddled the horse I usually rode, a docile, roan mare called Ivy. As the gates cracked open and Braithe and his men rode out, I nudged her after them.

'What do you think you're doing?' Braithe scowled at me.

'I've as much right to be here as anyone, Captain,' I told him. 'We're all free people. One of the sisters' rules, isn't it?'

'Things are changing around here,' Braithe said, and his men grunted agreement. I ignored them and heeled Ivy into a trot, focused on staying in the saddle. Sitting a walking horse is easy, but I'd never been a natural horsewoman. It was only when I was a hundred feet from the walls of Dalnesse that I saw the red coats among LacCulloch's party, and my jaw locked tight as winter.

Niven LacCulloch was a young man, his desire to prove himself to the world written across his face. His mail was polished, and a helm with an ornate faceplate rested beneath his arm. He and his bodyguard of four men and two women, carrying the branch that signified parley, would usually have looked imposing, but their highland horses hadn't the sheer size of those ridden by the men in the oxblood coats, which easily stood four hands taller. One of them was the fat young man who'd ridden by me, but for a moment I had to check that I wasn't seeing yet another deathless soul. The old man who'd burned away the snow was sitting aside another monstrous charger behind them. His eyes were closed, and his head and hands were scraped with a dozen small cuts and bruises, but there he was, no ghostly vapour around him, solid as an oak. Very much alive.

Nobody should have survived a fall into that torrent. Those rocks. What nature of man was he?

'Still not sending Marthella out to speak to me in person, Braithe?' LacCulloch called as we drew to a stop three horse-lengths away.

'Somehow I doubt you'd be sitting so cordial if I had,' Braithe said. 'This has gone on long enough.'

'You must be getting pretty hungry in there,' LacCulloch said. In a display that spoke of forward planning, his bannerman took a piece of meat from a sack at his belt and bit off a chunk. I had to admit, it had the desired effect and my stomach tightened painfully.

'Our beliefs feed our souls,' Braithe said. 'You wouldn't understand.'

'Your beliefs are written in grave dust,' LacCulloch snapped.

'No,' Braithe said. 'You've been misled by a fever-driven mind. There is no finger of the grave upon the sisters, and no evil in their hearts. Sister Marthella speaks only the wisdom she reads in the colours. I cannot permit harm to come to them.'

'So you intend to sit here forever?'

'No,' Braithe said. 'Help is on its way. What do you want?'

'I've nothing more to say to you,' LacCulloch said. 'They do.'

I pulled my hood up to cover my face. The old man looked asleep in his saddle, but I'd seen him catch an arrow, had seen him melt the snow. That he'd also survived the fall into the river left me chilled. If he recognised me, my silence could become a noose of my own making. I'd lied to Braithe. I shuddered even at imagined fury.

The young man in red tried to speak, and his voice emerged as a squeak. He cleared his throat.

'We are here on business of Redwinter,' he said. Despite his girth, he seemed like a child among these growling men. Even so, mention of Redwinter made Braithe and his men shift in their saddles. 'You are harbouring a criminal, who must be returned to us at once.'

'Sister Marthella is no criminal,' Braithe said, and I sank further into my saddle. Braithe had been right, though he couldn't have known it. Coming out here had been a mistake.

'We have no interest in your soothsayers,' the young man said. He looked about as certain of his place here as a hen in a fox's den. He glanced back at the older man, who remained immobile, breathing slowly. 'We are here for Hazia LacFroome. She is an apprentice of Redwinter, and wanted for the gravest of crimes.'

'You're Draoihn?' Braithe asked.

'I am Novice Ovitus LacNaithe,' the young man said. 'This is my uncle, Ulovar LacNaithe, Draoihn of the Fourth Gate and van of Clan LacNaithe. We have pursued her all the way from Harranir.'

A freezing chill dripped down my back as if an icicle were forming between my shoulder blades. I felt the world spinning away from me, as though I rose up, up and above it from a great height, staring down at the impossible juncture I had brought us to. I had sought to help. To show mercy.

What had I done?

If the young man was telling the truth, then I'd loosed an arrow at one of the most powerful men in the kingdom. Harran was not the wealthiest nation. Too much weak soil, too much rock and wind. Too cold. A client kingdom of our great southern neighbour, Brannlant, Harran was lesser in wealth, in culture, in most of everything. But LacNaithe was an old clan, with roots that twined down to the bedrock of the land, and within the clanlands few could challenge her for influence, or for power. The young man's proclamation had a similar effect on Braithe and his men. Dealing with a small-clan highland thail like LacCulloch was one thing. Refusing a command from LacNaithe was another.

'What do you require, Van LacNaithe?' Braithe said quietly.

'We've no part to play in this sad quarrel,' the young man, Ovitus, said. 'I hope for all concerned that there is a happy resolution to be had. But Hazia LacFroome must be delivered to us.'

'If she's moved, she'll die,' I said. The words were out before I could stop them. Ovitus looked pained.

'I don't want her to die,' he said. 'She's my friend.'

The old man, Ulovar LacNaithe, van of his clan, stirred, his eyes still closed. 'Then you must take us to her.'

Something changed in Braithe at that moment. I'd seen it in him the day before. He would not be commanded. Had he always burned with this desire for authority? What a little taste of power does to a man, I thought.

'No,' Braithe said. Ulovar's eyes opened a tiny fraction.

'No?'

'No.' His hands were hard on his reins. Ready to pull his horse around, ready to ride hard if he had to.

The old man's eyes closed again.

'Please,' Ovitus said. 'We've no wish for violence—'

'If she is not brought to me within the hour, your gates will fall,' Ulovar growled, 'and what befalls you and your people will be on your own heads. Bring her to me. Alive if possible. Dead if needs be.'

'I've heard enough,' Braithe said. He glared at LacCulloch. 'These imposter Draoihn were a bold move. But it takes more than a red coat to prove a man's from Redwinter. Try to take our gates if you can. You'll not find your reception to your liking.'

He sawed on the reins, bringing a snort of pain from his horse. I wheeled Ivy around as well, my heart pulsing a fearsome beat in my chest. We heeled the horses to a canter as we headed back into Dalnesse.

The moment we were off the horses I grabbed Braithe's sleeve.

'We have to get out of here,' I said. 'All of us. He's not bluffing. Those men *are* Draoihn.'

'I know,' Braithe said. There was a wild, angry light in his eyes.

'Shouldn't we give them what they want?' one of his men asked.

'I'll not give them shit,' Braithe snapped. 'I'm captain here, aren't I? I saw a Draoihn in action once. He took five men apart like they were nothing. I'll not let them pass a foot inside our walls.'

'And if he breaks the gates?'

'The Draoihn may be deadly warriors,' Braithe snorted, 'but they're still men. He comes anywhere near us and he'll meet a rain no red coat will hold back.' He gestured to his men. 'Make sure the bows are strung and the arrows close to hand. Just in case they try something stupid.'

'Aye, Captain,' his men chorused.

'Arrows won't stop them,' I said.

'Are you questioning me?' Braithe snapped, anger turning his pale cheeks as red as his beard. For a moment I thought he was going to strike me again. He controlled himself, brought a big, colour-dancing smile onto his face. 'We're blessed by the sisters. There's nothing to fear.' He raised his voice to address the worried folk all around. 'The colours shine for us, do they not?'

'The colours shine!' they chorused back. I looked around in horror at the smiles, the beaming faces. This morning they'd been dancing, shouting the names of rainbow hues as they did every morning. It had all seemed funny when I first joined them, and then after a while I'd seen what they took from it. Community, a sense of belonging. The colour dance gave them a place in the world, and the sooth-sisters gave them a focus. But it was only words. I had seen real magic beneath the pines. I had seen a man who could snap arrows from the air and turn snow to steam. They didn't understand what they were dealing with.

I begged Braithe to listen. In my desperation I even told him what I'd seen, but he shrugged me off. Dismissed me as he would a panicking child. Maybe I'd never been more to him than that. I was helpless, voiceless among them. He didn't want it to be true.

'You were never really a believer, Raine,' he said sadly. 'But these people are. They look up to me. I can't let them down.'

'We have to get out of here. All of us.'

He shrugged.

'The Light Above provides the colours of the world for us to dance. We'll dance them the way she intends.'

'You *want* them to come,' I said. 'You want to fight.' As I said the words we both knew I was right.

He strode away, ordering men to the walls. He'd found his place among these people, as I'd never found mine. They looked to him to lead them, and he would. He'd lead them straight into their caskets.

I sank back against the wall, as the wind tossed a skitter of fallen leaves through the air before me. I saw the pillars of my life flutter away on the same cold wind. The people here had been good to me. Had helped me, when I needed somewhere to turn. Had welcomed me though I had nothing to offer, asked little of me and given much. I wasn't truly one of them. Braithe was right about that. But I thought I had been happy among them. Thought I had found somewhere I could belong.

I was crying when Braithe looked back at me, and I saw myself as he saw me. A girl in a woman's body.

Just a child after all.

The sooth-sisters read an augury in the blood of a weasel. I don't know where they'd got a weasel from, but everyone gathered as they oohed and aahed over a bowl of its blood.

'The portents are good,' Sister Marthella said, pleased by what she saw. 'Lies have been told. We, the faithful who serve the Light Above in all her colours, shall be raised on high.'

Beaming smiles all round. Stupid faces with grins writ large, friendly slaps on the back. The sisters' faithful followers went back to their tasks with the relief that comes from believing absolute horseshit at a deep, resonating level.

I couldn't have looked much better than the weasel. My eyes stung, and my upper lip was raw from sniffling, but that didn't matter now. I felt more adrift, more apart from these people than any simple difference in belief could have achieved. As that gulf between us had widened, I saw them all spread out before me like distant places on a map. Places I had visited but could never be home. I had to go, I realised. Not just because LacCulloch had warriors, and Draoihn, but because my departure was inevitable. What pretty deceptions I had worked upon myself, to wear the colours of another person's life.

I stopped Lochlan as he headed to the wall. He brandished his dirk, with its bark-twine-wrapped hilt before him like a ward against evil, drawing strength from it.

'Come with me,' I said. 'Please.'

'Braithe said I have to stand watch on the wall,' Lochlan said.

'Never mind Braithe,' I said angrily. 'It's all over, don't you see it? Dalnesse won't protect us. LacCulloch has Draoihn among his men. Do you know what that means?'

'But they aren't on LacCulloch's side,' Lochlan argued. 'That's what Braithe said. They don't care about us.'

Lochlan looked very young to me then. He still believed, I thought. Still saw a road stretching out before him, a pilgrimage of fate that would continue beyond the next few hours or days with these people. He didn't see that it was over. I couldn't blame him. I had barely stepped from the path myself.

'Braithe isn't thinking clearly,' I said gently. 'He thinks he can find a way through this on a ship built of his own making. People are calling him Captain, filling his sails. But he's just a landlocked sailor who fancies the log he's sitting on is a ship. And he's going to sink us all.'

'He has led us well this far,' Lochlan said. So desperate to believe. So in awe of a man who knew more of sails and seas than he did swords and strategy.

'I wish I could believe you,' I said. 'I want to believe you. But if Braithe's cousins are all he says—will raise men to rescue us all—then why has he spent these years travelling with the sisters? Why would the Brannish overrule Niven LacCulloch? The Brannish don't care for us either, Lochlan. Nobody does.'

Lochlan looked at me as though I were a limping rabbit, struggling to hop away from a child's caring hands.

'I know he shouldn't have hit you, Raine,' he said. He hesitated for a moment, maybe drew more strength from the hilt of his knife. 'That was wrong of him. If you were my woman, I wouldn't hit you.'

I shrugged that aside. I felt the sting of humiliation in the stiff, swollen lump over my cheekbone.

'That doesn't matter now,' I said. 'Get your things ready, and take them down to the crypts. If everything goes south, then I want you to head out through the tunnel. Maybe you can climb down and swim across. Don't think about fighting them. We can't fight them. We don't have the people, or the weapons. Or the magic, if it comes to that.'

'The sisters have magic,' Lochlan said. He tried to reach out to me, but I brushed him off.

'Not this kind of magic,' I said. 'Please. Trust me.'

'You have to have faith, Raine,' Lochlan said. 'I'm sorry. I need to stand watch on the wall.' He turned and walked away, then stopped and looked back. 'He shouldn't have hit you, Raine. But you need to watch what you're saying.'

I stood there, numb, for a while. I couldn't even convince Lochlan. I'd never felt so powerless, so alone.

This was what it all came to in the end. The community I'd chosen to be part of. Mama had told me that I was nobody to anybody but her, and she'd been right. I'd left her cruel words, her resentment, her bitterness, but four years later her words drifted around me like circling crows. I had done what I could, had told the truth. Only my words were worth nothing to them, and I was worth less.

Out beyond the walls, I heard the sound of drums. Very distant, very faint. A repeating beat, soft and gentle. *Dhum, dhum, dhum.* A chill passed through me. Drums I'd heard before. My thoughts seemed to be falling into the same rhythm, words falling on the beats. Everything seemed very clear, very bright.

Shades of pink and yellow on the followers' shirts were glaring, almost painful to the eye. Everything was too loud. Footsteps on the ramparts above could have been hands clapping beside my ears. A massive headache was sure to follow.

I moved quickly, gathering what I could. Not much to show for the time I'd spent with the faithful. I'd lived alongside these people for four years, cooking for them, pitching tents, darning stockings and feeding horses. Writing letters for them, looking at bills of sale to ensure they weren't being swindled. Dancing their stupid colours, which wasn't even a dance, it was just throwing yourself about and wailing. For the last year, sharing Braithe's bed. I'd made myself useful. But I still wasn't one of them. I didn't believe, and I never had.

Dhum, dhum, dhum.

That, I believed in.

I entered Hazia's sickroom. The fire was dying, but the room held a thick, sweet-smelling heat. The young woman sat on the edge of the bed, sheened with sweat, her dark hair hanging lank around her face. The sisters had bandaged her side, but stains had forced themselves through, yellow and red. The smell was sickening.

'You need to lie down,' I said.

'No,' Hazia whispered. 'They're coming. Don't you feel it? The Third Gate is open. Ulovar is working something.'

'What does that mean?'

'Where is it?' Hazia said. She looked around, her eyes wild. 'Where is it?'

'Where's what?'

'The page,' she said. 'I carried it all this way. To bring it back, where it belongs. Where is it? What have you done with it?'

I'd left the seemingly indestructible sheet of paper in the room I shared with Braithe.

'We need to get out of here,' I said. 'They're coming for you. You need to dress.'

'I don't care about that,' Hazia said. She bared her teeth, and her fingernails gouged at the bedframe. 'Get me. The page.'

'Has everyone gone mad?' I demanded. 'What does an old piece of paper matter? They're going to kill you, Hazia. We can still get out. The way we got in.' And then maybe find another way to cross the mountain river. Maybe somehow get this sick, dying woman somewhere that she could heal. Maybe evade the Draoihn until we got clear. It was a lot of maybes, but I was damned if I was going to let them ride in here and murder her in a bed.

Hazia reached out and grabbed my wrist, her grip painful, squeezing my bones.

'Bring it to me. And take me to the crypt,' she hissed.

'The crypt?'

'Yes,' she said. 'Don't you hear it calling?'

'We have to go through the crypts,' I said. Down to the crypt, follow the old monk's ghost back to the underground stream, and out. But we'd need warm clothing first. Fur-lined hoods, heavy coats, something that might keep us alive if we were caught without shelter overnight or if the snow began to fall. There would be no trails out there. 'I'll get it for you,' I said. 'Just wait here. Put some clothes on and wait for me.'

I fetched the page, tucking it into my coat, then crossed the monastery's yard to the supply wagon. I found spare clothing, colourful shirts for new worshippers, winter coats and cloaks. No boots or shoes. I bundled what I could in a sack, tied the end off with thin rope. Made a good knot, a seafarer's knot that Braithe had taught me. Was I really going to do this? Leave him? Leave my few friends? The trumpet sounded up on the wall. Three clear blasts. Kella had been a court musician before she'd joined the sisters, and her notes were bright and clean.

Atop the wall the watchers looked aghast.

'What's going on?' I yelled, but they weren't listening, too busy wrapped up in what they saw. 'Damn it.' I took the stairs two at a time.

LacCulloch's men were charging us, on their highland horses, snow flying as the horses ploughed up the road.

'Ready bows! Ready bows!' Braithe yelled. His cloak streamed out behind him in the high mountain wind.

'What are they doing?' I shouted as the drumming of hooves beat through the earth. The sound of four hundred iron-shod hooves resounded from the mountainsides.

'They've gone mad,' Braithe muttered. 'Mad.' He shook his head. He plucked the string of his bow, felt the thrum. He shouted along the wall, 'Wait until you can't miss!' I heard a bite of joy in his voice, fearless behind his high stone walls. I saw Lochlan trying to string his hunting bow, a bow he'd only ever used to shoot crows on a farm whose name I couldn't remember. The string slipped from the horn nock, his fingers sweaty. There were only twenty men and women on the walls. Limited ammunition. The sisters had close to fifty followers, but some were old, some were children, others were just milling about below, unsure what to do.

The riders stormed onwards, swords and axes held to the shoulder, spears ready. No ladders, no ram, nothing they could use to storm the gate. For a single moment I understood Braithe's confidence. He'd been a sailor, heaving lines and loading cargo. A man who took orders. Here he was lord of the wall, and his enemies were going to smash themselves against it like a ship running aground.

Dhum, dhum, DHUM.

A great throb of force shook the wall, as if a hammer had fallen against it. I staggered, grabbed the parapet. A huge crack ran through the great double-gates. A second crunch rippled through them and on into the wall, and Lochlan fell back onto his arse. The gates collapsed outwards, hinges shorn away, crashing into the churned snow like toppled giants.

'Light Above,' Braithe whispered. He turned towards the horsemen rushing towards the breach, his eyes wild, and his bow fell from his hands.

I ran for the stairs, stumbling and falling to one knee as I made it to the courtyard floor. I launched up from my other foot, raced across the courtyard, fumbling my bow from my back as the horsemen began to pour into the yard, shields raised above their heads. A handful of bowstrings thrummed, arrows hammering into the wood. One rider cried out as the tip punched through to gash the arm beneath.

The horsemen saw the scattering people, and they went after them, or leapt from their horses and ran for the stairs. These weren't farmhands and musicians who'd played at stick-and-shield as children. They were sworn-swords and clan riders, men and women who had made violence their life's work, and the followers' terror was euphoric to them. One of the riders hurled his spear, taking a colour-shirted man in the chest. An old woman was too stunned to move as an axe struck her down. They swarmed up the stairs and onto the monastery's walls to reach her defenders, spreading across the compound like flame.

I burst into the sickroom.

Hazia stood over the body of Sister Anthra, a red knife in her hand and another woman's blood across her bandages, looking like some wild thing of the Night Below, black-nailed, tear-streaked, her whole body shaking.

She surged towards me, grabbing me by the hair and throwing me back against the wall.

'Where is it?' she shrieked hoarsely. 'Give it to me.'

The knife blade pressed cold against my neck. Panic welled through me.

'It's here,' I gasped. 'Here, take it.'

She relented, drawing the knife back.

I reached into my coat and pulled out the page of indecipherable writing. Hazia's eyes flashed, and I read the maddened, murderous intent there. She lunged at me, but I moved faster, dragging the page down, and the knife blade stuck hard into it, thudding against my winter coat with bruising force. I flailed a fist at her as she tried to tear the page from me with one hand even as she tried to drive the knife home with the other. I slapped at her face, and then balled my fist with a snarl and drove it against the wound in her side.

Hazia recoiled with a howl, lashing out with the knife, slicing across my face. The page slid from my hand. The madwoman clutched it against her chest like it was a child.

'I'm sorry,' she whispered in a hoarse, reedy voice. 'Tell them I'm sorry. I don't have a choice.'

She staggered over Sister Anthra's wide-eyed, throat-cut corpse and out through another door. My knees gave way and I slumped to the floor as the terror thrummed through me like a clamouring gong. Everyone was trying to kill me. Everyone would be dead soon. Lochlan, Braithe, Sister Marthella, and all the rest of these simple, innocent people.

A wispy, green-tinged Sister Anthra stood up, scratching at a boil on her back. The ghost went about the room, trying to find something she'd lost. She smiled as she lifted nothing at all, and then her shade dissolved into nothing.

I staggered out into a day alive with screams and the din of battle. Ghosts swayed among the living, confused, blundering through people. Ghosts of people that I knew, people that I'd danced the colours beside. People I'd called friends, people who'd fed me, people whose children I'd played with. Children I'd bounced on my knee.

'Hide!' a man roared at me, Farlan, one of Braithe's friends and a former soldier, Fergus alongside him, no less hardy and wielding a spear. 'Raine, run for your life!'

A voice boomed like thunder and along the narrow alley.

'Where is she?'

Van Ulovar LacNaithe, the heavyset old Draoihn, faced us, his sword resting on his shoulder, clean and bright in the light of fires that had sprung up across the yard.

'Stay back!' Farlan yelled, and Fergus levelled his spear.

'I only want the girl,' Ulovar said, and his voice shook dust from the shale roofs of the buildings around him. He pointed his sword at me. 'Bow-woman. Take me to her.'

Farlan and Fergus charged him. Farlan had fought in the bloody Kwendish civil wars, and I'd seen Fergus end more than one bar fight with a knockout punch. Ulovar was old, and he was heavy, and they were young and had him two to one. Then his sword cut the darkness, one, two, and both of my friends were dead, and he was striding towards me. Farlan's ghost didn't know his body had fallen, carried on fighting, swinging a sword that wasn't there as Ulovar strode through him.

I fumbled for the bow on my shoulder, but he closed the distance in a burst of speed far too swift for a man, any man, and his sword struck it from my hand.

'Don't make me hurt you,' he roared, and his voice carried beyond the air it filled, beyond sound into the thunderous beat of the drum in my mind. The point of his sword came level to my eye. 'Where is the woman you helped over the bridge?'

'She went mad,' I said. 'She's going to the crypts.'

Ulovar seized me by the arm as the younger Draoihn skidded around the corner, ducking under one hand as something arrow-shaped flashed overhead.

'Show me.'

Into the sept, through the ancient trapdoor and down into the dark below.

There was no light, but the young Draoihn, Ovitus, drew out a glass sphere and shook it. Motes of steel-blue cadanum awoke inside, spilling bluish light along row after row of sarcophagi. I was shaking as screams drifted down from above.

'What's down here?' Ulovar said.

'There's a way out,' I said. 'Back to the river.'

'That's not where she's going. She was coming here. Whatever she wants, it's here.'

'There's nothing here but the dead,' I said. 'Nothing but tombs.'

'Then that's what she wants,' Ulovar said. He released my arm. 'The dead.'

I needed to get out of here. I needed to find Lochlan and make sure he got away. But how was I going to do that? He might have been dead already. They all might have been dead already. Out of nowhere, the Draoihn had become my best chance of getting out of here alive. Every choice I had made had led to disaster. If I'd not tried to find the mountain path, if I'd not brought Hazia back here, if I'd not told my secret to Sister Marthella. It was all my fault. All of it.

The thought was too much to take in.

We hurried through the ancient crypts, splashing through overflow from the stream. Even that sound was too loud for me, and the cool cadanum light shone like noonday sun. Drums hammered in my skull, too loud, rattling my teeth. I was thankful that the sounds of battle and the piteous wailing of the ghosts faded as we descended further into the depths.

'Light Above, Uncle. She's in Eio,' Ovitus said.

'I can hear that,' Ulovar said. 'She's been exposed to something that's woken it in her. Keep her with us.'

The young man gave me an apologetic look as he nodded me to follow alongside them.

'I'm terribly sorry, miss,' he said. 'If you can possibly stop that sound in your head? The one that sounds like thunder.'

'I don't know what's happening,' I gasped. A piercing, stiletto-thrust pain was slowly driving itself into the front of my skull. I pressed a hand to my head, clenching my eyes against the brightness.

Ahead, the floodwater ended, and the light revealed wet footprints turning right, onwards between carved pillars. Crude gargoyles leered down at us.

'What am I doing?' I said.

'You hear this sound?' Ovitus asked, pulling me along and beginning to tap his fingers against my arm, a slow, deliberate beat. The rhythm followed the beat of my headache.

'That's not me,' I gasped.

'It's you,' he said. 'Light Above, you don't even know what you're doing. You're moving in and out of a trance.'

'I am not in a trance,' I said firmly.

'You are,' he said. 'You've passed the First Gate.'

'There's no time,' Ulovar called from ahead. 'Bring the damn light!'

Ovitus hurried after him, and rather than be left behind in the dark, I followed. I tried to concentrate on the rhythm, but it wasn't the only one. Steady, powerful beats pulsed from Ulovar, discordant, breaking-crockery clatter from Ovitus.

A louder crash sounded ahead, rending metal. Ulovar and Ovitus rushed on, and I chased after them into a burial chamber. Doors had stood here before, doors of long-rusted iron, but they lay fallen, twisted and bent.

A wave of something cold, uncertain and very old quested out towards us. The cadanum light spread, uncovering things which had lain undisturbed for hundreds of years. Maybe thousands. The air was brittle, tainted.

Across the chamber, five ornate sarcophagi of black, light-drinking stone ringed the chamber's single occupant. Hazia stood behind a dragon-carved lectern. Blood and pus slicked her side, and her hands trembled as she held that page before her.

'Five guardians,' Hazia said. Her voice was barely more than a whisper. 'Five souls to watch over that which was bound. But even the dead will die, given time.'

'Put it down, Hazia,' Ulovar said. His base growl had softened. 'Whatever you took from the Blackwell, it has taken your mind. This is not you. Let me help you.'

Five guardians. Each of their likenesses was carved into the stone sarcophagi. A proud man in armour. A woman, robed and crowned. A hunter with a dog at his feet. Ulovar took a step towards Hazia, his hand outstretched. Foulness emanated from the book that lay open on the lectern, an uncleanness that radiated out to touch skin, and teeth and eyes.

'No,' Hazia said. 'I hear him. I hear him in my bones. He runs through me like love. Imagine being bound here. Imagine being starved of light and air and love for seven hundred years.'

'You can still come back, Hazia,' Ulovar said. 'You don't have to do this.'

'No,' she said. 'It's already done.'

She pressed the torn page down onto the book, and a sound resonated through the crypts like the turning of a key in a lock, as heavy as time. The ceiling shuddered, masonry dust showering from the stonework, through the air. She spoke a single name.

'Ciuthach!'

There is a moment, when someone comes bearing news of a death in the family, that you see it in their face before they speak. You know the words that they are about to say are immense, and will change something, something that we mortals have never learned to accept as part of the natural order. A moment of hesitation, twined with the messenger's desperate need to press the awful truth into your reality. I had seen it many times. I saw it in Hazia's eyes now, as she looked at me, the mania that had driven her knife hand faded away, crumbling like old plaster to reveal what was built beneath.

Hazia shattered from within, her body erupting across the room in a riot of darkness and flickering light as a pulse of force emanated from her, and then I was flying through the air, through the dark, slamming back into one of the ancient black sarcophagi. The carved figure shattered like glass, shards of sharp, gleaming black stone raining down around me, rainbow hues playing across every surface. Ovitus crumpled as his head cracked against a wall.

Ulovar alone stood against the gale of howling, fetid air that blasted from the open pages of the book.

A deep, dark presence opened one ancient eye and looked at us. Darkness and light twisted together, a riot of flickering energy where Hazia's blood still misted the air. I felt the weight of a mind opening, a mind that had been chained all these long centuries, and a voice whispered itself through the cracks in my being.

I am returned.

I saw him. Saw the occupant of this room, standing proud in bright bronze scales. His hair flowed like a mane of rippling fire and polished silver, pale skin stretched tight across features that seemed spaced too wide, and he carried a long spear that dripped, dark and hissing. Something about him was human, but something was not. Changed, modified, a creature of war. Enemies came to him, and he fought. Sweeps of the long-bladed spear felled foe after foe. He ripped into bodies. He ripped into minds. He battled, surrounded, an impossible stand. And there it came, the blow that felled him, the bright sword punching into his chest, driving him down, down onto the rock. It didn't kill him. Couldn't kill him. He fought and bit as his assailants surrounded him, words too large to hear ringing in the air, unseen forces twisting, binding. He struggled, pinned to the white stone as they forced a book against his chest, and his spirit shuddered as it was torn from his body.

He was glorious. He should have been a king, should have been free to serve his queen. And his ancient enemies had bound him to the pages of a book.

The vision broke as bones and debris toppled from the broken sarcophagus behind me, smacking me in the head. A splay of bone and tattered cloth, choking dust and the broken boards of an ancient shield clattered around me. I rolled as a rusted sword clanged to the ground, got whacked again by a midnight-blue recurved bow. As I scraped tomb dust from my eyes, a yellowed old skull grinned up at me.

'It's coming,' Ulovar said.

A shadow figure began to coalesce in the maelstrom of energy. A tall man. Pale hair. This ancient warrior king had been bound here, watched over by the very people who'd killed him. Watching, holding, intent on ensuring that his name would never be spoken again. Because they knew what would happen if it was. And through the visions that had barraged my shuddering mind, I knew what would happen too. And it was happening.

Panic rose in me.

'You do not belong here,' Ulovar growled. Hazia's blood dripped from his face as somehow he steeled himself against the pulsing force emanating from the book. His jaw was set hard as rock.

'I see the world,' a deep voice said, the sound of ashes being scraped from stone. The shadow body filled out in pulses of night, overly lithe and overly tall, banded with scales that caught the light of the fallen lamp.

'You've seen enough,' Ulovar growled. 'You have no place in our world, demon of the past. You are dead and you will remain that way.' He began to mutter a quiet, insistent prayer.

'I am not bound by your mortal law, Draiohn,' the thing that had been Ciuthach laughed. 'I feel your power. A mere four Gates? Do the Draoihn send their children against me now? I served Hallenae the Riven Queen for more than a century. You cannot begin to imagine what I have achieved. I have summoned beings you would think of as gods and commanded them to my bidding. In my time we would have thought you unworthy even to carry a sword.'

Ulovar thrust his point forwards, staring down the length of the blade.

'And in my time, you are nothing but a blot on a page.'

And then it hit.

A single, mind-crushing wave bore down on me. It struck from above, the side, all around, a blanket of lead, driving me to my knees. My palms smacked against the flagstones, skin splitting. The breath was torn from my lungs; my vision blurred into swarming dots, a snowstorm of swirling flies obscuring everything.

A titanic drum-beat boomed directly from within Ciuthach's darkness, unleashed, thundering out into the world. In the centre of it, Ciuthach stood upright, uncaring of the forces he had unleashed. His bent back clicked, cracked, straightened as he stood tall in the world, rising as if he emerged from a glacier, cold and inexorable. Amber eyes burned through the tempest, pits of savage fire.

Ovitus groaned as he tried to lift his face from the ground, blood on his brow. But Ulovar remained standing, rooted in place as black wind raged around him, his sword point thrust against the ground, hands gripping the hilt to steady himself. Somehow he kept his footing against the onslaught, though sweat ran from his face in streams. His shoulders trembled.

'You will not prevail,' he managed to whisper, but even that cost him. He gasped and faltered, going down onto one knee. 'You are weak now. You will be contained.'

'Pride was ever the Draoihn's undoing.' Ciuthach's whispers floated directly into my mind on furnace heat. Mocking. 'What was clouded becomes clear. What was lost has been born anew. I have been waiting for you, you see.' He began to stroll forwards. 'Your forebears could not destroy me, only bind me. Your essence will guide me towards the final gate's opening.'

That wave of oppression swept out again, a billowing cascade of invisible stone driving me down onto my belly. Ulovar's shoulders trembled, the strength it took him to remain on one knee incalculable. As Ciuthach advanced, a black-bladed spear dragged behind him, lazily, carving a furrow through the dirt. There was a vast weight to his overlong body, his footsteps echoing in more worlds than ours alone. Only fifteen paces from Ulovar now. He would take his head. And then mine, and Ovitus's, and those of everybody else that stood in its path.

Ovitus had passed out. Or died. Drums thundered through my head, my body. The creature from the tomb cracked yellowed lips into a smile.

'You will know your place,' Ciuthach said.

I couldn't even speak, but the echo of Braithe's words stirred the embers in my gut to a blaze. No more lying down. No more being used by those that thought they were above me. No more being struck down. No. More.

I forced myself up, arms spasming as I gained my elbows and knees. Like forcing myself through rock. The steady beat radiated from Ciuthach, *dhum-dhum-dhum, dhum-dhum-dhum.* I focused on that, tried to ignore the exhaustion that threatened my limbs just for moving. I could barely steady my head to look at the deathless creature.

Ulovar raised his sword a few inches, then drove it down into the ground. A gout of fire roared up from the earth around Ciuthach, his grave-dry clothes flaring to ash. Unseen forces unleashed around him, blasting, burning. But he merely leered, or maybe that was just the effect of the skin being drawn so tight across his jaw. A volley of stone shards exploded from the earth, bouncing from skin.

The rhythm of the creature's life hammered in my head, *DHUM-DHUM-DHUM, DHUM-DHUM-DHUM,* as if it were trying to smash my skull open from the inside.

I fumbled around me, grasping among the tomb detritus. An ancient sword hilt found my hand, but the blade had long rusted, broken where it had fallen.

Ulovar tried to raise one hand from his sword hilt, fingers clawing forwards. Blood burst from his nose, running down his face in thick, twin streams of crimson, over his mouth, through his beard. His eyes bulged in their sockets, veins rising into stark relief. Lips peeled back, he forced his hand upwards. The struggle roared in every line of his frame, the desperation in his eyes as he battled the creature's will with his own. Some wordless cry strangled forth from his lips, and then it was gone. His hand slapped back down onto the cross guard of his sword; his head sank forwards. He tried again, raised his head only long enough to spray more blood from his mouth, bloody tears streaming from his eyes, before he crumpled. Fury raged in his eyes, fury and self-loathing at his defeat and vanquished pride.

Ciuthach continued to walk slowly forwards, hand stretched out in cruel mockery of Ulovar's attempts. His unchanging, burning eyes seemed to usher down into pits of molten stone, but his slow, dragging steps told me it was an effort to emit this terror-field. He wanted us to think it all-powerful. Its confidence demanded that we accept we were beaten.

I was not beaten. Not by Braithe's careless anger. Not by Hazia's knife. And not by some fecking corpse. A silent scream of hatred rang through my head. My fists clenched tight. I was no Draoihn; the creature had dismissed me. I was a little thing before it, a nothing, a nobody. I'd been nobody to Braithe. Nobody to anybody.

No more.

No.

More.

My fingers found the bow stave. As I touched it, the impossible, silvery gleam of a string took form, bending the limbs into shape. I forced my fingers to touch it and found an arrow there. Like it had been there for centuries, waiting for my hand to find it. Pain sizzled across every muscle, a low and simmering burn. That effort alone sapped at what little energy I had. I had to keep going. I had to fight, but by the Light Above and all the colours I didn't believe in, nothing had ever been harder.

Raise. The. Bow.

Draw. The. Arrow.

The shaft was white wood, inscribed with bronze. White dots filled my vision, clouding in the periphery. The dark blizzard blinded me. Pain ran rampant through my head, pounding behind my eyes, cracking at my temples, hammering the back of my skull.

I struggled to raise my arms as my sight faded. Even as I dragged the bow upright and put tension on the string, I was losing the Draoihn and the creature to a distant haze. I only had one chance. What little strength I had was fading; I would only be able to draw once. It wouldn't even matter. I couldn't hit him blind.

Dhum-dhum-dhum, dhum-dhum-dhum.

Only I didn't need to see him. I focused on that rhythm, the drumming sound in my mind. Beside it, I sensed Ulovar's slower, pulsing waves of un-sound. I let my hands move on their own, finding their way to aim for that triple-chambered heart which I could feel as clearly as I felt the stone beneath my knees, the cold, hard grip of entombed air around me, and before my strength could abandon me for the last time, I drew. I roared.

'Ciuthach!'

The bow boomed, lightning flared and the arrow sped away, released into a grey haze.

Light flooded the world, the distortion was banished and all became clear. I blinked for a moment, falling forwards as the pressure released me. Ciuthach staggered, the force of the arrow nearly knocking him from his feet, spear raised high but the arrow's shaft jutting starkly from the side of his head. Flaming lava erupted in jets, casting back the twisting shadows. Ulovar sagged forwards, blood running from his face, his eyes. Ciuthach rocked, regained his balance despite the arrow through his brain, and made to bring the spear down in the arc that would end us all.

Ulovar's arm lashed out, and a rope of brilliant lightning-fire burst forth. It lasted only half a heartbeat, a dozen coils of blue-white energy connecting Ulovar's hand to Ciuthach's chest. The demon was blasted from his feet, but instead of being hurled back, he rose two feet into the air, suspended, limbs convulsing.

Tap-tap-tap, the sound came again, but this time it was not the beat of a mind, but the thud of Ulovar's feet. He sped across the intervening yards, and his blade turned from yellow to red to white, blurring the air with heat as he drove its point into the nightmare's chest.

Fire rushed along the blade and into the creature, blazed into him. Ciuthach screeched, three voices binding together, rolling over each other in shuddering, hell-wrought anguish. He glowed with inner light, cracks running through blackened and charred skin as though he held a molten core. And then Ulovar tore the sword free and cut Ciuthach's head from his shoulders.

Silence.

Ulovar stood stock-still, framed for a moment in the pale blue light, face manic, blood-coated, and then slowly toppled sideways to the ground, crashing to the earth like a felled oak. Ciuthach remained upright, feet planted on the ground once more. But his body had turned grey, chalky. Stone. No. Ash. And then the body collapsed, into nothing.

Dust, blowing on unfelt wind.

'It should not be possible,' Ciuthach said. I stared at the severed head. Charred. Blackened. 'I served the Riven Queen. I am Sarathi.' The dead thing's amber eyes moved slowly in the sockets as if at a great effort. Perhaps it was. He looked at me, and instead of blazing pits of fire, I saw childlike terror. 'It has been so long,' the head complained, triple voiced and whining. 'It's not fair. You should have joined us, child of the grave. To reach the final gateway . . .'

I shuddered, climbed to my feet. The oppressive power was gone, leaving an emptiness that felt as unnatural. Something wet landed on my hand. Blood, dripping from my eyes.

'Honestly,' I said, 'I'm tired of old men telling me what I've done wrong.'

I drove Ovitus's sword down into Ciuthach's forehead with a crunch of splitting bone. The glow in its eyes died away, and a moment later, it crumbled into ash as well.

Everything seemed dead. The world had turned to corpses and ash, and I was alone, the last person standing in the world of the dead.

7

'I wonder when we'll get to go home,' Lochlan said. He sat beside me, watching LacCulloch's men loot our wagons. One of them had tied a many-coloured tabard to a spear butt and raised it like a flag. The mountain breeze couldn't bring the weight of stained wet cloth to life.

I was in too much pain to speak. My head felt as though anvils had been bouncing around inside it for hours. My body felt as though it had been ground between millstones. I shook my head to tell him I didn't know, and even that was too much for me.

'Do you think he'll let us go?' Lochlan asked.

I rested my head in my hands. It was all my fault. I'd brought this down upon us. I'd wanted a way out. Wanted us to escape this trap of pride and the foolishness of men. And I'd ushered our destruction inside and set it loose.

Some of LacCulloch's men glanced my way. They were hot-headed after their victory, such as it had been. Nearly everyone was dead. Their glorious charge had led to the butchery of a bunch of unprepared, badly armed followers of three charlatan sisters. LacCulloch's men had been swept up in the bloodlust, and they'd slaughtered whoever they'd found. They wanted the spoils now. Ovitus stood over me like a warden in his oxblood-red coat, and his presence kept them at bay, though I didn't think he realised it. He didn't fit into this new world around us, as much a stranger to war as I had been. But LacCulloch's war-riders had seen what Ulovar had done to the monastery gates. They weren't going to risk his ire over one idiot, idiot girl.

'Your hair,' Ovitus said. He had a puzzled, embarrassed look to him. He wouldn't look directly at the bodies.

'What about my hair?'

'It's white. It's gone white, I mean.'

I couldn't see it myself. My hair was short. I'd never seen the point in having long hair, just so that it could get tangled. I ran a hand across my head. It didn't feel any different. Didn't seem terribly important either.

'Your hair's gone white,' Lochlan said. He couldn't hear Ovitus. Didn't hear or see anything that was going on around him, though somehow he'd found me. He stood and began to walk away. Walked right through his own body, lined up with the others. That shiny dirk Braithe had given him was still clenched in one dead hand. The blade was clean, I saw, and I was glad he hadn't used it. His spirit went off to stumble around with the rest of the dead. He shouldn't have been able to speak to me. That wasn't what the shades of the dead did. They followed the paths and uttered the words they'd known in life. Until the feather-crowned ghost had spoken to me on the bridge, I had thought of them as disconnected from living things. Confused, shadowed echoes of by-gone lives. I hoped for Lochlan's sake that the misty, green-white shape stand-ing with its feet in its own corpse was not really him. The Light Above should have claimed him, drawn his soul up into Anavia. He was too simple a soul to be taken down into Skuttis by the Night Below.

I shivered and wrapped my arms around myself. The world was grey.

Kella sounded her trumpet atop the wall. They hadn't brought her body down yet. Fergus and Farlan seemed to be arguing with one another about the price of ham, but on opposite sides of the yard, facing away from each other. There were as many ghosts as there were living people.

Niven LacCulloch wore a conqueror's smile. The faceplate of his helm was raised, and his pride and blood-glory were writ large as he strode around Dal-nesse. He spoke to one of his men, punched him lightly on the arm, and they shared a joke. A joke. Among all this. I must have looked disgusted. He saw me, walked right through Lochlan and gave only the slightest twitch to show that he'd felt anything at all. Maybe he'd felt a chill. Maybe I'd just imagined it.

'The leader's girl,' he said. His eyes took me apart, measuring me as though he were going to try to guess my weight. 'I'll be taking you with me. I place the terms of your indenture at ten years.'

'The girl is coming with me.'

Ulovar appeared from the sept, walking slowly. He carried a small, dull lead box beneath one arm. The whites of his eyes were stained a vivid red. I was not the only one to carry the battle with me.

'My lord van,' LacCulloch said. 'The traditions over spoils of battle are very clear. She served with the enemy. As the victor—'

'You call this a battle?' Ulovar barked. 'What you did here today will stain your name from now until your clan no longer walks the earth. Do you think you fought a war here, LacCulloch? You slaughtered innocent men, women and children to catch three harmless old women.'

LacCulloch's smile fell deader than a drowned rat. His tongue ran over his lips.

'But, my lord—you helped us. Your mighty power sundered the gates.'

'I did what I had to,' Ulovar said gravely. 'And the screams of these innocents will haunt me to my last day. Were you one of my thails, I'd see you blinded and hobbled for your actions today, but this is not my land. When the king hears of it, you had best kiss the dirt to save your neck. And this girl is mine. If you want to fight me for her, then choose a grove of ash trees, cut the runes into their trunks and let's have done with it.'

LacCulloch's slaughter-pride waivered on his face, then retreated behind the mask all Harran thails wore when admonished by those who sat on higher branches.

'Of course, Van LacNaithe.' He didn't even look at me as he stalked back to his men. I felt a gentle hand on my shoulder. Ovitus. I blinked at it, unsure what I was supposed to do. Everything seemed very far away. Sounds seemed muted.

'Get your things, Raine,' he said. 'We have to go.'

'I've nowhere to go,' I said.

'You're coming with us,' he said. 'To Redwinter.'

'It's the middle of the night,' I said quietly. 'I need to cook for Braithe. And Lochlan will want to play cards.'

They left me alone for a few moments, and I watched the dead going about their business. Living, dead, all jumbled up together. Lochlan didn't speak to me again. Perhaps I had imagined it. It was hard to keep track of time, of people, of who was alive and who was dead, unless I stared hard enough at the bodies to make them seem like real people again. I looked down and found that I held a knife. I tossed it from one hand to the other. Ulovar had taken the midnight-blue bow from me before Ovitus dragged me from the tomb.

'What happened to the book?' I asked.

'It's still there,' Ulovar said. 'And it won't budge. I don't want to risk trying to force it from that pedestal, but I managed to remove Hazia's page again. It must be returned to the Blackwell.' He held the box at arm's length. 'I don't want to touch this for longer than I have to. Come. Once I've closed the crypt, we ride day and night until we get there.'

The stiletto point had driven through most of my mind and was coming out of the back. The drumming wouldn't stop.

'Peace, now,' Ulovar said. He reached out and placed a finger on the back of my hand. The reds of his eyes swirled, black patterns and shapes among the colour. When he took his finger away the world closed around me, dull, opaque, matted. I couldn't hear the rats scuttling anymore. Couldn't feel the wind before it reached me. No more drums, but even scowling was too much effort. 'You did a brave thing today,' Ulovar said. I shrugged. I hadn't felt brave. I'd just been so angry. 'I know the pain of losing family. I'm sorry for your loss.'

I looked across the ranked bodies of the sisters' followers, lying uncovered. The crows would come for them with the dawn. A blanket of soot-cast feathers, jostling for scraps.

'They weren't my family,' I said. 'I don't have any family.'

Lochlan's ghost looked confused as he tried to drink from a bucket that wasn't there. He flickered, growing insubstantial. And then he was gone, blown away on the wind. One by one, the last remnants of these people were fading from the world.

'It was a spirit lock,' Ulovar muttered to Ovitus. 'Hazia called him Ciuthach. The name is recorded in Autolocus's *Lessons on the Spirit War*. He was one of Hallenae's creatures, a warlord in his own right. Dead, these past seven hundred years. He lies dormant again, but his power will rebuild, and he'll return if he's allowed to. The five in the tombs around him were Draoihn. The old kind. They're supposed to keep his soul locked in the Afterworld. If he even has one.'

'He can't be destroyed completely?' Ovitus asked.

Ulovar shook his head. His eyes were ringed with crusted blood.

'Some things are bound too tightly to the world to be destroyed. Bodies can be reformed, or it can find a new vessel. Grandmaster Robilar has been killed before, and that hasn't slowed her down much. Better to keep his soul trapped and locked here. I'll do what I can to see that it goes undisturbed.'

My mind was empty. Everything was empty.

'You can cry, if you want to,' Ovitus said. He'd found Braithe's wine, grimaced as he drank. Could hardly blame a man for drinking just then, though. He offered it to me, but I shook my head.

'I will,' I said detachedly.

I began to laugh. His eyes narrowed and I laughed more, and I had never hated to laugh so much but it was too funny not to. Ulovar watched me without speaking.

. . . . . .

I seemed to jerk awake some time later, standing over the body of a small child. I remembered the day he was born, the celebrations where I got drunk on barley wine for the first time. There had been singing and stories, the babe's parents exhausted but happy as the sisters proclaimed good fortune for him. It was the first time that I'd really noticed Braithe, first time I'd wanted to kiss him. The child's head was broken now. It was a strange thing. I found that I was still toying with that knife. It wasn't my knife, and I didn't recall where I'd found it.

I looked up at the three sooth-sisters, swaying on their poles. They'd even hanged Sister Anthra, and she'd already been dead.

Lies have been told. We, the faithful who serve the Light Above in all her colours, shall be raised on high.

They'd been right, after a fashion. Maybe there'd been more to their portents than they'd realised.

Braithe lay beneath them, his hands bound behind his back, his face a mess of bruises. They looked better on him than they had on me. Of all those who had deserved to survive this, he had not. I had loved him, but I had been filled with something else, so heavy that there seemed no room in the world for love anymore. He was still so solid, and the life that filled him felt like an insult to the bodies of the fools who had believed in him.

'Should have listened to you,' he said through split lips. His eyes were swollen to slits. 'Should have got out when we had the chance.'

'And what then?' I said. I couldn't look at him as I spoke. 'Everybody else would still have died. Lochlan would have died. Kella would have died. They'd all have died.'

'Wasn't our job to protect them,' Braithe said. 'What happens to me now, Raine?'

'I don't care,' I said, and a giddy laugh escaped my lips. 'You led us here. You said there was help coming. You let them call you *Captain,* and I supported you. Look what we've done. I brought Hazia here and brought all this down on us. I didn't even believe any of it, did you know that?'

An ugly chuckle escaped Braithe's lips.

'Neither did I.'

I threw back my head and screamed at the sky. Tears turned the stars to blurred smears of cruel silver light, and I howled and I howled. Anger raged through me, fury at the sheer unfairness of it all. I rocked forwards, pain coursing through my shoulders and back, and I pounded my fist against the earth. I punched until my knuckles split, the pain nothing compared to this horrible, blinding grief. Breathing became hard, ragged. I couldn't draw air, couldn't stand to be alive in this bleak and dreadful world.

It wasn't fair. I'd had nothing, and even that had been taken from me. I couldn't inhale. We hadn't even buried them. I fell to my side, muscles giving up, letting me topple to the same treacherous ground that had drunk my friends' blood. I lay still. I lay shaking.

I don't care, I thought. *Let me die now. Let me shake my eyes from my head. Let it all just end, let everything end and take me away so I don't have to know it. Take me so I don't have to think on this ever again. Let me die. Let me die.*

What did anything matter now? Panic, anger, horror and torment flurried like a snowstorm around me, my mind unable to grasp the impact of one before the next took it over. I saw the yawning maw of madness stretching wide to envelop me. I welcomed it, thanked it, pleaded with it to take me. Anything. So long as I didn't have to know what I had caused. I took hold of the knife in both hands.

A shape loomed over me, a heavy, dark shadow. Ulovar's voice floated to me from the darkness.

'Warrior of the north, the Crown has need of you. You will destroy yourself with this. The Crown must be served.'

Thick, callused fingers gripped my skull. An image blazed in my mind: Ulovar, knee bent in the lunge, his sword striking as fire blazed along his sword. A moment of victory.

And then, something flowed from Ulovar's fingers and into my skull. It cut like a knife. I screamed as it seared across my mind, gouging a canyon a thousand feet deep and filled with flame, a raging, cauterising glow. And then it drew closed, sealing, walls crashing shut. I heard the thunder of his trance as four Gates rose silent and hollow over the scar driven through my mind.

And then it was all gone. Gates, scar, fire. Gone.

And so was I.

Before we left, Ulovar brought the great sept of Dalnesse Monastery down on the catacombs. He worked through the night, hunched over heavy books, drawing patterns in red, green and gold ink, chanting invocations in sounds that didn't mean anything. The mountain howled, the ground trembled, waking me from a sleep I hadn't known I'd entered. I limped outdoors without feeling a thing as stone dust filled the air.

It must have been a monumental feat of magic, but I was essentially dead to the world.

The days that followed I remembered only as a decaying tapestry dredged from a river. Parts of me had rotted through; others remained miraculously whole. But all were dark, and sodden, and gave no joy to look back on.

The dreams, I was aware of. I saw the depth of fire in Ciuthach's molten eyes shining at me from every dark corner. I had stared into the burning, hungering soul of a creature of bygone power. The sooth-sisters used to say that evil was nothing but a matter of perspective, but they were wrong. I had stared into its hungering maw, and I knew the sharpness of its teeth. To close my eyes was to awaken that fell presence back into the world, as if even remembering it revived some part of its existence. By daylight I was little more than a blank, staring clotheshorse. Two days after I began to refuse to sleep, the hallucinations and visual distortions began, and I could seldom remember what I was doing. Eventually my body forced me to stillness through sheer exhaustion, and that sallow oblivion was still better than waking in a pool of hot sweat with a scream on my lips. I slept only when my body forced it upon me, and my mind was all the more shadowed for it.

There was a journey. We went from stopping place to stopping place, sheltered by lords or wealthy townsfolk who seemed only too happy to gift us with food and wine. There was a nervousness in their voices as they greeted us, bowing and scraping to Van Ulovar of Clan LacNaithe and commonly thinking me some kind of servant. I had no energy to correct them.

Twice we sheltered at a Brannish governor's residence, where soldiers in orange and white opened the doors with a strange combination of obeisance and disregard. They were the strangers here in Harran, though their tithe-houses and governor's halls had been part of our land since long before the time of my grandparents, whoever they might have been. And yet, the Brannish knew themselves a thing apart, the soldiers rotated in and out so that they never put down roots, or took their spouses back with them along the thick mud of the road leading south. Their casual indifference suited me. They were not part of Harran, not really, and neither was I.

The world held no interest for me. Not now, not after what I had seen. Though I had travelled the High Pastures extensively with the sisters, there was much that was new to me. Men in the south shaved off their beards in the Brannish fashion, and the women gathered their skirts above the knee to display garishly embroidered woollen stockings. There was less beef, more mutton, less ale and more cider. Even the houses were different, thatched roofs instead of slate. I didn't care. I didn't care about anything. It was enough to simply exist through each day, dreading the coming of night. I found succour in drinking until terror could find no purchase in the sodden wreck of my mind. Ulovar did not approve. I could see it in his eyes, and the way he denied Ovitus the same release, but he paid for the wine all the same.

It was three days' ride out of the High Pastures, leaving behind Van Niven LacCulloch, leaving behind the bracken and the open moorland. Ovitus sat beside me as I swayed dozily in the saddle, reading aloud from dry books about the Evoline Kings, who'd had too many sons. Most of them had murdered one another. Or recounting the ill-fated rebellions that had flickered in and out of existence over the last century. I knew what he was doing. The guilt was written plain on his thick features as he tried to jostle some interest in the world back into me. At one town he took me to a shop which sold jewellery, where he talked for a solid hour about his sweetheart, Liara of Clan LacShale. She was fair as the morning is bright, small but well-proportioned, her hair the envy of bonfires. She was kind and magnanimous, gentle yet strong in nature. She was also a Draoihn apprentice in training at Redwinter, under Ovitus's uncle's tutelage. When he was finally done boring the shopkeeper, he bought a golden locket. I'd never seen so much money change hands in one place. Ridiculous.

When I thought of Braithe, there was no grief there. There was nothing there at all.

When food was placed before me, I ate, but the fine cuts of meat and sweetened vegetables the inns served tasted plainer than water. A boarding house provided rotten goat in the stew, and though I noted it as I began to eat, I said nothing. Ovitus made to protest, but his uncle silenced him and chewed through it all the same. His eyes were still red as blood.

'We must choose a path south,' he said as the serving boys kept their distance. The lead box containing the page that had unbound Ciuthach lay beside him on the common room table. 'They will be watching for us on the road.'

'An escort would be no bad thing, Uncle,' Ovitus said. 'Not with what you are forced to carry.'

'I will not risk it,' Ulovar said. 'Think, boy. Hazia passed through the wards on the Blackwell, though it should have been impossible. She stole the means to resurrect that thing, and knew precisely where to find it. She was a good girl. A good apprentice. It was not her own will that drove her there.'

My eyes rested on the plain, dull-metal box on the table. I had held that page. Had shown it to Lochlan, toyed with it. I'd experimented on the means to unleash nightmare upon the world.

'All the more reason to surround it with loyal Draoihn,' Ovitus said.

Ulovar's left eye wept thin, bloody fluid.

'Hazia cannot have entered the Blackwell alone,' he said. 'Someone in Redwinter had to help her. And if so, then they will be the first to have pursued us. I will return this to the Blackwell myself, or I will place it into Grandmaster Robilar's hands, and no other's.'

They talked of mountain passes, lesser travelled roads and rivers I'd never heard of. I only half listened as I drank myself a blanket to cover the terrors that lay in the night.

Ulovar's caution saw us board a trading barge in a backwater town, and for two weeks we passed quietly along the water. The landscape gradually became less mountainous, then less hilly, then less forested until we disembarked and rode through the peaceful central heartlands where the long, golden wheat was being harvested and stone bridges spanned swift-flowing rivers. Herds of longhorn cattle sometimes wandered in the distance, their musky stink carried on the wind.

I awoke one morning with a stiff neck, the run-down tavern's pillow barely stuffed, and I winced as I sat up to rub it. I felt hunger properly for the first time since Ulovar had stabbed my mind, not just knowledge that I should eat, but a desire for fatty sausages and boiled eggs. Sadly, breakfast only consisted of a stodgy porridge with bacon lardons and some crumbled goat cheese. I blinked a few times, wondering at the sensation of feeling before it slipped away again. But little by little, I began to return. I did not want to. Grief found no purchase in my mind, but fear—that remained.

Ulovar set a terrible pace, fourteen hours a day in the saddle, though he finally allowed a day of rest at a town on the banks of a river. Great mills lined the waterside, and I watched their wheels turning as Ulovar went down to see the dockmaster about taking another passage. Ovitus waited with me for a time.

'Your hair's getting longer,' he said.

I'd avoided mirrors since the journey began, maybe afraid of the girl that would look back out at me. I was a new thing, I thought. If I was new, how could I bear blame? When I finally looked, I did not like what I saw. A thin scar began along my nose, slicing down my cheek to my jaw. I'd faced down Ciuthach, but it was Hazia's knife that lingered in my skin. Not that Ciuthach had left me unmarked. My hair had been dark before, but even at the root it now grew an icy blue-white. It made me stand out, and I wore a scarf over it when I remembered. But it was the person behind the changes that I disliked the most. I had taken those scars in a crucible of change. It was the child who bore them that I didn't recognise.

'Hair grows,' I said.

'I like it.' Ovitus beamed a rosy smile at me, the golden locket destined for Liara LacShale's neck playing in his fingers.

His eyes moved from the locket and then to my own neck, and for a horrible moment I thought he was going to give it to me.

'I'll probably cut it off again soon,' I said. I felt that should be enough.

'Of course, as you prefer,' Ovitus mumbled. He sounded embarrassed. The locket vanished into a pocket. Maybe I'd misread a friendly gesture. It seemed impossible that he'd think I'd be thinking about romance just then, but then, there was little on my mind at all. I hadn't even found the strength to ask why they were dragging me along with them.

One night I stood at the rail of the barge that was floating us down from the north, and watched the insects gliding across the river's surface. I stayed there a long time. I stayed there until the sky grew black, and my shawl couldn't keep the cold from my arms. I needed the silence. Needed the quiet. Time to let my mind steady itself, to catch on to anything that would hold it from tumbling down into this crevasse. Everything was different now. Everything had changed, but I didn't have the energy or the strength to control it. It was all I could do to keep standing.

She appeared on the dark, far side of the bank across the water, rippling in blue light. A shawl of dark feathers draped her shoulders, a wreath of them above her ears. She shouldn't have been here. She was from the river. Even the ghosts that lingered didn't travel, no more than trees do. It wasn't what they were.

'You don't need to be afraid, Raine,' the spirit whispered. Her voice was as clear as if she were standing next to me, heavy and lush.

'There is nothing left of me but fear,' I said. 'And I am nothing without it.'

'Fear is natural,' the ghost said, her words a rustle of skirts, an autumn wood throwing leaves against a window. 'Do not fear to fear. You are moving through the world now. You leave change in your wake. It has been a long time, but I feel it. Feel the stirrings of something that will leave us all changed. You must grow stronger. You must prepare.'

A boatman yawned behind me, shifting in his heavy winter coat. I mouthed my response back to her. There was no point in saying the words aloud. She didn't need sound to hear them.

'You helped me,' I said. 'What are you?'

'I am the dream that was, and the echo of what is still to be.'

I thought that I detected a hint of mirth in her voice. Teasing me.

'You need not fear me, Raine. Had I meant you harm, you would not be here. But you must keep yourself secret. You must keep yourself safe. At all costs, you must not reveal what you can see to the Draoihn. They will seem generous at times. They will woo you with warmth and song and the offer of respect and position. But if they know your true nature, they will destroy you.'

'I'm not a fool,' I said.

'Learn what you can from them. You will need it.'

'What are you?' I asked. 'You're not like the others I see.'

'No,' she said. 'I'm no lost soul, Raine. I'm something else.'

'Are you one of the hidden folk?'

'You say something?' the boatman behind me asked. I'd spoken aloud.

I turned back to the figure across the water, but if she had been there at all, she was gone now. I stayed there, staring over the water, until my fingers turned white with cold. I did not remember finding my way to my blankets, but the wine I had put out for myself was untouched in the morning, and my mind had lain dark and empty.

Whatever murderous pace and small, unknown roads Ulovar chose, we could not travel every day. There had to be rests, for the horses at least. It made no difference to me whether we rode or remained in place. To be a journey, a period of travel must have a beginning and an end; something must have transitioned from one place to another. But how can something that has no form begin in one place and end somewhere else? If a crow begins flying south, but what arrives is a swan, then the crow never undertook a journey. I puzzled over this, and found that the philosophy engaged me where other worldly concerns could not. I knew that I was not the girl who had left Mama's scribe-house, nor the girl who had followed superstitions across the High Pastures. I was not Braithe's woman, not even the girl who had sought to help a fallen woman in the snow. I didn't know what I was. I was ill-defined, uncertain in my constancy, like an image reflected in a pool full of ripples. As I looked around me at an unfamiliar world, I found myself no more recognisable than the strangers who filled my cup, or those that rode beside me.

On one of those rest days, Ovitus urged me to walk in the sun. He thought it might do me good, or else he wanted some time alone with his uncle, who despite all his muscle, bulk and title, seemed to be fading at the edges. I did as I was asked without much feeling about it. Inside, outside, warm or cold, it mattered little. There had been a dawn, and later there would be dusk, and tomorrow the process would repeat itself. I existed, and that was all. We had rooms at a Brannish tithe-house, which had seemed cleaner than the inn and cost nothing for a lord like Ulovar LacNaithe. The relationship between them all was foggy to me. The Brannish owned Harran, as they owned many other countries, but Harran ruled itself. The Brannish took tithes and kept soldiers in little garrisons around Harran, but Harran provided soldiers to the Brannish's royal armies when they went off to conquer somewhere else, so that they could put Brannish governors there as well. The Harran lords were owed respect and outranked the Brannish governors, but the governors conveyed the king of Brannlant's rulings, which were more important but didn't actually seem to have any effect. I found the whole system entirely senseless, which sat as well with me as anything else.

I walked, as Ovitus had said that I should, choosing a path away from the village at random. It was a dirt track, leading up along the hillside where sheep wandered aimlessly. I'd gone five or six miles with only sky and the occasional eagle for company when I met a man in the livery of a Brannish tax collector coming the other way. He was limping.

'You there, miss,' he called to me in that strange accent the Brannish have, which sounds like they don't come from anywhere. 'Give me a hand here.'

'Why?' I asked. The question could have had a number of different meanings.

'A bloody cow trod on my foot,' he said. 'Help me back to the governor's residence.'

I looked down at his foot. I couldn't see anything wrong with it. Naturally, I was wary about men begging help from young women on the road, but he was thin and ageing, and I didn't fear him. His limp looked genuine.

'No thank you,' I said. 'I'm not going that way.'

'Come on, girl, I need help,' he said.

I stared at him a moment and tried to think why I ought to do as he asked, and if it was sensible, or good, or anything at all really. But in the end I just shrugged at him and carried on walking. He shouted some things behind me, but I wasn't really listening. Somewhere over the hills somebody was burning something. There was wood smoke in the air. The Raine who had arrived at Dalnesse, fearful and penned in by walls and obligations, would have helped him. I knew that. I found her hard to understand now.

I walked quite a long way, and Ovitus had to come and find me on his horse.

'Where are you going?' he asked, as though I had an answer for him. I didn't. He'd sent me out to walk, so I'd walked. He tried to make small talk as I rode behind him on the way back, but I wasn't really paying attention, so he ended up talking about Liara LacShale again, as he often did. I didn't really pay attention to that either.

There were other days like that one, but none worth remembering.

· · · · · ·

'We're approaching the city,' Ulovar told me one night when we sat alone together in an inn's common room, long after the other patrons had retired to bed. He looked old, drained, the lead box never far from reach but seldom in his hands. The fire was banked to sweltering proportions, but he added another log all the same. I couldn't tell if it was the heat he wanted, or to keep the shadows at bay. 'I'm taking you to Redwinter, Raine. That may not mean much to you. But it will be your home, if you want it.'

'Why?' I said.

He shifted in his chair, more now a man deep in his fifties than the warrior who had brought down a nightmare.

'Do you think you are ready to hear?'

'Yes.'

'We have spoken little on the road. But that does not mean that I have been unobservant,' he said. 'You are in great pain.'

'I don't feel it.'

He shifted, fingers toying with the end of another log. The shadows gathered in the reds of his eyes. The crackling fire would never be enough to drive them out.

'You saw what Hazia stole. A page from a book. She took it from the Blackwell, the vault that lies beneath Redwinter. A place so heavily guarded with ancient power that it should not have been possible to steal from. The grandmaster of my order forbade me to pursue her. But I did anyway. Hazia was my responsibility, and I must confess to what transpired. To the lives lost as a result of my failure.'

'You nearly caught her. On the bridge.'

'"Nearly" is seldom enough. I should have killed her, when I had the chance. I could have done it. A killing spell at that range is no simple thing, but not beyond my ability.' He frowned as he stared into the fire, trying to replay details from memories that had not been focused on them. 'The bridge should have held me. Perhaps the page itself protected her. I had hoped to break whatever twisted compulsion it had inflicted upon her. Had hoped to bring her back.'

He didn't know, of course. It had not been Hazia, had not been whatever evil power lay within that book. That power had erupted from a word, a word spoken by a woman dressed in blue. I could see the mystery of it in the bruise-like hollows beneath his eyes, the slow motion of his lips.

'What will happen now?'

'We shall see when we arrive at Redwinter. I broke the grandmaster's command. It will be for her to decide whether my actions were for good or for ill.'

'You need me as a witness,' I said, finally understanding why I was here. He nodded.

'And what do you want?'

I wanted it all to be different.

'I don't want to be afraid anymore,' I said. I looked up slowly. 'I want to be strong. Can I be like you?'

'You would be Draoihn?'

'Yes.'

'I will not deny that I have thought on it. You have the talent,' Ulovar said, his bloody eyes narrow. 'To become Draoihn is no easy path. It is a life of service to the Crown, and comes with great sacrifice. To be Draoihn is to become a weapon. I do not know if I can ask any more of you than fate already has.'

'To be anything has to be better than being nothing,' I said.

A shadow crossed Ulovar's face, as though all the shadows that had hidden in the webs around his eyes and canyoned across his cheeks had been only the vanguard of a greater darkness.

'You are far from nothing, Raine, though it may feel like that at the moment. You have a right to life, and a right to choose its direction.'

'I chose my own life when I left my mother and ran away with the sisters. But if not for me, you would have caught Hazia. Then you wouldn't have broken the gates. Everyone would still be alive. I gave them no choice in that. Why should I choose now?'

'Nobody knows where their choices will lead. We can only hope that our intentions are pure,' Ulovar said softly. His gentleness crawled against my skin. There was no place for it within me. 'The failing was mine, and I shall be the one to pay its price. But you are more than just the sum of your choices. There is power in you, Raine. I saw it in the crypt. If you would harness that power for duty, for service, then I will do what I can to help you. The decision is not mine alone. But there is a place for you in my clanhold. And it is all I can do for you, having failed you so completely.' He tossed the log onto the fire, sending sparks billowing into the flue. 'What do you feel?' he asked, and even against the stacks of clouded grey panes that separated me from the world around me, I knew he was no longer asking about my choices.

'I'm alive,' I said.

'And?'

I just shrugged. There was no 'and'.

'You don't say much, Raine. You just eat, drink, and do what you're told.'

That sounded true, so I shrugged again. 'Perhaps that's what I should always have done.'

'For some that is enough,' Ulovar said. 'But I do not think fate intends such a life for you.'

9

I could feel Ciuthach in the dreams that floated at the far edge of my mind. He was sealed back into his book, buried beneath hundreds of tons of broken mountain and fallen monastery, but somehow he had followed me deep into the world. Nothing can track a person with greater tenacity than the horrors that broke them.

Another sleepless night clouded my sight, and the depth of weariness was closing in hard enough to ensure that I wouldn't wake screaming from those furnace eyes, so I was glad when the road through the pines brought us to a cluster of buildings around an inn.

'How can they do enough trade here?' I wondered aloud. The forest was thick around the crossroads, and the roads were barely worthy of the name. Ulovar's desire to keep from commonly travelled paths had taken us a long, circuitous route cutting east as well as south. Ovitus pointed to drying racks, hides stretched out across them.

'Trappers and hunters,' he said. 'Boar, wolf, bear, beavers too, by the look of those pelts. Harranir is barely a league away now. The forest is dense, but it's well-trodden ground.'

We dismounted. Whenever I climbed down from Ivy's back, her big brown eyes seemed full of sympathy. Like she knew something was wrong but couldn't have said what. You and me both, horse.

Ulovar looked like a padded cushion that had been beaten for spring cleaning and hung from a line. He moved delicately but with a great weight calling his whole body down towards the ground, that lead box tucked beneath one arm. He staggered after dismounting, caught himself on a hitching post.

'Don't touch me,' he hissed at Ovitus, breath dragging hoarsely in his throat. 'Not until this is done. Not my clothes, not my skin. Don't touch me at all.'

'You're fading, Uncle,' Ovitus said. 'This can't go on.'

Ulovar pushed back up from the post. He grunted. 'It won't. Not long now. See to Raine. Make her eat something.' He moved slowly into the inn's interior, a wash of roasted-meat scent escaping on a wave of warm light.

'He's not well,' Ovitus said.

'It's that thing he's carrying,' I said. 'Hazia was injured when she came to Dalnesse. Maybe it's inflicting the same on him?'

'No,' Ovitus said. I had not spoken of those events with him, not in all the days we'd been on the road. 'It made Hazia stronger. It was Draoihn Dhoone who wounded her.'

'Who was he?'

'A Draoihn in service to my uncle,' Ovitus said. 'He caught up to her first. But that artefact she carried didn't weaken her. It made her stronger. Strong enough to kill a Draoihn of the Second Gate.'

'If I'd known what she was, I would have cut her throat,' I said. The words left me before I'd thought them through, as words often do. They sat comfortably on my tongue. But Raine-in-the-snow—the Raine who had helped Hazia—they weren't her words. I had struggled just to draw an arrow on Ulovar, even in the throes of desperate self-preservation.

'I was supposed to, if I caught up to her,' Ovitus said. He adjusted the front of his oxblood coat, shifted his sword around at his waist. He'd lost girth in the weeks on the road. My own belt was looser than it had been too. His uncle looked beaten down; Ovitus just sagged. 'I'm supposed to believe that I could have. But I don't know. I really don't.'

'The thing in that box isn't making your uncle strong,' I said. What did it matter who was capable of killing whom? Everyone winds up dead in the end.

'I can only guess,' Ovitus said. 'But I think that's because we're taking it the wrong way. Away from where it wants to go, anyway. Hazia got stronger the closer she got to Ciuthach's tomb. The further we travel from Dalnesse, the more it's trying to tear my uncle back north. It's one of the reasons he doesn't want to encounter anyone else.'

'He's accepted the burden.'

'Sometimes I think my uncle was cut from pure duty. It's why he had to go after Hazia, even when the grandmaster forbade it.'

It didn't matter. It would be over soon.

Ovitus took my arm, began to lead me inside. I didn't need his hand on me, shrugged it off. My attention had been caught by a spectral figure standing half in and half out of a tree trunk. It was a young tree, had probably grown long after she'd died. She seemed to have a burden on her shoulder, looking around as if unsure where to put it. She didn't see me. Didn't see anything. Just an echo of someone.

'What is it?' Ovitus asked.

I shook my head. 'Nothing. Let's eat.'

The inn was busier than I expected. I let myself be seated at a communal table, and Ovitus wasted little time in ordering large helpings of whatever they had. A hunter's lodge always has the best fare, and there was venison, boar and fowl. Ulovar had acquired rooms for us—they would be little more than cupboards with beds, but they were private—and he did not come down to join us. I listened to some of the other diners talking, ears pricking at their accents.

'They sound like they're from the city,' I said. 'From Harranir.'

'We're close,' Ovitus told me. He had laid waste to a whole string of sausages. 'We might even be there tomorrow night. Then we'll have to decide whether to ride through or cut around.' He rested his fork on his plate, gently, in the manner of a man who wishes to pause for breath but is not yet finished. 'You've been there before?'

'Once, when I was young. With my mother. She was looking for work. It was a long time ago.'

'Harranir used to be called Delatmar,' Ovitus said. 'During the years of the Yanni Dominion.' It was hard to listen through the blanketing weariness, and the haze of exhaustion was causing me to see things that weren't there. Colours were going wrong. I saw blues as black, yellows as brown. Spiders danced in the seam of a wall, birds could disappear and reappear in the sky, and I saw swirling letters in an old man's beard. Even so, I did not want to be lectured. I did not want to be taught. Mostly I wanted to be left alone.

'I know,' I said, cutting into Ovitus's lecture. 'Before Hallenae was defeated and the Succession Age began.'

'It was!' Ovitus said. There was a twinkle in his eyes that I hadn't meant to put there. A spark of puppyish engagement. I had failed to discourage him. 'Where did you read about that?'

'In books,' I said. 'I forget their names. They had histories in some of the scribe-houses we boarded at when I was young. I used to read them to Mama in the evenings.'

'It's fascinating, isn't it?' Ovitus said excitedly. I had pierced some bubble of his personal interest, and he wanted to squeeze what he knew out of it. He was a good-natured enough boy, but for a Draoihn apprentice the same age as me, he seemed younger. 'Harranir is the only city in the country that predates the Succession Age. It actually predates the Yanni Dominion as well. It was buried during the Age of Soot—that was over fourteen hundred years ago! But lots of the buildings still stand. Isn't that amazing? We'll see them tomorrow.'

'I know,' I said. I sounded weary, even to myself. 'As I said, I've seen it before.'

Ovitus continued on about the rising of the great primal demons of the Age of Soot, and the kingships of Haddat-Nir and Delac-Mir that got trampled on, and all the way back to the Age of the Faded Lords and the Bronze Kings and everything else that hadn't mattered for three thousand years. He spoke about it with great authority, because he'd read it in a book, while I would have struggled to tell anyone what I'd eaten for supper two weeks ago, and it had always seemed implausible to me that anyone could really know what had happened so very long ago. Impossible, and of no real relevance. I hadn't read the histories in the scribe-house because they were fascinating; I had read them because my mother insisted on keeping me by her side, and there was nothing else to do when the long evenings drew in.

'Ciuthach was from the Riven Queen's time,' I broke in. 'I saw him. Fighting. Saw him killed there. He said he served her for a century.' I fixed Ovitus with a direct stare. Enough of his history. If he wanted to talk directly of things from the past, I would do it on terms that made it relevant. He shifted uncomfortably.

'That thing—Ciuthach—was just a remnant,' Ovitus said. 'A shadow of what once was. It was not really—not a person. It was old magic that has nowhere else to go, magic that thought it still had purpose. That's what my uncle said.'

'It thought it was one of the Riven Queen's warriors,' I said. 'Thought it was fighting a war that ended seven hundred years ago. Or wanted to start it over again.'

'That sounds like them.'

'Did—did any of them look beautiful and wear crowns made of feathers?' I asked. The riverboat meeting with my fairy ghost mother had slowly worked on my mind. Everything inside my head was dampened, muddled, but she had helped me. She had nearly killed Ulovar, and he had never even seen her. She was not the same foul, dead thing that Ciuthach had been, and she was not one of the empty, staggering spirits that lingered around the site of their own death. She could speak, and she could move, but I thought she was dead all the same.

'If there were, I doubt they'd be very beautiful now,' Ovitus said. My question had been an odd one, but he didn't seem to notice. 'The Crown endures. All else is dust.'

'Nephew.' Ulovar had changed his clothes, removed his mail, though he had donned his oxblood coat and wore his sword again. He flicked his head towards the door. 'I thought I saw something through the window. Come with me.' Ovitus's face seemed to lose all colour, as if a tap had opened beneath his double chin and it all drained away.

'What is it?'

'I don't know,' Ulovar said. 'Maybe nothing. Come.'

Ovitus rose with the stiff back of a man who has eaten too many sausages too quickly, but he followed Ulovar. I had not been summoned, so I remained seated, staring into the dram of whisky that remained in my cup. It was cheaper and took less drinking for whisky to do its work than wine, and I had developed a taste for it. If there was one thing the people of Harran did very well, it was whisky.

'Top you up, darlin'?'

A man had sat down opposite me. He was about thirty, with a ragged, un-kempt look and a long beard that should have belonged to a much older man. He wore the thick, warm clothing favoured by foresters, but there was a pow-erful, bitter, mouldy odour to him. Ashium leaf. It was hard to come by in the north. Braithe had acquired it whenever he could, then fallen into a bleary-eyed stupor for the rest of the night. It was strange to think, now, that I'd looked forward to it.

'I won't object,' I said, pushing my cup towards him. He had a whole bottle of whisky, and since I didn't have any money, declining would have meant waiting for Ulovar and Ovitus to return. The man's clothes were cleaner than I'd have expected if he'd spent the day rolling around finishing off deer in the forest, and there was no smell to him. Or maybe that was just the whisky in my nose. He took out a packet of Ashium leaf and put it into a pipe.

'Smoke?'

'No. But thank you for the drink.'

He used a candle to get the pipe bowl glowing, seeming happy to sit in the silence that surrounded me. I drank the whisky, then reached for the bottle. Paused before my fingers touched it.

'Go ahead, mate,' he said. 'You won't owe me nothing for it. Those like us, we ought to share what we have with one another.'

'I'm not a trapper,' I said.

'Never mistook you for one,' he said, leaning forwards in the chair and suck-ing on the pipe stem. He blew a long stream of white smoke into the air be-tween us. He spoke quietly, low and inaudible to any listening ears. 'You gotta be careful, mate. Got to know who you're seeing. Got to know *what* you're seeing. Plenty of things here aren't what they seem. Places. People.'

Despite the sleepless weariness and the whisky, I found my mind coming back to full alertness.

'What do you mean?'

The man smiled, and I saw that beneath his overlong beard, he had a snaggle to his lip.

'I saw a woman in a tree today,' he said. 'And so did you.'

'Anybody can climb a tree,' I said. But I had placed my hands on the table edge, ready to spring. I knew what he was speaking of.

But the bearded trapper just sat back, his eyes dancing. He spoke quietly. 'There's a difference between a woman in a tree and a woman in a tree, though, ain't there? That's what really matters, isn't it? Seeing what's real. What's true.'

Had I possessed hackles, his words would have raised them.

'Seeing the truth, you mean.'

'The living truth,' the trapper said. Beneath the fox-fur around his neck, I saw he wore a dirty yellow warrior's coat. His nails were clean. He was neither a hunter nor trapper. I didn't know what to make of him, but his words had chilled me. He sucked on the pipe again, blew out a cloud. 'Truth of the living, and the truth of the dead. No, no, don't worry. I'm not here to spill anyone's secrets. We all got our own, don't we?' He tapped his pipe, then used his free hand to lift a small charm, carved in the shape of a bird, that hung tangled in his beard. 'I know where you're headed. You need to take care here, miss. You got a rare and powerful gift. But the penalty for having it is just the same down in Harranir as it is anywhere else. Anyone finds out that you know the difference between being in a tree and standing in a tree . . . well. Don't know how they do it where you come from, but in Harranir they do the stoning in an arena.'

I should kill him, I thought. The sooth-sisters had died because Niven Lac-Culloch had suspected they saw the dead. This man was telling me that he knew that I did. Perhaps I had stared at the ghost trapper woman too long. I should take him out the back with the promise of a kiss and put my knife in his chest.

The rise of that violent thought sat cold and alone in my mind for a moment. It wasn't me thinking it. I wasn't that person. Or I hadn't been.

'Who are you?'

'I'm a friend,' the man said. He smiled, the scar across his lip peeling back to show good white teeth. 'A friend who sees the truth of the world, like you. There's a feller, real old wise feller, wanted me to have a look at you before you reach Redwinter. Those of us that see what we see, we got to stick together. Those Draoihn you're with—you don't have to go with them, you know that, don't you? No matter what they say, there are ways out.' He drew back his fur-cuffed sleeve, displayed a lattice of old white scars. 'Evil doesn't always wear fangs and rage.' He leaned in close, pipe smoke and whisky on his breath. 'Redwinter sits on the peak above Harranir. You have friends there, if you need us.'

'My friends don't tend to fare so well,' I said.

'Perhaps you've been choosing the wrong friends.'

I furrowed my brow.

'Don't ever speak to me again,' I said. 'I don't care what you think you know. I want no part of it. Leave me alone.'

The door opened with a gust of cold air, and my travelling companions returned. The trapper cast them a glance and rose.

'I'll be taking my leave,' he said. 'The offer still stands. Keep the bottle.' He skirted the edge of the room at a distance from Ulovar as he headed to the staircase that led to the rooms in the eaves, and stepped out into the gathering darkness. He did not look back at me.

'Who was that?' Ovitus asked, sinking down into the warm chair the trapper had just vacated, frowning after him.

'Just a man,' I said.

'What did he want?'

'He wanted to hear what I knew about the ancient history of Harranir,' I said. 'What do you think he wanted? What do men *always* want?' It wasn't fair on the trapper, who had been nothing but cordial, but I couldn't say *He sees the dead and knows that I do too.* The cold air from the doorway pulled through the room in the closing door's wake.

'You get any trouble like that, you let me know,' Ovitus said. He settled back in his chair, hands placed on the table edge, trying to look stern. I might have smiled had I not felt the twinge of possession in his voice. It was the kind of thing that Lochlan would have said. I didn't want, or need, to be looked after.

'Don't worry about me. I can take care of myself,' I said.

'Yes,' Ovitus said. 'I suppose you can. I'm sorry. Some of the girls I know— well, Liara really—she needs a hand now and then. It's hard on her, on account that she's so beautiful. She draws a lot of eyes.'

He was about to lapse into another lengthy tale of his sweetheart's many values, so I cut him off.

'What was outside?'

'Nothing, by the time we were there,' Ovitus said. 'My uncle thought he saw a couple of horsemen in colours we want to avoid. But they were gone. Nothing for you to worry about.'

When the whisky was drunk, the hunters and trappers were drunk, and people had made their way to bed, I was left alone beside the dying fire. I stared into the embers and dwelled on men who see ghosts, and ghosts that had spoken to me, and the burning eyes of a thing long bound to the pages of a book. I was still staring into the embers when dawn's light began to draw a paler blue against the clouded windowpanes.

10

The horses were saddled and the sun had almost dragged itself over the distant mountains when the trouble began.

Ulovar looked like a cooling corpse. I had not slept at all, but if he had, it had done him no good. Ovitus tried to help him into the saddle but he pushed him away, growling. I could not equate the grey-faced, exhausted old man with the bull-chested warrior who had steamed away the snow, survived a fall into an icy torrent, torn down the gates of Dalnesse and done battle with a demon in its crypt. The sooth-sisters would have fared better in a boxing match than he would just then. If they hadn't been dead.

I was removing my horse's feedbag when three riders came up the south road at an urgent pace.

Ulovar brought his horse around, red eyes glinting in the weak dawn light, and placed one hand on his sword hilt.

The riders wore cloaks of dark blue-and-white breacan over oxblood-red leather coats that fell to the knee. Two of them carried crossbows, wound and bearing bolts in the slot, and neither woman looked unsure about using it. But it was the man at the fore that drew all attention, pushing his horse ahead until it was steaming and blowing thirty feet from Ulovar.

'Keep back, Raine,' Ovitus murmured. He stepped ahead of me, shifting his cloak so that his own sword hilt was freed of its confines.

'Ulovar LacNaithe! You are hereby under arrest, by order of Grandmaster Robilar!' the lead rider barked. He was a thin-necked man in his later forties, the shining dome of his pate marred by three vivid green gouges that furrowed the flesh of his forehead. He had cold eyes, the careful consideration of a stoat before it savages your hand. 'I have to say, I'm surprised to see you crawling back. Lay down your weapon and surrender.'

His eyes roamed across Ovitus, then me, dismissing us instantly.

'Haronus LacClune,' Ulovar said grimly. 'I thought I spotted some of your half-trained pups on the road last night. They've spent a long time watching for my return.'

'You're a renegade, LacNaithe,' Haronus LacClune said, not without a little enjoyment. I was no politician, but everyone knew that LacClune was a clan to rival LacNaithe in both power and wealth. 'Surrender your sword, and submit to me.'

Ulovar tried to rise higher in his saddle, but he moved as though his spine had frozen in the night, every motion having to crack away shards of ice. His voice rasped, filled with winter cold.

'You know I won't be the one that stands down. And you know that I don't have to.'

Dhum. Dhum. Dhum.

Ulovar's trance pulsed through me. I could feel it in my chest. There were other trances beating in the morning chill, different rhythms, different paces and tones, but Ulovar's dwarfed them all, the slow, steady beat of a war drum.

'There are three of us, LacNaithe,' Haronus said. The furrows on his face almost seemed to glow, ghost-green against the peach and azure hues filling the horizon. He looked like the kind of man that knew how to use the big sword at his belt, and while I felt the press of the trance emanating from him, it seemed a quiet, sober thing compared to Ulovar's thunder. The van of Clan LacNaithe looked across the riders. He grunted.

'You haven't passed six Gates between you,' he said. 'I can take you all single-handed if I have to.'

It was posturing, blustering. Nobody cared what I was doing. I put the horse between myself and the riders. The midnight-blue bow stave had slipped free of its ties and fallen from Ulovar's saddle, lying before me like it wanted me to hold it again. I knelt and took it, felt a slight tingle against my palm as it touched the dark shaft, and my right hand plucked for the moonlight string. It was barely visible in the weak light, but the bow gave the faintest creak as it flexed to hold it. Yes, it had wanted me to hold it again. Slowly I began to draw a handful of arrows from a quiver beside the saddle edge. No bronze inlaid phantom arrow this time, just wood and iron.

'Your Fourth Gate is worth nothing if you can't get a hand on me,' Haronus said coolly. 'But if it makes it easier on your pride, know a dozen Clan Lac-Clune Draoihn follow in my wake. Look at yourself, LacNaithe. You're in no condition to raise your Gates against us.' Haronus plastered a mirthless smile across his face. 'You can barely sit your horse. Will you defy the command of the grandmaster a second time? Must I carry you back to Redwinter trussed up like a feast-day piglet?' His eyes moved to the lead box that Ulovar clutched against his chest. 'I feel it through the Gates, Ulovar. You will hand over that which your apprentice stole from the Blackwell, and you will hand over your sword.'

If he had not been enjoying himself so much, or had he not been so focused on his old rival, he might have noticed me nocking an arrow to the string and stepping around the horse.

'You do not know what you ask, Haronus,' Ulovar said gravely. 'What I carry, I will entrust to none but Grandmaster Robilar herself. I will place it back into the Blackwell with my own hand, if she permits. I am barely containing the urge that emanates from this. You command but three Gates, and only the Fourth grants me some measure of protection. It would take your will, just as it took my apprentice.'

I drew on the moonlight string, felt a thrum of power within the shaft. It wanted to fly.

'The excuses begin,' Haronus said. 'I've not ridden through the night just to argue outside some mud-shack tavern.' He waved a dismissive, arrogant gesture. 'Take him.'

Ulovar's trance roared, a wave of unseen force emanating across the mud, but Haronus was ready for it. Something met it head-on, and a line of mud erupted upwards between the two Draoihn, blasting high into the air. Two thumps sounded, and then Ulovar was reeling in his saddle.

I could have slipped away in the confusion. Perhaps it was instinct, or perhaps I felt some sense of misplaced loyalty, but I didn't. I drew back on the string, aimed for where Haronus LacClune had been, and released the arrow. It sped through the falling rain of mud and was rewarded with a shriek. Dirt rained down, a falling curtain.

'Raine, go,' Ovitus said. He offered me a boost onto the horse's back, and I vaulted into the saddle, thrust the balls of my feet into the stirrup irons. As the rain of dirt cleared, Haronus LacClune was clinging to his saddle, my arrow high in his shoulder. One of his riders lay motionless against a tree, blood on her scalp, the other lay half-buried beneath an unmoving horse. We didn't wait to see what they would do next, but turned to the east road, through the forest, and heeled at our horses until the inn was a distant memory behind us.

The horses galloped for a bit, slowed to a canter, and then to a walk as we headed east. East, away from Harranir, away from Redwinter and our destination. I could feel the dual trances of the Draoihn pulsing. Ulovar's powerful bass slowed to the breaths of a hibernating bear. Ovitus's rhythm battered back and forth, irregular, discordant. Those sounds forced hard memories to the surface. In all the moments of my life in which I had been most afraid, those Draoihn trances had filled my mind. Eventually they faded.

We stopped at a bothy, not much more than a wayfarer's shack with a damaged roof. An old trough gave the horses a drink after we sagged out of our saddles.

'We can't rest long,' Ovitus said. Ulovar said nothing. His eyes were half-closed, one hand pressed to his leg. There was blood there. He probably ought to have it looked at by someone, but he hadn't said anything, so neither did I. It was his business.

'You think they're coming after us?' I asked.

'Haronus will wait for his men to catch up with him. He won't underestimate me again,' Ulovar said. He coughed, breath ripping at his throat. 'I'm worn thinner than a moth's wing. I won't be able to stop them a second time.' His face was streaked with red tears.

'We can't run forever,' Ovitus said. 'We have to make it to Redwinter.'

'East and south,' Ulovar said. Every word cost him a grunt of pain. 'I won't let Haronus bloody LacClune stop me now. We make for the circle tor at Tor Marduul. From there, we can get a message to our kin.'

'What—' Ovitus began, but Ulovar cut him off.

'Concentrate on what's around you, boy,' he said. 'My head's light. I can't hold the First Gate any longer. Be our eyes. Stay in Eio. Sense what's around us in these damned trees. It's on you now.'

'I can help,' I said. 'I can make the drums in my head. You said I'd passed the First Gate.'

'Keep your mind silent,' Ulovar said. 'Now is not the time to go opening it to the world. The First Gate expands you outwards. You will give us away as soon as give us an advantage.'

'It's all right to put the responsibility on me, though, is it?' Ovitus muttered sulkily. His uncle did not appear to hear him, and that was for the best. I felt a stab of irritation. If something could have given me a better view of who was coming, I would have taken the risk.

'I should tend to your leg,' I told Ulovar. 'You're still bleeding.'

'We don't have the time,' he said.

'Can't you just'—I waggled my fingers in the air in front of him—'Gate it better?'

'Healing requires the Fifth Gate,' Ulovar said. 'And I have seen only to the Fourth.' He looked back the way we'd come. The road seemed quiet. 'We do not have time.'

'You can't hold on to that fecking box if you pass out,' I said. 'Or bleed to death.'

He grunted. 'Do it fast.'

There was a wound in Ulovar's thigh, deep and dark. I'd brought down enough small game with my bow to know an arrow wound when I saw it—or in this case, one dug out by a crossbow bolt. He'd torn it open further pulling the bolt out. When I tried to push my finger inside it to test the depth of the wound, Ulovar seized my hand with a hiss.

'Light Above, girl, that's bloody agonising. Think before you act.'

'I'll know more about it if I poke it,' I said.

'And I'm half likely to faint right out of the saddle if you do,' Ulovar said. But the anger had drained from his voice and he sounded as weary as I did. 'There's a needle and thread somewhere in my saddle pack. Stitch it up as best you can. It doesn't have to be pretty,' Ulovar said. 'Just seal me up enough that the edges meet and I'll do the rest. No more arguing.'

I was no surgeon, but every highland lad and lass know how to darn a sock, and darning a person wasn't so very different. Still, it wasn't my leg that was going to end up uneven and badly tied together. The confrontation, the violence, none of it belonged to me, but I knew what lay in that lead box. I would not touch it, and I could hardly entrust it to Ovitus. If losing the box risked it finding its way back to Ciuthach's crypt, no matter how many tons of rubble lay atop it, then it was a risk I couldn't afford to take.

I fished around in Ulovar's pack, found a curved, brutal-looking needle and thick twine. They had never been intended for delicate jobs.

'This is going to hurt a lot,' I said as I threaded the needle and went about tying it up. Ulovar grunted.

'It can't get much worse.' He was right. I probably shouldn't have tried to stick my finger into the wound. Blood was still running from it in dark, sticky rivulets.

'Talk to me while you do it,' Ulovar said. His head was bowed, his broad shoulders sagging. Ovitus faced back along the road, his mind a small, tinny rattle in its trance.

'What about?'

'Anything at all. Who you are, where you come from, what you like to do.'

'I don't know,' I said. 'I just followed my mother around, until I joined up with the sooth-sisters. Then you got them all killed, so now I'm here.'

Ulovar winced as I forced the head of the needle through his skin, pinning both halves together.

'What did your mother do?'

'She was a scribe,' I said. 'She didn't like it.'

Another grunt as I pushed the length of the needle right through him.

'You read well, then?'

'I've read a lot of things,' I said. I didn't feel like sharing that part of myself. It felt better to cut myself off from everything that had happened before, as though I could rebirth myself each day anew. I felt the irony: my mother would have been thrilled for a clan lord nobleman like Ovitus to have praised her learning, but in some ways it had been the cause of her great unhappiness. Other than me, I suppose. Perhaps I sounded snappy, but only because I was concentrating on trying to drag the thread through. Blood oozed over my fingers.

'No offence was meant. The highlands are not known for their schooling. And you have the colouring—had the colouring—of the High Pastures.'

'My mother was Pastures,' I said. 'I was born in the Dunan Highlands.' I jerked the thread all the way through, and Ulovar honked like a goose.

'Keep talking,' he said. 'And don't stop until I tell you to.'

I darned.

'Knowing letters gave my mother her living. Poisoned her against the world, though. I think she only taught me because it was all she had, really. Probably still is. I learned because reading was an escape. The scribe-houses weren't much fun for children.'

'How did it poison her?' Ulovar's gloved fingers jerked against the saddle bow as I drew my second stitch.

'Customs. Status. The usual.' I jerked the needle through again, harder than necessary. Another grunt from Ulovar. 'In my mother's village, about as north as you can go into the mountains, there weren't many books. Their custom is for the village clerk to pass her learning down to her children, who assume her position when her final winter comes knocking. Not as fancy as it sounds. The village clerk writes bills of sale, receipts, has dealings with the merchants and peddlers who pass by. Most people up there sign their name with an X. Reading and writing might as well be wizardry.'

I waited for Ulovar to say something more, but he just stared stonily back along the trail, his eyes half-lidded. You get used to pain after a while.

'My mother liked a little power,' I said, finding that once I had started, it came out easier. I had never talked about my mother with Braithe, not even with Lochlan. I found bitterness, and old resentment, where I thought there had only been emptiness. 'She felt important, I think. It steamed up through her head like hot mead. Her mother told her she was special, which can be a dangerous thing for a child to believe, so when it was her turn to scribe for the village, Mama left Dunan to seek a brighter life. She thought her literacy somehow made her suited to a life of greater things, away from sleet storms in winter and clouds of midges in summer. She never said so directly, but everyone could hear her acid tone when she spoke of that life. She thought she knew so much, thought everyone else so backward. Then she came south and discovered that her special skills, which had made her prized and vaunted for their scarcity in the High Pastures, were not so special. She found that wealthy lowland children attended schools, that a low-paid clerk was valued less than a wealthy crofter. She must have thought of going home—anybody would. But I suspect pride never let her feet carry her back to the high north, and when I came along, she was stuck there.'

My needlework was intricate, exact and precise, I thought. The edges of the muscle I had drawn together and the torn skin above matched perfectly. Ulovar's quiet, laboured breathing ushered back and forth like waves across a beach. I could almost feel its warmth.

'Raine,' he said quietly. 'Stop it.'

'I'm nearly done,' I said.

'No,' Ulovar said. 'You've opened the First Gate again. Close your mind.'

I looked up from my bloody handiwork. In the morning light I could make out the individual needles on each bough of the trees that filled the world to either side of us. Beads of sweat on Ulovar's neck gleamed like diamonds.

'It's helping,' I said. I didn't know how I was doing it, but the world was clear and bright. I redoubled my efforts, a second row of identical stitches. I talked about Mama. Told Ulovar about her temper, and how she'd resented me for taking her legs. I talked about the day I'd decided to leave. We were in the latest in the series of scribe-houses she had taken us to, and I'd known that, as with all the others, they would not tolerate her vicious tongue forever. There had been no planning on my part, no grand scheme. I had thrown myself out into the world like a kite on the wind.

'I'm done,' I said.

Ulovar looked down. He nodded slowly.

'Close the Gate now,' he said. 'That's enough, Raine. You've done enough.'

'I don't know how.'

'Just let it go. Like waking up and realising that you've been caught in a dream.'

Ulovar reached down to the wound on his leg, and there was a sudden smell of burning meat. His eyes bulged, wide and red in his straining face. When he removed his hand, the wound was fused shut, blackened and burned. I felt a pang of annoyance that all my neat stitching had been burned away.

'I thought you couldn't heal yourself,' I said.

'It's not healed. It's cauterised,' he said. His voice sounded, impossibly, thinner than it had been before. He wheezed like an ancient. 'The Gate of Taine, the Third Gate, commands the elemental energies of the world. Fire, cold, that sort of thing.'

'Can I do that?'

'There are not many who can. You have passed the First Gate, Eio. The Gate of Self. You have pushed your awareness out into the world, made yourself a part of it where you were not a part of it before. That's why everything looks and sounds so clear. The Second Gate is Sei, the Other. The Third is Taine, and the Fourth Gate, Fier, is that of the Mind. I am one of only six who have that power. To heal requires the Fifth Gate, Vie, and those who have seen it are fewer still.'

'Is there a Sixth Gate?'

'The Sixth is Skal, which is forbidden. And the Seventh, Gei, is the Gate of Creation. It is merely theoretical, however. The Faded, the lords of the hidden folk who once were, could open themselves to it, perhaps.'

'Why is the Sixth forbidden?'

Ulovar shook his head.

'Because it is the trance of death, and it was the mark of Hallenae's Sarathi.' He turned his face to me, head twisting as though his neck were as stiff as an oak's trunk. 'Wake from the dream, Raine. Your head is going to hurt very badly, very soon. Stop trying to see the world so hard. There are many routes into Eio, but you should not plunge yourself into it headfirst. Close your eyes, breathe in and out, and think of nothing at all.'

I tried. I did as he asked, and I could feel the pain building in the back of my head. The autumn air felt exceptionally bright and sharp against my skin. I still knew precisely where the other horses were, their warm breath thick as porridge. I struggled my own in and out, but the world was heavy and full of being. Ahead of us, the life of the trees, silent but at work growing. A mouse in the undergrowth, the marten that crept slowly towards it weighing up whether we would notice it. Ulovar beside me, utterly drained, clinging to consciousness by a thread. Ovitus behind us, doing his best to hold on to his focus, his mind as loud and noisy as a tin box full of rattling coins.

It was a wonderful world. If it hadn't been for the people coming to hurt us, it would all have been very exciting.

11

Night was falling as we approached Tor Marduul. The forest grew sparser, and then there was no forest at all and we rode upwards across barren hillsides, mountainous and jagged with rock. The night-cold sat deep around us, and our tired horses pumped steam from their noses. The moon hid behind the cloud banks, and we were forced to continue by the ghostly light of a cadanum sphere. It was weak, but it gave the horses something to see by.

I rode close on Ulovar's left, with Ovitus on his right. It went unsaid that we were there in case he fell from the saddle.

Tor Marduul was not a stronghold as I had expected, nor even one of the bothies we'd passed. It offered no shelter at all. At the crest of a tor, a double circle of tall stones stood twice my height, ringing a fallon like royal guardians. The standing stones were rough-hewn things, but the fallon in their midst was four-sided, a thirty-foot-high obelisk that wasn't stone or metal or earth but something else entirely. Fallons dotted all of Harranir, dating back long before Hallenae's war, before the Yanni Dominion, even before the Age of Soot. They had been raised in the Age of the Faded, the lords of the hidden folk, those distant times which were remembered only by priests and the kind of barely legible ancient scrolls that no sane person tried to decipher. The rough stones that protected it seemed older still. I looked about nervously for ghosts. It seemed the kind of place where ancient people would have buried their dead, but the hilltop was empty of spirits.

This was not what I had expected.

Ovitus helped his uncle down from the saddle, having to catch most of his weight as Ulovar slumped. His horse staggered. Ulovar was a heavy burden, and we'd ridden the horses harder than we should. Ivy's legs trembled as she bent her head to crop at the long grass.

'I'm fine,' the older man grunted.

'You've lost a lot of blood, Uncle,' Ovitus said.

'What are we doing here?' I demanded. It occurred to me to wonder what in the name of Skuttis I was doing with them at all. This wasn't my fight. I didn't owe them anything, and Ulovar's people didn't seem that interested in his story. Perhaps Ulovar had put Ciuthach back in his tomb, and yes, they had protected me from Niven LacCulloch, but it was Ulovar who had broken the gates and let LacCulloch storm through in the first place. I looked out into the darkness. I could see lights over on the horizon, a vast sea of tiny, twinkling gold and blue stars. The city of Harranir. I could lose myself there. The false-trapper at the inn had said I had friends there if I needed them.

I found it hard to believe in them. Ovitus thought he was my friend, and somehow now I was running for my life and I'd put an arrow into a Draoihn.

'There's a ley-channel here that runs right to Redwinter,' Ovitus said. He sighed, looked out beyond the city. 'We're so close. We might even see it in daylight.' He shook his head, rummaged in his saddlebags and found a bottle of whisky. Ulovar sat with his back to the central stone, took the bottle and drank. He clutched the lead box containing Hazia's artefact to his chest. Ovitus eyed it but did not move to take it from him.

'Do the invocation now,' Ulovar said. His eyes had closed.

'Yes, Uncle. I'll try,' Ovitus said. He took three scroll cases from Ulovar's packs and began sorting through them. He found what he was looking for. The cadanum sphere was dying, its waxy light beginning to sputter. He had me hold it in one hand as he spread the scroll out. The page was vellum, scraped calfskin, illuminated in gold, green and red inks. The artist had drawn dozens of overlapping circles, joined by lines that ran riot seemingly at random, flanked by complex sigils and devices.

'Are you doing magic?' I asked. I shook the little light sphere again to keep the embers within alive.

'It's an invocation,' Ovitus said. 'A spell, if you like. Prepared in advance, for emergencies. I can try. It should send a message to my uncle's people at Redwinter, asking for help. Someone might hear.'

'They *might* hear?'

'It will depend if anyone is listening,' Ovitus said.

For several moments nothing seemed to happen. Then I heard Ovitus open up his clanking trance, and I thought I saw a lintel appear briefly between two of the standing stones, a gateway opening. The inks on the page flared, hissed, and then the whole page erupted into flame. The vellum curled and crumpled inwards, flaking away in tatters of ash. I felt nothing. Ovitus's trance dropped moments after.

'Is that it?' I said.

'I think it worked,' he said with an uncertain nod. 'The range is short. But anyone who was listening should have heard it. If we're close enough to Red-winter, then maybe we're in luck.'

'Should have used it to get a fire going,' I said. Ovitus looked at his uncle, who seemed to have fallen asleep or passed out. They were one and the same, really.

'Can you make a fire?' he asked. 'Keep him warm?'

'It might not be such a good idea,' I said. 'If that Haronus LacClune is near, he'll see it.'

'They must know we're headed here anyway,' Ovitus said. His face was pale in the dying light of the cadanum sphere, the shadows turned blue beneath his eyes.

We piled our horse blankets over Ulovar, and I tried to work up a fire while Ovitus encouraged his uncle to eat some neaps and blood pudding. The wind was too high and I couldn't get the kindling to stay aflame. I had been raised in the cold comforts of scribing houses, and Braithe had not prioritised my outdoor-survival skills.

'What now?' I asked.

'Now we have to hope that help comes. We should huddle together for warmth,' Ovitus said. I cast him a sidelong glance in the last of our blue-steel light.

'You can get nice and close with your uncle if you like. I'm a highland girl. I'll be fine.'

I walked a slow perimeter of the stones, treading in soft, hunter's steps. I was a night-hunter here, prowling, keeping myself to the shadows. Braithe had taught me that at least, and I had always loved the quiet tension of the hunt. Even after thousands of years the stones were still rough, not even the hill-top wind able to wear them smooth. Some ancient people had probably wor-shipped their gods here, when the Faded walked the earth alongside mankind. Perhaps that was why they had raised the fallon at the centre of the ring, to show the bronze tribes whom they ought to be sending their prayers to. There seemed to me a colossal conceit in that. I wondered what kind of kings could be so insecure that they needed men to tell them how magnificent they were. The kind that ended up destroying each other, I supposed.

I kept the midnight-blue bow with me, the quiver at my waist. The horses were cropping the long grass and didn't seem to care what I took from the packs.

'You won't hit much in the dark,' Ovitus said as I looked through the quiver. There were only six arrows in it.

'Better than nothing,' I said. 'If we have to fight, we have to fight. Your uncle can't run anymore.' And the truth was, neither could I. Dreams of Ciuthach had kept me from sleeping. Even holding the bow felt difficult. Like my eyes could close at any moment, without my knowing, and I'd be dead before I woke.

12

Harran is a cold country. Our southern neighbour, Brannlant, whom we somehow belonged to, was a warm land of grapevines and golden wheat. But summer in my birthland was cold, and winter was worse, and winter at night was worst of all.

I put on every spare piece of clothing we had available. Ovitus seemed to be faring better, but looked no less exhausted than I felt. We repeated our efforts to get a fire going as Ulovar lay immobile, breathing quietly beneath our piled blankets. If he'd been a horse, I would have put him down. The fire-making was frustrating and came to nothing. It was just something to do to pass the time.

'I'm sorry that you got involved in all this, Raine,' Ovitus said.

'I can leave if I want to,' I said. 'Maybe I will.'

'I know,' Ovitus said. A more gallant man might have tried to persuade me to, would perhaps have reminded me that this wasn't my fight. But Ovitus wasn't a hard, granite-browed man like his uncle. He still had puppy fat in all the places where hardship is wont to burn it away, but his gentleness stretched deeper within. Whether he could open the First Gate or not, he was ill-suited to this life.

'I've never seen Harranir like this before,' I said, looking out towards the myriad lights that swarmed together like a colony. 'I remember it being dirty. Crowded. From all the way over here, there's a sort of beauty to it.' I breathed steaming breath over my hands, but they were cold again a moment after the wash of heat.

'I didn't mean sorry that you're here,' Ovitus said abruptly. 'I mean—about what happened in the north. At Dalnesse. Your friends. All those people.'

I shrugged. It didn't seem to matter terribly much anymore. Their bodies were a long road away. It would be even colder there, I thought. I was glad not to be there anymore.

'Don't worry about it.'

There was such concern written across Ovitus's face that although I didn't really care what he thought of me, I had to raise an enquiring eyebrow.

'Weren't those people your friends?' he said. Like I'd shocked him somehow.

'Some of them,' I said. 'Lochlan was.'

'Then how can you say not to worry about it? They died, Raine. All of them. Doesn't that burn inside you? My mother died—and—and . . .' He could not complete the sentence.

The truth was, I didn't care. It wasn't just that I'd discovered that the sisters were full of shit and that Braithe was a bastard. I couldn't find the feelings that, if I was honest with myself, I knew that I ought to feel for them. Braithe had got them all killed through his stubbornness, and I had a measure of anger for that, but he'd also shared my bed. There had been tender moments between us: the time he lagged behind the whole caravan to pick flowers for me, just because. The time he arranged a candlelit picnic in summer twilight. When I'd fallen sick with a bed-fever, and he'd fed me with a spoon. He was the only one who hadn't died, dragged off to whatever fate Niven LacCulloch reserved for men who defied him. The only one who could still suffer. My mind reached for something to connect to that and found only fields of barren stones.

I looked at Ovitus's sagging face. His voice had broken at mention of his mother. I should have felt something at that too. I could feel something, deep in my mind, a ridge of scar tissue that formed a wall between my waking self and the things I knew I should feel.

I felt fear. Fear of Ciuthach's burning eyes, worry over where my next meal would come from. I found interest in new sights, new sounds, new roads. But when I tried to share the grief in Ovitus's eyes, or reach for the feelings which were mine by right, I was blind. They weren't there. I felt nothing. I thought back to the Brannish tax collector with his cow-trodden foot. He'd been angry at me for not helping him. The old Raine would have helped him. The old Raine would have cared.

I did not care. I smiled as I realised that I didn't care about anybody anymore. Ovitus misread my expression, and turned his head fiercely away, swiping his sleeve across his eyes. A link of his mail sleeve caught him, and he winced.

'I'm sorry about your mother,' I said, trying the words on. They sounded right. Sounded like something Old Raine would have said. I didn't feel any differently after I'd said them, though, and it wasn't true. People died all the time.

'Thank you,' Ovitus said. 'But I meant it too. We needed to stop Hazia. If my uncle hadn't brought down the gates, Ciuthach would have been released fully. If he'd had time to marshal his power, I don't think we could have stopped him. When one of the Sarathi rises, they seem crazed at first. Berserk. But then when their rage subsides, they slip away into darkness and begin working to—Well. This wasn't the point. That monster would have killed everyone in Dalnesse anyway. But I wish things could have been different.'

'That was sort of an apology,' I said, standing up. 'And sort of telling me that you didn't do anything wrong. Like I said. Don't worry about it.'

'Look,' Ovitus said. 'Torches.'

There were two of them, burning brands held aloft in the darkness by riders on fast-moving horses. I flexed my night-cold fingers. They moved slowly, as though they had to think about my instructions separately before they responded. I felt for the silvery bowstring, and it gleamed into existence as I probed for it, the midnight-blue wood flexing to hold it. I liked the bow. A little magic in just the right place. I nocked an arrow.

'Maybe they won't see us,' I said.

'They're Draoihn, Raine,' Ovitus said. 'They can see as well in the night as in the day. They could still see us if someone took the eyes from their heads.'

'Maybe we can test that,' I said as I tensed the moonlight string.

'Wait,' Ovitus said as I began to draw. 'It's not LacClune.' He let out a pleasure-filled gasp of steaming night-breath. 'It's Wildrose! And Esher is with him.'

'Friends?'

'Better,' Ovitus said. 'Kin.' His expression said the rest. He looked jubilant.

The two riders rode up the hillside towards us, yellow light flaming from pitch-soaked brands held aloft. I eased off the bowstring, and it winked out into nothing.

'Cousin!' Ovitus said. He beamed, held his arms open wide in greeting. 'You've come!'

The man that Ovitus had called Wildrose had five or six years on me. There was something in his features that reminded me of Ovitus, though where Ovitus was plump and soft, this man had been carved from the heart of a mountain. The jaw beneath his straight-set mouth was strong, darkened by a day's growth of stubble. His hair was a tangle of black curls, catching lines of torchlight and hooking them into rings. If Ulovar had produced a surprisingly tall, broad-chested, sleepy-eyed son, it would have been this man. He wore mail like a second skin, and I had no doubt that he would be formidable with the longsword that hung from his saddle.

The woman beside him was no less striking. Her long golden hair was bound back, but even in the crackling light of a torch, it seemed to shine. For a moment I thought that this had to be Liara LacShale, the beauty who Ovitus never seemed to stop talking about, but somehow I knew that she wasn't. Her shoulders were broad as a man's, strong, and though she had a face to rival the richest emperor's courtesan, I did not think that Ovitus could have talked about her that long without mentioning that her left eye was blighted a milky blue-white. Besides. Liara LacShale had red hair and green eyes. I'd heard about them a lot.

'Where is Ulovar?' the man demanded as he swung down. He strode forwards, long legs clad in black leather devouring the intervening distance. Ovitus was practically dancing on the spot. He didn't sense any threat in the annoyingly handsome man's advance, but I did. Each movement was sharp and intentioned, like a pine marten about to pounce.

'It's good to see you too, Sanvaunt,' Ovitus said. Wildrose, Sanvaunt, Draoihn, lord of the clan, these people had too many names.

'Where is he?' Sanvaunt said. 'Do you have it?'

'Yes! We got it back! Thank the Light Above you're here. Haronus LacClune is coming, and he says he has men with him. He's . . .' His voice trailed away. Perhaps he saw what I saw now. The two young men looked one another in the eye, stood a few feet apart. 'You didn't get our invocation. You were coming anyway.' Ovitus swallowed. 'You're with LacClune.'

'I'm with Redwinter,' Sanvaunt said. 'LacClune sent me on ahead.'

The girl whom Ovitus had referred to as Esher was emitting a muted, step-by-step rhythm that seemed to alternate left and right. She had noted me, cast her eyes across me and disregarded me. They both had. She stepped forwards now.

'Come quietly, Ovitus,' she said. Her accent spoke of some land to the south. Maybe everyone there had hair that shone as hers did. 'Make this easy on everyone. Don't make me hurt you.' Her one eye flashed bright, a jagged ferocity in her stance.

Ovitus was lost for words. His jaw flapped open and shut like a door blown to and fro by the highland wind. I didn't react. It was not time to react yet.

'I'm sorry it has to be this way,' Sanvaunt Wildrose said, though his tone was devoid of empathy. 'Surrender the artefact to me, and I will take both you and Uncle Ulovar into my charge, where you will be returned to Redwinter and presented before the grandmaster for questioning.'

'We can't,' Ovitus said. 'You need to let me explain. It's dangerous. Only Ulovar can carry it.'

Sanvaunt drew his sword in one fluid motion, and then it was levelled at Ovitus's chest. He moved so fast I didn't even have time to find the moonlight bowstring.

'Don't think that being kin means I can allow you dispensation from the grandmaster's command,' he said. 'Light Above knows that I love you as my cousin, Ovitus LacNaithe, but I am sworn to Redwinter. The Crown is our life; all else is dust.'

I slipped an arrow to the string and raised the bow. Tried to raise the bow. Sanvaunt LacNaithe of the many stupid names turned and threw his sword at me like a spear. It struck the upper arc of the bow stave with such force that it snapped out of my hand, spinning away into the dark. Ovitus tried to draw his own sword, struggled with it, and Sanvaunt swept his leg low, crumpling Ovitus's knee. The big apprentice crashed down with a cry. I turned and ran for Sanvaunt's sword, but by the time I had it and turned back, Esher stood between me and the men, her own sword drawn. Her hair was loose and it streamed out towards the distant lights of Harranir like a sheet of gold.

'Don't interfere, *Fiahd*, or I'll cut you in half!' she said in that silk-sheen voice. 'This is Draoihn business.'

Fiahd. A highland wildcat.

I scowled. I did not like being disregarded. I'd told myself I wouldn't allow it again.

'Your trance sounds weird,' I said. 'Like you're dodging left and right.'

Her eyes widened, but there was a vivid determination in her one good eye. I didn't know how to wield a longsword, and despite the hardstanding tendons in her neck and the way she settled like a coiling snake into a high guard, I knew that she'd put in her hours. It didn't matter anyway. Behind her, our no-longer saviour, Sanvaunt, had dragged Ovitus upright, disarmed him, and had forced his cousin's arm behind his back.

'Enough.'

The word cut through the scuffle on the hillside, drew all eyes up towards Ulovar. He had risen from his blanket pile and leaned against the big fallon obelisk at the centre of the ring of standing stones. He had his sword at his side, one hand resting on the pommel as he limped down towards us. The torchlight played across his broad face, settling his eyes into even deeper hollows.

'Look down the hill, Uncle,' Sanvaunt called up to him. 'I had hoped to bring you gently, as I love you as a nephew should. You know this. But the time is up, and your flight is over. You must surrender to Redwinter.'

Horsemen waited in darkness at the foot of the hill, a dozen of them in shadow-red Draoihn coats, but their swords were drawn as they began the ascent.

'Light Above,' Ovitus said, his voice quavering as Sanvaunt shoved him away.

'Stay where you are, or so help me I'll send you all to the Afterworld,' Ulovar said, his voice a solid block of oak. Gone was the slouch-backed, weary traveller who had sunk slowly into his own exhaustion. He was straight-backed, bull-chested, and pulsed with the steady, measured beat of an opened Gate.

I didn't have anywhere to go, so I followed his instruction, even if it was meant for the horsemen. They did not.

The Draoihn spread out as they closed, forming a half circle around us.

'Van LacNaithe!' Haronus LacShale bellowed, the vivid gouges across his forehead glowing green in the night. Old wounds, the flesh around them smooth and shiny but not entirely healed maybe. Of all of them, he had not drawn his weapon, one arm held in a sling. Hostility rippled through his words. 'This is your last chance. Close your Gates, or I'll bring you in any way that I have to.' He smiled coldly. 'I do not fear you.'

Dhum. Dhum. Dhum.

Ulovar's trance pulsed through me, deep in my chest. There were other trances beating in the night, different rhythms, different paces and tones, but Ulovar's dwarfed them all, the slow, steady beat of a war drum.

'I will permit no other to touch the artefact,' Ulovar said. 'You cannot contain it.'

'There are twelve of us, Ulovar,' Haronus called back.

'Surrender, Uncle,' Sanvaunt said. Imploring. 'Don't die for nothing on this barren rock. I wish things were different, but as you have always taught me, my duty is to Redwinter first, and my clan second. The Crown matters; all else is dust. The grandmaster has ordered you arrested. It is your duty to comply.'

'You should listen to your nephew, Van LacNaithe,' Haronus agreed. 'You might just live out the night.'

Dhum. Dhum. Dhum.

Ovitus had gone deathly pale. The horses pawed the earth. I had nothing to do here, no part to play, and I didn't think that around all these Draoihn I really counted for much. My bow was several yards away. Maybe this was the end of this journey for me, and this was my time to run. The one-eyed girl, Esher, who was probably no older than me, kept her sword between us. I didn't think she'd let me run far.

'Who are you?' she asked me quietly.

'Raine,' I said. 'Who are you?'

'Esher. Apprentice to Van Ulovar.'

'Why are you trying to capture him, then?'

'Because the grandmaster ordered it,' she said. Surrounded by all these loud-voiced men, who smelled like horses and iron, her voice was like the scent of fine wine. 'I don't want to fight.'

Up and down the slope, the posturing and the boasting continued.

'You know I'm no easy prey, Haronus,' Ulovar called. 'You might give me a

few moments of battle. The rest of them? Inconsequential.' He reached down
and lifted the heavy lead box that had never been far from his hand since Dalnesse. 'Escort me to the Blackwell, and when I have thrown this back where it
belongs, I'll allow you to clap me in manacles, if you must.'

'You will surrender?'

'I am Ulovar LacNaithe. That you doubted I would only makes you a fool.'

'You rebelled against the grandmaster's command, Uncle,' Sanvaunt shouted
up at him. 'You cannot be permitted entry to Redwinter whilst you bear your
sword.'

'You know I don't need my sword to unmake the lot of you,' he growled.

'I know, Uncle,' Sanvaunt said in a clipped tone. Imperious, like he'd never
spent one day of his life having fun, but there was sweat on his brow. 'But I
have to demand it all the same.' He looked calm and his words were even, but
behind them all I could feel the patient, melodic rhythm of his mind. He was
caught between Haronus and Ulovar, a kitten between lions. 'My duty insists
that I take it. I love my clan, but we swear our allegiance to the Crown even
before Redwinter. I won't beg it of you. But I will insist.'

Ulovar's face was a bank of rock. His hand hovered near his sword. To draw
it, or to hand it over? Pride lay thick in the crow's feet around his eyes. The
weight of these entwined, honour-sworn loyalties wound around them all like
lead serpents, demanding that they all go down to the mud and lie still and
dead together.

I was bound by no such oath. If anyone started throwing fire, I was going to
run. Harranir's lights called from across the valley.

'You cut the turf from your own grave,' Haronus LacClune snarled. 'So it
must be.'

A rippling explosion of light and flame erupted midslope. Snaking coils
of blue and yellow fire lashed out, caught in a dozen different winds as a new
voice roared, far greater and more terrible than any of them.

'Lord Draoihn Ulovar of Clan LacNaithe, you will stand down!'

The wind seemed to hold its breath for a moment as a black silhouette appeared in the roaring flame, a hunched, bent figure leaned on a staff that was
taller than she was. As the roaring flame dissipated, she stepped out into the
world, the grass around her red-tipped and smouldering. She wore a deep red
robe, bordered with gold embroidery that seemed to glow as it caught the dying sun. Long white tresses hung down from the shadows within her cowl,
while silver light reflected from eyes hidden deeper within its depths.

All the strength, all of the fight, drained from Ulovar. He fell to his knees,
his head sagging forwards.

'Grandmaster Robilar,' he said, bowing his head. 'I surrender myself to you.'

'You have displeased us, Lord Draoihn,' she said. She was old, but her voice had a metallic edge, resonant with the same simmering power that smoked from her eyes. 'I gave a direct command that you were not to leave Redwinter. You have disobeyed me. You have broken the rule of law within the Order of Draoihn, and I should scrub you from the earth for it.'

Ulovar braced himself, but he did not look up to meet her smoking eyes.

'I have done what had to be done, Grandmaster,' he said. 'I am willing to accept my fate.'

'He should be taken to the Forgetting, Grandmaster,' Haronus LacClune said. His pleasure was masked as duty. The grandmaster ignored him, stalking up the slope, one foot dragging behind her, staff clicking against the ground. She glanced at Ovitus, me, as dismissive as though neither of us was of significance. 'What of the traitor apprentice? Where is she, and the artefact she stole from the Blackwell?'

Ulovar raised his head slowly. He held the lead box forwards like it was a holy relic.

'The apprentice is destroyed,' he said. Not dead. *Destroyed.* 'The artefact is returned.'

The grandmaster pushed back her hood. The dome of her head was hairless, her skin dark against the white of her hair. A web of metal bands encased her skull, and with a surge of queasy unease I saw that they were riveted to her head. A thin wisp of smoke leaked upwards from one of the cracks, tangling away on the breeze.

All around me the drum-beat rhythm of trances died away, one by one. Quiet stole back over the night.

'You will be tried, Van Ulovar,' the grandmaster said. 'The Council of Night and Day shall judge your actions. Until that time, you are under arrest. As both a councillor and Lord Draoihn, you will be given your freedom within Redwinter's walls until judgement be upon you.'

'Grandmaster, this man has—' Haronus LacClune began, but she waved a clawlike hand at him, and his words died.

'Summon Van Merovech from your clanhold, Haronus,' she said. 'I am sure he will want to ensure his seat is occupied when Van Ulovar stands before the council.'

Haronus LacClune's face became a hard leer, but he restrained his tongue.

'I ask one thing only, Grandmaster,' Ulovar said. He still had not raised his head to look up at her. 'The road to reclaim this was hard, and it was bloody.

Let me return this cursed thing to the Blackwell, where it can bring about no more devastation.'

The grandmaster's eyes faded, their glow dissipating.

'Draoihn Dhoone rode with you. Where is he?'

'Fallen, Grandmaster.' The gathered horsemen sucked in breaths, eyes widening, scowling.

'Come,' the grandmaster said without missing a breath. Ulovar straightened, brushing dirt from his knees. The grandmaster looked towards Ovitus. 'Young LacNaithe, I do not hold you responsible for your uncle's actions. You are not yet sworn to be Draoihn, and so your duty still stands to your clan before our Order. But if you wish to enter our ranks, you would do well to follow your cousin's example. The Crown is our life. All else is dust.' She looked around at the cold, dead hillside. 'Somebody get me a horse.'

She turned on her heel, heading down the slope, beckoning Ulovar to follow. He rose groggily to his feet but followed her, head low.

'Light Above,' Ovitus muttered. He shook his head slowly. 'Not as bad as it could have gone. But a whole lot worse than I'd hoped.'

I watched the old woman as she was helped into the saddle. She had appeared through fire, but it was her command of these men of violence that slowed the breath in my throat. Did she truly command so much power? I'd read the stories of magic and myth, of the Faded Lords and the nine primal demons and the terrors they unleashed on the world. I stood now surrounded by those who were capable of working them. These people, these cold and brutal men and women, could do things I had never believed possible. Old, deep things that most of the world had let slip through its memory.

The world had forgotten, but the dark things like Ciuthach did not. My thoughts squirmed and reordered themselves away from it. I knew I shouldn't allow that, but his visage lay beyond a line that seemed to score right through me.

'Come, cousin,' Sanvaunt said. He clasped a hand to Ovitus's shoulder, as though they had always been friends and the fighting no more than cousins at play. 'It's good to see you again.' He walked past me, retrieved his sword and, I noted with a frown, my bow.

'We shouldn't have broken the grandmaster's decree,' Ovitus said quietly to me. 'But honour demanded that we put things right.'

'No,' I said, heat rising to my face. 'No. You did the right thing, even if it broke the rules.'

'We could be in a lot of trouble.'

'Not me,' I said. 'I didn't do it.'

13

Ulovar rode ringed by riders in dark red leather, and I trailed along with Ovitus at the back.

I was glad to be the least important part of the group. There was comfort in knowing that if I timed it right, I could take my chance and disappear into the gloom. Head off to the city and its lights, where a person could lose herself amid the myriad lives that would go on around me unknowing what walked among them. I had abandoned my mother, had sought to abandon even the sooth-sisters at the last, and my latest travelling companions had only been selected by chance. I dropped back in the group, letting Ivy slow her weary pace, wondering if I could just fade back from everyone else's attention and out of this dangerous twist of fate for good.

'Keep up,' Sanvaunt Wildrose said, his horse falling back alongside mine. 'You'll get lost in the dark.' I wasn't quite as invisible to everyone as I'd thought.

'I've been lost for a long time,' I said. 'Besides, I want my bow back.'

He nodded, solemn-faced, but he didn't speak to me again.

By the time dawn bloodied the skyline in a blaze of ultramarine and fire, we had skirted the city, heading towards the pine-crowded mountains that lay to the south. I was hungry, exhausted and struggling to stay awake in the saddle, but it was a new day and I wanted to see it. I fought sleep back one last time.

While it might have provided some level of possible safety, I was glad to avoid the city. So many people, so much history. It would be crowded with unhappy ghosts which I was in no mood to see just then. The dead were a reminder of the poison inside me. I had tried to convince myself that the grave-sight was harmless, that what I saw didn't matter. I had been a fool, and people had died because of it.

The land rose, a gravel-strewn path sloping steeply upwards between walls of dense trees. The air was sweet, but there was an edge of mist about it. I could hear things moving among the trees, but whenever I glanced towards them, the sounds stopped.

'It's just snatterkin,' Ovitus said, sensing my discomfort.

'What's a snatterkin?'

'You don't have them in the north?'

'No.'

Ovitus considered how to explain it for a moment. 'They're hidden folk. Wood . . . things. Like living sounds, I suppose? They don't do any harm. Annoying, though.'

'Living sounds,' I muttered. 'Ridiculous.' I tried not to let my anxiety show. As the blankness had slowly melted from my mind during our journey, my trepidation had begun to rise. I didn't know these people, not really, and they had turned on one of their own without hesitation—even Ulovar's nephew, Sanvaunt, had been prepared to fight him. Where did that leave me, a girl without clan or kin who had the grave-sight? I'd had no time to think about the warning offered by the not-a-trapper at that wayside inn. He had found me, picked me out. He knew what I was. If I ever saw him again, I had to kill him. It was the only way to ensure that I didn't end up like the sooth-sisters. But murder carried just as harsh a punishment as the grave-sight, so it was hardly a jolly solution.

It wasn't in my nature to think about murdering people so freely. I put it down to the weight of weariness that had settled over me like a leaden cowl.

The ascending path wound between the trees. The air grew colder still. Finally, as the path curved back on itself, Redwinter, famed stronghold of the Draoihn, loomed into view. The walls were dark in the rising light, silhouetted, the red-and-gold sky aglow behind them. The sleepy-eyed young man, Sanvaunt, drew us forwards into the ring of horsemen to fall in beside Ovitus.

'I don't blame you for going with Uncle Ulovar,' he said. 'I know he can be—difficult—to say no to.' He had a proud, distant look to him, but the turn of his lip spoke of affection as well. Wry amusement. He caught me looking him over, and I decided to stop looking at the shadow of stubble on his jaw. 'It's good to see you safe and sound.'

'I suppose we are,' Ovitus said. 'But a lot of people aren't.'

'Dhoone didn't make it.'

'No.'

'I see,' Sanvaunt said. His mouth was a dour, hard line. 'And who are you, lady?'

'Her name's Raine,' Ovitus said before I could speak for myself. 'Uncle Ulovar brought her as a witness.'

Sanvaunt glanced at me again.

'Welcome to Redwinter, Raine,' he said. 'As much as we can call it a welcome.'

He turned, all military straightness and hard angles, but there was a warmth underneath it. He began speaking with another of the Draoihn horsemen. There was something of the mistcat about him, and his jaw was more chiselled than a man who could also do magic deserved. Ulovar and Ovitus had treated me well enough on the road. For a moment I'd craved this Sanvaunt's attention, and that annoyed me. There were more spectacular sights to see than some man with glossy hair.

Redwinter. We entered.

The fortress-monastery of the Draoihn was not a castle or temple as I'd imagined, but a vast, walled compound much bigger than some of the towns we'd passed on the journey south. The walls rose twenty feet high and stretched wide, acres cordoned away behind walls of white marble and rosy quartz that reminded me of fat-strewn steaks. Great towers rose at irregular intervals, fronted with statues of robed figures dispensing wisdom or staring majestically into a past that only they recalled. The low gates were closed as we approached but swung open as we drew near. I was disappointed that this was no enchantment but rather the work of a vigilant, grey-robed servant beyond. We rode through. The arch of the gateway was inscribed with geometric sigils and constellations. Maybe they meant something to the Draoihn, but not to me.

Beyond the walls, open grounds stretched out into the distance, covering the mountain plateau. Enormous structures, each the size of a small castle, spread around the edges. Greathouses, they called them, and clanhold flags flew from their three-or even four-storey roofs. Gardens and courts of sand lay between them along with dozens of smaller buildings. More of a walled town than a monastery. If the scattering of greathouses and outbuildings conformed to any kind of greater plan, then its design was beyond my understanding. There were wide open spaces, gardens of carefully sculpted bushes and the season's last flowers, stables, pens of quiet livestock, sheds.

At the centre of it all, a squat, single-storey building with a low conical roof kept its distance from the others. Ovitus had told me about the Round Chamber, the heart of Redwinter, nearly sacred. Ulovar was led beyond it, off towards whatever the Blackwell was, disappearing from view long before he reached it. I hadn't truly grasped the size of the grounds from the outside. There were many great buildings, in styles that I had never seen in the north or even on my brief tour of Harranir. Scant few had any light in the glazed—glazed!—windows, and the whole place was a great deal sleepier than I had imagined it would be. Whatever I had expected, this quiet place was not it. Save for the crunch of our horses' hooves on the gravel, the only sound issued from a water cradle raising and dropping its load peacefully into a bucket, the working of some machinery off in the dark.

'I want to wait for Uncle. Before we go to the greathouse,' Ovitus said.

'I doubt she's going to turn him into a statue,' I said.

'Don't joke,' Ovitus said quietly. 'She's done that to people before.' I couldn't tell if he was joking or not, but Grandmaster Robilar had erupted from thin air in a ball of fire, so it didn't seem implausible. Ovitus sighed, rubbed at his belly. 'I don't want to face the others without him. They'll bombard me with questions. Will you wait with me?'

I shrugged. Where else was I supposed to go? We dismounted, and grooms appeared as if from nowhere to take my mount. Ivy had been a decent companion on the journey south, and I patted her neck and promised her an apple that I didn't have. The other horsemen of the arrest party dispersed, save for Sanvaunt and the blonde girl, Esher. Watching over us?

'Will that Haronus cause you more trouble?' I said, thinking of the man with the greenish furrows carved into his forehead.

'Clan LacNaithe and Clan LacClune don't see eye to eye on many things,' Ovitus said. 'Haronus is their representative here. LacClune's van, Merovech, commands the Fourth Gate, but he doesn't come to Redwinter. Not unless he has to.'

'Probably for the best, if his representative is anything to go by.'

'Merovech hates my uncle even more than Haronus does,' Ovitus went on. 'It's personal as well as political with them. But Merovech is on the Council of Night and Day. He'll come here for the trial.'

We waited for nearly three hours. There seemed too few people for such vast buildings, most of them grey-robed servants, only a few in Draoihn red. The sky was clear for a change, sunlight overtaking the glass globes set on posts that glowed with a blue-white light. They continued to glow throughout the day. I'd never seen its like. Light wasted, light that nobody needed.

Sleep was coming on fast, but I fought it back. Sometimes I faded in and out.

'You can sleep if you want to, Miss Raine,' Sanvaunt said. 'You look like you need it. Both of you do.'

'Thanks,' I said. 'But no.'

He got up and crossed over to me, all tall and broad and annoying. He produced a small silver hip flask.

'Take a drink of this,' he said. 'It will keep you awake, if that's what you want.' He removed the stopper.

'What is it?'

'Just water, laced with rose-thistle,' he said.

'Uncle doesn't allow it,' Ovitus said. 'It's not good for you and you won't like it.'

'But it will help,' Sanvaunt said. 'The offer's there if you want it.'

I'd not heard of rose-thistle, but I hadn't seen a place like this before either, and it was hardly the strangest thing that had happened since the previous day. I took it, swigged—and my mouth was filled with a bitter, ditch-dirt foulness. Ovitus was right, I didn't like it. But I swallowed anyway. Sanvaunt and Esher each took a swig, while Ovitus declined. It took about ten minutes for the rose-thistle to kick in, but the dark shadow that had covered my mind eased back, and the world turned clear again. Edges that I hadn't noticed were blurry became distinct, and all the colours were back to normal. Maybe I did like it after all. With enough of that on hand, maybe I'd never need to sleep again.

'Where are you from, Raine?' Esher asked.

'The far north,' I said.

'Do many people have hair like yours there?'

'No,' I said. 'Just me, I think. It wasn't like this before.' I pulled a strand forwards to look at it. White, almost bluish. I must have been a strange sight. A young woman with an old woman's hair. 'I like your hair better,' I said. 'You're beautiful.'

'One thing to note about rose-thistle,' Ovitus said wearily, 'is that you might end up saying some rash things.'

'I don't care what people think of me,' I said.

'That's probably the rose-thistle talking too,' Ovitus said. He had lain down with his head resting on his heaped-up cloak. I didn't want to lie down anymore. I wanted to walk around.

'Is that why they call you the Wildrose?' I asked Sanvaunt. His face changed, hardening back to that pouncing marten I'd seen at Marduul. Esher looked away, embarrassed.

'No,' he said. 'Who called me that?'

Clearly I had put a foot wrong, and I didn't feel like spoiling this newfound good mood by saying that it had been Ovitus.

'Haronus LacClune,' I lied. 'What does it mean?'

'It means he has his head up his arse,' Sanvaunt said. Conversation after that turned to a mundane account of our journey south. Ovitus dozed off, and the rest of us took occasional nips from Sanvaunt's flask. It was a strange conversation. Half-dazed, half-buzzing from the rose-thistle, and only a few hours before, Esher had presented me with four feet of oiled steel while Sanvaunt tried to arrest us. But at least they were new people to talk to. I lost track of the conversation more than once, though. I got distracted when other people passed by, perhaps wondering what the four of us were doing out on the dew-damp lawn in the morning cold.

At last, Ulovar returned. He was alone.

'Let's go home,' he said.

'I'm sorry I had to oppose you, Uncle,' Sanvaunt said. He hadn't spoken in hours.

'Back with us now, are you?' Ulovar said. I felt he would have glowered if he'd had the energy.

Sanvaunt bowed his head, but there was bitter iron in his voice. 'What would I be if I had done anything else, Uncle?'

His uncle relented.

'You did your duty,' Ulovar said grimly. 'I knew the penalty when I went after Hazia. I will endure the blows as I must for it. Haronus LacClune wants me tried for Hazia's deeds. I'll need to convince the council that she broke into the Blackwell by herself, though the Light Above alone knows how she managed that. The grandmaster was fair. I'd do the same in her position.'

'I'm glad you're home, Uncle,' Sanvaunt said. He did not look up.

Ulovar nodded and looked around.

'It's over. For now. It's good to see you too, Sanvaunt.' He led us on through the grounds. I suppose that I should have felt a lot more fearful about what had just happened, but in all honesty, everything was still pretty confused in my head. I'd seen too many new things of late. And for the first time since leaving Dalnesse, I desperately craved sleep.

'It *is* good to be home,' Ovitus said with a yawn. 'No more bugs in the beds. Real food. An actual library.' He smiled as he reached up and fussed with the clasp of his cloak.

'And training,' Ulovar said. 'Don't think that my predicament lets you off the hook. You're back at practice first thing tomorrow. And you'll be present at dawnsong, noonsong and evensong.' He turned red eyes away from his nephew, his piece stated and no argument to be considered.

'Well, yes,' Ovitus said. 'That too, I suppose. What is life without hardship?'

We approached a greathouse that was even bigger than the Dalnesse Monastery. Three storeys tall, cut black stone and thick dark beams, it seemed perhaps my belief in the absence of a castle was ill-founded. The whole vast structure was shrouded in thick evergreen ivy. Green against black. The clan colours of Clan LacNaithe. As before, the door opened ahead of us to reveal an elderly man in immaculate robes. How he had anticipated our arrival, I had no idea.

'Welcome back, Van Ulovar,' he said. 'Greetings to you also, Thail Ovitus.'

We were admitted and our cloaks taken by a scampering of younger servants. They came and went without even offering their names.

'I need a change of clothes,' Ulovar said. No greeting, only business. 'Send a boy to advise the abbot that I'll be calling on him shortly. My soul is in need of absolution.'

He looked just about ready to collapse, but nobody contradicted him.

'I had presumed to have the girls lay out your best, my Van,' the old man said. He had a dignified air, his voice as smooth as his shiny bald head. 'Do you wish to speak to the apprentices when you return?'

'Maybe,' Ulovar said. 'Tarquus, this is Raine. She's entering my service.'

Oh, I was, was I?

'A pleasure, Miss Raine,' Tarquus said. He was less fawning than the inn-keepers we had stayed with but eminently respectful in demeanour. 'What role will she fulfil?'

'I don't know,' Ulovar said. 'Put her with the apprentices for now.' As Ulovar strode away towards a wide staircase flanked by ornately gilded bannisters, Tarquus called after him. 'My Van, if Miss Raine is to be housed alongside the apprentices, there is only one suitable room. Its last occupant's belongings have not yet been cleared away. We had hoped for her return.'

Ulovar paused on the stairs.

'What's done is done,' he snapped. 'Give her Hazia's room.' He began to stamp up the stairs, heavy boot heels snapping, but he paused halfway up by a wall-mounted painting. He reached out to run a finger down the portrait's face. 'I'm almost glad you aren't here to see what's become of us,' he said qui-etly. Then he swung around and disappeared into the dark of the landing.

'The other apprentices are at noonsong,' Tarquus said. 'Would you like to change before you eat?'

'Food first, please,' Ovitus said, cheeks bulging as the broadest smile I had ever seen him give crossed his face.

Tarquus led us into a dining room. Grand paintings of imposing, hard-faced warriors hung across the dining room's wooden wall panels, alternating with busts of creamy marble. The decadence might have dazzled me if the unusual had not become mundane after a day of oversaturation. The table it-self was covered with a thick cloth patterned with black and green breacan. Within minutes, bowls of steaming, exceptionally bland soup were presented along with soft rye bread rolls and cups of chilled cider. Ovitus set to with the appetite that I had come to expect, and though he ate with a cultured dignity, he had wiped his bowl clean by the time I was halfway done. Somehow food didn't seem that appealing, though I had been starving before.

'That's the rose-thistle,' Ovitus said as his fingers drummed in anticipation for the next serving. 'You won't want to eat until it wears off. Like I said, it's bad for you.'

A second course followed, meats fried until they were as dull tasting as the soup. Ovitus's cup was refilled by a quiet girl the moment it was dry, the cider poured through a silver strainer, but it seemed that due to our widely differing status, I was responsible for filling my own, so I got bits of pulp. Apart from the cider, it was a remarkably bland meal.

'Delicious,' Ovitus said, chewing his way through what I supposed was fried turkey.

'How many people live here?' I asked. Ovitus had to pause his eating to count.

'In the greathouse, or in Redwinter?'

'The house.'

Ovitus began ticking names off on his fingers. 'There's Uncle, me, and I suppose you now. Then my cousin Sanvaunt, and Liara that I told you about. Colban, Gelis, Jathan, and Esher. And Adanost. They're all apprentices like me. I think that's all. Ten?'

Ten people in a place this vast?

'The servants don't live here?'

'Oh yes. I forgot them,' Ovitus said. 'Tarquus and about—er—ten others, here? But most of them go home at night. There's separate quarters on the far side of the grounds for them, and the day servants mostly live in the city.'

'How many servants are there in total?'

Ovitus shrugged. He didn't know. It didn't seem to matter to him. He didn't speak to the young woman who filled his cup, almost as though she were just another eating utensil, the strainer an extension of her arm. I wondered how that felt, to treat people like that. To have so much money, so much authority, that you didn't have to care what anyone thought about you. There were breadcrumbs in Ovitus's three-day stubble, grease on his chin as he sucked the meat from the bone. Was he oblivious to how he came across, or just too rich to care? The notion of having so many people's lives at your disposal that you forgot they existed turned the bland food sour in my mouth. It was something Braithe had wanted: people giving him a title, doing his bidding and looking up at him with fawning eyes. I had been one of those people to him. People deserved more than that.

I didn't understand this place, or its people. My appetite was weak, and I found myself growing tired of forcing food down long before I was full, only to have a further course served the moment I pushed my plate away. The girl served us bowls of warm custard with chunks of crystallised sugar bobbing within. The custard seemed far too sweet to me, and Ovitus eyed my bowl as he scooped up the last of his own. A quick switch of the bowls and he was wolfing mine down as well.

'Your uncle stopped at a painting,' I said. 'Halfway up the stair. Who was that?'

Ovitus's face grew sombre, and he put his silver spoon down. He pursed his lips.

'It's a portrait of Ulovaine. Ulovar's son. He was killed serving in the Winterra, fighting to expand the Brannish border, two years back.' He sighed, pushing back the bowl, appetite finally defeated. 'He was my uncle's second son. His eldest, Ulovir, died in a duel nearly seven years back. My aunt lost her health after Ulovaine died. She'd already lost two girls as infants and when Vaine died, she just gave up. The world's a cruel place.'

'So Ulovar has no heirs?' I said.

'He does,' Ovitus said. He milled his spoon around in the bowl. Sickly sugar, disintegrating into the yellow-white sludge.

'Sanvaunt?'

'Sanvaunt is Ulovar's sister's son, but he's nobody's heir,' Ovitus said. He dropped his voice low when I looked blank. Ovitus whispered: 'He's not legitimate.'

'So if not him—it's you?'

'Much to Uncle Ulovar's great frustration,' Ovitus said. 'Ulovaine and Ulovir were cut from his mountain. Fighters, with quick swords and quick tempers. I was destined for an absolution house and a life of worship, but now he has to try to make me fit to lead the clan. Do I look like the van of a clan to you?'

'I don't know,' I said, 'I've only met one.'

'Trust me, I don't,' Ovitus said. He gave my unfinished custard a last look as if trying to summon the will to resume battle with it, but finally, it was beyond him. 'Come on, I'll show you to the room.'

He led me upstairs and I followed. The last of the rose-thistle was dissipating from my blood, and every stair seemed to cost me. It was all I could do not to climb on my hands and knees. But I had made it here. I hadn't known what awaited me, still didn't know, really. But as I ascended higher, and higher again, I knew that something had ended, and something new was about to begin. The tapestry on which my old life was stitched was burning away, disintegrating into so much worthless ash. But perhaps there was value to be had here. A new life, in which I might come to understand the things that had happened to me. A life which might offer more than the lash of my mother's tongue or the back of Braithe's hand.

Who was I, here? Who or what would I be if I let these people change me? I had found myself among people who commanded power that I had never dreamed possible, but already I had seen the price it exacted. Ulovar, grey and spent. Sanvaunt, duty-bound to turn against his own kin. Even my hair had paid a price.

I didn't know if this was what I wanted, or what I had been looking for these past years. I didn't know what this was. But I was here, and I was going to choose my own path.

14

A dead person's room holds something of their spirit, the detritus of a life scattered across surfaces, dangled on hooks, stowed silent in drawers. Either Hazia had been scrupulously tidy or somebody had been doing some tidying for her. Two pairs of boots sat beside the door, the leather gleaming black and brown, one pair for riding, one for walking. A small table beside the comfortable bed held two books in an even stack, on which a trio of untouched candles nestled within a pewter candelabra. I looked through both of the wardrobes; they contained a variety of exquisite clothing, all with silver-worked buttons and gold-threaded embroidery. A fortune in silk and wool. The small chests at the bottom of the wardrobes I left alone; there are some things that are too private for investigation.

The room's furnishings were finely crafted, but the décor was sparse. The walls were panelled in dark wood, the floorboards padded with thick animal-fur rugs, too exotic for me to recognise. The hearth had been lit while we were eating, smoke drawn away into a stone chimney. My mother's scribe-house quarters had never been so large as this one room. I'd imagined a monkish cell, perhaps a bed and a washbowl, not this luxury. I even had a wide, glass-panelled window. A glass-panelled window of my own, even if it was only temporary.

I was in a dead woman's room. A woman that I'd seen die, her body torn apart by eldritch force. It should have felt stranger than it did. It should have felt like something. But there it was, that ridge of scar running from one side of my mind to the other. I couldn't feel sad for her. Couldn't feel remorse for what I'd seen done to another living person. There was want in me, and need, and fear. But that was when it really hit me: where empathy once lay there was only a cold, empty moor.

Looking around at all this corpse-gift splendour, I wondered if Hazia had once felt the cage forming around her as I felt it now. A prison of silver bars and silk sheets. It had taken all my strength, all that was left of me, to keep moving. Part of me wanted to run, but another stoked ember was uncoiling its flame. So much wealth. So much possibility. I'd already touched their First Gate—what more might I become if I allowed myself to throw it open?

If I had power, true power, the kind of power that Ulovar had shown me, then I wouldn't need anybody else ever again. Wouldn't need to rely on anybody, wouldn't fear anybody, wouldn't have to feel shame or rejection. I wouldn't have to fear Ciuthach's burning eyes in the night. With that kind of power, I could reforge myself into a person who never had to be afraid again.

Food had been placed beside the bed on a small silver tray, as though the courses we had been served might have been insufficient. I ignored the twin bowls of salted nuts and honeyed figs but poured myself a mug of small beer from an earthenware jug as I climbed into the oversized bed. It made no sense that they were trying to feed me again right after dinner.

I lay and stared at the ceiling, my overtired mind rambling. I thought of the grandmaster, the scintillating aura of power around her. I thought of Ulovar, reading words from a book—just words—as he brought the monastery down in a crash of stone. I had never known such power could exist.

I needed that power. I wanted it, so that I could taste true freedom. Only the powerful ever know what that means.

I didn't want to be a servant, pouring drinks for an oblivious diner, like I barely existed. It wasn't enough. For seventeen years I'd barely dared to dream. But I'd seen things. I'd shot a nightmare in the face with the bow I'd taken from its tomb. I'd brought that bow with me, even if I'd lost it again at Tor Marduul. It was mine. I wanted it back.

I wondered what my mother would have thought of me, if she could see me lying here. Maybe she would have been proud . . . but I doubted it. She would have found some fault that had brought me here, or told me that I was flashing my legs at the old man, or that they only wanted to use me for their own ends. No. Mama would not have been proud. Even my smallest achievements had brought her pain. To Braithe, they hadn't mattered at all. I hadn't been a person to him. I had been something he wanted, something to possess and use, like a horse or a blanket. There had been no room for me to have a life of my own with either of them.

Perhaps there was room for me here. Somehow. But as what, I didn't know.

·   ·   ·   ·   ·   ·

A servant knocked to rouse me. Ehma seemed baffled when I asked her name, apologised and provided yet more food. I thought it was no wonder Ovitus had managed to attain such girth if he was constantly being fed this way, but I didn't complain about the blood puddings or soft-boiled eggs she brought to my room. Now that the rose-thistle had worn off, I was ravenous. Along with my breakfast she delivered a message; I had slept a day and the night that followed, and had only half a bell until a tailor would come to take my measurements.

The greathouse was quiet, too many rooms for too few people; Ehma informed me that Ovitus and the other apprentices were attending dawnsong at the chapel. I tried to engage the servants in conversation, but they were reluctant to speak to me. They didn't know what I was. I didn't know what I was meant to be either, and that made conversation difficult. Making them uncomfortable would avail me nothing, so I left them to it. They all wore grey robes, belted at the waist, with the Clan LacNaithe crest, a stylised wyvern, picked out in green thread on the breast, collar and cuffs, and they wore their hair tied neatly back or cropped short.

I was anxious. Mama and I had sewn our own clothes. Braithe had bought me a pretty dress once, pale yellow, but it hadn't fit. He'd had a tailor come to take it in around the waist and bust, and she'd pricked and prodded at me, talking about my body like it was an obstacle to work around. What would this tailor dress me in? I feared it would be a grey robe with a wyvern on the breast.

The tailor turned out to be a stylish woman, her hair stacked in coils atop her head and her eyes painted in such a way that it looked as though exotic feathers had settled over her eyes, their quills extending out to her hairline. She brought two girls with her, journeymen, whose eyes were similarly adorned but with less glimmer in the paint. A city fashion from Harranir, I supposed. She had her journeymen strip me down and tutted that she could see my ribs against my skin, and I needed more meat on my bones, and what a shame that scar had spoiled my face. When they were done prodding and poking me, the tailor asked whether I had any preference for colours or styles.

'A dress?' I said hesitatingly. I'd seldom worn dresses. In the scribe-house, Mama had allowed me only the same scratchy black robe she'd been made to wear, and I'd never been able to wear the sisters' colourful uniforms with a straight face.

'My dear, I am to supply you with a *wardrobe*,' she said. 'There will be *dresses*.'

I thought that she and her girls were sharing little smiles behind my back, but I couldn't really blame them. My accent said I came from up in the High Pastures, a smoky, up-and-down sway to the way I spoke. The voices I'd heard as we travelled south were heavier somehow, and some of the words they pronounced so strangely that it was a wonder that they were the same language at all. But I was the outsider here, and couldn't help but feel that I was the one somehow speaking incorrectly.

'The fashion down in town is the Murrish cut,' one of the journeymen said. 'The queen of Murr may keep on sinking Brannlant's ships, but the city folk love everything Murrish—their operas, their table etiquette, and now they

want to dress like them. Fanning skirts that stop below the knee, tall boots
and tight bodices. We can make a lovely-looking lady of you.'

'I've not come across hair of this colouring before,' the tailor mused, pluck-
ing at strands of my hair as though it were an accessory and not part of my
body. It was long enough to reach down to my ears now. 'It's so silvery it's
almost blue. I'll have to search for some unusual bolts of cloth to match this.
Do tell your master that. I wouldn't want him to have a nasty surprise when
his accounts come through.'

Your master. I'd never had a master before, and I didn't know how I felt
about that. Or perhaps I was kidding myself. Perhaps I'd always kidded myself.
Braithe had been my lover, and I'd been too young to realise being his woman
didn't bring me any status, but a kind of ownership. I'd seen it at the last, but
maybe that's what love was. I hoped not. Ovitus had talked of his adoration for
Liara LacShale all the journey south, but that didn't feel like love to me either,
or at least, not a kind that I wanted. At least he respected her. Somehow I didn't
expect there to be love here, not in this place of grand houses and endless
mealtimes, but the prospect of a whole wardrobe of clothes made to suit me
was something I'd never tasted before. I'd owned five tunics, stockings and
kilts, a skirt. One pair of shoes. I hadn't owned a wardrobe, let alone clothes
to fill it.

By the time the tailor was done taking my measurements and telling me I
was too thin, even the prospect of soft wool and a warm winter overcoat had
started to wear. I put my old clothes back on. Someone had laundered them
while I was asleep, and stitched the tears. I headed down the flights of stairs,
pausing to look at the portraits of dead LacNaithes. Ulovir, Ulovaine, Ulovost.
A lot of glowering and stern-eyed stares. I had just reached the foot of the great
central staircase when Ovitus and Ulovar returned from their prayers, and
with them a flurry of young apprentices. Most were around my age.

Jathan was a Kwend, with skin the colour of a fox's coat, black hair tightly
curled, a playful grin that spread his wide mouth across a round face. I'd never
met anyone like Adanost before, dark as coal, gold rings in his ears. I stood
at the side of the room, without any real idea what I was doing. None of them
paid me a great deal of attention.

'Raine, this way,' Ulovar said, ushering me through to the dining room.
He looked weary, his cheeks sagging, as though he'd been holding his flesh
upright all this time, and in the safety of home he'd finally allowed himself to
exhale. Sadder. Older. He frowned at the clothes I was wearing. The launder-
ing hadn't been able to deal with the sweat-and-travel stains I'd brought down
from the north. 'Did you meet with the tailor?'

'I did. She said it will be a while before she can send things for me.' I paused. 'Thank you. I haven't been given such gifts before.'

'Don't mention it,' he said, in a way that told me that it wouldn't matter to him if I actually didn't. He looked across his apprentices as they attacked a lunch of cold meat, olives and pickles, laid out for them by the servants. 'You need something to wear now. We've an appointment. Esher, come here.'

She approached. There was something unnerving about the milky whiteness of her left eye, the way it sat so calmly and so utterly out of place among all that beautiful hair.

'How tall are you?' Ulovar asked, appraising her much as the tailor had me.

'Five nine, Lord Van.'

'You're about the same size. See if you've something that Raine can wear. Formal, but not too austere.'

'Of course, Lord Van,' Esher said. She smiled at me, a dazzling display of white teeth, white as her eye. By her deference, I would never have thought that just two nights ago she'd brought arms against her own lord. She led me from the room, up towards the stairs and along a corridor.

'Feeling rested?' she asked. Light as anything. Light as though this whole place weren't as strange and outlandish as a circus.

'Some,' I said. 'I could sleep some more.'

'You've been through the rivers of Skuttis and back.'

Despite her weird eye, and having held me at a sword's length, she seemed easy enough to talk to, but conversation faltered as we ascended the stairs.

'Ovitus has been telling us all about you,' she said. 'You two obviously get on well.'

'I suppose so,' I said. Another pause. My turn to offer something. 'I thought you were Liara, when we met,' I said.

'Liara? Why would you think that?' Esher said.

'The way Ovitus describes her, she's basically been yanked out of a painting,' I said.

Esher made a bemused frown.

'We don't look much alike. She's away on her rite of passage roam-around. She's due back soon. You'll meet her soon enough if you stay.' She hesitated. 'I'm sorry for calling you a fiahd. I may not have seemed it, but I was pretty scared out there. I guess I was trying to be tough.'

'There are worse things to be called than a wildcat,' I said. 'The highland wildcats are beautiful.'

'They are.' Esher smiled. She hushed her voice, conspiratorial. 'Are you staying? We're all wondering if you're joining us as a Clan LacNaithe apprentice.'

'I don't know,' I said. 'I don't know what's going to happen to me.'

'It would be great if you stayed.'

I just shrugged.

'I was sorry to hear about your people,' Esher said.

'Don't be,' I said. 'They were mostly shits.'

Esher raised her unusually slender eyebrows at my language, but she didn't complain.

'We could do with some more girls around here, if I'm honest,' Esher said.

'I don't know,' I said. 'I feel strange. Like I don't belong here.'

'Who does?' Esher said. 'My mother tended the bar at an Ashium leaf-den down along the waterfront, right when parliament voted to shut the dens down. It was Ulovar's initiative—he doesn't like that kind of thing. He brought some men to shut my mother's den down and heard me trancing. Now I'm here.'

She showed me into a room—not her bedroom, but a room that appeared to be intended for nothing but clothing. A whole room of clothing. Ridiculous.

'You had to leave your mother?' I said. 'What happened to her?'

'Oh, she lives down in the city now,' Esher said. She gave a little smile as she cast her eyes across the luxurious array of silk, wool and fur. 'Ulovar bought her a house, set her up running a decent stew kitchen, and she's much happier for it. They buy us, Raine. You knew that, didn't you? I think my mother did her best to make it happen. Here.'

She drew out a sleeveless, knee-length pale blue dress and held it against me. She found a belt to cinch it in, long black woollen socks, a shirt to go under the dress in the same colour. I put it on, feeling odd in another woman's clothes. Her shoulders were a little broader than mine, and there was a healthy muscularity to her that my thin frame couldn't match. The tailor's words returned to me, and heat filled my cheeks. Maybe I needed to start following Ovitus's eating regime if I was going to fill out. That unusual feeling almost made me smile. Just a short time ago there had been nothing but fear in my mind. Now I wanted to look like this beautiful girl before me and was ashamed that I didn't. Somehow that was better.

Esher's feet were smaller than mine, so I was going to have to stick with my scuffed old ankle boots.

'Well,' Esher said. 'If you do stick around, I'm going to have to keep an eye on Jathan. You look fantastic.'

'Jathan?'

'Reddish skin, curly hair. But bear in mind that at best he's a snack.'

'I thought you were with Sanvaunt.' I didn't know where that came from.

An assumption I'd made because they'd turned up together, or because they seemed so at ease with one another's company.

Esher laughed.

'That man doesn't scabbard his sword inside Redwinter. Too afraid of what people would say about him. He worries about things like that.' She cast an approving eye over me, then passed me a waist-length cloak. 'Here, take this too. It's cold out.'

I'd never worn clothes like those. The stitching was so precise, so well done. I could feel the quality settling onto me, and the shirt didn't itch at all.

'Nearly there,' Esher said. 'Do you want me to do your face?'

'My face?'

'Glamours,' she said.

'Is that a kind of magic? Like the hidden folk do?'

Esher laughed, and it was a real laugh, the kind that started at the back of the chest.

'Oh, Raine, we're going to have fun, I think. No. Just some powder and eye paint. Glamours, you know?'

I didn't know. I let her do it, sitting before her huge, silver-bright mirror, trying not to keep blinking as she accentuated my eyes with a little line of black, dusted a little powder across my cheeks. It didn't hide the scar that Hazia had put there, but neither did Esher comment on it.

'I look strange,' I said. Glamours, as she called them, were a town custom. Not for High Pastures folk. Esher laid her hand on my shoulder, sensing my uncertainty.

'You look fantastic,' she said. 'There's nothing wrong with taking care of your appearance, or wanting to look nice. And you do. Jathan really is going to have a fit.'

'I—well—thank you,' I settled on at last.

Her hand stayed on my shoulder.

'You really are safe here, you know,' she said, and I was so sure that I was going to burst into tears that I practically ran from the room.

Ulovar was waiting for me at the foot of the stairs, short, broad, his hands clasped behind his back. He gave a single nod of approval.

'Very good,' he said. 'It's time to see what the future holds for you.'

'Be polite. Speak only when you're asked a direct question,' Ulovar said.

'What should I say?'

'Be honest. She will know if you're lying,' he told me. We crunched along a gravel path that ran through one of the many gardens within Redwinter's walls. The size of the place was no less astonishing than it had been on my arrival. Huge manors sat around the edges, while sandy practice grounds, lush gardens and pools filled with fat orange carp jostled for space around the low, conical roof of the Round Chamber at Redwinter's heart.

'I thought you were my master now,' I said. I didn't even like saying the word.

'The decision is not mine. Not altogether.' He stepped back from me, smoothed the lines of the clothing that Esher had cobbled together for me. He nodded. 'You'll do.'

I swallowed down the wave of anxiety building around my gut. The grandmaster was impressive in the way a thunderstorm is impressive. She may only have been small, but I'd sensed the vastness about her. And she would decide my fate. I had passed the First Gate, more than once. This place should have felt safe, but I didn't feel safe here. Too much that should have been settled still tumbled through the air, like leaves caught on the wind. It felt a long time ago that Ulovar had suggested to me that I might join these people. That I might be counted among them, trained as Draoihn. Ulovar and Ovitus had helped me, and Esher seemed kind. But I wondered about the risks of placing myself here, among these gifted, dangerous people. I may have been able to open the Gate, but I was not like them. I saw the truth of the dead, and they would kill me for it if they knew. But then, wasn't that true anywhere?

The grandmaster's greathouse was one of many vast greathouses within Redwinter's grounds, but in an entirely different style to Ulovar's. It rose in pyramid tiers, stacked one over the other, slate roofs overhanging the red wood beams. Ulovar held out a hand to stop me.

'She may not be quite as you remember her,' he said. He was about to say more when the doorway slid open, and a powerful scent of lilac flooded outwards as a servant admitted us.

'What do you mean?' I asked. But Ulovar shook his head.

'It would be rude to speak of our host in her own home.'

I fretted as we waited in a comfortable parlour, served sweet tea in yellow glass cups. I drank nothing, sat in silence, and my tea was cold by the time we were summoned up the wide central staircase. An open door ushered us into a richly furnished stateroom, sliding shut behind us moments after we passed through.

An astonishing-looking woman awaited us, her face blank.

'Grandmaster,' Ulovar said, bowing and stepping forwards to kiss an offered hand.

There had to have been some sort of mistake. I looked around for the terrifying old woman who had appeared from fire. Grandmaster Vedira Robilar was more than unrecognisable: she seemed to be an entirely different woman. The bent-backed, white-haired crone from Tor Marduul was nowhere to be seen. This woman sat neatly in a high-backed chair and looked to have barely ten years on me. Her hair was thick, lustrous brown locks falling straight before they spiralled into white-gold across the shoulders of her silver-satin gown complemented with jewelled slippers. The lattice of metalwork across her head was nowhere to be seen. Full lips, a straight nose, flawless skin and a light application of greenish colour across her eyelids. Glamours, indeed.

'Lord Ulovar,' she said in an accent that was as odd to me as everyone else's, but which also told me that Harran wasn't her native tongue. Her voice was a soothing lullaby. 'I must be softening in my dotage to even allow you to bring a potential apprentice before me, given that you are still to stand trial for your last apprentice's actions. But your punctuality is always appreciated.'

I had been prepared for the old woman whose head was held together with metal straps. I was not, for this elegant, desirable, almost repulsively perfect woman. I fell to mimicking Ulovar's etiquette, hoping that it was right and that she wasn't about to turn me to stone or melt my bones for getting it wrong. I made a bow, took her hand and kissed the ring finger, though it lacked a ring. It was marble-cold against my lips, like kissing the hand of a corpse.

I snapped a lid shut on thoughts of corpses. Don't think about the dead, or ghosts, or seeing anything that I wasn't supposed to see. Perhaps she could see straight into my mind and rip out all my secrets. Perhaps I had come all this way only to meet a horrible, excruciating death after all.

The grandmaster smiled, gave a near imperceptible nod. It seemed that I'd done the right thing.

The grandmaster's stateroom was filled with strange items of learning. Maps were drawn on balls, and those balls mounted on angled, rotating sticks. Books

were stacked and shelved in impeccable order. Charts depicting the insides of
bodies, grotesque diagrams showing muscle and exposed sinew, were framed
neatly on the walls alongside dream-laden watercolours. Cases of knives, little hammers, bone saws and other surgeon's tools were arrayed neatly along
the walls beside viewing lenses and vials and bottles of dull-coloured liquids
whose origins I shut away with corpses and ghosts. A diagram showing six
circles, each within the next, overlaid with six circles, each overlapping two
others, filled the entire back wall.

'I'm told that your name is Raine. Your mother was—is—a scribe, in'—she
glanced down at a paper in front of her—'Dunan. A village in the High Pastures.' She pronounced it wrong. *Doon-un,* rather than *Dhoo-nan.* Nowhere
she'd ever heard of. Why would she? I thought about correcting her. People in
positions of power always loved that. 'Lord Draoihn Ulovar has told me of the
circumstance of your meeting. And of your part in defeating Ciuthach.'

She looked me over, assumptions and conclusions forming silently. There was
something peculiar about her eyes, and the subtle shading of her skin marked
her distant heritage. Her lineage was not native to Harran. Home seemed very
far away, and in this place of strangers it was probably better to stop trying to
guess where anyone hailed from. Everyone is a stranger somewhere.

'Answer the grandmaster, Raine,' Ulovar said.

'I did what I could, Grandmaster,' I said. She squinted at my hair and touched
a hand to her own. Right where those metal rivets had nailed the old woman's
head shut. This radical transformation was more than just glamours of paint
and a wig. Maybe it was an illusion, and the real Robilar sitting before me
was bent-backed, cracked and scarred. Maybe she could do that. I mentally
shrugged. Why not? Not much else made sense.

'Make your case, Ulovar,' Robilar said.

'For more than seven hundred years, we have fulfilled our sacred duty to
serve the Crown,' Ulovar started. 'Every apprentice that we can—'

'I need no history lecture, Ulovar,' Robilar said irritably. 'Just speak plainly.'
Ulovar cleared his throat.

'Raine has already demonstrated the aptitude to open Eio,' Ulovar said.
'Whether that comes naturally or was awakened by proximity to the Sarathi
magic is a matter for scholars. What counts is that she has the ability to open
the Gates. Without her intervention, I would not be here.'

'You feel that you owe her?'

'We all owe her, Grandmaster,' Ulovar said. There was a growl buried behind his tongue. 'The Crown owes her.'

'The Crown owes nothing,' Robilar drawled. 'We are honoured to serve.'

She turned to me, fixed me with those hard, sharp eyes. 'Has Lord Ulovar explained to you the importance of what happened in the north?'

'I understand some of it,' I said.

'The weight placed upon you is vast. It is unfair. You have glimpsed the darkness that lingers, even after all these years. Do you understand it?'

'No, Grandmaster.'

'Do you know what you fought in the crypt at'—she paused a moment to scan her notes—'Dalnesse Monastery?'

The most important events of my life had taken place at Dalnesse, if I didn't count being born or the midwife resuscitating me. The grandmaster's world was so big and full of grand things that to her, it was just a word on a piece of paper. I swallowed. I remembered Ciuthach's baleful, roaring eyes. I remembered seeing him in battle as a living man, slicing left and right with his spear. I remembered seeing his death, his soul torn from his body and bound into a book.

'Maybe. Not really. I don't know.'

'Then come,' she said. 'Let me show you.'

Grandmaster Robilar reached out and placed a single, delicate finger against my wrist.

At once, everything was different. I stood alone with her on a podium of bare, smooth stone no more than twenty feet wide, looking into an endless gulf of nothing. Blackness, a cloud-cast night sky. Not a star to be seen, not a glimmer of light, but the grandmaster and I were well lit. She was even younger here, as though we were of an age, a vestige of puppy fat around her sharp cheekbones. I looked around helplessly, feeling something like nausea, but there was no physical sensation. It was as if my mind expected there to be and was trying to reproduce it.

'What is this?' I breathed.

'This is your waking mind,' Grandmaster Robilar said. 'Do not fear. You are quite safe here.'

Nothing could have terrified me more, her assurances bouncing off me like sleet. She might be safe here, with me, inside my unclean mind, but I wasn't. Here with all the ghosts I had seen. With my secrets. She looked off behind me, and with wide eyes and clenched teeth, I followed her sight. Distant in the blackness, something red and black was scored across the utter darkness. She pursed her lips, brows drawing in with displeasure, but turned back to me.

'We are here so that I may show you the world. Not the quiet world you have lived most of your life in, but the real world.' She gestured, and beneath us on the podium, a vast expanse of purple clouds swelled forty feet below.

'You aren't real,' I said. I had to keep her talking. Had to keep her thinking, anything but riffling my mind.

'Here? No. I am a projection of thought. An impression of myself.'

'I saw you at Tor Marduul, and you were old,' I said. 'Then you were younger, and now younger still.' She smiled. She could have been an apprentice, if not for the complete authority that emanated from her. There was danger here.

'The Fifth Gate has its advantages. Call it vanity, if you will.' She pressed a hand to the place where the crone-form's skull had been broken. 'I have been struck down twice during my duty. The first time was my own error. The second, I cornered one who serves the Night Below, corrupted by the Faded beyond the veil. Our battle was long, and my wounds grave. But the Fifth Gate is Vie, and it offers the powers of life and healing. I held my shattered body together, though I should have been destroyed. I am very old.' She smiled, could have been a girl sharing gossip. 'It is nice to reforge myself to be young and pretty, without aching bones, when I wish to, but to show my true face has its advantages as well.'

'Which is the real you?'

'We all wear many faces,' she said. 'I just show mine more easily.' She looked down at the soft, young skin of her hands. 'But this has not been my natural shape for more than a century.'

She waved her hand, and the darkness around us changed. I stood alone with her in a vast, domed stone chamber. The walls were alive with tens of thousands of tiny blue-white lights, stars moving across the surface like fireflies, colliding, combining, diverging again. A thousand people holding hands could not have reached from wall to wall.

'What is this?

'This is the Crown,' she said. 'It lies beneath Harranir. This is what we are, Raine. This is what we serve. Look down.'

She gestured to the surface of the podium on which we stood. A chain of six silver circles lay with six more concentric circles beneath our feet, star-lights moving in slow, beautiful rotations.

'I don't understand.'

'These circles represent the spheres of existence, Raine. Self, other, energy, mind, life, death, creation. They are all bound together, and they are all one. The world is both the Light Above and the Night Below. It is you and me and the rocks and wind. It is belief and life and death.'

'Then it's everything.'

'Everything is everything. The power of the Crowns holds everything together, as it should be.'

'Then there's more than one?'

'There are five Crowns. Our overlord, the king of Brannlant, holds the second. The third is in Dharithia, my homeland. The serpent queens of Khala-clant to the south hold the fourth, and Ithatra, which has been inaccessible since the western ocean became too turbulent to sail, nearly a century ago, held the fifth.'

'It's beautiful,' I said, watching one of the stars, detached from the wall, begin to make its way across the chamber.

'I have seen it only once,' Robilar said. 'But yes. It is a great work. The world came close to breaking once. The Crowns hold it together. Without the Crowns, our world would collide with the hidden realm, and the Faded, the demons, the hidden folk, even the dead could return. Our world would be shattered. So we protect the Crown. We serve it with our lives, our bodies, even our deaths.'

Service. It's what everything seemed to revolve around. I saw what was happening here, the point of the mirage she had planted in my mind. Serve my mother, serve Braithe, serve the sisters, serve the Draoihn. This majestic, impossible dream-edifice of stone was another iron in the wall to which chains could be bound. I wondered if perhaps there was anyone in the world who simply got to *be*, to exist as they wished to. There could not have been many in Harranir who commanded authority like the grandmaster, and even she chose to bind herself down. What a thing it would be, I thought, to just be alone. To step back from everyone and everything and simply live.

'Why would anyone want to destroy it?' I asked.

'There are worse things than people,' Robilar said. 'Though that is sometimes hard to believe. What do you know of the Faded?'

'Only what they say in church. They were evil. Demons,' I said. I thought it was what she wanted to hear.

'The church has long struggled to put the unbelievable, and the dreadful, into words,' the grandmaster said, but wearing the kind of smile a mother would reserve for a child who thinks they're invisible when they close their eyes. 'The Faded were not demons, but they were driven beyond the veil long ago, before the kingships of Haddat-Nir, even before the Delac-Mir. The hidden folk that still remain are little more than whispers of the past. But seven hundred and forty-nine years ago, they reached out and consumed Hallenae, the Riven Queen. The Faded had gifted her with terrible power. She came close to destroying the veil that divides the world from the hidden realm beyond the veil. Even after her defeat, the circles of the world had become unstable. The Draoihn of that time raised the Crowns, to bring back stability, and restrained the Night Below's reckless thirst for annihilation.'

Myth and legend. Monsters and people long dead. The chains reached out from the distant past, entangling, constraining. But behind them—within them—there was something I wanted. Needed, maybe.

The star-lights swirled and danced across the walls, waxing, waning, winking and binding to one another.

'I thought that the king wore the crown,' I said, wondering how this world of lights and magic, of fey lords and demons could exist even in the shadow of our own and remain so unseen.

'The Crowns must bind to mortals,' Robilar said. 'When the Succession comes, the king is led down, into the Crown, there to accept its responsibility. It is a terrible thing, Raine. Many do not survive. It is the price one must pay to rule our land. The shadow of the veil is ever in their mind. It is a punishing, relentless nightmare of shadow.'

'Why would anyone want that?'

I did not want that.

'We tell the heir, before they attempt to take the Crown. Most often, they do not believe us. But never underestimate what an ambitious heir will tolerate. Why would any fool ride into a hail of arrows? It seems inconceivable, and yet, men will do it in their thousands. And there are even those who would see the Crowns unmade. In their hate, and their malice, they would bring an end to all things.'

'People are idiots,' I muttered.

'But I did not bring you here to teach you our history. I should like to see the one called Ciuthach. Would you imagine him for me?'

The fear all returned at once. I didn't want this woman in my memories. If my mouth had been real in this mind-trap world, it would have dried, but I didn't seem to have saliva here.

'You can't just pull him out?'

'The Fourth Gate can shape or alter the mind of a living person. But I cannot use it to delve into a past that has already happened any more than I can force you to take actions you do not wish to undertake. There is no past anymore; there is only now. Your memories are as much your own construction of the past as things that truly happened. We overwrite them with what matters to us, or we never understood what we saw, or even choose to alter them. Remember him as best you can.'

I swallowed with my not-throat. If she was telling the truth, then I was safe enough, even with my mind under occupation. I didn't want to do this. I wanted to go back to the room where my body was waiting for me. But it occurred to me that if my mind wandered, I might show her anything, and if I lingered, that accident became more likely.

Ciuthach emerged into the light of the Crown, a dark shadow, long spear reaching, his eyes ablaze with hatred. I took a step back, pushing through a swirl of drifting star-motes.

'Nothing can hurt you here,' Robilar said. 'He is merely a construct of your imagination.'

I couldn't look at him. Couldn't stare into those eyes again.

'Thank you,' she said. 'Even an imperfect recollection, warped as it is by your fear, is helpful in understanding the enemy. It pains me to think that he was counted among the Draoihn, once. This is the darkness that the Sarathi path would bring us to.'

'He was Draoihn?'

'Ciuthach was one of Hallenae's lieutenants,' Robilar said. 'He was Sarathi, a Draoihn traitor who served the Night Below. Those who felled him buried him, locked him with spirits, and entombed him for what they hoped would be all time. But even those powerful magics will fade, given enough years. Hallenae's creatures have but a single aim: to prevent the Succession and destroy the Crowns that hold the Night Below in check.'

'The Crown is our life; all else is dust,' I said. I'd heard it said more than once. It brought a smile to Grandmaster Robilar's lips. I watched for signs of cracks in her face, as though this beautiful visage might flake away as powder when she moved.

'That is our creed,' she said. 'We won a great victory, when we sealed him away in Dalnesse, Raine. We are ever in a race against the darkness. To deny the rise of a Sarathi may well be the most important thing you ever do in your life.'

Her fervency grated against the ridge of scar that divided me, the barrier that Ulovar had thrust into my mind as it teetered on the edge of collapse. Something hot cracked along the barrier, a single hair of fire. That distant red-and-black line hissed.

Everything vanished. Dizzy for a moment, I swayed in the chair. I found Ulovar's hand steadying me, and the grandmaster sitting opposite me. Faintly, four Gateways receded from my mind's eye, fading until they vanished.

'Grandmaster,' I said, clenching my fists. 'Innocent people died because of that thing. To stop it, Lord Ulovar sacrificed everybody I cared about, and I only survived on the spin of a coin. His eyes are full of blood, and your Draoihn nearly turned their swords on one another. If this was a race, we only crossed the finish post by tripping over our feet and smashing our faces into it.'

'Raine!' Ulovar snapped a warning.

'It's all right, Ulovar,' the grandmaster said gently. Gentle, but firm. Calculating. 'I am not without sympathy for your suffering. What you have endured has been immense. I mourn for your people. We all do.'

'Those are just words,' I interjected. 'I don't need your pity. I need what you can teach me.'

The words shot out of me like dragon's breath. I hadn't known that I meant to say them, or when that desire had fully formed. But they erupted now like liquid rock bursting from a volcano. As they flowed from me, that hairline crack in my mind steamed and burned bright with a fierce, white-hot light. 'I want the power to bring down the mountain, and the power to appear out of fire. I want to burn things with lightning and break people's minds. I don't want to have to be afraid, not now or ever again. You owe me. You all do!'

Vedira Robilar, Grandmaster of the Draoihn, laughed. A hard, cruel laugh, but a laugh nonetheless, and through it I thought I heard some of the woman she had appeared as before.

'We owe you?' she said. 'Dear girl. You are a child still, and a child who has suffered. But you cannot even begin to grasp the insignificance of those lost lives. You saw Ciuthach in a primal, emergent form. Had he escaped, he would have gathered his power, and disappeared. The Faded do not work against us by mindless violence. By preventing Ciuthach reaching a subtler form, a great disaster has been averted.' She smiled. Cold as a viper. 'You have questions. Ask them. You think they will shock me. But you *are* owed answers.'

She was right. I had a question.

'How many people was it worth?' I said.

'To bring down a single creature of Ciuthach's power?' Robilar answered instantly. 'Forty-six thousand, six hundred and fifty-six.' She stated it like an accountant ticking off parcels of beans being delivered.

We stared at one another for a moment.

'Right.'

'That sounds fair to you?' Robilar asked.

'I think it's right that you have a number,' I said. 'Why that number?'

'Six to the power of six,' she said. 'Six spheres of existence. Self, other, energy, mind, life, death. Circles within circles.'

'And how many Draoihn would it be worth?'

'The Draoihn are the bulwark that ensures the Crown is passed from monarch to heir,' Robilar said, a smile displaying even little teeth. 'Each is rare, and precious.'

'Worth more than other people.'

'You may not like it, but yes.'

'Is this necessary?' Ulovar asked.

Robilar turned sharp eyes in his direction. Her voice cracked like a whip. 'What is it that you object to, Ulovar? Her impropriety or her bluntness? You think I can't see what you've done in there? The scar? You want this girl to form part of your little army, but what is she? Half a person? Less? You've buried her grief, but do you see what you've left behind?'

The scar in my mind. I'd felt it, running the fingers of my mind across it. I'd wondered what Ulovar had done to me that had left me so blank, so empty all the long way down from Dalnesse. It seemed obvious, now that someone said it out loud. He'd cut through my mind as if with a blade, slicing away something that had once been a part of me. He had made me something else.

Ulovar bristled but bowed his head before the grandmaster's anger.

I just sat there. The anger I'd felt earlier was ebbing away, running sidelong against the crack that ran through my mind. I could see it now, see what it was, what it held back. Grief for the people taken from me, and with it, my sorrow, my ability to feel for them as I once had. In a way, he had taken those people from me too, even if they were already dead. If only he had also taken away the curse that had blighted me since childhood. I had always known there was something wrong with me, the grave-sight sullying me. Making me a target.

'You are a hero, Raine,' Robilar said. 'Though I am afraid your glory will not be sung.'

'I don't care about glory,' I said.

'You are angry, that I do not care enough for those you have lost? Would a show of tears appease you? I have shed tears, from time to time, and they have never brought anybody back. The enemies of the Crown have tried to kill me many times. I have been torn apart twice by creatures more terrible than Ciuthach, and both times dragged myself back together to continue my service. I have trained men and women and they have died, horribly, souls torn from their bodies, immolated, drowned, cut to pieces on foreign battlefields. And all of it has been worth it. You believe you have suffered more than any, yet you say you want to join Redwinter in its fight. You are wrong. You do not seek to serve the Crown. What do you truly want?'

I thought about it, spooling phrases through my mind. I had been so numb ever since Dalnesse, I had bounced from moment to moment like a fledgling bird leaping into its first flight just as the hurricane struck. What was the truth?

'I don't want to be afraid anymore,' I said. 'I want what you have.'

'Power? Wealth?'

'I want to be free.'

Robilar pursed her lips. I noticed that her fingernails were immaculately manicured and painted, tiny roses picked out in green and red against a black background. Green stones sparkled in her ears, on a bracelet around one wrist.

'Van Ulovar wishes you to become an apprentice, and to be trained here. But I do not see the commitment to the Crown within you that is required. There is great danger in training a Draoihn who does not wish to give themselves over to service. We do not teach power for personal gain.'

'None are born to serve, Grandmaster,' Ulovar interjected. 'We admit those from Clan LacClune—though Merovech LacClune barely communicates with us. Clan LacShale bred a traitor, and his daughter is out right now preparing for her Testing. This girl has done more for Redwinter—for the Crown—than any of them.'

'What would you have us use her for, Ulovar? A diplomat without education? A rune-smith without languages? A warrior without martial training?'

'Not every Draoihn is a warrior,' Ulovar pled. 'If she can reach the Second Gate, there is artificing. Even if she only ever masters Eio, there is cartography, art, teaching. I would have use for her in my clanhold even so—'

'*Your* clanhold, indeed,' Robilar said coolly. 'Even were she to display some special aptitude that I am unaware of, there is the matter of the scar you have inflicted. Enter the trance of Fier.'

Ulovar sighed. 'Give me your hand, Raine,' he said.

I trembled in my seat. I didn't move. I didn't want anyone else in my mind. Not again. No matter what the grandmaster had said, there were things in my mind nobody could know. I willed my thoughts to still silence.

Ulovar placed a warm, weathered hand over mine.

I became aware of something new, something brushing against me as though I were clay on a potter's wheel, spinning, hands fitted smoothly around me, testing my shape. I gasped at the intrusion. I made to stand up, but my legs wouldn't move. The Draoihn had closed their eyes.

Two presences pressed in on me. Ulovar, his mind a big, solid mass, ground forwards like a rolling millstone through the connection of our skin. Robilar was different, only half-substantial, and yet far more formidable. I spun within their grasp as they caressed my being, almost tenderly.

And then the illusionary hands lifted from me and my vision was left filled with stars. I sucked in a loud, rasping gasp of breath. Sat panting.

'The scar is deep,' Robilar said. 'I cannot unmake it.'

'But—'

As my vision cleared, I looked into Ulovar's blood-filled eyes, and the fear began to gentle. The grandmaster had been telling the truth. They could not read me like a book. They couldn't pick apart my memories. *They didn't know what I was.* 'He did it to protect me,' I said. Desperate. 'And I'm stronger for it.'

The grandmaster's eyes narrowed as she considered me. Ulovar made to speak, but she stayed him with a wave of her hand.

'What Ulovar has done to you is forbidden. He has altered your mind. Cut part of it away and sealed it. You have not been your old self lately, have you?'

'I don't want to be my old self,' I said. 'My old self was useless. I'm better this way. I can serve the Crown. I can be whatever you need me to be.'

'There is great danger in dividing a mind so,' the grandmaster said. 'He has taken all the pain you should feel at the loss of your home, all those people. The terror. What are you now? Something less than a whole person?'

'No,' I said. 'I'm something more.' I met her eye for as long as I dared.

The grandmaster smiled for the briefest of moments. It was a lovely smile, but only a fool would have taken it for an expression of love.

'My answer is no,' Robilar said. 'I am sorry, child. I can see the fire in you, but our flames ring the Crown. You do not seek to join us, but to take what you can. You do not have the making of a Draoihn.'

I glowered as I stood, the chair grating across the floor. I could beg. I could demand to be tested, to prove myself. Or I could be on a horse and gone from this place in less than an hour.

'Wait, Raine,' Ulovar said. 'Grandmaster, I object to your decision, but if I cannot change it, I will keep Raine on in my clanhold as a retainer. I owe her my life, and on my honour I will see that debt paid. That much, you must allow me to do.'

'Do you forget that you are under house arrest here, Van Ulovar?' Robilar said, and a storm rose behind her words, heavy and filled with cloud. 'Do you forget that one of your own apprentices breached the Blackwell, and cost this girl's family their lives?'

I hadn't had any family, but the point seemed moot.

'You must allow me this, Grandmaster,' Ulovar growled.

Robilar considered me. She was startlingly beautiful, as beautiful as a clash between night and day.

'Keep her on as a retainer,' she said. 'But you'll not teach her the trances. If I discover that you or any of your people are doing so, there will be a price. You will not wish to pay it.'

I stumbled from the grandmaster's house into a world that seemed colder than it had before. I had come all this way, had suffered so much, and at the end of it all they would have me wear a grey robe, and I would still be the same terrified girl who couldn't close her eyes for fear of what lay in the darkness.

Ulovar walked some of the way with me, but at some point I just began walking another direction, and he didn't stop me. There was kindness in that, or maybe shame for what he'd done to me. I suppose I could have felt angry about it, but now that I'd had to confront the truth of what he'd done to me, I didn't resent it. I didn't feel sorry for him—couldn't feel sorry for him—either. I was a broken thing.

I owe her, he'd said. Duty and honour. To Ulovar, my life was a debt that he had to pay.

I sat beside a carp pond and watched the fish nibbling at the surface. Easy to be a fish, maybe. Better to be a fish. I sat there a long time, until it got cold, and the dark drew in around me.

16

It was no new thing for me to feel sadness. What settled over me on that cold afternoon, as the winter light died and the pale blue cadanum light took dominance over Redwinter, was different to the gentle sorrows I had known. It was a blanking, a pall of empty, hopeless grey. I had lost my family, not once but twice, and there was no true place for me in the world. I passed through the night like a half-living thing, as I had been when Ulovar first took me onto the road. Food tasted hollow. I would have preferred to be angry, but I was too tired to find the spark.

For a moment I'd thought I'd found an answer I hadn't known I was looking for. A flickering candle in a dark world, guttering in the first wind that touched upon it. Perhaps this is how a painter feels after decades of futility, hanging up a paintbrush, resigning himself to the notion that his art would never hang on a clanhouse wall. Opportunity, snuffed. Ulovar had said he would keep me on. For the time being, it was all I had, and the journey's toil still lay heavy on me. What stretched out before me now was a daily routine in Redwinter, devotion, work, devotion, some more work, some more devotion, and then either sitting doing work or being devoted or possibly, maybe, turning it all silent in sleep.

· · · · · · ·

The day after the grandmaster's rejection, I rose to the sounds of movement around the greathouse, apprentices readying themselves for dawnsong. I opened my door with bleary eyes to find them trooping out wearing thick, starched grey robes that looked like the ones that travelling friars wore. Since I wasn't permitted to become Draoihn, at least I didn't have to endure sermons. I went back to bed.

A few extra hours in bed. I'd heard people talk about it before with a kind of reverence, but having never had a comfortable bed before, I hadn't really understood. Hazia's old bed was different. The mattress was stuffed entirely with feathers, which I'd discovered when the point of one pricked through the fabric and I pulled the downy feather free. A whole mattress of feathers— the sheer number of geese, or ducks, or whatever they had come from—was impressive, especially when I realised that everyone else in the vast house must have had one too. The covers weren't some thin, frayed blanket either, but soft and thick, and there were enough of them that even after the fire had died down, I didn't get cold. I resolved quite firmly that I would stay in bed for as long as I was allowed. Maybe forever.

A knock on my door. I ignored it. The person outside evidently decided that my silence meant that they ought to come in. The hairless servant, Tarquus, appeared.

'You are late, Miss Raine.'

'I can only be late if I'm trying to go somewhere.'

'On the contrary. Van Ulovar insists that you attend dawnsong with his apprentices. Hurry along. I shall show you where to go.' He placed a thick, starched grey wool robe over the back of a chair.

Bed seemed far preferable, but I could hear Tarquus puttering about beyond the door. I rose with a groan, struggled into the itchy robe, wondering why anybody with all this money would choose such a dismally uncomfortable garment, and allowed myself to be led to a vast church. Coloured glass rained shades of rainbow across rows of what I'd thought were seats. Tarquus prodded me inside and shut the door behind me.

Rows of hooded worshippers in similarly unpleasant robes stood in ranks as an elderly priest droned on from the front beneath a stained glass window showing Our Lady of Fire, her voice scarcely making it halfway across the nave. I stood dumbly, not knowing where to go. A tall man on the end gestured that I should come over to his pew, then nudged others aside. I slotted in gratefully. I still couldn't really hear the priest.

'Put your hood up,' the man whispered. Sanvaunt. I realised I was the only attendee—'worshipper' would have been too strong—with their hood down.

'Why do we have to wear our hoods indoors?' I whispered back.

'So the Light Above can't see our faces,' he said.

'Why can't the Light Above see us?'

'I don't know.'

'It's silly.'

'Yes.'

'Shhhh!' Someone along the row didn't like our whispering.

'I heard about the grandmaster's decision,' Sanvaunt said. 'For what it's worth, I think it's a shame. You've already proven yourself.'

Across the church floor, there was some kind of exchange between three priests, and a dark man even bigger than Ovitus cleared his throat and began to sing in a powerful, beautiful voice. The rest of the grey-robed congregation joined in with the droning chant. One group sang a counterpoint. It sounded horrible.

'I think it's wrong too,' I said. I didn't know the words, the tune, or any of the rest of it. 'I wanted to learn.'

Sanvaunt turned to look at me. His eyes were very pale, the fronds of unruly hair that hung around his face black as night. He stopped singing. 'The grandmaster can't be seen to allow Ulovar a new apprentice right now. Not after Hazia. But things could change, if you show that you're able to dedicate yourself to the Crown,' he said. 'Maybe in a year she'll change her mind.'

'Vedira Robilar doesn't strike me as the kind of woman who softens,' I said.

'Shhh!' a woman hissed in a lull in what I suppose was a song but sounded more like some kind of battle chant. 'Sing, you heathens!'

Sanvaunt fell back into the song. After another couple of rounds, the prayer, or hymn, whatever, it cut off abruptly. Several people failed to hit the timing correctly, and the church lapsed into awkward silence. The old priest started up her mumbling again, words like 'duty' and 'obligation' reaching me, telling everybody how they ought to be living. My mother had never had time for religion, neither the outlander deities of the mountain clans nor the Light Above that the Brannish insisted we say we loved.

'A word to the wise. Call everyone by their titles. It'll be better for you in the long run.'

'Should I call you Draoihn Sanvaunt, then?' I asked. He smiled at me. Up till now I'd struggled to find pleasure in anything at Redwinter but the sausages. Apparently that had changed. I felt a little sick.

'It's better than Wildrose,' he said. Mocking me, reminding me of the insult I'd inadvertently given? No. Teasing me. Telling me it was all right, and he'd forgiven the slight?

'I still don't know what it means.'

Sanvaunt joined in a few words of droning chorus, and I thought the conversation might be over.

'A wildrose's mother wasn't married to his father. Scandal! And not so good for inheritance.'

'I didn't know,' I said. 'I'm sorry. If I'd known what it meant . . . nobody says that in the north. They aren't so fussed about marriage there. I'm a wildrose too, I suppose.'

He glanced at me from beneath the hood, reached out and gave my hand a little squeeze. It was a warm, simple gesture, so casually done I should never have felt the surge of heat as blood rushed to my face. I actually thanked the Light Above that the hood hid my ears, which had to be redder than poppies.

Oh, Light Above, had I just enjoyed that? Just a person putting their hand onto mine to say it was all right that I'd called them a bastard?

'Roses are the best flowers anyway,' he said.

'Either be quiet or leave!' the exasperated woman hissed. Leaving didn't seem to be an option, so we passed the remainder of the service in silence. My mind was not on religion. It was on the warm hand on mine, and heavy-lidded, sleepy eyes, and beds of rose petals. I hadn't expected to enjoy being in church, but I had such a sense of this man standing next to me—knowing that he was so competent, that he'd been able to disarm and overcome me by throwing a sword, which I was pretty sure wasn't the conventional way to use it—but that he was showing me kindness behind it. Kindness without expectation. Ovitus was kind, but I always sensed that he needed something back from me, whether it be affirmation, acknowledgement or just company.

When at last it was over, we filed out and someone stopped Sanvaunt to ask him to stand in for a swordsmanship instructor who'd gone down with a cold. As I wandered out, I scratched at all the spots where my stupid robe itched. I wasn't the only one.

'You never get used to it,' Ovitus said as he walked back to the greathouse beside me. 'But you can wear something underneath. That helps.'

The robe was already heavy enough. Roast alive or scratch yourself to death. If I was going to stay here, then getting out of this absurdity needed to be high on my list. I wondered whether I could get back into bed, but Tarquus stopped me.

'Van Ulovar has dictated that you be shown your duties,' he said.

'Duties?' I said. I hadn't had duties yesterday. I didn't want any today.

'Everybody earns their keep here, young miss,' Tarquus said, as though his near infinite patience had already been worn thin in the earliest hours of daylight. 'You are to be named First Retainer,' he told me. 'I am also a First Retainer.' He said the words as though they deeply offended him. 'The scullery girls are deemed Fifth Retainers, the kitchen hands are Fourth, and so on and so on until we reach First. Just we two. Isn't that wonderful?'

'If you say so. I have to change.'

He stood outside my door, whistling a tune to let me know that he was waiting. I put on Esher's clothes—still spectacular—and noticed a little tray of glamours on the nightstand, the set Esher had left for me. Partly because it would delay being given chores, but also because there was something nice about the little tray of coloured powders, with its dark little eye pencil, I tried applying them. It was a lot harder than I'd imagined, and I ended up looking like a theatre clown and scrubbed it all off before facing the inevitable. I headed out and Tarquus showed me around the greathouse, the big kitchens, the three parlours, including one that had a strange little footbath in the middle of the room, the actual baths at the back, the stores.

'What am I actually being asked to *do*?' I asked.

'If the van lets me know, I shall be the first one to inform you,' Tarquus said. His irritation had only been growing as the tour continued. 'For now, I suggest that you wait on Van Ulovar, Thail Sanvaunt and Thail Ovitus at table. I shall demonstrate how.'

What followed was an instructional course on how dinner was supposed to be eaten, how wine ought to be poured, and the various preferences of the lords, which Tarquus seemed to know in excruciating detail. It was deeply tedious, and my heart sank further as I imagined what it would be like, pouring drinks for the masters of the house. When Ovitus had counted the people who lived in the house, he'd forgotten the servants altogether. I felt myself shifting backward against the wall, as though I would become a part of it, invisible, unnoticed. Only yesterday I had faced the grandmaster, and opportunity and life had spread ahead of me like some vast unexplored map of a world I'd never dreamed of. Life had snatched that away again, and reduced me to a mobile piece of furniture.

At some point the apprentices had returned, eaten their breakfast and gone off to study Eio, the trance of the First Gate. I thought that I could hear it, very distantly, the faintest rhythm in my mind. It was distracting, and I tried to shut it out.

'I suppose you can learn as you go along,' Tarquus said. 'Since Van Ulovar has already elevated you to the highest rank within his clanhold, I doubt he's going to dismiss you for carving his lamb incorrectly.'

'Wait. Do you mean I'm doing badly at this?' I said.

'I have seen boys of twelve do better on their first day,' he said, in a tone that dug fingernails into my spine. I was sick of being treated like an adult by men when it suited them, and an incompetent child when it didn't.

Anger. It came like a crackling forest fire, eating me alive.

'We're the same rank, is that right?' I said.

'That is right, Miss Raine.'

'Then you can go fuck yourself,' I said, and strode from the room with that fire trailing in my wake. I lay on my bed and sulked for a while, until Tarquus reappeared as though nothing had happened and said he had more to show me. I was still cross with him, but he was a servant too, and I had come to realise that maybe I was treating him like one. I couldn't quite bring myself to apologise.

It took hours, late evening by the time we were done. None of it was hard, just dreary. I hadn't eaten. At least, I thought, the day would be over soon.

'There is a task that I am going to put into your hands,' Tarquus said, long after I'd had enough. 'It will be your task, and yours alone. You must do it once per week, without fail. Put on some outdoor shoes and meet me in the garden in ten minutes.'

It was cold out, and I wrapped up warm with a scarf and hat I found on a hook by the front door. I'd had no time to explore the garden that lay behind the greathouse. There were no cadanum globes here, and the rows of sculpted trees and empty flower beds lay in darkness. A light shone from within a maze of tall hedgerows, a warm, natural yellow light. I slapped my gloved fingers together to warm them up as I headed through the chill.

Tarquus was crouched in the middle of the maze, beside a circular plot of earth where things had been allowed to grow wild. The central tree was leafless, but the bushes clogging the earth around it competed fiercely with one another for space. A little path of flat stones led through them to the tree, in which a little door had been fitted—a door for hedgehogs, maybe. I made to speak, but Tarquus held a finger to his lips for silence. He had a tray bearing a jug of milk, a jug of ale, a pot of honey, a plate of small cakes and a raw, bloody steak. He carried it to the tree, knelt and laid it in front of the door.

'For the hidden folk, whichever of you may find us by sun or by moon, we make this offering. Be happy around us, be unseen, and if you must visit us, be quiet.'

He stood, his knees creaking, back stiff. Maybe the duties he'd been showing me were taking their toll on him. Perhaps he should have been glad of the help, although if he was, he certainly hadn't shown it today.

'You think there are hidden folk here?' I asked.

'Oh, there are. Many. You heard the snatterkin on your way here? They like the magic, I suspect. Or perhaps it's merely that Redwinter is very old, and the hidden folk have a great sense of history. Have you ever seen one of them?'

I'd seen something an awful lot worse than a powise or a brownie, and I saw plenty of other things that I shouldn't. I didn't want to go into all that. It was such a relief knowing that the Draoihn couldn't pull my memories and thoughts out of my head, that I'd been doing my best to ignore the spirits that inhabited Redwinter's grounds.

'In the north, we say that everybody sees a goblin at least once when they're a child,' I said. 'But I never did.'

'The hidden folk rarely look as one expects them,' Tarquus said. 'I saw a black cat once, but I would swear it was some fey thing.'

'It was probably just a cat,' I said.

'Perhaps. But this duty—setting out gifts for the hidden folk—is one which I wish you to take seriously. If we provide for them here, the hidden folk will keep out of the house. The previous First Retainer forgot once, and for days there were bites taken out of the cheese, tears in fresh laundry, and all manner of spillages. The hidden folk are like Apprentice Esher—they become very enervated, very quickly, about very little which leads to all sorts of problems.'

'So I just bring out some biscuits, some milk and some honey and put the tray by this little door once a week?'

'Once a week, come rain or shine.'

Even I had to admit this was not a duty that I minded doing. Mama had put out a tot of whisky for the hidden folk once a week, though I'd always thought it was just an excuse to buy whisky when she was low on money. The fey creatures of the world preferred deep forests, lonely hilltops, and deep rivers to cold accounting houses.

'Should I open the door?' I asked.

'No, never open the door,' Tarquus said firmly. 'And whatever you do, don't forget to put out the meat.'

'What's the meat for?'

Tarquus gave me a sidelong glance.

'That's for the one that lives behind the door.'

17

I began to have a life. It was not a life I had wanted, but it was the one I was living, and one cannot always swim against the tide.

Redwinter was a place of luxury the like of which I'd never thought existed. In my travels I'd seen thails and minor lordlings, who seemed all sharp edges and gleaming cloth, but it's only when your eyes are opened to the sky that you see what lies beyond the clouds. Compared to these people, they were rustic. Uncultured. Large dogs in the pack, but dogs nonetheless.

It was easy to be overwhelmed by the grandeur. My heart pined for forest trails and secluded pools, but I was not immune to luxury. They felt further away here than they ever had, and a mist had begun to fall down upon me, blanking my eyes. The seduction of gold.

Some minor agreements were made. I received a small stipend at the start of each week, purportedly enough to cover basic living costs, but since my food and board were covered, it was just disposable coin. A buyer was sent to the horse fair to select a suitable palfrey for me. Ivy was not in the stables when I looked. The hard ride down from the north had not been easy on her. I chose not to ask what had become of her. My beautiful, midnight-blue bow had not followed me into the greathouse either. Ulovar had spirited it away. I wanted that back even more than I wanted my horse. I'd found it—had earned it. It was mine. When I found it, I planned to take it back.

'Retainer Raine,' Tarquus called after me on a morning during which he'd shown me how to rearrange napkins. He didn't really raise his voice, merely inflected it. 'When you are done, your master has asked that you call in on Draoihn Sanvaunt. Third door to the left, second corridor on the right from the main hall.'

My master. The word made me want to hiss like a cat. Tarquus's blasé tone did nothing for my temper, and a week of waiting at table and checking that silver had been polished had only intensified my reluctance to bow to it. I stamped my way through the halls. Was that what this whole journey had been for? It wasn't enough that I'd been dragged hundreds of miles south, but now I was supposed to scrape and fawn and pour wine? On the journey, I'd started to believe I would become one of them, would learn from the Draoihn. Would harness the rhythm in my head, and use it. I stalked through the corridors, second corridor on the right from the main hall, third door to the left, and stomped in. At least Sanvaunt had seemed to be friendly. Ovitus was leaving his cousin's room, looking terribly cheerful.

'Ah. Raine. Beautiful day, isn't it?'

'I never wanted to be a servant,' I said. It wasn't fair to take it out on him, but he was the person in front of me, so he got it. 'Your uncle told me I could be Draoihn. Now all I do is pour wine.'

'I don't really like wine all that much anyway,' Ovitus said. He was red-faced, sweating, though the house was always cold.

'Are you all right?'

'I'm fine. Busy, apprentice work, you know.' He wiped his brow with his sleeve. 'Do you want to walk me to the baths?'

'Let's say no?' I said, ignoring the absurdity of the suggestion. 'I have to see Sanvaunt.'

'Ah. Well, like you, he's in quite the bad mood.' He ambled off down the corridor. I pushed open Sanvaunt's door.

I interrupted him in the middle of something. Sanvaunt startled at my arrival, knocking an inkwell across the desk, blue-black night spreading over the fine wood. He grabbed a small, leatherbound book from the table, ripping it from the ink's path, and thrust it into his coat as the blue-black tide swept outwards.

'Damn it all!' he snapped, a flare of hot anger. Then he looked over at me. 'Can't you knock?' Then the anger melted from him, and he looked weary. Drained. Nothing at all like the quiet-smiling man who'd beckoned me across the church to join him just a week back. I'd been looking forward to seeing him again, but he'd been busy with something. His smile was missing, as though he'd been bright silver and had tarnished to tin. Now he was covered in ink as well. I ran off to find a cloth. When I returned, he was trying to push spilt ink back with his hands to prevent it from getting on the carpet. I mopped it up as best as I could, but it was ink, and the drawing table was going to be stained.

'I'm sorry,' I said.

'It's nothing,' he said. So tired. 'Just ink.'

He held up his hands, blue-black and dripping, but he didn't raise his head to meet my eyes. Didn't look at me directly. His dark hair was disorderly, thick and curling around his neck, two days' stubble on his jaw. We hadn't met under the best circumstances, but where had the friendly, advice-giving, hand-touching man from the church gone?

'I was told you wanted me?' I said uncertainly. It hadn't been much, that service in the church, but he'd been easy to talk to. He poured his own wine at table and had smiled at me a few times. I'd been looking forward to talking to him again.

Sanvaunt looked down at his hands, palms and fingers black as tar with ink. Servants appeared to try to save the drawing table. He spoke quietly, all that easy confidence gone.

'I've been asked to show you around the grounds,' he said. 'Come.'

I had noted that apart from the three times a day when the apprentices all went to sing the hours in the chapel, they wore whatever seemed to suit them best, and those that I guessed to be Draoihn going about their business could have passed easily for the better-dressed citizens of Harranir. Aside from the grey worship robe, I hadn't seen Sanvaunt in anything but the deep red leather coat that signified his position, even sat at dinner.

'I hope I didn't ruin whatever you were writing,' I said as he led me across the grounds.

'You didn't.'

'What was it?'

'Nothing of value.' He still hadn't looked me in the eye. I'd not imagined after our brief meeting that we were fast friends, but I felt myself shrinking. Had my initial outburst towards Tarquus caused some graver insult? This was a far cry from sharing his flask of rose-thistle or whispering in church.

'What's that over there?' I asked, pointing. 'And that, what's that? Who lives there?'

Sanvaunt gave brief, functional answers to my questions, until I came in sight of a span of stone that stretched out from the plateau on which Redwinter sat—a bridge across a gulf of space, a gulf of nothing. On the far side, a wide stone spire reached up to connect to the bridge.

'That,' Sanvaunt said, 'is the Blackwell.'

'Where Hazia stole the page?' I could see what looked like a very small building on the far side—but it was barely big enough to be used as a latrine. Hardly a vault. 'There are no guards,' I said.

'No. There are no guards anywhere in Redwinter,' Sanvaunt said. 'Although since Hazia walked right into the Blackwell without challenge, that may well change. Not that it needs to.'

'Why not?'

'It's protected, just not by people. There's something called a soul-web that runs the length of the entrance. A Draoihn who has attained the Fourth Gate—and there are only six of them living—can shield themselves against it.

That's what makes no sense in all of this. Hazia should have been torn apart just trying to enter the tunnel.'

'But she wasn't.'

'No. Ulovar wanted me to show it to you so you'd know to stay away,' Sanvaunt said. 'So do that. Keep to your duties and don't poke about.'

I stopped him.

'Have I done something to offend you?' I asked. My voice sputtered. 'Are you angry because I made you spill your ink?'

Sanvaunt stared out across the drop on either side of the Blackwell's narrow bridge.

'No. You've done nothing wrong. What you do, and how you do it, is not for me to judge. Follow me. Please. This is the quartermaster's office.'

The quartermaster was a woman with rotting teeth, apparently not Draoihn herself but responsible for overseeing the accounting of the whole place. It seemed that for every Draoihn or apprentice in residence there were two dozen servants or functionaries ready to bow and scrape, of which I reluctantly had to count myself as one. Even if most of the Draoihn didn't wear their battle-reds within Redwinter's walls, the staff's grey robes, bowing and subservience made the distinction obvious. Ulovar hadn't told me to start doing all that bowing, so I hadn't started, but I knew that it was coming. The quartermaster was a little different, however. She looked me up and down, didn't like what she saw and wrinkled her nose.

'A little young to be First Retainer, isn't she? A little on the thin side to be anything, I'd say.'

'First Retainer Raine is to be extended the Clan LacNaithe line of credit on the same provision as the apprentices under Lord Draoihn Ulovar's care,' Sanvaunt told her. He said it like someone had died.

'She's not an apprentice?'

'No.'

'But she's getting apprentice credit?'

Sanvaunt gave a curt nod.

'If that's what Van LacNaithe wants,' the quartermaster said with a frown.

'It's what he wants.' Sanvaunt said.

'What's apprentice credit?' I asked. 'How much do I have to pay back?'

'You can draw one hundred pel per day at any of the counting houses in Harranir, for anything that you need to conduct your duties,' Sanvaunt said. To the quartermaster: 'She'll need a signet ring cast. Can you arrange that?'

'Of course,' the rotten-toothed woman said. She took hold of my hand and inspected my fingers. She tried different-sized tin rings on my finger, noted it down. 'Don't go splashing the Lord Draoihn's credit all over the place, I know what you rustic types are like. The less scrupulous merchants will honour whatever you ask for, but I won't, so unless you want to be working off your debts in a stable, don't go blowing it on horse races. Credit won't be taken at the gambling halls or the baiting pits, so don't try it. If you need more than that in a day, I'll need to see it in writing from the van. And no flushing it all away on Silk Street either.'

'What's on Silk Street?' I asked. The quartermaster grinned cruelly and sucked on her teeth.

'Houses of ill repute,' the quartermaster said. 'They'll not charge you there if they think you're from Redwinter. But it ill becomes us if those associated with the clan—'

'Why wouldn't they charge?' I asked. My question was only made of curiosity, but by Sanvaunt's pained grimace and the quartermaster's cackle I could see they thought it less than innocent.

'Because if they think you're an apprentice, they'll think you can give the "night-gift." That if they bed you, magic will rub off on them.'

'Does it?' I asked, intrigued. Sanvaunt stiffened.

'Tell her the other thing as well. Van Ulovar wants her to have everything she needs,' Sanvaunt said, and then stepped outside.

'Those Draoihn men,' the quartermaster said. She smiled, all brown teeth. 'They'll put a sword through a man and eat breakfast off his dead back, but the way a woman's body works terrifies them. You're a lucky girl, being in the LacNaithe house. That wildrose could melt a glacier with those eyes of his, and that young Jathan's blooming rather nicely—I'm sure you've noticed.' She ceased assessing the young men of the LacNaithe household and gave me a serious look. 'You don't know about the night-gift?'

'No.'

'It's practice in some parts for villages to send their most beautiful into the beds of passing Draoihn. There's this foolish belief that bedding a Draoihn, boy or girl, might rub their magic off on you. They want a shot at all *this*.'

'Why would they do that? Villagers, I mean.'

'They don't teach you much in the north, do they?' the quartermaster snickered to herself. 'Well, the girls on Silk Street know it. A thousand a day. That's your limit.'

'One thousand *every* day?' I said, wrinkling my nose. My mother hadn't made that scribing accounts or letters even in her best weeks. 'What would I even spend that on?'

'Ask your master's fat nephew,' she said with a leer. 'He seems to manage it.'

'What was the other thing Sanvaunt mentioned?'

'Ah. Yes. Wait here.'

The quartermaster disappeared from her desk, heading into a vast storeroom. When she returned, she had three small wax-sealed vials in her hand. Black liquid sloshed glutinously around inside.

'What is it?'

'Linny seed extract,' she said. 'Although on Silk Street they call it Maid's Freedom. You know what it does?'

'I know,' I said. I turned the vial in my hands. Braithe had given it to me, the first time we lay together. I should have felt something about that, but in the end I was just glad I'd never got with child. I certainly wouldn't miss feeling like someone was stabbing me in the guts once a month.

Sanvaunt showed me where the laundry was located, the water pumps, then the armoury. He didn't speak to me other than to name the places, and he seemed so run-down it was hard to engage him further. What did it matter, anyway, if some handsome boy had changed his mind about talking to me? I'd lost far more. I told him I didn't need any more assistance, and he walked to the armoury doorway before glancing back at me.

'I understand that you suffered, in the north. I'm sorry for that. But if this is your path, and Redwinter is where you want to be—be here for the right reasons.'

'I'm sorry about the ink,' I said, because it was all I could think of to say. He gave a quiet, joyless smile.

'It was just ink.'

He walked away, and I walked away, and I didn't think that I could have become sadder still and yet, I was.

The armoury was an impressive building. Suits of polished steel stood on scarecrows, and racks held countless swords, spears, knives and pole-hafted weapons I had no name for. I took a leather wrist guard, a bow and some arrows from the armoury, and heaved a practice butt out to one of the courtyards to shed some steam. An ordinary bow felt like a mundane thing in my hands. I hadn't expected to find my own bow there, and I didn't ask. Better that nobody knew I'd been looking for it.

I found it hard to focus, my mind only half on what I was doing, and I struggled to land arrows even at forty paces. Not helped by the spirit of some long-dead Draoihn—hazy, so indistinct I couldn't even make out their features—who was trying to do the same. Redwinter was old, and I'd counted a dozen or so spirits thus far. One thought himself very grand, and was always hurrying off into the Round Chamber insisting that he had urgent business. Two of them were children, who seemed happy enough, or at least as happy as an echo can be. None of them had spoken to me as Lochlan and the warrior ghost had done, and for that I was grateful. I was wary of them now, though, kept checking that the archer wasn't watching me shoot. But he wasn't. He was just dead.

I stopped worrying and just loosed. I pushed all these people from my mind and focused only on the target. I breathed in and out, releasing the string between beats. Braithe had taught me that trick, his hand pressed against my chest, counting it with me. Creeping through the undergrowth with me, lying down beside me. I wrinkled my nose at those memories, annoyed that I'd been so naïve, and imagined his face in the centre of the target. Whatever was happening to him in the north now, he would probably have welcomed an arrow. The thail-lords were not known for their mercy. There was no sympathy for him in my heart. I loosed arrow after arrow, varied the ranges from the target, loosed while walking. I wasn't a champion archer, but I wasn't bad either. I plucked the bits I needed from Braithe's tutelage and discarded the rest, uncaring that I scattered bits of memory to dissolve on the wind around me.

Grandmaster Robilar thought the scar was some great wrong that had been done to me, but it felt good not to care.

'You're pretty good with that. I'm glad you didn't shoot me at Tor Marduul.'

Esher, golden haired and one-eyed, stood a little way behind, watching me.

'It would be awkward now if I had,' I said. My arms were tired. 'Thanks. For the case of glamours.'

'It's nothing,' she said, and she smiled and I believed her. Having learned about all that credit, it really was nothing to her. Easy to be generous when you have everything. 'Who were you shooting at?'

'Stupid men,' I said.

'Plenty of those around,' she said. 'I guess they were lucky it was just the butts you were hunting today. If you're done wiping out fools, I'll show you where the baths are.'

I nodded. Hot water sounded good. She led me to a squat, low building divided for men and women by hours of the day. Warm air greeted me as I stepped inside, welcoming as summer and filled with hanging steam. A wide pool filled the room, stone steps leading down into it. We were the only bathers.

'How is it heated?' I asked. There were no tin kettles or buckets over fires.

'There are heat orbs beneath the floor,' Esher said. 'Draoihn of the Second Gate make them.'

'How?'

'I wish I could tell you,' she said. 'If I ever reach the Second Gate, perhaps I'll understand. They use the Gate to manipulate the Other. Change the nature of things. They made them store heat.'

The First Gate affected oneself; the Second Gate reached out to the other. Of course. It made a kind of sense, I supposed. More importantly, when I disrobed and lowered myself in, the water was beautifully warm around my legs, then my thighs, and then I was up to my shoulders. A vague floral smell filled the room, soft and welcoming. Esher watched me from the side of the bath as she shed her clothes. She was pale and smooth, but the muscles of her arms and legs were well defined, her shoulders broad. She stepped down into the chest-high water, slowly propelled herself across the bath towards me.

'What?' I asked as she came closer. She was studying me through the water.

'I'm sorry,' she said. 'I don't mean to stare.'

'But you were.'

'Those scars you have, on your ribs and legs,' she said. 'Where did you get them?'

Oh. The scars. Esher's hair floated around her in the water, a spread of polished gold. Self-consciousness welled up through me, and where I'd been naked and uncaring a moment before, now I wanted to cover myself. It didn't seem fair to be naked beside such beauty.

'I'm sorry,' she said. 'Everyone has a right to privacy. I shouldn't have asked.' She settled close to me, her head resting on the bath's edge, and closed her eyes.

'Hard to have privacy in here,' I said.

'I've used these baths so many times, I don't even think of it,' she said. 'But you don't have to feel the same. I didn't think you'd be self-conscious about it. Around here, people tend to show their scars off rather than hide them. Accept my apologies, please.'

Being naked around other women was hardly something new, but this felt different somehow. Esher was just so perfectly made.

'No. It's fine,' I said. But beneath the water, my hands moved of their own volition, covering the scars on my ribs and leg. 'I was a child, and my mother and I were crossing a fallen tree over a river. I fell off and bounced off most of the rocks on the way down. My mother had to pump all the water out of me. Said that I was cold as death for a while, all full of river water. It's not a good memory.'

That wasn't the entire story. That morning I'd seen a dead man, at my mother's accounting house. I told her, and that same day she'd resigned her position, packed and we were off. Looking back now, I wondered if she'd feared I'd told others as well. Protecting herself, protecting me too. She'd been angry with me, though she wouldn't say why, telling me it was my fault. I'd cried, blinded myself with tears, and lost my footing. Bounced, drowned, breathed again. I'd never told her—never told anyone, how could I possibly?—but after that I saw the dead even more clearly, more substantial than they had ever been before. Or so I remembered it, and remembering what you saw before you were seven years old and comparing it to what you saw after is not terribly reliable. I may have invented it. I had, when I allowed myself to think about what I was and what I could see, wondered whether it was my first death—throttled by my own birth-cord as I entered the world—that had given me the grave-sight, and drowning had only made it stronger.

'Isn't a fiahd always meant to land on its feet? You don't have to hide them, you know. I think they're becoming,' Esher said, smiling, her eyes still closed. I wished she hadn't seen them. Was she picturing them again now?

'I guess I can't hide my scars now,' I said. Hazia's knife had bitten deep across my face. The wound had scabbed, hardened, and now that line was as much part of me as the dents the rocks had put in me. I hated them all. 'It must be nice to be whole.'

'Other than my eye, you mean?' She smiled. 'You can ask me about it, if you want to.'

Esher's left eye was clouded and milky, a hard flaw in her otherwise flawless countenance. Leaving it in sight almost felt like she was issuing a challenge. Her head resting back against the side of the bath, her eyes closed, she breathed in steam.

'Why don't you wear a patch over it?'

'Because it's me,' she said. 'A bit of me, anyway. If I can't see out of it, I don't think it's fair that I have to cover it over too. Sometimes I catch gross old men staring at me, and then they see my eye and they stop. That's useful. Anyone worth my time won't dislike me for it, I think.'

I swallowed. Hard. No, they wouldn't. That proudly worn imperfection only made her more lovely.

'I have another scar,' Esher said. 'Just the one.' She opened her eyes, almost as though she was daring me to look away from them. I didn't. She pushed a little from the side so that she flowed through the water. She showed me the palm of her hand where the skin was overly smooth. 'From when I was little. I put my hand on a stove. My mother thought the burn would infect and I'd die. But I didn't, and I don't like to hide who I am.'

I took her hand in mine and traced my fingers across the smooth skin. Sanvaunt's hand had been big, and warm and rough against mine. This was different.

'It's not a bad one,' I said. Esher's fingers closed around mine as the steam rose around us.

'Yours aren't bad either, Raine,' she said. 'They're the story of who you are. What made you. Written in your skin.'

She was very close to me. She held on to my hand, but she reached out with the other, and her fingers played over the new scar that crossed my nose and cheek. The world was too full of her, her polished-gold loveliness overwhelming in the scented water. Her knee brushed against mine as gentle fingers played over my scar. I swallowed the lump in my throat. This must be what the hidden folk were like, I thought, the fey Glaistig, enchanting, dangerous.

Esher lowered her hand, her fingers moving across the old river-scar on my ribs.

'Does it hurt?' she asked.

'No,' I said. My voice was stuck in my throat.

'Most Draoihn arrive with scars of one kind or another,' she said gently. 'And we'll all have them one way or another by the time our lives are done. Don't fear yourself, Fiahd. You're beautiful.'

The glistening water on her skin. The gentle curve of her jaw. She leaned in and my heart was suddenly kicking like a bee-stung mule in my chest. My breath was a heavy thing, locked low in my lungs, unmoving.

'I think we shall be good friends, Raine,' she said. 'It's nice to have another girl around the place.'

And then she splashed water in my face, and the spell broke in a shower of warm droplets. Esher moved away. She smiled at me. She meant nothing sensual, I told myself firmly. We were just two girls in a bath. But I felt as though I stood naked before a market-day crowd. My hands itched to reach out and touch her, but she'd already released my hand as she closed her eyes and propelled herself back across the water. She seemed something different, something I shouldn't be looking at.

'The full moon's up soon,' she said. 'Some of us girls will go out on the moor. You should come with us.'

I closed my eyes, breathed out and sank into the consuming warmth of the water.

First Sanvaunt was my friend, and now he was as distant as Dalnesse. First Esher raised a sword to me, yelling like she was possessed, and now she was soft as silk and sweet as honey. I didn't need Sanvaunt to be my friend, but I still felt like something that could have been good had been reft from my grasp. Maybe I'd thought that there was a little spark there, and yes, if I was really honest, maybe I'd wanted there to be. Only now Esher had made me nervy, and she was only trying to show me it was all right to be myself, and Light Above but I didn't want to feel any of this right now. I was fine on my own, although I had to admit, it would be nice to have a girl for a friend for a change. Perhaps that was why I'd suddenly felt so uncomfortable when she drew close. Maybe? Probably. Best to say that was it and not think about it again, ever.

18

An initial hearing was held against Ulovar, among the members of the Council of Night and Day who were in residence at Redwinter. As his anxious clanhold awaited his return, I poured the stupid wine for the ungrateful apprentices as they sat around a table that would have seated five times as many.

'There's only Grandmaster Robilar and Lord Draoihn Onostus here to sit,' Jathan said. He was usually a happy young man, a year my senior, but that night his expression was sombre. They all were. Their patron's fate hung over them.

'Lord Draoihn Kelsen won't leave the king's side. Not even for this. His seat is only a formality,' Esher said. She swirled the dregs of her cider miserably. 'Merovech LacClune is off at his holdings, like always. Hanaqin is the Light Above only knows where, and Lussaine is off fighting for the king of Brannlant.' She looked around at her peers. 'We need to do something. What can we do? Let's do something!'

'Uncle has few friends on the council these days,' Ovitus said. He had drawn a big letter L in leftover gravy with his knife.

'Don't start moping for the dead,' Esher said. 'Kaldhoone LacShale's actions bought him his fate. There have to be rules, even for us.'

'There are,' Sanvaunt said as he entered the room. 'And we're following them, as we must.' He sounded tired. I didn't look at him. Our budding friendship had died and been hung up on a thornbush, and it prickled like a burn. 'Esher, careful with the careless words about Kaldhoone LacShale. He was executed as a traitor, but his daughter is our friend. Your best friend.'

'I wouldn't say it if Liara was here,' Esher said. But she looked away, chastened, all her hot temper fading.

'Then don't say it at all,' Sanvaunt said. He stood over them, looking so much older and wiser than the rest of them, even if he was only twenty-three. Sanvaunt was a full Draoihn, Tested and proven, and when he spoke, the apprentices listened. 'Since Ulovar is predisposed tonight, he's asked me to lead you in the observances.'

The apprentices managed to withhold their groans. I did not, and for just a moment the dark-eyed Draoihn closed his eyes as if holding something back.

Then he blinked, and he was back to being sleepy-eyed and handsome and not noticing me at all. The observances were readings, all about the Light Above and the Faded and how they'd taught people things in the Age of the Boring Faded, and then had a Boring Faded War, and then there were kings and the Haddat-Nir and the Age of Soot and the Age of Rebuilding and the Age of Can-I-Please-Sit-Down-Now. It was all very well for the apprentices not to have groaned—they didn't have to stand around holding a jug of wine like an idiot. I watched Sanvaunt, wondering how this man had ever whispered with me in church that morning. He took out the heavy, well-thumbed book of liturgical verse and passed it to Ovitus.

'Start us off. Yes, it's dry, but it makes us better Draoihn. Choose something interesting, if you can find it.'

Ovitus was not a natural performer. The previous night's reading had got to a part where three brothers of the line of Delac-Mir rose to power and made kingdoms. He began to read a list of who had sired who, and who they had sired, and on and on it went. All of this had happened nearly two thousand years ago, and why it was important that anyone knew who the second wife of some long-dead king's favoured third son was, I had no idea. The Order of the Draoihn was like that, though. They seemed to think that tradition excused wasting a lot of their time, and somehow it was important that I stood by the wall and did nothing while they did it.

After supper, Ovitus caught my eye.

'Come sit with me?' he asked. 'We haven't spent much time together since I got back.'

Ovitus thought we'd become friends on our journey south. I was a retainer, and he was more than capable of ordering me around, but he seemed to forget that. I didn't see how people from such different worlds were meant to be friends, but I welcomed the company. The evenings were long as winter came down, and so I wrapped myself in a borrowed scarf and a heavy coat and went out with him to sit on a bench in the manor's private garden, and look up at the stars.

Ovitus didn't say anything. He just looked up at the sky. They were the same stars, I thought. We'd come all this way south, but the stars hadn't changed.

'What will the council decide?' I asked.

'I don't know,' Ovitus said. 'Part of me doesn't want to know.'

'What's the worst that can happen?' I asked. 'Your uncle is a powerful man.'

'The council will have to determine whether his actions were a threat to the Crown,' Ovitus said. He shook his head. 'You must have heard what Esher said, about Liara's father. He commanded the Fourth Gate too, but he ended up floating in the harbour. A single Draoihn of the Fourth is more precious than gold, but if the Crown was endangered—well. The Round Chamber dispenses justice quickly.'

'He did the right thing,' I said. 'They'll see that.'

'Perhaps,' Ovitus said. He shifted uncomfortably.

'What is it?'

'The grandmaster is no fool,' he said. 'She's old. Old enough to know much that others don't. I've wondered about her order to stand down, what she knew about that page that Hazia stole. Did she know what it might do to my uncle if he actually got hold of it?'

'He resisted it. He was strong enough.'

'He didn't know that,' Ovitus said quietly. 'Nobody did. What if he'd brought Hazia down, only for Ciuthach to corrupt him too? Ciuthach alone would have been a terrible danger in the world, but how much more so if Ulovar had succumbed? The grandmaster keeps things close to her chest.'

'You seem to have as many enemies here as you do out there.'

'Merovech LacClune hates my uncle with a vengeance. Maybe he'll take this as an opportunity. Either way, it— You know, can we talk about something else?'

'I don't know,' I said. 'What do you want to talk about?'

'Liara will be back soon,' he said. 'I can feel it. I can't wait for you to meet her, Raine. She's not like Esher, all full of herself. She has this inner beauty, and it shines. It really shines.'

I rather liked Esher. Liked her more than I was comfortable with, in fact. She was a cool breeze on a warm day, and sometimes a hot wind in a desert. She was confident, and pretty, and when I was around her, I felt that I could afford to be soft as well as hard in this place of iron and stone. I didn't see whatever perceived aloofness he saw in her. As Ovitus stared up at the stars and began to wax on about the perfection that was Liara LacShale, I realised that perhaps I had misjudged just how boring those dinnertime readings on the Delac-Mir had been. Perspective is everything.

Ulovar seemed drained the following morning when he joined us at the formal breakfast after dawnsong. The apprentices ate in silence. I was expected to wait on them, and I wasn't any good at it, which is an embarrassing thing to have to admit about what is essentially a child's task, but they didn't complain.

'Summons go out to the other council members today,' he told them. 'Life continues as normal. Be attentive to your studies. Work on mastering Eio. And don't let me hear from Master Hylan that any of you are slacking at your martial studies.' He looked intently at Ovitus as he said this, but his nephew chose to stare intently at the bread and butter before him instead. The rest of the meal was completed in a stilted, awkward conversation.

'I have new duties for you,' Ulovar said to me when Fifth Retainers came in to clear away the plates—many still half-full of food, all of which I would gladly have eaten—and the apprentices had gone to change from their formal breakfast wear into clothes more suited to the training court. 'I need someone I can trust to run messages for me, since I'm pinned down here. I can trust you with that, can't I, Raine?'

'You can trust me,' I said. Ulovar smiled, half-flattened by weariness.

'My messages aren't always simple. Sometimes they require a little pressure. A little convincing. You'll get the hang of it, I'm sure.'

'I could do with a break from all this standing around. I haven't left Redwinter since we got here.'

Ulovar held my gaze for several moments, longer than most people would have been comfortable with. Maybe it was the scar he'd put in my mind, but it didn't feel uncomfortable to me.

'Some of your duties may not seem terribly interesting,' he said. 'I'm aware. I had to act as a page, when I was very young. Mostly you're just standing around listening.'

'I know,' I said, wondering why he felt the need to explain it to me, since I was doing it every day.

'Mostly, listening,' he said. 'You keep on doing that. It won't do you any harm to listen.'

I passed the morning being instructed in various forms of greeting and polite etiquette by Tarquus. I had come to regret being so rude to him, and to acknowledge that he probably thought I was an ungrateful little shit, but he went
about his duties as though nothing had happened at all. A hard man to read
in many ways. There were so many different ranks and relationships between
southern people it was a wonder anyone could remember them.

'Each district is minded by a reeve, and each reeve deputises to five or more
quarter-reeves,' he said.

'Why are there five if they're quarters?' I asked.

Tarquus frowned.

'I don't know. There just are. As a First Retainer, you'll address a quarter-
reeve as "good sir," but a full reeve as "honoured sir."'

It all seemed pretty unnecessary to me, but Ulovar had said to listen, so I
listened. Maybe I was being ungrateful. I was well-fed, I had more money than
I'd ever seen in my life, and I could take baths in the evening, although I'd
become careful to make sure that I only went when they were quiet, or when
other retainers were using them.

'. . . and if they are from Dharithia, always bow.'

'Got it.'

Tarquus looked sceptical, but if he thought that he could bore me into sub-
mission with his list of honorifics, he'd find I was entirely the wrong person
to try it on.

Another week passed. Now that I knew Ulovar was going to start sending
me down to Harranir, I began to force myself to go down the mountainside, to
face the city head-on. Ovitus insisted on coming with me, ostensibly to show
me around, but I thought he was just lonely. It was as bad as I had imagined it
would be: ghosts walking through walls, ghosts sailing down the river on non-
existent boats, ghosts lying mewling in the street. Hundreds and hundreds of
ghosts, their misty green-tinted forms complaining and arguing with thin air.
I learned to keep my head low, my eyes on the ground. None of them noticed
me, which was just how it should have been, but I feared that one day one of
them might look right at me.

The quiet days in Ulovar's greathouse had given me more time to reflect
than I wanted. I was able to think of Ciuthach now without wanting to curl
into a tiny ball and disappear—maybe it was my proximity to the likes of Ulovar and Grandmaster Robilar. There couldn't have been many places that were
safer. I still had more questions than answers. The Draoihn's most pressing
question was whether Hazia had acted at Ulovar's direction. I had no doubt

that she had acted independently, and my questions were more about who, or what, the feather-crowned spirit had been. She had helped me, had come to me again on the road. Spoken to me, as though she were a person. Denied being a ghost.

She had worked powerful magic. As powerful as the Draoihn. Maybe she was one of the hidden folk? A Queen of Feathers, a creature of legend among them? The hidden folk lived beyond the perimeter of our world, crossing in and out. I preferred to think of her that way. The dead were predictable, unnerving at times but ultimately powerless. I didn't want the rules I had understood since childhood to muddy. There is comfort in understanding the world, and she had shaken my understanding to its core.

I had survived the grandmaster's probing, but the longer I thought on the Queen of Feathers, and every time I saw a harmless old ghost, I felt a mental flinch. The man at the hunter's inn had told me I'd find friends in Harranir, but that was the last thing I wanted. Rather, I knew that at any moment I might have to run, and so I prepared for it.

I began to ensure that I took Ulovar's messages down to the city when Ovitus was required in a lesson or church service, and bought whatever I thought was easiest to sell on using the clan credit I'd been extended. Then I took my new goods and pawned them. I tried to vary the amounts, sometimes large, sometimes smaller. Sometimes I used the coin to buy jewellery, gemstones, anything small and highly valuable that I could stash away easily. Initially I feared that someone would come and ask me where my fine silks were, and I even bought an old horse once, but nobody seemed to pay any attention to it at all. I bought travelling supplies, and hoarded them beneath my feather-stuffed bed in a backpack. My hoard gave me some measure of control. I could abandon these people with enough wealth to start over, if I chose to.

Clothes began to arrive from the tailor in neatly wrapped packages. I'd never seen anything quite like them, and they all fit me in a way that clothes never had before. Predominantly they were in blue, grey, white and a silver material that shimmered like metal but was as soft as silk. The buttons shone. There were no over-knee skirts for me, whatever the city fashion said. The tailor had provided snug breeches, shirts and riding boots that rose to the knee. Esher said that I looked good in them, and that both meant more to me than Ovitus's clumsy compliments and made me want to avoid her. I stood out among the servants like a cat trying to hide among dogs. Pouring wine at table was certainly tedious, but I was getting better at it, and it didn't take up that much of the day. A dull little part of me began to think I would eventually get used to all this. Everything had changed so fast.

And, fate decided, it would all change again soon enough.

. . . .

Ulovar's errands broke the monotony of clanhouse life, even if it meant facing the myriad dead souls in Harranir. I had to deliver a missive to another nobleman's estate down in the town, and I now rode a horse of my own—sort of my own, technically Ulovar's I supposed—chosen for me at the fair. I called her South, since that's where I'd got her, and she was a big beast with an easy temper and a calm stride. Ivy would have looked like a nag beside her. I liked to imagine Ivy was off cropping grass somewhere, living out a peaceful retirement, but I rather doubted it. It seemed a waste. I wasn't a natural rider, but I had come to like horses. There was something deeply calming about sitting up high, letting another creature do all the work for you, and the horses didn't seem to mind.

I tried not to feel too grand, wrapped in a thick woollen cloak of fine green-and-black breacan, the Clan LacNaithe wyvern across the back, long riding boots, sitting tall on a beautiful horse. I did an awful lot of complaining about what were really some rather simple duties, I thought, given the advantages that were being given me. The snatterkin whispered and clicked as I passed them by, but once I was through the pines, I was glad of the road towards Harranir. It was peaceful, the constant beating of the First Gate trances that so frequently pattered around Redwinter were gone, and I could let myself melt into South's easy tread.

The delivery was a simple enough affair. I arrived in the wealthy district on the east side of the city and located the broad, refuse-free street. It was a stark contrast to most of the city; there weren't even any hogs rooting around, and a bored-looking young man with a staff seemed to be patrolling up and down this one stretch of cobbles. The streets to the west and south were like a foreign land, where pleading beggars sat in the corners and the feral pigs fought street urchins for the best gutter pickings. I threw back my cloak as I arrived to display the Clan LacNaithe wyvern on the breast of my bright blue tunic.

The message was headed to a thail, a landholder from the south who preferred the bright city life to managing his rural pastures. The nobleman took the message, licked his lips and stood in the light of a broad window to read. His house was cold, and his servants scurried from sight like nervous vermin as I waited for him to draft a response.

'The king of Brannlant demands yet more soldiers? Does he intend to bleed us dry?'

'I wouldn't know.'

'There used to be more stomach for resisting the Brannish,' he said. 'King Orthanac LacDhune rebelled, you know, in the time of my great-great-grandfather. Now we send our young people out as war fodder so the Brannish conquest can continue.'

Actually, there had been two Harran rebellions against the Brannish monarchies since Queen Atta Mathea of Brannlant conquered us, their poorer northern neighbour. The first was crushed after two years in 655 and the second even faster, in 677, almost seventy years ago. The Draoihn refused to participate in the first, following the poor guidance of Grandmaster Adnac LacFroome. In the second, they sided with the Brannish and overthrew the would-be-king, Nuncan LacAud. Some said overthrew, others said assassinated, but it was the same thing, really. As far as the Draoihn were concerned, the Brannish occupation was good for the Crown. Brannlant held one of the five, Harran another. Better to be united, following one religion, fighting the same wars.

It seemed that in all my listening I'd learned a few things after all. Perhaps by assigning me to pour wine, Ulovar was inadvertently giving me some of the learning he'd been forbidden from giving me. Or perhaps it wasn't as inadvertent as appearances indicated. I hadn't considered that before.

'I'm not sure why you're telling me this,' I said.

The thail looked annoyed, but he didn't bother me with any further history. He sighed.

'I will do as Van Ulovar requests,' he told me. 'I shall call yet another twenty strong young people away from their homes, and they'll go east to join the next Brannish expedition come spring.'

'I shall let him know,' I said, rising from the threadbare chair. Despite the size of the house, the nobleman didn't seem to have much of quality. He was old money, plenty of land but little income, and it showed. I glanced at the sky as I took my leave, hoping to be back at Redwinter before the rain struck, when the thail asked me if this would be the prince's final request for men.

'I'm already funding more than a hundred. My accounts hold only sand and chaff. Surely the king of Brannlant has enough of our young men doing his bidding now?'

'If you wish to write a reply to Van Ulovar, I can deliver it for you,' I told him neutrally. He thought for a few moments. He didn't want to provide yet more soldiers, but admitting weakness before his van was worse. He was a

LacNaithe, but if he failed to do as the van ordered, he probably had a cousin or a brother who'd be more malleable.

'There's a rumour that Van Ulovar may not be van for very much longer,' he said. He swallowed. 'Did he do it? Was he responsible for the slaughter in the north?'

The news had followed us quickly. I felt my belly tighten.

'What do you think?' I said coolly.

'No, no, I'm being foolish of course,' he decided. 'Please say nothing of it to the van.'

'Of course,' I agreed. 'I am sure that Van Ulovar appreciates your commitment to our ongoing good relations with the Brannish.' I took my leave with a smile. That had been fun. For a few moments, I felt as though I'd spoken with the authority of the clan behind me, and I'd enjoyed the little tingle of power.

A moment later the truth reasserted itself: I was still Ulovar's errand girl, whether I was First Retainer or Fifth. I wondered if this feeling was what had led Braithe to his ill-fated decisions. Just a taste of power, for a man who in truth deserved none.

. . . . . .

As I rode back through the city, a man appeared on horseback alongside me, grinning at me as though I were some kind of carnival show. For a moment I was at a loss, staring blankly back, until I realised he was somehow familiar. He was clean-shaven, about thirty and sitting easy in the saddle, and then the stink of Ashium leaf emanating from him told me who he was. It was the kind of deep-set smell that meant he spent day and night cloistered away in some leaf-den, soaking in other men's smoke. With everything that had happened, the soft lull of feather beds, warm hands and baths with pretty one-eyed girls, my memory of him had started to fade like a bad dream.

'How's it going, darlin'?' he asked. It was the sound of his voice that finally connected the pieces for me, and I had to stop myself heeling at South's sides.

'It's you,' I said. 'Leave me alone.'

'Only ever been friendly, haven't I?' he said. The thick beard was gone, his hair clipped down to a layer of fine sand. His upper lip was twisted, two of the teeth behind it missing. An old injury, long healed. The trapper's furs had been replaced by a loose linen shirt, leather bracers and riding trousers. 'You and your Draoihn friends caused quite a scene at that inn. Glad to see you made it here in the end.'

'I told you already: leave me alone. I don't need anything from you. I don't know you, and I don't want to.'

'Name's Hess,' he said, ignoring me. 'Figure you're called Raine, and you made First Retainer to boot. Here I figured you were heading to become an apprentice.'

'No,' I said. His change in appearance made me uneasy. Maybe he'd just found his luck on the horses, but the abruptness of the change, and the strange things he'd said to me on our first meeting ran cold fingers along that ridge of scar in my mind. I couldn't make a scene. He knew too much about me, could denounce me as one who had the grave-sight. Even a rumour would be bad enough.

'Can't imagine it feels safe up there. The Draoihn hate those like you and me worse than any. They catch you, they'll think you're one of their Sarathi.'

Sarathi. The Draoihn who served the Night Below. For all the Draoihn histories I'd been listening to in the church and at mealtimes, they were seldom mentioned. A stain on the Draoihn's history. They'd been wiped out long ago, hunted down in the years after Riven Queen Hallenae's defeat, but I felt a chill pass through me nonetheless. Ciuthach had been Sarathi.

'Just leave me alone. I have work to do.'

'I work for a feller. He wants to meet you. Knows some things he thinks you'll want to hear.'

A second rider pulled alongside on my right. She was older than me too, thick wrists and short hair beneath a tan scarf, a bone bird pendant around her neck. Her skin was dark as best-quality ink. She didn't look nearly so friendly as the man on my right, and she wore a sword. I didn't like the situation that I'd just found myself in, flanked and out positioned.

'Who are you?'

'Najih,' she said, as though that explained everything.

'I'm on business for Van Ulovar LacNaithe, Lord Draoihn of Redwinter,' I said. But these were just names, it seemed, and they didn't hold power here. 'I'll be missed if I'm not back soon.'

'That's what we all like to think, darlin',' the former hunter said. 'But it's seldom true for anyone who wasn't born with a golden arse. Let's take a ride down to the river.'

'I'd rather not.'

'You're riding to the river,' the woman said. 'There's something you need to see.'

I had a dagger on my belt. I thought about using it, but I'd already spotted that Hess's dirk was much longer than mine. The woman looked like she knew a thing or two about blades too. I let the knife sleep. For the first time I saw some advantage in the number of people out on Harranir's streets.

A crowd had gathered on a broad plaza facing the river. Seating had been erected in tiers around it.

'Take the horses,' Hess said to the woman as we dismounted. She wouldn't be stupid enough to steal a Draoihn horse: there wasn't a buyer in the city foolish enough to take an animal with that brand. It would have been a death sentence, which was, I judged by the prisoner in the cage, what we were about to observe.

Hess led me along to one of the front benches where a bent figure wearing a heavy scribe's robe beneath an even heavier cowl was already seated. A couple of butcher's apprentices budged up to let us take space. The benches were poorly constructed things of cheap timber and nails, thrown up in a hurry.

'Is this her?' a stretched, reedy voice ushered from within the hood. A man dying in a drought would have sounded healthier.

'Yes, gaffer. The northern girl,' he said.

A gnarled, twisted hand poked out from one of the robe's heavy sleeves. The fingers were twisted and bent, and a huge X-shaped scar marred the hand's back. More claw than hand, a child's nightmare. It groped for me, settled atop mine. The fingers were unable to close around it.

'Good,' the drawn voice said. I could see nothing of his face within the depths of his hood. The sun was riding surprisingly high for winter, and it was warm until it vanished behind banks of heavy cloud approaching from the west, but the hand was cold. 'I want to show you something, girl,' he said.

'I'm not interested in what you have to show me,' I said. I looked across the plaza to the cage, a gibbet mounted atop a wagon. The prisoner within was a woman, ordinary, dressed in homespun. She looked like someone's mother. She looked terrified. Royal guards in fine coats of gleaming mail and Clan LacDaine's breacan pushed back a line of people who wanted to get closer to her. She seemed very alone out there. Behind her, the river wall rose ten feet.

'And yet, I will insist that you see it,' the hoarse old voice said. I gritted my teeth. I was an envoy of Clan LacNaithe and I didn't have to tolerate all this mystery. I made to pull back the broken old man's hood but Hess caught my wrist.

'Wouldn't do that if I were you, darlin',' he said quietly. Could have been scowling, but hard to tell through his mangled lip.

'Who are you?'

'We are Those Who See,' the old man said, his voice dropping even quieter. 'And as I am so shall you be. So you already are. My name is no longer spoken in this city. But you may call me Veretaine.'

I became aware that the thick-wristed woman, Najih, had found a place behind me on a higher-tiered bench. I was going to watch whether I wanted to or not.

'What do you want from me?' I asked.

'Only to show you the truth,' the old man said. He coughed, a dry, hacking sound. 'You have been swept from your feet and borne up the mountain to those red marble walls. But here, you will see the truth of those that give you shelter.' He gestured towards the prisoner, slumped at the foot of her cage.

'What crime did she commit?' I asked.

'She has committed no crime,' the man who'd named himself Veretaine said. 'She simply exists. She does not deserve to die. She does not deserve to be punished. But the Crown and Redwinter insist that she must be. And so shall it be. We are here to pay witness to her passing. To honour her in death.'

'She must have done something.'

'She sees what you see, darlin',' Hess said. 'What we all see. Nothing more, nothing less. Only she let on about it. Her neighbour's child fell in the river and drowned. They caught her talking to him.'

I sat stock-still, hard and straight as if I'd been nailed to the bench. She was like me. She saw the ghosts of the dead when they rose.

'What we all see?' I whispered.

Men feared what they didn't understand, and what they feared, they destroyed. I had kept my mouth shut since I was small, and then I had opened it, and the sooth-sisters had paid the price. Everyone in Dalnesse had paid the price. My stomach curled up like a woodlouse, tightening into a ball, a nausea inducing cramp that weakened my limbs.

'I've seen the price of careless words before,' I said. People had died because of me. Foolish, selfish, trusting me.

There was fanfare, speeches, lawyers—none for her, she couldn't afford one—witnesses, and the dead child's mother. They were driven by fear and ignorance and maybe in some cases, greed. The crack on that mental scar prickled, and I felt the heat rise there, a late-night ember, a fire that began in my brain. Pain. There were faces beyond that crack, faces of the dead, faces from Dalnesse and the life that had been cut away from me. I found a rhythm playing in my mind, *dhum-dhum-dhum, dhum-dhum-dhum*, and I latched on to it, focused on that instead of the pantomime before me. It didn't help. It only made the scene before me brighter. Colours intensified, the sweet smell of age and bed-sweat that rose from Veretaine, the horse shit in the road.

'Easy, Raine,' Veretaine whispered to me. 'Close your mind down. Now is not the time, nor the place, for you to be entering that state of being.' I looked at him, or more appropriately, at the folds of cloth that hooded him away.

'You're Draoihn?' I said. I knew what I was doing. I heard those rhythms and silent drums all day long in Redwinter.

'No,' Veretaine said. 'Like you, I hear the trances, but they do not count me among their number. And I hear your trance, Raine. Like heavy footfalls on a bed of moss. But you will not wish to be within that trance for this. And you should not let on to the Draoihn what you can do.' He raised a broken hand towards the woman in the cage. 'And now see the truth of your new friends.'

A Draoihn man in oxblood-red leather arrived on horseback and took the centre of the stage. Haronus LacClune, bald-headed and his brow scraped with three greenish furrows. He scanned the crowd, perhaps hearing my trance, but his own Gate was not open. His search was interrupted by a functionary handing him a ledger. He skimmed the page. Just skimmed it, though the trial had taken nearly an hour.

'This assembly has determined that this woman possesses the grave-sight,' he proclaimed. 'For the good of all Harran, the sentence is death. Blessed be the Light Above.'

Haronus passed the book back to an attendant, almost tossing it offhand. He did not stay to watch.

I did.

They stoned her. The crowd was carrying rocks. They were not the kind of small, smooth, river stones that kids fling at each other. They were half bricks, sharp edged, heavy. Men threw them with all the force they could muster. Women hurled them with both hands. The prisoner could only stand for the first few. When she went down, they carried on throwing. Maybe fifty people in all. The royal guards stood there, looking fine as the gates of Anavia in polished metal and the pale-blue-and-yellow breacan of Clan LacDaine. The king's own clan. Sanctioning the bloodshed on his streets.

The prisoner didn't last long, and there wasn't much left of her when it was over, smeared across the flagstones.

A single tear escaped me. I had not shed one since Dalnesse. I felt the scar across my mind flex and settle.

'I've seen it,' I said. 'Can I go now?'

'You haven't seen it. Not yet,' Veretaine said. The crowd began to dissipate. Who was going to clean up the mess the stoning had left was anybody's guess. The wild pigs and dogs that plagued the streets, maybe. The woman behind me placed her hands on my shoulders.

'Watch,' she hissed.

The ghost rose, green and white, insubstantial, vaporous. She looked twenty-five, twenty-six. Wore a shawl, a dress. Maybe ghosts manifested the way they had been at death, maybe nature chose their visage for them. She didn't weep, or howl, but she stared down at her lost body with so much sadness that it almost reached through to me. Almost. Her name had been Nairna LacMuaid. I promised myself I wouldn't forget it. That was all I could do for her now. I made to rise again, but the woman pressed down.

'Wait,' she hissed again.

A second ghost crossed the plaza. A child. He ran to the woman with open arms, as wispy and green-tinged as the first had been. As they met, the two of them disappeared. And I knew that only the four of us, still sitting on the benches, had paid them any heed.

'That is what she died for, Raine,' Veretaine said. He showed me both of his hands, twisted, ruined. 'I was more fortunate than most. They took my hands. My feet. My eyes. But I lived. When you return to your Redwinter luxury, remember that this is their work. Remember it when they speak of their sacred task to protect the Crown, as they try to bring you ever deeper into their service. The Draoihn place the king on his throne. The Draoihn might sit apart from the king's chamber, but make no mistake that they rule here. All that goes on in the name of the Crown is their choice.'

'Worth more than other people,' I muttered as the grandmaster's words returned to me. I wondered what lay beneath the cowl, how mutilated this old man must be. But I couldn't take away his dignity. 'How did you find me?'

'We have a friend in common,' Veretaine said. 'A woman, crowned in feathers and painted for war. She knows. She seldom comes to me, but when she does, it pays for us to listen.'

'Who is she?' I asked. '*What* is she?'

'There are more things to understand in this world than the Draoihn's black-and-white view permits. She is a friend, one who has helped those like us for a very long time,' Veretaine said. He coughed, shoulders shaking, hands twitching. So very frail. 'I'm sorry,' he said. 'I must retire. Even this little exertion exhausts me. But it has been good to meet you, Raine.'

'But I need to know more,' I said. 'You know more than you're telling me.'

'Trust must be earned,' Veretaine said. The racking cough hit him again, and Najih caught him. 'But you will earn ours. I believe it.'

Najih interposed herself between us and began to gently lift the old man from his seat. I stared at the cobbles, while a man of the court was sluicing with buckets of river water. Washing away the red. Since Dalnesse I had thought that nothing could touch me. That there was no empathy buried in my heart, that Ulovar had cut it from me. But I had been wrong. I felt more for that poor woman than Haronus LacClune had, and all I had to offer her was a single tear.

'Come on, darlin', I'll see you back to your horse,' Hess said. He drew me back to my feet and led me away to the horses, hitched up to a post. He was gentle, but I could have used some of the Ashium leaf he'd clearly been smoking that morning.

'That was awful,' I said. 'I always knew what this—this power—means about me. That I'm a broken thing. That I'm corrupted. And people have died because of it. But she didn't deserve to die that way.'

'It's an awful world, darlin',' Hess agreed. 'A girl could do worse than find a few good friends. Friends that understand who she is. What she is. Friends who don't think it's wrong, or unnatural.' He rubbed at an old tattoo on his neck, the kind soldiers got with their friends when they got drunk and stupid. A trio of swords wrapped in flowers, badly inked. 'What we showed you today, you understand it can't be shared? The names we gave you ain't real anyway, and you'd never find us unless we want you to. Not in this city. Don't go getting a half ton of rocks banging into you, like that poor gal.'

'Why did you show me this?' I asked. Hess smiled, or would have had the curl of his mangled lip allowed it.

'Times are hard, and harder for those like us still. Good to have friends, ain't it? There'll come a day when you need to escape all this. Might need friends to see you away, to find your own life. One that isn't gripped in Redwinter's iron fist. Anyway. Get off with you. Day's a-wasting.'

I mounted South and kept my eyes firmly on her neck as I picked my way back through the city. Back towards the source of the bloodshed I had just witnessed. My clothes didn't feel so fine anymore, the steps of the horse beneath me an experience that belonged to somebody else. There were good people in Redwinter, I was sure of it. Ulovar, Ovitus, even Sanvaunt seemed good at heart, even if he would no longer look me in the eye. But they shared their home with men like Haronus LacClune, with women like Grandmaster Robilar, who would condemn a person to death for no more than their own tragedy. I did not think that I was in danger, not unless I made a mistake. But the people who had sought me out, who had identified me—they were just as dangerous. They knew.

The Queen of Feathers had done this to me. She had told those people who I was, maybe even where to find me. She had protected me once, but this didn't feel like help. It felt like somebody else had an agenda, and I was a piece being pushed into a game I didn't understand. I kept my face pointed downwards, lest I caught a glimpse of a deep blue dress and a flash of corvid wings.

20

They'd been clever. There was nothing for me to say, and nobody to say any-thing to, without revealing that I was cursed to see the dead. And in their moment of showing me, they'd reinforced the fate that awaited me if I risked it. I'd been cursed this way since childhood, and I was accustomed to ignoring the dead. Like feeling a pain in your head, year after year, invisible and of no consequence to anybody but you. Another of life's ways of reminding us that though we may exist in proximity, we are in fact, always, alone.

Their cunning ensured my silence. Day bled into day as my routines reas-serted themselves, but I began glancing into alleys, jumping at shadows. The glamour of the Draoihn's fine existence had begun to swaddle me. They fed me, clothed me in silk, gave me more money than I could spend. If they knew what I truly was, they would kill me. But then, that had been my daily exis-tence since I was a child.

'She's back! She's back today!' Ovitus declared in excitement as I joined him on the stairs.

'Who is?'

'Liara!' Ovitus said. 'A runner came in during the night to say that she was returning today. I just heard it from Sanvaunt.'

'I see,' I said. I had to confess, if only to myself, that I was interested to meet her. Since meeting Ovitus I'd heard far more about her than I ever really needed to. Mostly about how good she was. And how kind. And dedicated, and gentle, and all the rest.

'Should I give her the locket straightaway or do I wait a bit?' Ovitus fretted as we walked from the LacNaithe greathouse to the chapel for dawnsong. It had become a daily routine for him to wait for me on the stair, and his self-doubts filled the morning air as he listed his options. Apparently, one of my duties as First Retainer was to accompany him to chapel. A lot of my duties seemed to involve following Ulovar's nephew around.

'What locket?'

'The one from that river town,' Ovitus said. I could scarcely remember it. Everything had been so hazy back then. The scar on my mind had been at its strongest, casting the world into deepest shadow. I felt clearer now. I knew I wasn't right, not completely, but I treasured that single tear. Maybe there was something left of the old me after all. 'Or maybe I give her the brooch?' Ovitus went on. 'Or that Iscalian brandy? She likes brandy, did I tell you that?'

'You did,' I said. I seemed to know an awful lot about Liara, given that I had never met her.

'Strange isn't it, for a girl to like brandy? Do you like it?'

'Never tried it.'

'The grandmaster drinks brandy, but then I've heard a lot of people say she should have been born a man.'

'Men say that about women who intimidate them,' I said.

'But what should I do?' Ovitus went on, skating over my words on a layer of obliviousness. 'About Liara.'

'Think about it during dawnsong,' I said.

Dawnsong was only one of the three daily verses sung by Redwinter's resident monks. They devoted their lives to the worship of the Light Above and the cults of her Lords and Ladies, but apparently that wasn't sufficient without some singing, and it was the worst part of my day. I didn't stand beside Sanvaunt again, but I found myself glancing in his direction from time to time. He'd treated me differently that first day. I wondered what had changed to cause him to withdraw into himself so much, and then I got angry at myself for caring. He never even looked at me anymore.

Ovitus's chatter continued as we plodded along. I preferred the mornings to be a time of quiet thoughts and gradual acclimatisation to the day, but Ovitus's mind was already pumping with worry about the return of his beloved.

I'd thought that I loved Braithe. He'd had position, even though our community had been small. It had made me reckless, stupid. Maybe that was what love was really like. A consuming sickness that made you endlessly dull.

'I don't want to seem too eager,' Ovitus said. I didn't reply, since his pre-chapel conversation had been the same for several days. 'Have you managed to learn the dawnsong for this morning?'

'Not yet,' I said. Of all the duties that had been assigned to me, singing praise to the Light Above, who neither listened nor cared, seemed the most wasteful. Anything seemed better than spending hours making meaningless noises in a language I didn't speak to someone who probably didn't exist.

'So what should I do? I can't seem too keen. Some women don't like to know that you like them at first, that's what I heard. From some men anyway.'

'You told me that she was your sweetheart,' I said as we passed beneath the stone archway.

'Well, no,' Ovitus said. 'I mean yes. Sort of. She would be, she just doesn't know it.'

'In my experience, if someone wants you, then you just know it,' I said, thinking of Braithe. Braithe on top of me, hard bodied, warm. Braithe lying bruised and broken. Braithe's hand cracking against my cheek. Lochlan, following me with his puppy dog eyes. Esher, her hair fanning behind her in the water. Wait. No. Giving a few items of clothing, some powder and a bath was hardly an indication that I lit her candle that way. And what did it matter to me if she did? Mama had called those women dead ends. I cast those unwanted thoughts away, angry that I was even thinking about it.

Since the stoning of Nairna LacMuaid, I had found thoughts of the dead came to me with growing frequency. I locked them back, beyond the scar that ran across my mind. Not because they could distract me—I had no grief for the dead. I knew that they were gone, I knew that what had happened to them had been awful. I just felt nothing. I was grateful for the scar Ulovar had laid across my mind. Sympathy, pain, anguish: they belonged to some other Raine, a different girl who'd fallen down. I was the Raine who had got back up.

'That's the problem,' Ovitus said. 'I have no idea.'

'My mother was a terrible person, but she said a helpful thing to me, once,' I said. '"If you aren't sure about something in life, the answer is no."'

'That's hardly optimistic,' Ovitus said, and, ignoring my words entirely, began listing Liara's graces. Again.

Even if he could be as repetitive as the daily absolutions, Ovitus's company suited me. There was something of the lamb about him, a trusting kind of innocence. Sometimes I felt that I was more cynical with him than I was with anyone else. He was only looking for happiness, and he looked for it in gentleness and small pleasures: food, warmth, a good book at the end of the day. He wasn't suited to the life he'd been placed into, whatever its advantages.

We sang dawnsong, a salute to creation and all that came after. We sang of the Light Above and her kindness in forming the world, and how she left man freedom of mind so that good could exist, for without choice there can be no good and no evil. We sang of the twelve Lords and Ladies, who had taught us all about the Light Above, for all the good that knowing about it did us. I nearly knew all the words now, though I mostly just mouthed them. I had no voice for singing, and the rise and fall of the melody touched nothing of my soul. Esher, frustratingly, had the best voice. She'd lucked out on her looks, her voice, and with the magic which had made her rich. She was even nice to me.

She confused me. Everybody knew that some people turned their sheets that way, but the Light Above didn't approve. I didn't like that I even asked myself that question, so I did the sensible thing and ignored it. I certainly admired her. Maybe I just wanted to be her.

I stifled a yawn. I'd stayed up late, trying to read by candlelight, which was hard on the eyes and left me with a headache. I'd managed to borrow a book from Ovitus that outlined different meditations that could assist in entering the first trance, Eio, although *borrow* was a loose definition, since he didn't know. So far though, it had proven impenetrable.

'I couldn't decide,' Ovitus said as we filed out of the chapel. I'd hoped he might have started worrying about something else. Despite having agonised over what to buy her in the metalworking shop along the river, he had subsequently bought a number of other trinkets as potential gifts. I hadn't tried to count them, but he was cultivating a sizable collection of women's jewellery out of an affection I now suspected he had never confessed to Liara.

But who was I to try to tell a man how to love? I'd chosen Braithe. That said a lot about how good I was about making decisions in that arena.

We stopped and I watched the Draoihn undergoing martial practice, as I did most mornings. I could hear the rhythm of their trances at the edge of my mind, soft and controlled, *dhum-dhum-dhum, dhum-dhum-dhum,* as they worked in unison. Within Redwinter's walls I heard it nearly constantly, whether from the apprentices practising in the greathouse or the Draoihn training on the martial field. Ovitus kept talking while I watched the warriors at their weapon practice. There was a supple grace and beauty in their movements that called to my desire for calm. There were six of them, clad in laced white shirts and baggy pantaloons bound tightly to their calves with thongs. Blades flashed brightly as the ghosts in the steel caught the light, moving together in perfect synchronisation whether they drifted lazily through the air or sliced swiftly through it. Four men and two women moved as a delicate unit, spores on a breeze, swords coming to guard and then cutting down, drawing the blade back slowly before lashing out again with lethal speed. There was nothing to draw comparison between these adepts of the blade and the warriors who had stormed Dalnesse. The Draoihn were artists, painting the air with beautiful sword strokes. I wanted to be part of the display, to weave the patterns with them.

'Light Above, look at him move,' Ovitus said despondently. 'How am I ever meant to live up to that?'

I grimaced.

I watched Sanvaunt's sword-dance. He had a fluidity of motion that made him seem one with the weapon in his hands, its steel an extension of his arm. He was long limbed and tall, and the hard panes and angles of his face matched his finely muscled physique. He flowed in time to whatever invisible rhythm spurred the swordsmen's invisible foes.

Since the day he'd had to show me around the grounds, he hadn't spoken to me once. The few times I'd tried to fill his cup he simply placed a hand over it. He was polite when he had to be, but he didn't look at me. That was fine by me. I didn't want to speak to him anyway. As generous as Ulovar was to me, these were not my people. I didn't have any people. If they really knew me, they'd close ranks and toss me to the dogs. I'd spent too many years wishing for the people to open their arms to me. Too many hours wishing somebody else would want me, or like me, or call me daughter. Ridiculous.

'He's not the best of them,' I said. 'The tall woman is better. But he's very good.'

'They all look like they're doing the same thing to me,' Ovitus said.

'Shouldn't you know swordsmanship already?' I asked as he prodded me back toward the greathouse to change from our robes into daywear. 'I thought all sons of the clans learned it.'

'Ulovar's sons did,' Ovitus admitted glumly. 'Ulovir won the Ruby Sword when he was only sixteen. They tried to teach me, but I was always meant for the church, so nobody much minded that I wasn't the bloodthirsty type. Now look at me. Can you imagine me doing that?'

I really couldn't. I gave him a sympathetic smile, an expression I was growing better at falsifying daily. Where Ovitus had no desire to train, my greatest frustration was being unable to learn. I had imprinted a single image in my mind: Van Ulovar, standing stock-still, his sword stretched out, Ciuthach's head falling from its shoulders. I had stamped it into myself, frozen in time like stained glass, and I had to keep it in sight. Behind it lay Ciuthach's burning eyes, and I had come to enjoy sleeping again.

'If they make you learn, will they make you go fight battles for the Brannish?' I asked.

'Draoihn don't fight in proper battles,' Ovitus said cheerfully. 'We're far too valuable to be hit by stray arrows and whatnot. That's something at least,' he said, and wrinkled his nose at the thought.

'Even in the north we'd heard of the Winterra,' I said. 'Don't they fight?'

'Well, yes, I suppose so,' Ovitus agreed. 'If you don't unlock the Second Gate, they send you off to join them. Nobody wants to, but it will be the fate of most of us. Well. Not me. They can't make the van of a clan go.'

'If they don't fight battles, then what's the point of them?' I said.

'Large-scale battles aren't common, and there hasn't been a full-scale battle in Harran since the last rebellion, but there's always a place for scouts, advisers, and so on. Feuding thails might do a lot of burning farms and raiding each other's borders, but nothing comparable to the civil wars down in Kwend a few years ago. They'd never send me into the thick of it, though. Not a proper battle. I really hope not. I can't imagine anything worse.'

'You've already seen worse,' I said.

'I know. And I hope never to see it again.'

The idea seemed to be agitating him. Whatever life had intended for Ovitus before, he had not settled well into fate's twist. I suggested that we get break-fast, and at once that turned my friend's mind to more pleasant imaginings.

. . . . . .

I left Ovitus eating and took a bath, alone, then headed back towards the great-house. As I crossed what they called the magpie lawn, I saw something gleam-ing in the glass. Someone had left a sword behind. I picked it up. Five feet long, with a twine-bound grip that fitted both my hands and could have taken two more. I went to place it on a wall so that its owner would find it, but just before I put it down I turned. I held it out in front of me, trying to mimic the pose I'd seen the Draoihn taking when they came to rest.

I immediately felt stupid. What did I know about swords? But it felt good in my hands. I raised it above my head and cut down through the air. The motion felt awkward. The sword wasn't heavy, but it felt foreign. Braithe had taught me to hunt with a bow, but this was different. I tried to imagine someone else with a sword in front of me. How would I hit them with it?

I'd been hacking the air for a few minutes when a voice interrupted me.

'Excuse me,' Sanvaunt said. 'I see you found my sword.'

'This is yours?' I asked.

'I left it here after training.' He stood uncertainly, and then had no choice but to look at me directly. I met his eyes, and we stood silently for a few mo-ments. He was dressed more informally than I'd ever seen him in a loose, sleeveless white shirt and a green-and-black kilt. He was tall but had neither his uncle's bullish bulk or his cousin's weight. His arms were powerfully mus-cled, but there was more of a wolf than a bear about him. There was sweat in his hair.

'I'll bring it back later,' I said.

'I don't mean any offence, but I'll take it now,' he said. 'The blade needs oiling after handling. It's cadanum steel, but even so, I don't want the blade to mark. I've already embarrassed myself enough by leaving it here.'

Where was the powerful, determined man I'd met back at Tor Marduul? He was so annoyingly calm, even as he let that unbreachable air of discomfort linger between us. I didn't know what I'd done to offend him, and his manners were impeccable, but he clearly didn't like me. I shouldn't have, but a sudden desire to kick the beehive rushed a word onto my lips.

'No.'

A ripple of surprise passed across Sanvaunt's face. Annoyance? He walked swiftly towards me, stalking like a cat. On instinct I held the sword back, and then he swept in on me. There he was. There was the confidence-filled warrior who'd threatened his own cousin with a blade. I wasn't sure what he did exactly, but one moment I was holding it and the next it was twisted from my grip, he had the blade tucked beneath his arm, and I was on my backside. I rubbed at my wrist and glared up at him.

'What was that?' I snapped.

'This is not a toy,' he said. His eyes were flinty. 'This steel dictates whether I will live or die. This art is not a game, and antagonising me won't get you what you want either.'

'You think you know what I want?' I asked as I picked myself up.

He looked away. All that tingle-inducing fire drained out of him.

'I try not to judge,' he said. I fought down a scowl. What did he think he knew about me that would let him? I had enough to cope with to deal with whatever preconceptions he had of me.

'Wait,' I said as he turned to go. 'How did you get it off me? What did you do?'

He seemed surprised by my question. Floundered for an answer for a moment. For the first time I noticed the bags beneath his eyes. He was tired. Exhausted, maybe.

'I trained under Lady Datsuun. It's a Dharithian technique.'

'How do I do it?'

Sanvaunt frowned. He shook his head.

'It's an advanced technique. I don't know that I can explain it to you if you're not trained to the sword. To explain would be like trying to teach you the Fourth Gate before you've experienced the First.'

He was trying so hard not to sound patronising, and that only made it all the more irritating because what he said made sense. I picked myself up and dusted off, my cheeks reddening. I turned to march back to the greathouse.

'I can show you the First Principles, if you wish.'

I turned back. Sanvaunt didn't look at me. He was staring off towards the dogfish lawn, as though he hadn't said a thing.

'Why?'

'Because you're brave, and my uncle believes in you, and you want to learn.'

'You don't want to rest?' He looked like he needed rest. Like he needed a good night's sleep.

'The world doesn't wait for us. You want to learn, learn now.'

I grunted. He put the sword down carefully on a wall, then took a posture. 'Copy me. Left foot facing forwards, back foot halfway forwards and halfway to the side. No, not all the way sideways. Still going forwards. So you can walk. Good. Now walk with me.'

We walked about the lawn, making those strange steps that kept us both upright and low. When I was doing it easily enough, he made it a game, facing me, taking steps towards me or back, and I had to follow along with him, forwards when he went back, retreating when he advanced. We didn't use our hands. It almost felt like some kind of dance.

It felt good to be doing something physical, exerting my body. It wasn't hard exercise, but it was constant. Eventually my thighs started to protest, but Sanvaunt showed no signs of slowing up. We moved that way for an hour. He seldom spoke, seldom met my eye. It didn't matter that he hadn't given me the sword. I was learning something, at least, even if it wasn't magic. I was quite lost in it, until Sanvaunt straightened up.

'That was good. You learn fast.' He looked away, to where Ovitus was sat on a wall, watching us. He coloured, coughed into his hand. 'I am very busy today. If you'll excuse me.' He took his sword and headed back towards the house. I stared after him for a few moments, wondering at the abrupt end to his lesson, and then went to sit beside Ovitus.

'You actually want to do that?' Ovitus asked.

'Why not learn something new?' I countered. 'There's beauty in it. In the movement.'

'You're all sweaty,' he said. 'You should clean up before evensong.'

. . . . . .

When noonsong was done and the praises of Our Lady of Fire had been sung, Ovitus managed to persuade me to wait with him near to the gate.

'I need to be there doing something. I can't just hang around there by myself,' he told me when I suggested that I probably ought to find something useful to do.

'Why do you need to see her at the gate? She'll be coming to the greathouse soon enough, won't she?'

'She's been preparing for her Testing,' Ovitus said seriously. 'She'll need to see a friendly face as soon as possible. The preparations can be harsh. Or so I hear.'

'What happens in the Testing?'

'I don't know,' Ovitus said, sweating anxiously. 'Nobody speaks about the Testing. It's forbidden.'

'What did Sanvaunt have to do for his?' I asked.

'I don't know. He passed it easily enough, though. He's annoying like that.' Ovitus shrugged.

'Annoying how?'

'He's good at things.'

We gathered a few books so that we could pretend he was teaching me El-gin, a ridiculous dead language, and sat huddled in cloaks near the gate. More than a few passersby gave us strange looks, but none of the servants would have dared to question him, and most Draoihn were sensible enough to be indoors avoiding the chill. The winter hadn't come down hard, but it was still winter.

'That's them! That's them!' Ovitus said, hopping up excitedly as a pair of riders appeared at the gates on powerful Draoihn horses. They were cloaked, but dark red leathers peeked from beneath. The man she was with clapped her on the shoulder and headed off as the girl rode on towards us.

'Sit down,' I said, hiding a smile. 'You're bounding around like a puppy. She won't be impressed.'

Ovitus went white as milk and dropped down to his arse faster than I'd ever seen him move before.

For a few moments, I found it hard to believe that this was the legendary Liara of Clan LacShale that I had been hearing about for nearly three months.

There was nothing wrong with her, but how the girl on the horse could reasonably be linked to anything that Ovitus had told me about her took a deep stretch of imagination. She was very short and broad, slumped low in her saddle like a precariously balanced sack of cabbages. The shimmering waves of fiery hair turned out to be ginger curls, peeking from her hood. She stifled a yawn as she rode on into the grounds.

Ovitus stared as if he'd seen a vision of the Light Above Herself. He was struck to mute stillness for several moments, mouth hanging open as if the awe of her presence was simply too much to comprehend, before lurching up and towards them.

'Hey, Ovi. Might have known you'd be avoiding work somehow,' Liara said when she spotted him, raising a weary hand to wave. She reached up and pushed the hood of her cloak back. She was a similar age to us, with a round, plump face and a liberal spray of freckles across her nose and cheeks. As she noted where we had been sitting I thought I caught a glimpse of weary resig-nation pass over her rounded features.

'Welcome home,' Ovitus said enthusiastically. 'Can I help with your saddlebags?'

'It's fine. If you carry my things, then I'll be indebted to you, and then my horse will be envious, and there'll be a whole month of horse-envy and then you'll end up feuding, and the horse will win and we'll have a new van Lac-Naithe,' Liara said.

Ovitus didn't seem to be following what she said, or maybe just wasn't listening. He was doing a lot of staring, though.

'We'll come with you,' Ovitus declared, and immediately began packing up the books. Liara glanced my way.

'So either you stole Tarquus's First Retainer pin or he finally got eaten by that thing in the tree, right?' Liara asked me. She had a dry manner of speaking, but it was somehow welcoming.

'Yes. A month ago,' I said. 'He forgot the steak and it came right out and ate him.'

Liara snorted as she laughed. It was rare to hear such an honest sound in Redwinter.

'Yeah, we'll get along just fine,' she said. She seemed to be embarrassed by what she'd just said, freckles hiding behind a flush. 'But seriously, he's gone?'

'No, he's fine,' Ovitus said. 'Raine's sort of in an honorary role.'

'Sounds like there's a story there.' She looked genuinely interested.

'What have you been doing?' Ovitus cut in. Liara turned serious.

'Training, mostly,' she said. 'Eio, in the main, but other things as well. You know. *Those* things.'

I didn't know what she meant, but since she didn't elaborate, I had no time to ask for clarification before Ovitus moved right up beside the big horse, beaming up at her like an overfond puppy and plying her with questions. It had been gruelling and hard. They had ridden all the way south, through Brannlant and into Murr, where they had met with scarlet priests and scared off some marsh riddlers. Ovitus's interrogation was relentless, and I caught the look of relief on Liara's face as we reached the LacNaithe residence. Ehma and Howen, two of the house servants, were waiting as if somehow summoned by magic, taking her horse and handing her a warmed cup of wine.

'An Iscalian red,' Liara said, closing her eyes and sighing. 'Tarquus remembers everything. Bless him, he's a treasure. Thanks for walking me in. I need a bath, but I'd like to see Sanvaunt if you run into him. It was good to meet you, Raine.' She gave me a brief smile and then vanished inside.

The moment that Liara was out of sight, Ovitus slumped against a wall.

'Oh dear,' he said, 'I feel so overwhelmed. She looked well, didn't she? I thought she looked well. A bit tired and dusted by the road, but well? Yes. I think so.'

'Why did you ask her so many questions?' I said.

In a blink, anxiety set his face rigid. I had said the wrong thing.

'Do you think I did? I thought . . . well, girls like questions. Questions about themselves, don't they? That's what I was told. I heard that, I think. Did I ask too many? Will she think me intrusive? Oh dear, do you think so?' He looked genuinely distraught.

'She looked tired to me, that's all,' I said, aiming for tact but perhaps striking only condescension. 'She's funny. I see why you like her.'

'Funny?' Ovitus said. He looked like he had no idea what I was talking about. Almost as if he hadn't heard a thing she'd said.

We made our way into what we called the resting room. Like all of the rooms in Ulovar's greathouse, the furnishings were minimal but finely crafted. The resting room had a wide hearth with room for spits over the fire that I'd never seen used, and a series of comfortable chairs and divans around a foot-pool. There was a plug in the centre of the pool, only a few inches deep, and one of my worst daily duties was to replace the water. Other people's foot water.

Sanvaunt was already there, a leg slung across the arm of one of the less comfortable chairs with that much-used book resting on one knee and a pen poised over the page. He snapped it closed as we entered, jerking upright and shoving the book into his coat as if we'd caught him at something illicit. He looked like some kind of soldier-poet, all ragged but full of life, run-down and trampled but pulling himself back up, dusting off the mud.

'Liara's back!' Ovitus declared. He adopted a triumphant stance, as though he'd somehow won a long-awaited victory. Nobody seemed to be expecting anything of me, so after a few moments I slunk down onto a stool at the edge of the room.

Sanvaunt looked up and glanced at me, then leaned forwards to drop his pen into an inkwell.

'I hope you gave her time to get her boots off before you started pestering her,' Sanvaunt said. He rested his hand on his coat, pressing the book against his chest like it was some great treasure.

'Boots?' Ovitus said, dropping onto one of the divans like a falling tree. 'She's back, though. She just arrived.'

'I am aware,' Sanvaunt said.

'She wants to see you,' Ovitus continued.

'Maybe later,' Sanvaunt said. He didn't look at me, instead picking up a small lap desk covered with pages and directing his pen to it. I had taken a seat near the fire, letting the winter's chill retreat from my fingers. 'Does she know about Hazia yet? I asked Uncle if I could be the one to tell her. They were friends.'

'I know,' Ovitus said. 'I didn't say anything.'

'The news will hurt,' Sanvaunt said without looking up. 'It may be best to leave her alone for a time.'

'Of course. Naturally,' Ovitus said.

I wasn't sure how much I believed that. Ovitus was as lovestruck as a fox staring at the moon. I resolved to do what I could to keep him occupied for a few days, at least. An odd thought—trying to manage the life of someone who was so superior to me in rank that I sometimes had to change his foot water. Neither of the LacNaithe men seemed to have noticed that I wasn't standing to attention. On a whim, I leaned against the wall and put my feet up on a pouf. I tingled, wondering at what their reaction would be. But nobody seemed to care.

'Aren't you going to see her now?' Ovitus asked. Sanvaunt took up his pen again and wrote for several moments before he replied.

'I've had reports come in from some of the thails about some disputes back home. There's a lot to get done. "The Crown matters," and all that.'

'Disputes?'

'Land, money, workforces. You could help me, if you've a mind to.' He held a sheaf of papers out to his cousin, only for Ovitus to wrinkle his nose at them.

'Isn't that Uncle's job?' Ovitus asked. Sanvaunt gave Ovitus a hard look.

'He has enough on his mind. It won't hurt if I take on some of the less important tasks. You could help, if you've finished bothering Liara.' He looked worn at the edges. His hip flask lay on the table, the same one we'd shared on that first morning in Redwinter. I wondered if he was resorting to rose-thistle, and how long it had been since he last slept. I'd come to learn that staying up on rose-thistle was regarded as a very bad habit.

'I'll leave it to you. I have a lot on,' Ovitus said.

There was a dangerous gleam in Sanvaunt's eyes, and for a moment, I wondered if he hated his cousin. The papers sat between them like a threat, but one that Ovitus remained utterly oblivious to.

'Sanvaunt,' I cut in before the tension could thicken any more. 'Maybe you should get some sleep.'

He stared at Ovitus a few moments longer, then retracted the papers and turned those dark, sleepy eyes on me. I'd thought that something had changed that morning. That an hour walking around a practice field could have undone whatever offence I'd committed. That hope evaporated around me now. His anger didn't diminish as it turned from his cousin to me. But it changed, from disgust to—to *what*? Light Above, I just couldn't read him at all. I took my feet from the pouf. Sat up straight, like a good servant should.

'I appreciate the advice. But I'm fine. There's still work to be done.'

He gathered his papers and left.

I sat looking at the door. Sometimes I felt so alive around him. When I was by his side, I felt like I was part of something—I didn't know what, but it was definitely something. Maybe it was the way he was always focused on his duty, even making the apprentices listen to dry old histories over dinner because it would make them better Draoihn. Striving for excellence in everything he turned his hand to. And yet, it was those rare moments when I caught him off guard that I saw another side to him. He seemed to wear other people's concerns on his shoulders. Helping without having to be asked. He was kind.

He had forgotten his rose-thistle flask. As I picked it up the door opened and Esher grinned in at me.

'Come on, Raine, get your riding kit on. It's full moon tonight.'

'You're not supposed to go do that anymore,' Ovitus said. 'It's dangerous.'

Esher grinned, all even teeth and golden hair.

'That's why it's such fun.'

21

South was not pleased to be saddled up in the dark, but an apple is an easy bribe. We followed the girls onto the moors that lay west of Harranir. It was a beautiful land by winter night's full moon, the river cutting through the darkened hills and catching the light of endless stars.

I was the seventh of the group; all the others were Draoihn. Esher, Liara and Gelis were Ulovar's apprentices, while the three eldest girls had all been Tested.

'What a day. What a three months. I'm glad I made it back in time for full moon,' Liara said. Her horse looked like it disagreed and would have been happier off stabled after its long journey. 'I've missed everyone. Draoihn Eiden is a dour old fish and he's been my only conversation.'

'And now you just have to put up with Ovitus mooning over you again,' Esher said. She swayed wildly in her saddle and threw her head to the side. 'Oh, Liara, your hair is so red. Oh, Liara, you smell like the very essence of nutmeg. Oh, Liara, your tits are so perky.'

'Hah. He's harmless enough. I'm not really a woman to Ovitus. I'm just the idea of one,' the short girl said. 'Light Above, I'd hoped he might have moved on to someone else by now.'

So much for Liara being Ovitus's sweetheart. I decided not to tell her how he'd intimated that they had a much closer relationship than I now saw was true. What was the harm in it, really? We'd been far away, and it was just a little make-believe.

'He was sort of heroic. In the north,' I said, feeling a need to defend him. He'd stood with me in Ciuthach's chamber, and that counted for something. He'd done his best to help me on the road south, and that counted for something else. Ovitus seemed different now. Perhaps necessity had forced some of those stronger qualities from him. They didn't reply, and then I realised, like a fool, that Liara had only just learned of Hazia's death. Hazia would have been with us, I realised. I slept in her room, and I had taken her place here too.

'First time looking for moon horses?' Liara asked me. A swift change of subject.

'I have absolutely no idea what we're doing,' I said.

'I told you, we're looking for moon horses,' Esher said. She'd helped me pick out suitable riding clothes and helped me do my glamours—which seemed to be referred to as 'putting on a party face' between the girls. All of them had come out looking like they were about to ride to a banquet at the king's own table, their hair curled or straightened with warmed irons, jewelled and wrapped in fox-fur or mink cloaks. I had never been among such exquisite-looking women before. One of the fully fledged Draoihn was wearing a split-legged riding dress that was practically a ball gown. She was magnificent, a queen taking the vanguard position.

It was still bloody cold, though.

'I don't always like surprises,' I said.

'You'll like this one. Did you bring something special like I told you?'

Esher's instruction had been to take along some little thing that mattered to me, something that spoke about who I felt I was. It was the kind of thing the sooth-sisters would have said before people started warbling and dancing the colours, and while I didn't take it very seriously, I didn't have anything like that. Everything I owned was new, bought with Redwinter money. So I'd brought a pot of honey that was intended for the hidden folk who lived in the garden behind the greathouse, because that was the duty I looked forward to the most. And that's who I was, really. A First Retainer who gave honey and cakes to things that were probably not even there. I felt out of place, as much as these girls were trying to involve me, but it was a good out-of-place. Like I was being invited to something exciting, something rare.

'Everyone else here is Draoihn,' I said.

'We're not Draoihn until we've been Tested,' Esher said. 'But we can all open the First Gate. That's the important thing.'

'Why is it important?'

'After you open the First Gate, you're more—I don't know the right word, I'm sure some book in the library would have a special term for it—more *entangled* with the hidden realm. The moon horses just kind of know. And whether you're Draoihn or not, I've heard you trancing,' she said. She was grinning. 'It's bloody cold tonight. Let's get a move on!' She nudged her heels against her horse's sides and he took off. South started to speed up then, realising that Esher's horse wasn't fleeing from danger, fell back to her preferred speed, which was plodding. Esher streaked away, whooping in the night, rising up in the stirrups with a crimson cloak and her golden hair fanning out behind her. She was a fantastic horsewoman.

'That girl is such a bloody show-off,' Liara said. Her horse seemed content to clomp along with South.

'Are we really looking for a moon horse?' I asked.

'Believe it or not, we are,' she said. 'We do it every month.'

'Do the boys ever try?'

'Moon horses won't come for a man,' Liara said. 'They're all female. And you wouldn't want to meet a stallion. They aren't the same at all.'

'We have a legend in the north,' I said. It was a fireside tale, the kind twelve-year-old girls tell one another after dark. 'About the moon-horse-man. They say never to admit a black-eyed stranger after dark on the first night of the month, or he'll have his way with you, turn you into a horse and take you away to the hidden folk's land to bear his moon children.'

'Yep,' Liara said. 'That's the stallions. Like I said, you don't want to meet one.'

I couldn't tell if she was serious or not.

'If that's true, then I'm a pink-spotted duck,' I said.

'Hah. Maybe. But good advice about dark-eyed strangers all the same!' She squinted at Esher's dwindling back. 'Ah, to the Night Below with it, we can't let her get too far ahead. She'll take all the best moon horses!'

She put her heels to her mount, bashing at him until he finally decided she wasn't going to give up, and South finally found her hooves and went after her. All these miles out from the city, the stars painted the witching sky in their millions. I hadn't been so far from Redwinter's protection since the night on Tor Marduul, but I wasn't afraid. I felt freer riding that horse through the bitter night air than I had for a long time. Maybe I'd never felt so free. I could turn her head, ride off into the darkness if I chose to. But I didn't choose to, and I wanted to follow this reckless pack of women.

And who didn't want to see a moon horse?

The miles were done when we reached a spring, gushing happily out of the hillside, sparkling in the dark. There were signs that other people had come here with offerings for the hidden folk, little waxed cloths weighed down with stones, but there weren't even crumbs there now. Of course, a few crows or a wild pony would have munched through most offerings anyway. But if there was a time and a place to see the hidden folk, then maybe it was here and now, lit only by the dazzling brightness of a star-filled sky, the gurgle of a freshwater spring and the cold moorland air our companions. The branches of a fallen tree served as a suitable tethering spot for our actual horses, and then we went looking for the moon's.

The woman in the ball gown, Draoihn Lioslaith, took the lead. She'd braided her auburn locks into a crown around her head, and in the moon's silver light she could almost have passed for one of the hidden folk herself. The moon sat wide and pale in the sky above, holding court among the cosmos. Lioslaith had us all form a circle, linking hands close to the spring.

'Mother Moon, we've come tonight to pay you tribute and to ask for a chance to win the hearts of your children. By the Light Above, let it be so.'

'Let it be so,' the others repeated, and I joined in belatedly. Lioslaith looked up and cracked a grin. 'All right then, have a drink and let's get started.'

I had not expected there to be bottles of whisky. I had thought that perhaps we were about to conduct solemn rituals and chanting, but whisky was better. It was a fourteen-year-old single malt from the High Pastures. I tasted peat, and warmth, and it was delicious. I took my swigs and found myself sputtering. I'd lost the knack of drinking.

'I'll go first,' Gelis said. The most I knew about her was that she got annoyed if I didn't strain her wine well enough. She produced a little doll from a pocket and went to kneel down at the centre of the circle. A little meanly, I hoped she'd fail, even if I wanted to see the horses.

'She always uses the doll,' Esher whispered to me. Her breath was warm in my ear; her scent was sandalwood and wildflowers. 'It never works.'

Suddenly nervous, I watched Gelis do whatever it was she was doing. She held the little doll out in front of her, an old thing made from scraps of fabric and homely stitching. Nothing happened, and the rest of us remained silent.

'It's not my night,' Gelis said after a while. 'Now, where's that bottle?'

There was more drinking, which was good because it was really bloody cold, and though we might all have looked fantastic, we were paying the price for it in the night chill. Esher offered me a spare cloak she'd packed—a veteran's move. Between the cloak, the whisky—further bottles of best-quality malt appeared when the first was done—and the camaraderie, I managed to stay warm.

Liara took her turn with a ring that had been her grandmother's, and Esher had a tunic she'd worn the day she came to Redwinter, but neither of them summoned the moon horses. When there were only two of us left to go, I was ushered into the centre.

'Your turn now,' Lioslaith said.

'I'm not Draoihn,' I said. 'I'm not even an apprentice.' I was nervous. It sounded exciting, but did I really want to start messing with the hidden folk, after everything I'd seen?

'You're a daughter of Redwinter all the same,' Lioslaith said. 'We all know how you tried to save Hazia and helped Van LacNaithe destroy one of the Sarathi. You deserve to be here as much as any of us.'

'Just try it, Fiahd,' Esher said. She bit at her lower lip, put a hand on my hair.

'You never know until you try it.' I'd thought that the hand on my head might be some sort of gentle stroking to coax me, but it turned out to be a way of pushing me into the centre and to my knees. The mud was cold. 'You can do it.'

I glanced across the faces all around me. Strong, proud, a little merry. I took out the pot of honey. Someone giggled, but there had been a lot of giggling since the whisky started going round, and I didn't think it was aimed at me. I'd listened to them talking, giving each other advice. You were meant to focus on the thing you carried, let your being expand into the realm where want, need and sentiment were as real as clay and thistle. The moon horses were of our world, and of the hidden realm, and they'd smell us and come to look. If we did it right.

'All right, honey pot,' I whispered. 'Bring me a horse.'

I knelt there for a while, thinking about who I had become, and what I was required to do, and how I was kneeling in the cold mud with a jar of very cold honey in my hand, and began to wish I could eat the honey. If there were any horses out there, then whatever I was thinking evidently wasn't very smelly.

'Drink!' one of the older girls demanded. 'Before my eyes freeze shut!'

It didn't matter that I failed at it. Succeeding didn't even seem to be the point of the expedition. We were young, and we were out in the night, and we were exciting and dazzling. It was a long time since I could have said that I'd been having fun. A conversation with Sanvaunt in the church, a bath, a lesson in moving around with bent legs. Not much to show for recent times.

I was pretty drunk by the time Lioslaith took her turn, which was a shame, because she actually managed to do it, and I might have liked to remember it more clearly.

Nobody mentioned what the significance of the knife she clutched to her chest was, but it must have mattered a great deal to her. It mattered enough that from the dark below, the most beautiful creatures I had ever seen began to emerge from the dark along the spring, washed in moonlight. There were five of them, perfect beneath the stars, bodies shimmering and translucent, but they were not cold, dead echoes. There was so much life in them, though they were apart from the world even if they were in it. They were only fourteen hands or so tall, rippling, ephemeral shapes of gold and silver, their glittering manes long, straight and smooth.

Lioslaith climbed slowly to her feet. There were tears in her eyes as she walked down the slope towards a silvery mare that left the herd and approached. She reached out a hand, and the horse sniffed it. They stood assessing one another for almost a minute, and then the horse slowly lowered a knee and bowed its head as if offering her a place on its back.

'Oh, no. I know your game,' she said. 'But thank you.'

The horse snorted and righted itself. Lioslaith placed a hand on its nose, and for a final moment the two of them just stood there, shaded in moonlight and stars, silent against the babbling spring.

The moon horse turned with a flick of its ears, trotting back towards her companions, until a strong wind gusted across the hilltop and they disappeared upon it.

The women erupted into a riot of cheering, arms hurled around necks, tin cups thrust to the sky spilling malt that suddenly didn't seem to have all that much value after all.

'Did we really just see that?' I asked.

'We saw moon horses!' Esher was screaming it, her good eye wild and her blinded eye gleaming, and so much joy on her face that when she grabbed hold of my collar and kept screaming 'we saw moon horses!' into my face I thought I might go deaf.

'How did you do it? How? How?'

'I don't know, not exactly,' Lioslaith said with a victorious but weary smile. 'I just told them a story of who I was, and that I really, really needed to see them tonight.'

'Why didn't you get on its back?' I asked, which turned out to be a stupid question.

'You don't get on a moon horse. It'll carry you off to the hidden folk's realm, and then you'll be a moon horse too.'

It was meant to be scary, but I thought that actually sounded quite nice. Maybe if everything went wrong at Redwinter I could find a moon horse and have it take me away. But not just now. That had been something worth seeing. Life had not been kind to me lately, and I was thankful for this. It had been something truly beautiful.

We celebrated with what was left of the whisky and were singing songs as we passed back beneath the gates in time for dawnsong.

22

I had friends. That wasn't normal for me, but there they were. Some nights Esher, Liara and I would sit up when my duties were finished, playing pebble board games, reading to one another, or simply talking. They didn't seem to want anything from me, and I looked forward to those late-night gatherings. Ovitus was envious, I could see that easily enough, so I made time for him as well when Liara went down to the city to practice for something she kept to herself. Esher knew what it was, and perhaps I felt a little jealous about that, but they'd been friends long before I had arrived.

I was playing a card game with Ovitus in the largest parlour when Ulovar summoned me. The greathouse had a single high tower, a sky-piercing pillar of stone, the vanity of an architect long passed into the grave. Step after step after bloody step up and my legs were aching by the time I'd climbed the seemingly endless stairs. The highest level barely had walls, the conical roof supported by twelve thin columns around the edge. The apprentices went up there to sit and meditate, working their minds through the Path of Awareness and Self as they sought to master the First Gate. But there was no meditation today. At least, not the usual kind.

Ulovar sat with his legs over the edge. Three bottles sat beside him, two of them empty, one rolled onto its side. I could smell the whisky. He muttered to himself, staring out at the city in the valley below. Distantly, the Dead Sister and the Maid lay huge and silent against the lower mountains that flanked them. The view was beautiful, but the night was cold, and the wind whipped my hair across my face.

I had seen little of him lately, though he was confined to Redwinter's grounds. He didn't notice me, and I was wary of approaching any drunk man when I was alone. But I'd been called here and I had a task to do, and the biting air insisted that I get on with it.

'My lord.'

He turned to glance back over one shoulder, red eyes winking in the pale blue-white cadanum lamplight.

'Raine. Good. I had a task for you. What was it?'

'I don't know.'

He laughed, mirthless.

'Neither do I.'

He was as broad as a bear, but his shoulders were hunched, his shirt un-tucked. He turned back to look at the city lights, the vast dark shape of the castle dominating the lesser spires.

'Should I leave you?'

'No, no,' Ulovar said. 'I came up here for some space to think, but it feels like I've finished thinking for the moment. Drink never did agree with me.' He put a fourth bottle down carefully, away from the edge. 'How has it come to this?' he said.

I walked to the edge and sat down a few feet from him, hooking my legs out over the wall. I had to admit, the view was majestic. I didn't know what to say, but I could tell from his tone that Ulovar wanted to talk. He wasn't slurring—he held his alcohol better than he seemed to think, but maybe that was just the advantage of being made from spare pieces of bear.

'My whole life has been spent in service to the Crown, and for the good of Clan LacNaithe,' he said, his voice low. 'The castle over there—the Crown lies beneath it, beyond the Final Seal. I've never even seen it. Not once. King Quinlan took the Crown when I was only a boy and I have never doubted, or questioned. I sent my sons off to war, to foster the unity between Harran and Brannlant. Protect the Crown, serve the kingdom.'

He shook his head slowly. It was a ramble.

'Sounds better than most people's lives,' I said.

'I don't lament my life,' Ulovar said, though I thought he'd been doing ex-actly that. 'And yet I will stand trial for holding to my responsibility as Hazia's guardian. She had to be stopped. It was my duty. Even if it meant killing a girl I'd known since she was ten years old, I was ready to do it. I'd hoped—hoped that there was some kind of mistake. How could she do it, Raine? Why would she do it?'

'I never knew her,' I said.

'But you met her,' Ulovar said, an edge of anger in his voice. Blaming me for his mistakes, maybe. 'She must have said something to you. Something to indicate why an apprentice of the Draoihn, a child I raised beneath my own roof, would seek to raise something like Ciuthach.'

'She didn't know either,' I said. I couldn't remember her exact words. That's not how memory works, most of the time. 'She was confused. Didn't know why she'd stolen it, what it was or where she was going. Is it possible—could Ciuthach have compelled her?'

'Ciuthach was dead,' Ulovar said. 'Locked away in his tomb. It's not impossible, perhaps. A Draoihn who has passed the Fourth Gate and achieved the trance of Fier can influence the mind. Implant suggestions. Manipulate emotions. But to do so requires a physical touch, a connection between the Draoihn and the recipient. I cannot simply stare across a room and command a man to throw himself into a fire. I have considered that Ciuthach, or possibly the page that Hazia stole from the Blackwell, could have had that power. But the Blackwell has its own binding wards. No magic passes in or out of it. It is where the most dangerous artefacts of our past are locked away. I do not see how even something as powerful as Ciuthach could reach beyond it. And that page lay dormant there for more than seven hundred years. Why now?'

'Could you make a man throw himself into the fire if you touched him?' I asked.

Ulovar turned drink-blurred, scarlet eyes on me.

'I have never tried, nor will I ever,' he said. 'The fourth trance is to be used only when the need is vital. It is no light thing to dominate another's will.'

I looked out over the city. Yellow lights for oil and fire, white-blue for the globes that the rich had access to. The city didn't truly sleep. Redwinter was quiet in the night, but down there, the hive swarmed and worked.

'But you did it to me,' I said. 'You cut my mind in half. You changed who I am.'

Ulovar picked up the last, half-full, bottle again and took a deep drink. He did not offer it to me, rolling it between his hands.

'Desperate times, Raine,' he said. 'People are not designed to suffer such grief. I thought to bury it, seal it away.'

'You didn't give me a choice,' I said.

'No,' he acknowledged. 'That was, perhaps, more selfish than I would like to admit. I need you. You are the only living witness to what Hazia did. I have not told my nephew the full extent of the accusations levelled against me. There are those that believe I consorted with Hazia to steal from the Blackwell, some may even go so far as to believe that I instructed her so. There are those that feel that, with four Gates open to me, I risked too much by exposing myself to that power. That perhaps I even sought it for myself. It is not merely disobeying the grandmaster that I am to be tried for. I will be tested as a traitor.'

Good intentions, innocence, guilt and treason. It was hard to know where one ended and another began. It wasn't my fault that the Queen of Feathers had prevented Ulovar from stopping Hazia reaching the crypt. But had she been saving me, or helping Hazia on her journey? I had to choose not to be-lieve that. The Queen of Feathers had stepped in late in the day, if that had been her intention. But had I not helped Hazia through the snow in the first place, Braithe, Lochlan, Sister Marthella—all of them would still be alive. If I hadn't told Sister Marthella that name in the first place, Niven LacCulloch would never have hunted the sisters down. If Mama had not made my life so full of tears and woe, I would never have left. Who had hurt her, I wondered, that she became so cold? It was a chain, linking error to foolishness, to pride, to failure. I had never intended to see the hidden spirit world beyond the sight of normal people, but I could, and people had died for it. I couldn't feel sorrow for the dead, but I could not help but curl my lip at myself in disgust. I saw the dead, and I brought death: I was exactly what people feared.

'What will they do, if they find you guilty?'

'They will break me, and throw my body into the harbour.' He took a long breath. 'I am sorry that I took the choice from you, Raine.'

'It's all right,' I said. 'I'd rather be scarred than dead. I don't want grief. I don't want that pain. It won't help me get what I want.'

'And what do you want?' Ulovar asked. I stared out into the darkness, at the lights of the town winking, changing.

'Sometimes, I just want to disappear.'

Ulovar raised the bottle out over the edge, looked into it for a few moments as if seeking truth in the liquid within. Truth, or maybe a way out. Then his fingers opened and the bottle fell away to shatter in the dark.

· · · · · ·

The colour storm struck the following day.

The sky was the hue of exposed bone, and a ferocious western wind howled across the moorland. Behind it came banks of bruised clouds, bearing the snow that had been due for many weeks.

I was sent down to the city to deliver a couple of messages and to pick up a new sword that had been forged for Ovitus. It was a beautiful thing, five feet long, engraved with the Clan LacNaithe wyvern, the grip bound with ray skin from the coast, held in a scabbard enamelled in the clan colours, green and black. I felt a stir of envy as I held it. I could take a sword from the armoury whenever I wanted one, but this was something personal, and precious.

The road was all but deserted. The usual stream of travellers—merchants, farmers, peddlers, monks and wanderers—had reduced to a marginal trickle. My heavy cloak, green-and-black Clan LacNaithe breacan, snapped behind me like a flag in the wind, and wearing my hood up to keep the wind from my eyes offered little protection.

As I reached Harranir's southern edge, I looked up at the sky and put out a hand to test the air. Clouds had blown in; tiny white flakes spiralled down to kiss my skin. I weighed up my chances of reaching Redwinter before the snow hit, found them poor. If the snow came in hard enough, I might find myself riding through a blizzard and lose my way on the moor. I saw the welcoming lights of a tavern on the last street corner, and glanced back to see the clouds had rolled in across the city. The broadening of the snowflakes signified that I was out of time, and as winter's promised snowfall began to fill the world around me, I crossed to the tavern. The stableboy took South and I stepped through the doorway. I had to duck beneath the low beam and then step down into the sunken room—it wasn't just northerners who preferred to dig down rather than build walls. Visiting a tavern didn't seem like such a bad idea anyway. I was still testing the freedoms allowed to me in this strange new life.

The aleroom was smoky, attesting to a poor chimney and the Ashium leaf being smoked in bowls at the rear. The smokers lay back in their chairs, eyes glassy and lips stained green, but they enjoyed their weed peacefully and were unobtrusive save for the musky odour. A trio of young Brannish merchants kept away from them, talking quietly amongst themselves, while a gaunt man sat alone with the unseeing stare of one who spends every hour of the day thinking how to afford the next drink.

At the best table, close to the fire, a young man in dark Draoihn red sat swirling a drink. Embroidery picked out a bright blue rose on his cloak. An apprentice; I'd seen him occasionally at noonsong and evensong, but never at dawnsong. He didn't seem to be in attendance to the praising very often. His dark blond hair glowed with a healthy sheen, as did his tan skin. He'd stretched out his long legs, a bottle of wine rested on the table, and there was a longsword propped against his chair. He spotted me just after I had seen him and gave me a wolfish smile. Beckoned me over. I hadn't been looking for company, but I didn't seem to have a lot of choice.

'Haven't I seen you in the chapel?' he asked.

'Yes, Master Apprentice,' I said. I gave the expected bow. A wry smile played over his lips. 'It's snowing now,' I added.

'I thought it might have started,' he said, a voice that spoke of high breeding. His nose was fine and aquiline, his hair loose and thick around his head. His only imperfection seemed to be that one of his front teeth slightly crossed the other. He offered a hand. 'Apprentice Castus, of Clan LacClune.'

Clan LacClune. I had put an arrow into Haronus LacClune's shoulder, and I didn't regret it. Not after his casual judgement of poor Nairna LacMuaid.

'Raine Wildrose, in service to Clan LacNaithe,' I said. Based on Haronus LacClune's imperious manner, I thought my dishonourable parentage might end the conversation, but instead he reached forwards and shook my hand. A rare gesture from a Draoihn to a retainer.

'Join me, Raine Wildrose. Have some wine,' he said, raising a hand to summon another cup. The serving woman was over before he lowered it again. 'You're one of Van Ulovar's?'

'I serve the van,' I agreed.

'LacClune and LacNaithe don't mingle a great deal. Seems a shame to me. We're all Draoihn, regardless of clan.' It didn't seem to bother him that I wasn't Draoihn. Castus poured wine for me, which none of the Draoihn apprentices in Ulovar's clanhold had ever done, despite often including me in their group. I felt unduly grateful for that small, simple act. I'd fallen into my servitude faster than I had expected, and though there were only about thirty apprentices in total housed at Redwinter, I had little contact with those outside the so-called Ulovar's Army. Not much of an army. Seven apprentices, one of whom was Ovitus, who, as he'd happily admit, was about as much use in a fight as a damp handkerchief.

We sat and drank the wine; it was sour and unpleasant. Castus talked freely, as though I were an apprentice too. He was a year older, but the city had been his home for a long time. He seemed to know something about everything.

Eventually though, I understood why he'd called me over.

'You were there when Ulovar killed it. The Sarathi, I mean,' he said.

'Yes,' I said. Despite the scar-wall across my mind, I was reluctant to talk about it. I may have relearned how to sleep, but some terrors never leave you.

'That must have been something,' Castus told me. 'It's what we're for. The Draoihn, I mean. I wish I'd been there.' I didn't meet his eye, and Castus frowned into his wine. 'Hazia was my friend. She used to spend time at our greathouse, when she wanted to get away from— Well. Tell me about it?' he said.

The memory was fogged, hazy, somewhere beyond the break wall. The wine tasted sharp on my tongue, brittle, and I hesitated. But he was an apprentice Draoihn, and I was just a retainer, even if I was First Retainer, and I couldn't deny him. I gave only brief details. Castus listened quietly, half a smile on his smooth-shaven face.

'Quite a battle,' he said. 'Seems that we should think of you as a hero, shouldn't we?' I couldn't tell if he was mocking or sincere, so I shrugged. Of late, shrugging was becoming my response of choice. I didn't always have answers that others would understand. 'You don't want to be a hero?' he asked.

'Heroes save people,' I said. 'I arrived too late for that.'

Castus's brow creased in what may have been intended as sympathy, but the smile never quite left his lips.

'I've shed my tears for Hazia. She was a good person. I used to see a good bit of her around Redwinter.'

'You were friends?'

'She was my sister's friend more than mine, and sometimes she wanted to avoid Ovitus's attentions. He carried a little flame for her, until he discovered the LacShale girl. I'm sorry about what happened to her. For all of them. What happened to all those people was awful.'

'They weren't really my people. They didn't want me.'

Castus sat up straighter in his chair, the casual laziness of his posture changing to one of intent interest.

'You don't feel anything for them? It must be hard. Isn't that painful for you?'

I knew exactly why I didn't grieve. But it was personal, and after last night's conversation, I didn't think telling someone from a rival clan what Ulovar had done to me was a good idea. The men of LacNaithe talked about Clan Lac-Clune as though they were some kind of poison.

'I try not to think about it.'

'I can understand that,' Castus said, though I got the strange sense that he was either enjoying himself or aware of something that I wasn't. 'So what does a girl like you do, down in the big city?'

I tensed at that. Whenever a man says you're a girl to your face, the conversation tends to start heading downhill.

'I'm not looking for a man,' I said quickly, and then regretted it. Saying as much often made men feel a need to try to convince me otherwise, to prove their worth. Didn't matter if they were young or old, they all did it. But I hadn't developed a better strategy than bluntness. To my surprise, Castus laughed.

'My heart aches to hear it,' he said, 'but unless you're planning to grow a cock in the next few months, I can assure you that you have nothing I want.'

He said it openly, plainly, clearly audible to anyone who cared to listen. I'd known men who liked men, and women who liked women, but those relationships had happened behind closed doors and went unspoken. Castus didn't seem to give a shit. He could see that he'd surprised me.

'I guess people don't care about things like that here,' I said cautiously.

'Oh, plenty of them do. Men get scared of men who might want to fuck them. Makes them feel that they're not the pack alpha.'

'But . . . ?'

'I don't care what people think, Miss Raine,' he said. 'And frankly I don't have to. So tell me. What do you want?'

'I'd like to ride a moon horse,' I said.

Castus gave me a look of mocking gentility. 'I bet you would.'

From another man, I would have been on my guard and heading for the door. But whatever I had seen of Haronus LacClune, I didn't sense the same from Castus.

'But I'd settle for a chance to learn. To be an apprentice. Become Draoihn. But I think I'm more likely to find myself up on a moon horse.'

'Nothing's impossible,' Castus said. 'Grief. This wine is dreadful. Hard to believe it's their best vintage, isn't it? So. If not Draoihn and not riding the hidden folk, then what?'

'I don't know what I want.' I paused, thinking. Maybe that wasn't entirely correct. I wanted my bow back, but it's best not to make it known you want something if you plan to take it regardless of the answer you receive. So why did I want it? Castus raised his cup and drank, the lower half of his face obscured by the cup. He had clever eyes. 'There is something that I want,' I said finally. That memory of Ulovar, sword out, knee bent, Ciuthach's head falling from his shoulders, stamped on my mind like a brand.

'And what's that?'

'I want to be stronger,' I said. 'I want to be more than I was. Greater than I am.'

'You want praise?'

'No,' I said. 'I want to be good at things. Not just good. I want to win. For a change, you know? I want to be able to stand up to the world and have a chance against it. I want to start from an equal position. To be able to defend myself, and not have to bow and scrape and depend on somebody for my life.'

'Aha,' Castus said with a grin. 'You're a woman after my own heart. Never accept second place, that's what my father used to say. "There are two types of people, winners and the corpses they step over." He was talking about warriors, but I've found that the principle applies to most situations.'

I thought about that as I drained my cup. He was right: corpses never did well at anything.

Across the room, a beer jug thumped down against a table, loud enough to draw every eye. Nobody needed to have a sense for trouble to know what was about to happen, how badly a drunk can ruin everybody's day. Sometimes the tension of imminent violence just bleeds into the air until you can feel it, coming on like rain.

The gaunt drunkard with the empty eyes had risen from his table and put his jug down in front of the three young merchants. His voice carried through the drifting Ashium leaf smoke, choked on beer and every bad decision that had led him to his love affair with it.

'You're recruitin',' he said. 'I want to be recruited.'

One of the merchants, a man in his twenties, offered a weak, pleading smile.

'Sorry, you've got the wrong people. We're just running tin down from Dulceny.'

'You're from Brannlant,' he said. 'Recruiting for your armies. I want to be recruited. I was a fighting man once. Inan the . . . something or other, that's what they called me.' He leaned forwards, tried to stifle a belch, then raised his arms to flex his muscles. He was a big man, mostly beer and pastry, but the Brannish are by fashion a slender people.

'We're really not,' the Brannish spokesman said. 'Please, we're discussing business, it's a private conversation.'

'This will not go well,' Castus muttered. His eyes had turned flinty. 'I despise drunks.'

The barkeep came over. Got involved, tried to persuade his customer to step away. Voices got louder, the Brannish merchants got to their feet and began to back away as Inan the Something or Other's gesticulations started turning to shoves, to a swipe of the hand that sent two mugs off the table.

I had always been told not to get involved in somebody else's fights, and for most of my life I had followed that advice. For one thing, I'd never had the size or skill to intervene effectively. This same story was probably repeating itself a dozen times over across the city. I stayed in my chair, watching as the man named Inan raised his fist over the young merchant.

Castus was across the room in moments. I heard his trance open, a distant, repeating series of waves on sand. He caught Inan's wrist before he could land a blow.

'You don't want to do that,' he said firmly. Inan looked startled that somebody had opposed him.

'You better let go of me, boy,' Inan warned, 'or maybe you want to do some recruiting too?'

'Look at his coat, Inan,' the innkeeper hissed from the floor, apparently keen to protect his customer despite the assault. 'He's a fecking Draoihn, do what he says. No offence, my lord, no offence!'

'I don't have to do nothing. I got the king's freedom to do as I please, don't I? Don't have to let these Brannish filth take what's ours.' The swerve in his motivation was of no surprise to anyone. Inan shook free of Castus's grip or, I thought, Castus released him.

'There are other taverns, and other fights,' Castus said. Calm as the falling snow beyond the window. A deathly quiet had fallen on the other patrons. Even the smokers had stopped sucking on their bowl pipes to watch. Castus looked Inan right in the eye. 'This spectacle is spoiling my drink. And I didn't plan on killing anybody today.'

'Go feck yourself, you cocky little appeaser,' Inan growled, and went about making the last mistake of his life. His hand went to the hilt of the knife at his belt. Every man and woman carries a knife. It's only practical to do so. The problem with carrying blades is that when tempers flare and the wine has flowed too long, the hilt is always in reach. His fingers closed around it, and he drew.

Castus had a knife too, and it was in Inan's neck, punching in and out so easily it seemed to cost him no effort at all. Blood spurted like wine from a punctured skin. Inan had only a moment to realise what had happened to him before he collapsed to the ground, legs shaking, grasping at the punctured vein. He shuddered, weakened, until he wasn't much more than a twitching sprawl of limbs. Groaning, sucking sounds. The wet gurgle of air dragged through an unnatural hole.

Castus cleaned his knife on a bar cloth. As unhurried as the coiling pipe smoke.

'I advise you to acquire a better quality of patron,' he said to the open-mouthed innkeeper. Inan lay dying on the floor and some of the customers got up to leave, but most sat stunned. Even the addicts had quit their pipes.

'I feel I should be getting back to Redwinter,' I said, rising. I was eager to be gone before those limbs stopped twitching. I'd seen enough ghosts for one day. It takes a long time for a man to die from having his throat cut open; he might have several minutes of life left to him before his inevitable expiration. Castus looked out of the window and frowned at the drifting snowflakes, but then shrugged and seemed to agree. Like the snow was more bother than the choking gasps coming from the body on the floor. As we walked towards the door, the innkeeper called after us.

'Master Draoihn, what . . . what should I do with . . . him now?' He indicated the shuddering body, the spurts of blood subsiding to a bubbling flow. The red spray across the side of the bar.

'You let him in here,' Castus said. 'You deal with it.'

．　　．　　．　　．　　．　　．

The stable hand passed us our horses' reins and we rode out into the growing snowstorm. It flurried down around us, turning my woollen hood cold and heavy over my head. I glanced back to see if anyone from the tavern was following us to raise a hue and cry, but there was nobody. Looking forward again, I saw a hooded man in a faded yellow surcoat standing in the road as if waiting for me. He looked from me to Castus and back, then disappeared down an alley.

Probably nobody. Probably nothing.

I still shivered. I had no desire to see Hess, Najih or Veretaine again and certainly never in the company of Draoihn.

I thought the guards might challenge us as we passed through the gates, arrest us and clap us in irons, but the one man standing miserably beneath the awning merely bowed to us as we rode by. There were no other travellers on the road. The ease with which Castus sat his saddle, his utter confidence, swept me along with him. He acted as though nothing out of the ordinary had happened.

'Shouldn't we report what happened to somebody?' I suggested.

Castus looked at me, a puzzled but tolerant smile on his handsome face. The scarlet lining of his hood cast his fine features in a bloody glow.

'Who?' he asked.

'The quarter-reeve?' I suggested. 'Won't he have to investigate what happened? Those people in the tavern all saw it.'

'The reeve will hear that a Draoihn killed a drunk.' Castus shrugged. 'Maybe not even that. You aren't worried about getting in trouble over this, are you?'

'The reeve won't do anything?' I asked.

'Of course not,' Castus laughed. 'I'm Draoihn. I could slaughter the whole tavern and not a lot would happen to me. That's part of what being a Draoihn is all about. We're free.' He looked at me sidelong, one eyebrow cocked. 'If that man had stabbed me, he would have been drawn and quartered for it. A Draoihn is far too valuable to the Crown to lose. Every one is worth a hundred men to the king.'

'More than that, I think,' I murmured.

Castus's smile had turned to a grin, despite the snowfall. It wasn't as thick as I'd feared, and it wasn't sticking on the frozen ground.

'Even if I wasn't Draoihn, my father is Merovech LacClune. He's the van of Clan LacClune. The law doesn't apply to us.'

Merovech LacClune. One of Ulovar's judges-to-be. I'd only heard him spoken of with scorn.

'That doesn't seem very fair,' I said.

'Only the weak insist that life be fair,' Castus said. 'Once they make themselves strong, they stop caring. The laws are there to protect those who have the money to help make them. There isn't a reeve I couldn't buy off if I had to. Fair.' He grinned at me. 'Really, whatever they taught you up north, Raine, they didn't understand law. Besides, who's going to miss one more ugly drunk? I did the world a favour today. They should be thanking me.'

I was silent for a time as we rode, the snow melting in the ditches at the side of the road, the path frozen hard ahead. The horses plodded on with heavy strides and I thought on Castus's words. I knew what he said was true. When I was eleven, the local thail had come to the scribe-house and seen a girl that he wanted. A beautiful girl, her hair long and glossy. She'd been fourteen. He'd given her a position in his clanhold as a servant and taken her away, and we all knew what she was really being taken for. The following day I'd cut my own hair away. I'd let it grow out again now, down to my jaw. It hadn't been so long in five years.

I wasn't horrified by what Castus had done. I ran the incident over again in my mind. The swiftness with which he had struck, the ease with which he had fallen into Eio, and the precision with which he had found the jugular: rather, I wished I had landed the fatal strike. Not because I had felt sympathy for the merchants or because the man had been a threat, but because Castus had demonstrated control. Control and action, together.

Ulovar, knee bent, sword outstretched. Yes. That was what I wanted to be.

Abruptly, without slowing or lightening first, the snow stopped. One moment it was falling, heavy flakes fogging the air, and then it was clear.

'That's better,' Castus said, pushing back his hood but glancing upwards at the clouds. The air had turned very still, and the cold settled deeper. Not even a blade of grass stirred in the wind, my cloak lying limp and sodden against my horse's flanks.

A gale struck us like an ambush. Our horses staggered, and I gripped South's mane hard to avoid being blown from the saddle. The wind was followed by a resounding boom, a deep and echoing rumble like apples being shaken in a barrel, growling and throbbing from the east. It kept rolling, like drums preceding an execution.

'Is that thunder?' I yelled. My voice was nearly lost beneath the sound.

'Thunder with snow?' Castus shouted back over the wind. The gusts grew fiercer still, flattening the grass and tearing at our cloaks. The noise intensified, still far away but rolling continuously on towards us.

A bright red flash lit the eastern sky. There was no light, as with a burst of lightning, instead the sky itself seemed to be flickering red. The grass around us suddenly flared blue and then white, the distant woodland grey, purple, yellow, and suddenly all the colours of the world were rampaging, changing, flickering from one to the next so swiftly that I couldn't call one from the other. I could see everything clearly, but nothing was as it should be, not the sky, the earth, not even my own hands as I raised them in front of my face. The soggy cattle up on the hill lowed in panic, turning this way and that in circles as they struggled to comprehend a world of shifting, flickering colour.

'What the feck is this?' Castus cried. The sky continued to roar, the hues of the world blazing non-stop as they altered and flickered. There was no rhythm to the changes, no pattern or sequence; the sky turned black as night for a heartbeat and the next moment a beautiful gold, swimming into turquoise, magenta, silver, blue. The booming roar grew louder as the colours flashed and blazed.

'This is not good,' Castus shouted above the drumming. We shared a baffled look as even the colours of our faces changed in rapid succession.

'You are seeing this as well, aren't you?' I asked, and he nodded. I was re-assured to know that I wasn't going mad. I studied my hand as it changed colours, growing faster and faster until the colours began to flicker and flash, unreadable. They seemed to be growing brighter, brighter and closer to white.

Across the heavens, a shape appeared. Too perfect to be natural. Shimmering silver circles filled the sky.

Six concentric circles, and framed within the largest, another six overlapping circles filled the space like interlinking rings. Six within six, exactly as the grandmaster had shown me. A gleaming, mirror-bright configuration, drawing slowly, inexorably inwards. I felt the sky's terror. Felt the world above constricting, twisting. Changing what lay beneath. A great gust of wind came howling from the east, smashing Castus and me from our mounts and bowling them over. A crash rocked through the sky, and the world flashed white as if from sheet lightning. I landed in the ditch, icy slush cushioning my fall, thankfully thrown well clear of South's bulk. The wind left me in a rush, and I struggled for breath as I blinked at the brightness in my eyes, vision hazy. As I finally sucked in a breath, the noise stopped; the wind died; the colours of the world ceased their violent flashing. Even the silver sky-circles were gone.

The spheres of existence. Self, other, energy, mind, life, death, creation. They are all one, both the Light Above and the Night Below.

As the brightness faded, I blinked a few times more, looking around me. There were no colours at all; everything was a shade of grey. The sky, the grass, my hands, my cloak, all of it was dull and lacked hue. The sky was clear. No more circles. Nothing.

Castus helped me to my feet, checked that I wasn't hurt. My leg snarled at me, wrenched in the fall, and my shoulder throbbed, but the slush had saved me from any serious damage.

'Come on,' he said. 'Whatever that was, we should get back to Redwinter. Or Greywinter, I guess it'll be now.'

23

Castus galloped through the gates in the blood-and-bone walls, and I followed him, clinging to South as best I could. The air was heavy with after-snowfall calm, but the world around us was grey, colourless and grim to the eye. There was light and shadow and shades of grit.

Redwinter's grounds swarmed as if the storm had been a foot scattering an ant's nest. An old man sat clutching his head, rocking back and forth, blinking and staring at his shoes as a younger servant tried to get him onto his feet. Draoihn were streaming towards the Round Chamber, apprentices and masters alike. It wasn't customary to wear the Draoihn coat within Redwinter's grounds—not unless you were Sanvaunt, and making a point of how committed you were—but they were now. And as though the thought had summoned him, there he was.

'What's happening?' I asked, jumping down from my mount. Sanvaunt's eyes flicked from Castus to me, taking in our arrival together.

'Draoihn LacNaithe,' Castus said, giving a polite enough bow.

'Apprentice LacClune,' Sanvaunt returned the formal greeting. 'I see you've met our First Retainer.'

'I haven't seen you since that night at the Crook and Lobster. Or that morning, anyway,' Castus said. Sanvaunt scowled at him. I'd seen him look fierce, at Tor Marduul, and I'd seen him carefree, and for a while I'd seen him uncomfortable around me. I wouldn't have enjoyed being on the receiving end of the look he directed at Castus.

'There are important matters afoot, Apprentice,' Sanvaunt said, stressing that last word. 'Only Draoihn will be permitted within the Round Chamber at this time. You should attend to your master.'

A paper-thin blade of tension flittered between them. I'd never known Sanvaunt to wield his Draoihn rank against the LacNaithe apprentices. Castus's demeanour was unchanged.

'You're not wrong,' Castus said. 'I shouldn't be seen around your kind anyway, should I? Not with the trial coming. Rumours about your van are flocking thicker than crows. But I'll leave his fate to my father and the rest of the Council of Night and Day to decide.' He flashed a look at me. 'If you get bored over there, come visit the LacClune greathouse. There's always opportunity there, and I promise you, we're a lot more fun.'

He hurried away to join his clansmen. Sanvaunt watched him through narrowed eyes for several moments before heading off towards the Round Chamber. Grandmaster Robilar stalked through the snow, surrounded by a thronging honour guard of Draoihn, though they were more likely the ones feeling the benefit of her protection. She wore her youthful appearance, dressed in a formal robe, her hair tumbling across her shoulders, its dual tones of rich chocolate brown and bright sunlight both muted to grey. She looked far too young to be addressing a hall of Draoihn, but I remembered the bent-backed old woman with the metal casing around her skull. She had told me that this was not her true shape, her Fifth Gate allowing it to be whatever she willed it to be. I returned to the greathouse. The grooms were not there, so I stabled South myself and spent a few minutes brushing her coat down, settling warm blankets on her back. I had spoken to no one of what I had seen. Nor was I asked. I had only just stepped through the door, was still stamping snow from my boots, when Tarquus collared me.

'I need to inventory everything we have in the stores,' he said. 'See that the apprentices have everything they need.'

'An inventory? Why?'

'It's chaos,' he said gravely. 'The grandmaster may order the gates of Redwinter shut whilst they ascertain what has happened. We may be under attack, or worse, it may be a plague.'

'I don't think a plague hits everyone at once,' I said. I only just caught my tongue before mentioning the bright circles I had seen in the sky. The same circles that sat within Grandmaster Robilar's stateroom. When had I decided to start blurting out the unusual things I saw? There was safety in silence.

'We do not know,' Tarquus said. 'We prepare for siege.'

He was right. We didn't know. Perhaps the grandmaster did, but until she had spoken, it was safest to keep my thoughts to myself.

It had not sunk into me quite how the apprentices were regarded, not until Castus LacClune casually rammed a knife into a man's throat and rode away without so much as a glance over his shoulder. He had got away with killing a man in the middle of a crowded room. The Draoihn were precious; they existed outside the common law. The apprentices understood that. So for the first time I understood them properly when they piled in around the dining table and began to make their demands. Cider, haggis, neaps and more cider. They held their own council. None of them could see a single shade of colour, and it frightened them, rightly. But not one of them mentioned the circles in the sky.

I had been right to keep it to myself. I was no stranger to keeping secrets, but I couldn't help but wonder whether somehow, even though ghosts and sigils in the sky were as far removed from each other as flowers and fire, that maybe my curse was why I saw what they did not.

The broken man, Veretaine, would know, as would Hess or Najih. Maybe I could ask, if I could find them. Or if they found me.

The apprentices ate and drank, filling their mouths to stop their fears spilling out.

I dismissed the other servants, freeing them to try to cope with what was happening to us all. It meant more work for me, but it didn't seem right that they should attempt to work amid all the uncertainty. Ovitus was comfortable asking me to get him things, as were Colban, Adanost and Gelis. Jathan had always seemed to enjoy asking me to do things for him. Esher and Liara avoided it when they could, but even if we were equals by a moonlit stream, we were not equals in here. Esher ate very little, pushing her food around her plate.

'It will be all right,' I whispered when I brought her another unasked for cup of wine.

'Will it?' she asked. 'Will it?' Her voice was breathy with desperation. The fear had struck her hardest, and the cup trembled in her hand. I wanted to stroke a hand across her hair, tell her that I'd seen far worse than this. That by comparison to Ciuthach, a little lost colour was nothing to worry about at all. But this wasn't the place, or the time.

I looked to Ovitus, willing him to take leadership. To see his place as the future van of his clan, to understand everyone needed reassurance. He ate. He drank.

Darkness had long since fallen when Sanvaunt returned.

'Is everyone drunk?' he asked. His eyes burned across the apprentices. 'You're all drunk?'

'It seemed the right thing to do,' Ovitus said.

Sanvaunt looked angry. Anger. That was another new one for him. Again I saw how tattered-looking he'd become. How deep the shadows beneath those sleepy-lidded eyes.

'The right thing to do was to stay alert. To wait for instructions. To act like Draoihn,' he said. 'What if we were mobilising, right now? What if there was a threat to Redwinter? To the Crown?' He strode forwards and slammed his fist down against the table. 'You train to be Draoihn. Do you think this is what life is about? Drinking and stuffing your faces?'

Nobody could meet his eyes. Sanvaunt turned to leave.

'Wait! What did they say?' Ovitus called after him. 'Where's Uncle?'

Sanvaunt paused, his back to them. It wasn't just that they'd made themselves useless with whisky and cider, I thought. He'd wanted to talk to someone. They'd spent the afternoon blurring the greys of their eyes and left him all alone with the problem.

'The Crown does not seem under threat. The Council of Night and Day continue to convene with the archivists. If you can still remember all that in the morning, Van Ulovar can tell you the rest.'

He stalked from the room in a swirl of grey coat-tails. It was very dramatic. I wanted to see him do it again.

The apprentices grumbled about him. Ovitus asked for more cider.

'I'm taking Draoihn Sanvaunt's feelings on the matter as an instruction to put a stopper in the bottle,' I said. 'If you want more, you'll need to get it yourself.'

'Are we idiots?' Esher muttered. She scratched frantically at her head. 'I—I think we might be idiots.'

I felt bad for them. They were young. Gelis was only sixteen; none of them had reached twenty. Getting drunk was what I'd have expected most people to do. But then, most people couldn't get away with stabbing a man in the neck and walking away. I left and headed upstairs to dead Hazia's room. I was glad to be away from them, even Esher—there is nothing appealing about a drunk person when you're sober. But I had nothing to do with myself in the grandly furnished bedroom. I went to the window and looked out at a new, light fall of snow. The flakes fell erratically, swirling and spiralling towards the lawns below. At least they hadn't changed colour.

There was movement on the lawn. Sanvaunt, in the garden. He moved through battle-forms, wooden practice sword in hand, bending and unbending his legs, striking through the air to slay the snowflakes around him. He was not dressed for the cold, doing invisible battle in his shirtsleeves. No words in my head made the decision, but I found myself going down the stairs, out the back door and onto the lawn.

'I don't think you can kill them all,' I said. Sanvaunt delivered a final blow, his fist quivering around the hilt.

'I can't execute them for being drunk and useless?' he said. I'd not seen this anger from him before. It could have melted the snow around him.

'I meant the snowflakes.'

Sanvaunt turned to face me. Black hair, wet around his neck and across his brow. Pale skin, hard arms.

'No. They'll just melt anyway.' He thrust the wooden blade down against the hard-packed earth. 'It's cold out here. You should go back inside.'

'Talk to me,' I said. 'I'm sober.'

'I'm training,' he said.

'So am I.' I took his practice blade, walked out and faced him. If Sanvaunt didn't want to be my friend, that was fine. He remained distant, not exactly aloof, but he closed himself off to me. Open, shut, open, shut. It heated my ears to admit that I wanted to win him over—maybe just because he didn't seem to want anything from me. Was that why I sought him out and needled at him, because I was so desperate for attention? Pitiful, Raine. Ridiculous.

Sanvaunt's expression remained dour, his eyes sharp on me.

'They've been given everything. Every opportunity. Money. One day they'll have power. Why is it only you, who has been given nothing but service, who cares?'

'Maybe it's because I haven't been given everything yet. So give me something. Teach me.'

A softening of the tension in his cheeks.

'Fine. Just do what I do.' He picked up a fallen branch and tested its heft.

Mama had not liked me to fight with other children, and other children had always been too wary of her whip-lash tongue to bother me. I had seen plenty of prizefights, boxing and wrestling matches at country fairs, though. Those fist fighters had always seemed incredibly fierce, swollen lips and cuts on their brows. They had bobbed on their feet, bouncing like hares in spring. Sanvaunt moved differently. He didn't duck and weave or throw jabs. He made deft, solitary strikes.

'What are we doing?'

'Killing snow,' he said. We slashed the air for a while. The movement got my blood flowing, started warming me, but the snow was cold and the night was cold, and it was all a bad idea a smarter girl would have avoided.

'Why are we killing the snow?'

We paused in our snow-murder and faced one another.

'Because I'm afraid. Because there will be riots in Harranir, and people down in the city will be dying. Because one day I'll rely on those apprentices, and they don't see how much responsibility lies on their shoulders.'

'Why will people riot?'

'Because we have no answers for them, and they're even more afraid than we are.' He stepped closer to me. 'Try to hit me.'

'It'll hurt.'

'Try.'

I did try, and my fears of hurting him were rapidly exposed as absurd. I cut and struck but never got all that close. Still, it kept the blood pumping through my veins, pushing back the snowfall cold.

'What did they say in the Round Chamber?' I asked. 'Did they know anything?' I thought the question might catch him off guard, might make him pause long enough for me to find a way to get a hand to his face. But he smiled as though he knew exactly what I was suggesting. He wasn't in the trance of Eio, no First Gate open, but even so, he was faster than me. He didn't try to hit me back; he just swayed and kept stepping back, infuriatingly out of reach.

'They don't know. Not even the archivists,' he said as I lunged in as fast as I could. He scooted back out of range. 'That kind of magic hasn't been seen since the Betrayal War. When the Draoihn fought the Hexen and the Tharada Taan.'

'The Betrayal War, the years 170 to 172,' I said.

'Good memory.'

I shrugged. 'I listen. Not that anyone has done much but mention it.'

'It's a dark period of our history,' Sanvaunt said. 'They were our allies against Hallenae and should have been protecting the Crown alongside Redwinter. But we fought them. We destroyed the Everstorm that gave the knights of Tharada Taan their power. The Hexen struck at Redwinter in retaliation, and the Glass Library was burned before they were overcome.'

'How did a glass library burn?'

Another flurry of swipes went nowhere but the cold.

'It wasn't all made of glass,' he said. 'With the loss of the library, and so many powerful Draoihn perishing, much of our own power died with the Tharada Taan and the Hexen. The Riven Queen had that kind of power, consumed as she was by the Night Below. And in the War of the Faded, powers we have never witnessed since were unleashed, but nobody in Redwinter—not even the grandmaster—could have attempted this. It goes far beyond the power we command as Draoihn.'

I was breathing hard. I held up a hand to stop the game. My arms felt heavy, but life was flowing through me. I could hear my own blood as it pulsed around my body.

'But why would anybody want to do it at all?' I said. 'You think they bought a shirt and were really displeased with the colour?'

Sanvaunt smiled broader than I'd seen him do for a long while.

'It wasn't a productive conversation. Clan LacClune's representatives disagree with anything Ulovar says on principle. LacDaine won't agree to anything, because they think it will commit the royal house to a path of action, and LacAud and Giln want to see where the pieces fall before making a decision. But they agreed that this working wasn't likely to be deliberate.'

'Then what is it?'

'A mishap? Or an unintended consequence. The result of something which used colossal power, and this was its byproduct.' He gave a short bow. I thought about hitting him in the face when he did it, but I didn't want the lesson to end, even if my feet were starting to go numb. He took this kind of thing seriously. 'What are we learning right now?' he asked.

'I don't know,' I said. 'That you're better at this than me.'

'No. We're learning distance,' Sanvaunt said. 'The most important skill in a warrior's repertoire. Knowing when you're in range of your enemy. Whether a step will bring you close enough to hit them, or leave you exposed. Whether you have the balance and footing to move out of range when the blow comes at you. There is no value in learning anything until you learn to control the space between you and your opponent. Now it's my turn. Don't get hit, but stay as near to me as you can. Deceive me.'

It was a lot harder than it sounded. Sanvaunt didn't use his full strength—didn't come close. I was very aware of the power in his arms, in his muscular shoulders. I knew if he whacked me full-on in the head, my skull would need iron bindings like the grandmaster's. But he moved gently, half speed, like he wasn't trying to use his stick to hit me at all. Just giving me something to work with.

'Not even the grandmaster wields the power to break the world this way,' Sanvaunt said. He caught me a light tap to the forearm, only hard enough to nudge it. I stepped away. 'Not even with our strongest ritual spells. Not even with the artefacts in the Blackwell.'

The point of Sanvaunt's stick brushed against the centre of my chest, then lightly rapped my wrist. It was infuriating to be so badly outclassed. He could reach me even using half, maybe less, of what he was capable of. I almost retaliated, but he would only have moved out of the way, and I would have felt worse about it.

'There must be others outside of Redwinter who know the trances.'

'The trances are Harran magic,' Sanvaunt said. 'The Brannish, the Kwends—they have their own ways. But no. Nobody living that we know of.' His movements seemed too gentle, given the danger of his words. 'But there were others who once had that kind of power. The Sarathi weren't truly destroyed.'

'Maldouen hunted the Sarathi down after the battle at Solemn Hill,' I said.

'Hunted, trapped and entombed. Yes. But the Sarathi control the Sixth Gate. They are beyond death.'

'Like the grandmaster?' I said.

'No,' Sanvaunt said. He stepped away from me, his arms dropping. 'The grandmaster has five Gates. The Sixth is the Gate to the realm of the dead. Do not even insinuate, not for a moment, that one among us commands the Sixth.'

A chilling thought came to me. A Gate that could break death itself. Perhaps this was what I was. The Queen of Feathers was a ghost, and yet she existed in our world. What if she was . . . no. She had helped me. She had protected me.

Maybe she had only protected me because I was like her.

Tainted.

'Beyond death. You mean like Ciuthach?'

A cold wind rolled through the garden, the snow dancing white against the grey. Sanvaunt was staring at me, his face dark. He gave me another short bow, then picked up his oxblood coat. He shook the snow from it, then took out his hip flask of rose-thistle and took a drink. He grimaced at the bitter taste, shivered.

'We're done?' I said.

'It's cold,' he said, 'and I have work to do.'

. . . . . .

I didn't speak up about what I had seen in the sky that day, the circles within circles. It was a piece of the puzzle that the Draoihn were missing, but Veretaine and his people had shown me all too clearly what happened to those that spoke the truth of the hidden world.

Over the next few days, books arrived in great stacks and the whole of Redwinter was put to work reading them. Even I was excused some of my duties, and assigned to read through the dullest and least likely tomes for a scrap of information. I was put to read a treatise on the use of magic in Brannlant to the south, dated two hundred years ago. Nobody expected me to find anything of value, though I scoured the pages in the hope of seeing a sign in silver, six linked rings within six concentric circles. Something I could use to vent the secret I silently clutched inside me. There was nothing.

The Queen of Feathers would know. I was sure of it. I just didn't think that I wanted to see her again. The safety of Redwinter may have let me bury Ciuthach's burning eyes deep beyond even my dreams, but I did not feel safe. She had already betrayed my greatest secret, to strangers.

For a time I had been hoping the Queen of Feathers would come to me again, whatever she was. Now the thought of her return filled me with dread. She wasn't like the other spirits that I saw, the common, greenish-white-tinted souls that didn't see me, didn't notice that I was there. I read furiously, skimming pages, looking for the words I feared. A painted face, a woman who wore a feathered crown. *Sarathi.* The books they lumped in front of me were useless. They taught me nothing I didn't already know.

In those days of futile study, we stuck to Redwinter's grounds and didn't venture out. Harranir was restless, a broiling beehive, chaotic with discontent and fear. The people blamed their leaders, looking to the king to somehow make right what had gone wrong. There were murmurings about his health and wellbeing—was this a sign of his forthcoming death? Others growled that he was seldom seen any longer, not even in parliament, and that his health was failing. Some began to demand Prince Caelan returned from his Brannish campaigning to the east, and calfskin banners advocating the worth and virtues of other candidates for the succession began appearing nailed to archways or hung over thoroughfares. The clan lords represented by the banners claimed they had no knowledge of the anonymous authors, suggesting some well-meaning citizens were desperate for them to be granted the kingship. That was no great strange thing to the citizens of Harranir, or to the apprentices. The political elite jockeying for position was always hotly discussed around the dining table as I poured wine. From what I understood, there was a fifty-fifty chance that accepting the Crown would cause madness and death, so I didn't really understand why they wanted it so badly.

Other more dangerous signs of discontent manifested in blood. A foolish mob destroyed two of the huge communal ovens in the centre of the city and had to be run off by the guard. Heads, taken in retribution for the chaos, began to adorn posts along Onebridge, and when the posts there were filled with the rotting warnings, along Leanbridge and Squirebridge as well. That didn't seem to slow the rioters, probably because it wasn't the ringleaders being caught. A group of priests had begun to proclaim the End of All Things, driving packs of self-flagellating fools to proclaim great dooms on all around them and whipping the fearful to acts of base depravity. One Draoihn was even assaulted, an angry mob trying to drag her from her horse as she chastised the priests in front of the crowd. That move proved instrumental in the mobs being brought under control, as Draoihn Amistaja of the Second Gate killed nine of them, including two of the priests. After that nobody was stupid enough to bother the Draoihn again.

The protests were brought to an end with less bloodshed. Matriarch Priseda, leader of the church, excommunicated the remaining malcontents, and they were branded across the forehead and exiled from the city. She proclaimed that she had received a dream from the Light Above, telling her that the colour of the world had receded in preparation for glories to come. This was good enough for most of the Draoihn: they saw themselves as an order that coexisted with the priesthood, symbiotes serving the Light Above in different but equally important ways. The matriarch's message was vague and made almost no sense, but the more I lived around the fervently religious Draoihn, the more I saw their faith preferred general notions of calm and prosperity to what I considered to be actual truth.

All things pass in time. It was five days before I began to see a pale lavender hue in some things around me. I was not the first, but as the colour began to come back into the world, so the fervency to research its departure waned. Sanvaunt entered the breakfast room one morning and announced, 'I can see blue today,' before sitting down to eat. Ovitus seemed to get his colours back last, Apprentice Adanost first, and I was somewhere in the middle. They were astounding to begin with. As they came back into my world I enjoyed the lushness of their shades, actually spending time seeking out things that had colour in them, until I was finally convinced that I could see all shades and colours once again. The end of the problem was such an intense relief that Ulovar held what he termed to be a celebration, and which everyone else except maybe Sanvaunt thought was a sedate and somewhat dreary evening listening to one of the monks singing religious verses in the dining room.

A more raucous affair was to be hosted by Tyronius LacClune, another of Castus LacClune's uncles, whose grand home lay on the richest street in the city. Tarquus delivered an invitation to my room one morning.

'That sounds interesting,' I said, reading the red and gold inks on the illuminated page. There was a list of performances, including a dancing bear, contortionists, classical dancers, two well-known minstrels and the infamous speed-eater, Hougal the Rotund.

The First Retainer lingered, a frown on his kindly, hairless face.

'I am sure that Tyronius LacClune's entertainments will be fascinating and diverse,' Tarquus said as he folded a shirt that I had let fall onto the floor, 'but the LacClunes are not Van Ulovar's favourite friends.'

'Are the others invited?' I asked.

'You alone have received an invitation,' Tarquus said. 'Shall I have the scribe draft your note of appreciation, and decline?' I opened my mouth to say that I was considering going, but Tarquus's expression left me in no doubt how that would be received.

'Why shouldn't I go?' I asked instead.

'One day, young miss, the world will shake and tremble, and fire will rise from cracks in the earth to scour the land of trees and beasts and men, and we shall all tumble into the Afterworld, to the freezing river of Skuttis or the warm mists of Anavia as our deeds and words dictate. But until then, LacClune and LacNaithe will sit in separate halls and dine on different fare. I'll have the scribe send your response.'

I was not content with that. I wanted to see Castus again, whatever bad blood lay between the clans. And yet, I could not fix my teeth around the hand that fed me. Instead of attending the LacClune party, I embarked on another day of reading alongside Ovitus.

Sanvaunt found me while I had my nose in some of the philosophies of Autolocus, which were dry and didn't mention any of the interesting nightcraft, Sarathi or the magic of the ancient Faded that the grandmaster really wanted to know about. Busywork, set by Ulovar, maybe. I only had two candles lit, and they provided poor light to read by.

'Raine,' he said, the same way he always drew my attention. I glanced up at him. I could see him perfectly in the dim light. The smooth, hard panes of his cheekbones, the bright blue of his eyes, which I could at last see again. The colour only showed off the weariness within them.

'How can I serve you, Draoihn Sanvaunt?'

'You aren't aware what you're doing, are you?'

'Reading?'

'You're in Eio. The whole house sounds like there's a horse galloping through it.'

I put the book down.

'I didn't mean to. Nobody will even show me how to enter Eio.'

'And yet, there you are,' Sanvaunt said. 'You're in a trance right now. How do you think you can even make out that page? It's nearly pitch-black in here.'

I shrugged. I fiddled around inside my brain for a few moments, and whatever it was I managed, Sanvaunt nodded approvingly, so apparently I'd managed to stop doing it. I looked back at the page and could barely see the words.

'Your trance is quiet,' Sanvaunt said. He leaned against the door post for support. 'Quiet, but heavy.'

'What does it sound like?' I asked. Everyone's trance had its own rhythm and sound, like the accents of those that fell into them. I heard them through Redwinter, constantly. Van Ulovar's was steady and powerful, like waves falling on a beach, a rise and fall that sighed out its strength.

'Like a draft horse's hooves on a bed of fallen leaves,' he said. He looked weary, dark hollows beneath his eyes. More than anyone, he was staying up late into the night poring over every book that the librarians could throw at him, and many that others had already trawled. He buried a yawn behind an embarrassed hand. 'You control it without thinking about it. Ovitus's trance is like a bucking mule kicking apart crockery.'

I smiled at the description. He wasn't wrong. But the smile died swiftly enough. I wasn't permitted to train with the apprentices, and I would never be Draoihn. Frustration gathered from the well that always lay at my core. I wasn't to learn to use this Gate that had opened within me, though I was still expected to control it. I wasn't to be an equal, or to attend parties when I was invited. I wasn't to do anything.

'Is there something you need me to do, Draoihn Sanvaunt?' I asked. My formality brought him back from the fog of weariness.

'No,' Sanvaunt said. He paused. Blinked once, twice, trying to order his thoughts as exhaustion strove to scatter them. 'My uncle requires something from Valarane. A book held in their archive, which might shed light on the colour storm.' Since I just stared at him blankly, he continued. 'Valarane is the monastic absolution house closest to our ancestral seat, Uloss. Since Van Ulovar is not permitted to leave Redwinter, he wants Ovitus to see to affairs around Uloss that have arisen during his absence. His party leaves tomorrow.' He drew a breath, then spoke the words as though—as though he didn't want to. 'That includes you.'

'Of course,' I said, clipping my tone the way that Tarquus did. I knew it was very annoying. 'I'll be ready at dawn.'

'After dawnsong,' Sanvaunt said.

'Fine by me.'

He made to leave.

'Will you be accompanying us, Draoihn Sanvaunt?' I asked.

'I will.' He hesitated. 'I believe my uncle hopes Ovitus might learn something of himself on the journey. Benefit from being in charge. This is a chance for him to show character. Help him to do so. Don't drag him down.' I didn't understand. I shrugged, but he wasn't finished. 'He needs a friend, Miss Raine. Ovitus has a good soul. But he is gentle, and easily bruised. Easily used, by those who don't value those qualities. Please keep that in mind.'

He left, closing the door quietly behind him, leaving me in a darkness that was barely touched by the candles.

The lands of Clan LacNaithe lay to the south and east, a full week's ride from Harranir. We rode through cold, snow-claimed farmland, the land flat and easy. The farmers working the fields wore thick, fur-lined hoods against the cold of winter as they tended flocks of sheep or made repairs to rough stone walls. Occasionally merchant caravans passed by, travelling north from Kwend and Brannlant, bringing the season's luxuries from warmer shores. They travelled without guards.

'These are Clan LacDaine's lands,' Ovitus told me, riding alongside. 'Van LacDaine scoured her lands free of bandits years ago. Her laws are very severe, and she is not a forgiving woman, according to the accounts one hears.'

'She sounds like a good van,' I said.

'Maybe,' Ovitus said. 'I think it was Jautulus who wrote that a van can choose either to be loved or feared, and to be feared is ever the safer. I think that on balance, however, I would prefer to be loved.'

Ulovar had sent all of his apprentices, saying it was good for them to get out of Redwinter for a change. But his confinement had made him brooding and reclusive, and I wondered if he simply wanted a quieter house. A train of servants and grooms trailed in our wake. We rode by humped mounds, sitting like warts atop the hills or along the road.

'Barrows,' Ovitus said when he saw me looking at them. 'The tombs of dead chieftains. There are tunnels beneath them, but most have collapsed in on themselves. Sometimes people try to break into them, but they've all been looted long ago. More often than not they just bring a heap of earth down on top of them. When we were children, Sanvaunt, Hazia and I sometimes tried to get into one. Children being children, you know? We never found a thing. But any treasures have to be surrendered to the clan anyway. The finder gets paid, but it's a lot of effort to go to given that we take it from them.'

It made a chilling kind of sense. A nightmare had slept beneath Dalnesse. Some things were better left undisturbed.

Inns opened their best rooms for us, and despite the considerable size of our party, there was rarely a shortage of space. Travellers were infrequent at this time of year. Even if the roads were safe, on the floodplains they were little better than bogs. Ovitus was well-known to the innkeepers, who fell over themselves to offer the best fare they had. Sanvaunt was unrelenting in his insistence that the apprentices practice Eio, demanding that they hold their trances while in the saddle, and in the evening made them sit and practice quietly together. I sat, and listened. Knowing Sanvaunt was alert to it, I didn't try to enter the trance state myself. Since I'd met Veretaine and seen the woman—Nairna LacMuaid, her name had been Nairna LacMuaid—stoned to death, I'd remembered to fear what it meant to be different. I tried to keep my mind closed, tried to seal out the sound of the apprentices' trances. When they spoke of the path of awareness and the path of serenity, I felt envy, and closed myself inwards.

Part of me wished that Sanvaunt would come over to me, and tell me the secrets. That Esher would tell me how to focus my mind, to control this ability that everyone knew I had. But none of them, not even Ovitus, would break the grandmaster's command and usher me into their fold. At times they spoke to me like I was one of them, but during their lessons I felt just how isolated I was. Once or twice, alone, I cautiously tried to open myself to the First Gate. I'd slipped into it by mistake several times, but only when it came unbidden. I couldn't open the door, and the apprentices had learned to enter it through paths of Awareness and Serenity. The grandmaster's ban on my training left the Gate infuriatingly out of reach.

If I wanted to run, if I truly wanted to escape this existence and the people binding me to it, this was my chance. Smuggled away in my pack were those small things I'd been hoarding. I could take my horse, and ride, and never look back. But I didn't. Events were turning. The world had changed around me, and I was changing with it.

The memory of the executed woman, the things that Veretaine had told me that I had tried to shut out, were wrapped like chains across my being. I could not equate what I'd seen of Haronus LacClune and his casual dispensation of Nairna LacMuaid's life with the generosity I'd been shown in the LacNaithe household. Ulovar had given me position, responsibility and more money than I'd ever even counted, and the comforts of that life, even the life of a servant, had already coiled around me. The world was in winter, but Harran never warmed. Niven LacCulloch had hanged the sooth-sisters for my careless words. They could not kill me for a secret that only I knew. If I kept my mouth shut, I was safe. But that silence pushed me further down an empty corridor. I could not afford to be alone, not forever.

Esher brought her horse alongside mine. We'd had little chance to speak since the moon horses, but I sometimes listened to her trance pulsing, like feet bouncing from drum to drum as she focused in the saddle. She looked magnificent, a sword at her side, golden hair tied back in a low ponytail.

'Are you well, Raine?' she asked. 'Ovitus hasn't been bothering you again, has he?'

'No,' I said. 'I'm fine.'

'I've never seen a person who was "fine" spend so much time staring at the ground. Not when the country is so beautiful.'

I needed to tell someone. Not everything. Not the parts that would get me stoned to death, but I had to let some of it out, or I'd explode like a kettle with a bung in the spout.

'I saw an execution. In the city.'

'After the riots?' Esher said. 'They got what they deserved. Innocent people were hurt by those thugs.'

'No,' I said. 'Before that. There was a woman. They said she saw the dead, and they threw rocks at her until she died.'

'Ah,' Esher said gently. 'Ovitus told me about those women you travelled with. The sisters. It's the same the world over.'

'I need to understand it. I have to, or I don't think I'll ever understand people again. Light Above, I don't think I understood them before, but it seemed different before I saw that. How can people claim to be good—how can they sit and eat supper with their families—and then bay for the blood of a harmless woman?'

Esher glanced back over her shoulder to the apprentices.

'Keep your voice down.' She looked to find Liara, who was being quizzed by Ovitus but had her eyes closed too. She noted her proximity. 'Ride ahead with me.'

She didn't explain further, but urged her mount to trot along the road. My riding had improved, but I hated the rise and fall of the trot, thumping down against the saddle.

'What are we doing out front?' I asked.

'Getting out of Liara's earshot.' Esher glanced about to ensure we were distant enough. 'If she opens her Gate, she'll pick out our words like bells ringing by her ears. Her family has a difficult history where grave-sight is concerned.'

'Liara's does?'

'It was years ago now, but her clan history is a boulder tied around her neck. Liara's father was Van Kaldhoone of Clan LacShale. He commanded the Fourth Gate, as powerful as Ulovar. Maybe the fifth or sixth most powerful Draoihn in Harran.' She lowered her voice yet further, barely even a whisper. 'But he committed the Sarathi rites, and began to speak to the dead. It's dangerous enough among the populace, but for Draoihn, it's the path to Skal.'

'Skal?'

'The Sixth Gate. The trance of death. You've seen what the Fifth Gate, Vie, allows the grandmaster to do. She reshapes her body as she wishes, and she's practically immortal. No Draoihn can possess both the Fifth and Sixth Gates. They diverge, life and death.' She took a deep breath. 'Liara's father was not Sarathi, nor did he seek the Sixth Gate. But when he learned how to speak to the dead, he began to walk that path. So Ulovar and the council captured him and put him to death. He'd murdered a man too, but that wasn't really the problem.'

'Then what was?'

The scar in my mind had cut me off from grief for the fallen. It had done more than that, perhaps, because I knew I should have felt afraid. It was like being told I had the makings of a murderer, or worse. I possessed the grave-sight. Was there a Sixth Gate at the back of my mind, waiting to be opened? It seemed an impossible dream. The Draoihn wouldn't even train me to open the First reliably, and would never show me the Second.

'Redwinter has no choice but to remove those that see the dead, because we cannot risk infiltration by the Sarathi.' She almost sounded proud of it, maybe just proud to be counted as Draoihn. Her mother had been born to the poorest of streets, after all. 'Ciuthach was Sarathi once. You've seen how terrible he would have been.'

'And that's what Liara's father was trying to become?'

'No. They never said that of him, anyway,' Esher said. She glanced back towards Liara again. 'The Sarathi are true servants of the Night Below, but the grave-sight is the first step along that path. There hasn't been a Sarathi in Redwinter since the Council of Night and Day unmasked Unthayla the Damned in 456. Liara's father was consumed with jealousy and grief. There was a murder—his mistress, it's rumoured. He spoke to her ghost, found the man who had killed her—her husband—and used the Fourth Gate to make him dive beneath a team of horses.'

'Sounds fair enough to me,' I said. But I thought of what I'd asked Ulovar that night he sat drinking atop the tower, whether he could command a person that way.

I have never tried, nor will I ever.

But maybe he could.

'The man he killed was just a cutler. Van Kaldhoone would likely have got away with it,' Esher said. Like Castus, he was beyond the law. 'But he'd stated before witnesses—Draoihn witnesses—that his mistress had identified her killer from beyond the grave. Was it true? Who's to know? But Grandmaster

Robilar took swift action against him. And he was a *Lord Draoihn*. There are only four Draoihn of the Fourth Gate left in all of Harran, now.'

'What happened to him?'

'He fought the council, when they went to arrest him,' Sanvaunt said. 'Robilar, Ulovar, Hanaqin. The battle brought down half a street. But they took him alive, tried him, and he was blinded, broken, and thrown into the harbour, to sink and rot with the rubbish. The grandmaster made a warning out of it.'

'You sound like you admire her,' I said.

'Of course I do,' Esher said. 'She's incredible. Only two living Draoihn have ever achieved Vie, the Fifth Gate. She's the most powerful woman in Harran.'

'But the woman I saw killed, she wasn't going to access the Gates, or sign up to become Sarathi and hurt people. She was just mourning a dead child.'

'To be Draoihn is not easy. No risks can be taken, even when it leads to the taking of life,' Esher said. 'Is that what's bothering you? About what you saw?'

'No,' I said. But I couldn't tell her the truth. That I'd begun to feel, as broken and torn apart as I might have been, that I could find a way to be content in Redwinter. That I'd begun to let friendship work its way into my veins. But how could Esher and Liara, even Ovitus, be my friends, if they would kill me over something I'd never chosen, or wanted, or even understood?

Esher sighed.

'Maybe you're fortunate that the grandmaster didn't accept you,' she said. 'When you swear your life to Redwinter, you act for the realm and the Crown. Everything else is dust. They gave me a life here, a life far better than I could ever dream of. But there comes a price, Fiahd. With everything there comes a price.'

 · · · · · ·

The journey couldn't fail to bring back memories of the last long journey I had made, the trip south from Dalnesse and the desolation we had left behind. When I tried to turn my thoughts back to the north, they wouldn't focus. There was a void, and the ridge of scarring, which felt like a desolate, barren plain where nothing would grow. There was something beyond it. A better world, maybe, or a worse one. I felt only a vague frustration that I was unable to think on it properly, but even that feeling was tired and grey. Whereas, I saw Ovitus's face light up whenever Liara gave him a pleasant acknowledgement. It was so easy for him to be happy.

There was nothing but a sluggish stream to denote that we were entering LacNaithe lands. The people looked the same; the wheels of the watermill churned icy water in the same lazy circles. Ovitus stopped to talk to them regularly, listening to stories of flooded fields, reports of stray dogs and rumours of mistcats in the woods. Some of them brought their children to see the fine lord passing by, which seemed to make him nervous, as though he might break the babes they placed in his arms, but whenever they did, he left them with a stack of coins for the child's future. It was easy to see why they courted his affection, and a more cynical watcher might have thought he was handing out coins as bribes, but he didn't have that sort of guile. He gave because he thought it was the right thing to do.

I had known that Ovitus was the LacNaithe clan heir, but Uloss Castle put that revelation into a new light. Though lacking the sheer size of the king's castle in Harranir, it was a seat not just of wealth, but of power. Massive black stone towers rose like tyrants from the gentle countryside, long stretches of toothy crenulations between them. A small town sat in the shadow of the towers and beyond the walls, a vast keep. Ulovar's greathouse at Redwinter was astonishing, but seeing this was like taking a plunge into a cold pool. I looked at the dreamer riding alongside me and wondered how Ovitus could ever be lord of such grandeur. This place demanded strength, and for all that I'd grown fond of him, I couldn't see Ovitus cutting a kingly posture.

A troop of soldiers, clean-shaven and pristine in green-and-black uniforms, met us along the road to ceremonially escort us to the castle gates, LacNaithe wyverns pinned to green-and-black breacan cloaks. A blare of trumpet song announced the van-to-be's homecoming.

· · · · · ·

'We're not going on to Valarane today?' I asked Ovitus as we drank cider in the main hall.

'Don't be sad,' he said with a burp, then bit into a piece of meat that had been cooked so long all the red goodness inside had turned grey. He enjoyed eating, but everything he ate had to be cooked until it tasted of nothing at all. 'There are a lot of steps up to Valarane. Sanvaunt can go and visit the monks. I've been asked to deal with some local business.' He waved at a nearby servant, whose name I'd not learned yet, and ordered bread and butter. I figured that if someone was being good enough to bring you food, the least you can do was ask their name.

'Have they told you what it's about?' I asked.

'No. Monks keep their mouths shut. I only know that they think it's urgent. Hard to see what a bunch of monks are having such a hard time with.'

'Don't get too comfortable,' Sanvaunt said, stooping as he ducked through one of the six doorways. He was dressed casually, out of his usual heavy dark red coat for once. He wore a simple white shirt, dark breeches, a bracelet of flat wooden beads wrapped half a dozen times around his left wrist. He presented a different face here, inside the walls he had grown up in. 'There are a lot of steps at Valarane.'

'I was just saying that,' Ovitus agreed through a mouthful of cheese, and Sanvaunt actually cracked a smile. He had been sleeping more on the road. I hadn't seen the flask of rose-thistle lately, and he looked better for it.

'If duty was easy we'd call it leisure,' Sanvaunt said. 'Feels good to be back, though, doesn't it? I haven't been here in three years. But it's all the same. Nothing has changed. Old Miller's still bossing the kitchen about like a field marshal, and the kennel hounds still try to lick your face off.'

'You sound like you miss it,' I said. 'I thought your life was all about Redwinter and duty.'

'It is,' he said. My little barb had failed to strike home. Needling him was becoming a bad habit. 'We grew up here. Ulovir and Ulovaine roaring around, smashing everything they could put a wooden sword to. Ulovar had boys, both his sisters had boys. I sometimes wondered if Hazia was fostered here to redress the balance.' He turned to Ovitus. 'Do you want me to take flowers? The winter garden is full of goldenrod and aster.'

'I suppose,' Ovitus said.

'Are you trying to woo the monks?' I asked. 'Because they're sworn to lives of chastity and inward thinking—'

'My parents are buried there,' Ovitus interrupted. 'Not everything's a joke, Raine.'

'I'm sorry,' I said, though mostly as a reflex. Even if I didn't feel the pain of the losses I'd taken, I could see them pinking Ovitus's cheeks. 'Truly.'

'The business I've been asked to conduct doesn't allow me to visit them,' Ovitus said, pushing his chair back. He'd left food uneaten on his plate. A first. 'Say a prayer for me.'

He left the room, shutting the door quietly behind him. I felt like I'd just doused the wrong person with a bucket of ice water.

'That wasn't your fault,' Sanvaunt said. 'He's still grieving.'

'How long has it been?'

'Not long enough,' he said. 'He'll be all right. He doesn't show it often, but it's still raw for him.'

'He should go with you.'

Sanvaunt stared towards the door Ovitus had left through.

'No,' he said wearily. 'It's not how he deals with it. Some people want to feel close to the dead. Others want to rage, and some would rather cry in their own space.'

'Nothing wrong with crying,' I said.

'We each choose our masks,' Sanvaunt said. 'Like you do. With your voice.'

'What about my voice?'

'You make it higher when there are other men around.'

I put a hand to my lips as though they'd somehow betrayed me. It was a habit that I'd grown so accustomed to that I didn't even think about it. But I didn't do it around Sanvaunt. I'd always spoken to him in my natural register. Strange, that.

'I just think Ovitus should cry if he needs to.'

Sanvaunt shrugged.

'Nobody can tell you how to deal with loss, or how you ought to feel about it.'

He stopped, suddenly nervous. He had to know what Ulovar had done to me: Ulovar trusted Sanvaunt, would have told him how he'd laid the scar across my mind. The atmosphere turned uncomfortable, and I made my excuses to leave the room, but I'd only passed down a couple of the ridiculously long corridors when I realised that I'd left my scarf on the table. I stepped back into the room to see Sanvaunt with that tattered old book in front of him, stained where he'd spilled ink across it, a pen in his hand. He shut it as he looked up at me. Like I'd caught him doing something that he shouldn't.

'Forgot my scarf,' I said. I was painfully aware of the sound of my own voice.

'I'll see you later, Miss Raine.'

· · · · · · ·

Rain lashed the castle that night. Sanvaunt retired early, and didn't even insist on history or religious verses during supper. This place suited him better than Redwinter, I thought. Perhaps the crushing sense of obligation was lessened here. My duties were certainly lessened, to nil, as the castle's own small army flurried through the corridors. I didn't even have to wait on the apprentices here. Somehow I still found myself in the dining room at mealtimes, sitting slightly to one side, not quite high enough to be one of them, not quite low enough to banish.

They were different, without Ulovar or Sanvaunt around. They laughed, threw things at each other in good-natured play. Jathan flirted outrageously with all the girls, and they gave it back easily enough, but I didn't think there was any real intention behind it. Not on the girls' part, at least. Ovitus was subdued, slumped in a corner of the room. He watched the others talking, laughing, listened to the rain as it spattered the windowpanes. Sometimes he frustrated me, seemingly oblivious to everything that was happening around him, but then his moments of melancholy reminded me of a person I had once been, cut off from those around me and desperately hurting inside.

'You're quiet tonight,' I said as I took a seat beside him. Liara was trying to sneak carrots down the back of Jathan's shirt, and Ovitus's eyes were locked on the pair of them, his face stony.

'It has been a long ride,' he said. There was an edge to his voice. A shadow beneath his eyes. I didn't like it. I tried to think of something that could distract him.

'This will all be yours one day, won't it?' I said.

'It doesn't matter much who the castle belongs to,' Ovitus said. 'I don't intend to live here.'

'I don't mean the castle,' I said. 'I mean the people. The other apprentices, they'll be yours. The servants and the soldiers, those people we passed in the fields, even the monks at Valarane. They'll be yours, when you're van.'

'I will belong to them, and they will belong to me. Sometimes I think I'd rather take a vow and wander off into the mountains to live as a hermit.'

'We're all bound to something, though, aren't we?' I said. 'By family, clan, Redwinter, even by the Crown. Nobody really belongs to themselves.' It was only after I said it that I realised that I was wrong about that. I didn't belong to anyone, or anywhere.

Ovitus smiled, a soft, sad expression on a soft, sad face. 'Have you been reading philosophy?' he asked. I shook my head. '"Man is ever bound by obligations, but to lose them gives no freedom but abandonment." That's Eudiricles. He was saying that it's our bonds to others that allow us freedom, that to be without ties is to be floating in chaos. Man must seek out obligations if he is to be whole.'

'Sounds good for those at the top,' I said.

'Doubtless,' Ovitus said, his smile widening. 'After all, Eudiricles was a king.' The softness left him as he looked back at Liara, who had risen from the table and was making her exit. Jathan hurled a carrot at the back of her head. 'What do you think she sees in Jathan?'

It was a trap of words. I knew from past experience that in this mood, Ovitus would dismiss whatever I said as having no value. I had heard Lochlan complain about a girl he loved often enough, a girl I had always suspected was me. But now, with the scar in my mind dividing me from those old, weak feelings, guessing what would hurt Ovitus's feelings was something I could navigate only by experience, not through feeling.

I knew what he wanted to hear: that there was nothing to see in Jathan. But that would only push his moping deeper.

Instead I decided to tell him a truth that I thought would be good for him.

'Jathan is handsome. He runs after dawnsong, and that's attractive. He's confident, isn't afraid of what she'll say. And he flirts with every girl he meets. If he really wanted anything more, he'd be upfront about it.'

'And you, Raine?' he asked. 'Is that what you think makes a man attractive? Not a kind heart, not being supportive, not being thoughtful? It's running aimlessly around the grounds and a pretty face.'

And there was the trap, sprung. Braithe would have baited it differently, and would never have allowed an implication that he wasn't a perfect man. But the sentiment was the same. *Admit that I'm the best man. Admit that I'm being wronged.*

'Ovitus,' I said, not gently. 'With all the respect due to a future van, who may one day dismiss me from whatever position I hold within your clan, those are not things that should make someone love another person. Being kind, supportive and thoughtful are the minimum level of expectation we should have for anybody.'

'So do you think he's attractive?'

The words I had carefully selected and spoken with good intentions had been firmly ignored.

'You spent the journey from Dalnesse describing Liara's flaming locks, her glowing eyes, and how skilled she is at Draoihn work. It's not one rule for you and another for everyone else.'

'So you think I'm ugly?'

This was going nowhere. I stood up and made my way from the room. A hand on my arm stopped me just past the door.

'Hey, Fiahd, what's bringing down that storm on your face?' Esher was a little merry, her cheeks rosed by southern wine. Since the colour storm, sometimes I still got caught up in colours.

'It's nothing,' I said.

'I'm glad I caught you. Want to see something fun?' She was pulling on a woollen hat, packing her hair beneath it.

Anything had to be more fun than Ovitus and his moping.

'So long as it's anywhere but in there, yes.' She took another hat and pulled it over my white hair.

'Come on!'

She took my hand in hers and began to run through the corridors. The castle was vast, and its corridors were long and made for dashing through. She released her grasp as we reached a spiral staircase, hammering down it in a joyous dash, but took it up again as we reached the lower floors. I had not been down here before.

'Where are we going?'

'You'll see!'

'What are the hats for?'

'So we won't distract her!'

In a subterranean level of the castle, a huge hall opened up. It was alive with smells of cooking, musky herbs, roast meat, baked bread. She'd brought me down to the kitchen. A cluster of retainers, fifth and fourth rankers mostly by the cut of their collars, lounged on the benches or sat on the long, knife-scarred tables, all facing the hearth. Up on a stage of stacked pallets, lit by the firelight, Liara LacShale stood over them, a ladle in one hand. A roar of laughter ushered from the servants.

'What's she doing?'

'Come on, find a space,' Esher said. She pulled me along, and we settled in on the edge of the gathering, behind a pair of broad-backed stable hands. 'Just listen!' The assembled castle staff were grinning, watching her with tankards of ale in hand.

'Don't even get me started on the monks. Have you seen the way they walk at night?' she said. She stuck her rear out and began shuffling backward along the crates. 'Hard to see where you're going that way, isn't it? Especially in the dark.' She straightened up. 'I mean, it's hard for the monks too. They're doing us all a favour aren't they?' She paused, giving her audience a very serious look. 'I mean, they think they are. They think it'll be much easier for the rest of us to see, given that the sun shines out of their arseholes.'

The servants laughed, and Esher laughed, and I was caught up in laughing with them.

'What *is* this?' I said. I was grinning. Actually grinning. 'What on earth is going on here?'

'What about farmers?' one of the scullery girls called out.

'Farmers? I have to be careful what I say about farmers,' Liara said. 'I'm a posh rich girl, aren't I. So I'll only talk about rich farmers. Not good solid farmhands, we all know they do a hard job. So. Farming—what do I know about farming?' Another pause for dramatic effect. 'Well, there's the mud. Do you ever look at a man who owns a farm and think, how did you *actually* get mud on you? It's not like they went out in the fields and did any digging, is it? So there they are, sitting indoors, counting up all the work other people have done, and somehow at the end of the day they always have this big old smear of mud across their face. I mean, how do you get all covered in mud without ever going outdoors? Let me tell you a little secret. People who don't actually do any work all carry a little jar of mud around. Smear it on their faces so you think they've actually been into their own fields. Imagine the nerve.'

She had the measure of her audience perfectly . . . and they howled with laughter as she took out a jar of mud and began to apply it daintily like a glamour.

Liara LacShale was shaped largely like an apple. Her hair was not the flaming glory that Ovitus had been so emphatic about, but a thin, unruly orange. But on that stage of crates, she glowed. Mesmerising.

'Look at them,' I whispered to Esher. 'They adore her.'

'She's wonderful,' Esher said. 'You could be funny like her if you weren't such a sourpuss.'

I kicked Esher under the bench with my heel. She elbowed me in the arm. We were both spellbound by this girl who had become something glorious on the stage.

'And don't get me started on the millers!' Liara said. She began to turn around in slow circles, her arms outstretched.

'Does she do this often?' I asked.

'Whenever she can get away from her duties,' Esher said.

'How long has this been happening for?'

'A couple of years, I think. She doesn't mind me watching, but sometimes she gets nervous if she knows the audience. Hence the hats. We're in disguise.'

I reached over and pulled Esher's woollen hat down over her face. Without pulling it back up, she reached back and did the same to me. I kicked her under the table again, and she retaliated, and suddenly we were wrestling on the bench, legs and feet dancing like snakes. And then they settled, and my leg was just behind hers, my ankle resting up against the back of Esher's leg. It stayed there. I was hat-blind, and my heart was pounding, and there had been wine. I pressed my leg slightly against Esher's, and it pressed back.

I drew the hat up. Esher had too and she was staring resolutely ahead at Liara, not looking at me, her face hidden behind a wall of hair. I fixed my eyes ahead. Light Above, my heart was pounding so hard it would have drowned out any First Gate trance. Where had my breath gone? No, why was my breath coming so fast?

Esher put her hand in mine, and I nearly made a noise of alarm. I flinched, and she began to withdraw, only that was the last thing I wanted, so I reached back and took it solidly in mine. Firm but gentle.

'. . . and that's where millstones come from,' Liara said. The audience bellowed its appreciation, but even the stable hands in front of us seemed distant.

'Fiahd,' Esher said, so quietly that I could barely hear her. 'I really like you.'

'I really like you too.'

There is something we're born with that tells us how to know when to lean forwards, which way to tilt your head. Nothing had ever been so clear to me, not even in the midst of a trance. The soft strands of her hair escaping the hat. The curve of her jaw, the white of her blind eye. I tilted my head.

The audience erupted into cheers and jumped off the tables, banging mugs and yelling their applause. The moment was shattered as one of the stable hands knocked into the table. Esher untilted, her face so red it could have averted a colour storm all by itself. The moment could have gone in any direction, teetered on the edge of disaster. And then at some unspoken signal between us we both burst into laughter. We hugged each other, fierce and warm and happy, and then we stood and joined in the applause for Liara.

As she descended the stage, a young man with gardener's hands made his bid to be the first to get a mug of ale to her. He was not the only young man that wanted to talk to her. She accepted the ale, declined everything else being offered, and strode towards us like a queen.

'You two! You're not meant to be here!'

'You were amazing!' Esher crowed, and threw her arms around her friend.

'You really were.'

We lifted a couple of bottles of whisky from the van's private cellar and went and got thoroughly drunk in Liara's room, and we laughed and talked, and perhaps there was something that I belonged to after all. That moment in the kitchen, the intense sense of closeness, of fun, of wonder, disappeared into the general bright spirits. It was easy to forget, in Redwinter's world of swords and threat, that we were only seventeen, and on some nights that needed to be embraced, and celebrated.

Valarane lay a half day's ride further south, but we were late setting out from Ulovar's mighty castle. The after-tang of whisky clogged my mouth to honeyed sweetness, a harsh rhythm of punches bashing away in my head. It had been a long night, and I'd felt no reason either to retire to bed or to stop drinking. I had snatched a couple of hours of sleep, but it had not been enough.

Sanvaunt had bags of winter-blooming flowers on his saddle, bright yellows and lush purples, a thrust of colour in the bleak, late-year landscape. We rode out from Uloss along the road to Valarane, passing a couple of farmers bringing carts full of food towards the castle. Ovitus didn't stop to talk to them, declaring he was likely to throw up, and his vomit-prophecy proved true before we were another hour down the road. We cut into thick forest, dense pines that had held their needles beyond the season's turn. I listened for snatterkin, the hidden folk and other things I sometimes heard on the path up to Redwinter, but if there were any here, then they were silent that day.

'Late night?' Sanvaunt said. He was not impressed.

'I'm never drinking again,' Ovitus moaned.

'Not until the next time,' I agreed. Sanvaunt didn't smile, and when the time came for our paths to split, he said nothing and rode away in silence.

'All this will be yours one day,' I said as we rode through winter fields, empty but for the birds. I still found it hard to take in the scale of the lands that Ovitus would rule. Ulovar just fitted right in: it was hard to imagine him as anything other than a clan leader. Ovitus seemed too unsure of himself, too eager to please. Nobody wanted an indecisive, easily led lord.

'It shouldn't be,' Ovitus grumbled, shielding his eyes from the cold winter light. 'Ulovar or Ulovaine ought to have had it, not me. Even my wildrose cousin would be a better choice. But he can't inherit, so I'm stuck with it. I've no stomach for it.' He had little stomach for cider either, I thought as we dismounted for him to retch noisily at the side of the road.

'I don't think you should call him that when he's not around,' I said.

'He gets to be handsome and charming, and gives us orders even though I'll be his clan lord one day. He can take it.'

'Is that what you call me when I'm not around too?'

'No, of course not. It doesn't matter who your parents were. It just pays for him to remember his place sometimes.'

'Like when he's not here and can't hear you?'

Ovitus shrugged. He looked likely to throw up again, and I hadn't the head for an argument.

'Will you govern from here, or from Redwinter like your uncle?' I said.

'From a nice cosy manor, I hope,' Ovitus said, wiping his mouth on a long shirtsleeve. 'Light Above, I feel like I could bring up my whole innards.' A few moments later, he nearly did.

Our health must have appeared questionable when we arrived, pale and clammy, at Thail Halman's estate. He resided in a fortified manor, with a big central hall with two storeys and a scattering of well-to-do farm buildings around it. There were no guards on duty at the gate—so deep into peaceful land it would be wasteful to employ men to simply stand around—but we were greeted by Halman's daughter, Halfera, a woman a few years our senior. She presented herself in a long blue dress, her auburn hair long down her back. The top laces of her straining bodice had come undone.

'My father is unwell,' she said. 'I'm afraid he suffers with stomach pains very often of late. Please, allow me to extend our hospitality.'

The wine we were served was not as good as Ulovar's cellarer had provided, but it washed the odious flavour of the previous night from my gums and teeth all the same. We ate bread with salt as was customary, and then asked when we might be able to speak to him.

'I understand that there's, er, some sort of problem with some, er, pastureland,' Ovitus said. Our hostess dismissed the servants and sat down across the table from him, her bodice and laces now distracting. Pointing it out would have been crass, so I just tried to keep my eyes on her face. My efforts to stay focused met with varying degrees of success, since the bright green of her eyes were barely less entrancing, like the coloured glass in Ulovar's windows.

'Did land ever change hands without somebody being unhappy about it?' she said with a sigh. 'I'm sure you must have experienced such pains yourself, my lord.' If Ovitus caught the hint of derision emanating from between her fine and very straight teeth, he gave no indication.

'What precisely is the problem?'

'I'm not sure what words were exchanged, exactly,' Halfera said. 'We acquired some land from Reeve Jon. It's good land. We intend to graze cattle there.'

'Reeve Jon indicated that there was some measure of unfairness, and violence, involved,' Ovitus said.

That was a considerable understatement. Ulovar had shown us the reeve's written correspondence, which accused Halman of having taken the land by force and murdering two of his men in the process. Halfera didn't blink.

'You're talking about his two shepherds? They disappeared, I'm told. I'd wager they ran away with some of the reeve's sheep, herded them off in the night and probably sold them down the river to the unscrupulous swine in Lagnesse. It happens sometimes. As the reeve it's Jon's duty to investigate such crimes. Have you met him?'

'Not yet,' Ovitus said. He seemed flustered. Though she couldn't be much more than twenty-two or twenty-three, Halfera was used to giving commands and being obeyed. I thought she had the situation entirely in her control, and the conversation was bending to her whim. Ovitus's difficulty in conversing with her was obvious, and I had the feeling Halfera's distracting bodice was deliberate.

'Jon's an obnoxious man,' she said. 'He thinks far too much of himself. He couldn't even imagine that some of his men might let him down like that. But it's all too common these days isn't it?'

'How does losing his flock affect the sale of the land, my lady?' I asked. Halfera turned her beautiful eyes on me.

'They are separate issues, as you note. When he lost his flock, he had debts he was unable to settle. My father paid those debts for him and took the land from his hands in exchange. I'll not deny, that was a fraction of its value. It's hardly surprising that Jon now regrets the agreement, but it's hardly something worth your time.'

I liked this woman. She was clever, and she thrummed with an intensity that wakened something in me, dragged across the wasteland that halved my mind. Bright, genteel, but cut from steel. Halfera reminded me of Castus Lac-Clune, although she wasn't as likely to open the throats of abusive drunkards. I smiled to myself; or maybe she was.

We stayed the night in Halman's hall without meeting him, his stomach pains keeping him abed. Ovitus and I had separate rooms, a luxury to have such guest chambers available even in such a large manor, and I'd just climbed into bed when there was a tap at the door. I called to enter, and a woman stepped into the room carrying a single-stemmed candelabra with a wavy light. She had to be thirty or older and wore a fur robe. Her hair was loose around her shoulders.

'Is the room to your satisfaction, lady?' she asked.

'Everything is fine,' I said. I expected her to leave right away, but she lingered. Then she crossed the room, knelt before me and pushed back her robe.

There was nothing beneath it but a nakedness that closed my throat. My whole body went stiff.

'Would you do me the honour of offering me your night-gift, lady?' She cast her eyes down, but her tone was husky, nothing meek about it at all.

I would have crawled up the wall and away into the thatch if I'd been able to. Instead, I dragged the rough blankets to my neck, as though they were a shield, and not a very strong one. Redwinter's quartermaster had told me of this custom, but the brazenness of it shocked me. I had never believed it would happen to me.

'What do you think you're doing?' I stammered. Something in my voice stopped her.

'I— It's the night-gift, my lady.' But she could see by the terrified-rabbit expression on my face that I had not expected this. 'Am I right in thinking, my lady, that you are training at Redwinter and that one day you will be Draoihn?' She had the southland peasant accent, her words lilting. Her face was sharp-boned, narrow. Dark hair framed knowing eyes and a coy curl of lip.

My thoughts had turned to quivering jelly, hammering randomly in a dozen different directions until none of them made sense as she gently reached up to stroke her fingers down the back of my hand. The breeze-soft touch of her fingers was like flame, like soft wind, like warm honey. Nothing at all like the way that Braithe had touched me. I could smell her, dried flowers and candle wax. When had the whole room grown so unbearably hot?

'No,' I managed to choke out. 'I'm just a retainer.'

'Oh,' the woman said. Her hand snapped back and she dragged her robe around her shoulders. A fleeting shadow of relief crossing her face and was gone. 'I'm so sorry. I'm so sorry, please don't mention this to Lady Halfera.'

'I won't say anything,' I said, my voice a strained whisper.

I lay awake for a while, wishing that people could stop making me feel so burningly confused. What did she think was going to happen? That magic was going to rub off onto her fingers? Maybe Ovitus had a woman in his room as well. I tried to listen but could hear nothing through the cut stone wall, and then felt icky for having tried. I hoped not. Everything about the concept seemed wrong.

· · · · · ·

A sullen dawn promised more rain and the sky hung heavy and expectant, but the moment there was light I dressed and hauled Ovitus from his bed to set out for the reeve's farm. As a law-keeper appointed by Ulovar, Jon monitored an area of land held by the thails, but he still made his living on a croft. It was an old system, separating the concerns of legality from the business of ensuring that the land prospered and it was designed to keep the thails honest. In practice the thails had the men, and they had the money for the bribes, and that Halman had not simply bribed his way out of this trouble suggested to Ovitus that something was amiss.

Halfera waved us off and had provided a man to guide us, dark haired with a thick jaw and thicker wrists. His name was Ollan. He was brawny and gruff, and wouldn't have looked out of place hammering iron at an anvil. He told us he'd served Van Kaldhoone LacShale before his execution for grave-speaking. When Van Kaldhoone had been cast down, many of those old retainers had moved to less-sullied lords. I guessed that he knew how to use the sword slung on his saddle better than he knew how to act around his future lord, spitting gobbets of phlegm and blowing his nose into his hand from time to time. I doubted that he would have been so disrespectful around Ulovar, but Ovitus seemed entirely oblivious, preoccupied with some other thought.

Jon's farmstead was four buildings, two halls, a barn and what could have passed for a townhouse, a symbol of past prosperity. The reeve himself was a skinny man of middle years without hair, beard or eyebrows. Ollan kept a distance as we approached. A feud is like a roasting pit, the fire brightest when first lit but getting hotter as the yellow flames sink to red embers. It would be important for LacNaithe, I thought, that this one be snuffed out.

'The bastards killed my men and stole my land,' Jon snarled after welcoming Ovitus and me into the out-of-place townhouse. He looked to Ovitus. 'Van Ulovar isn't coming, then?'

'He has asked me to adjudicate,' Ovitus said apologetically. 'The lady Halfera believes that your shepherds stole your flock.'

'Then she's just as much a liar as her father,' Jon said. 'Got her to talk to you, did he? He's a wily one. Hard to say no to those pretty eyes, isn't it? Those shepherds worked my land for more than ten years, and they have—they had—families here. I've had to put them out, of course, sent them off to relatives in the villages, since they can't pay their way. That old goat turd has ruined them as well. The land was mine. Halman has wanted it for years.'

'Is pasture in so much demand around here?' I asked.

'There's no end of stony fields, but good grazing land, with a watercourse? There's less of that than horse shit.' Halman said. His anger worked itself through the muscles of his rubbery face.

'Seems a lot of trouble to go to for some grass,' I said mildly.

'Grass means sheep, and sheep mean wool, milk and meat. You're not from around here, are you?'

'From the north,' I said.

'Maybe your land up there is better for it. Sheep need a lot of space, need to roam wide. And that means good pastureland. That old shit Halman stole my flock and had my men killed. Or maybe that daughter of his did. She's worse than her father: there's wolf fur beneath that dress.'

'Do you have any witnesses to the crime who can give oath?' Ovitus asked.

'Nobody saw it,' Jon said. 'If anyone had, I could have brought the charge direct. They did it deep in the night.'

'And then you sold the land to Halman?' Ovitus said with a frown. Jon looked bitter, his smooth hands rubbing together.

'Debts are a cursed thing,' he muttered. 'Got me a fool of a son too keen on gambling in Harranir. Supposed to be apprenticed to a lawyer and making money. Instead he spends his time losing mine. I had to pay off his debtors or see him lose an ear, and fool that I am, I'll not have him ruined that way.'

There didn't seem much more that we could learn from Jon; his account was more or less as Halfera had told us it would be. Ovitus suggested that we go and take a look at the land itself before any decisions were made. The brawny servant Halfera had sent with us, Ollan, had already ridden back home, so it was just the pair of us setting off again in the midafternoon.

'What will looking at a meadow tell us?' I asked. 'If there is a dispute here, it's about murder and sheep rustling.'

Ovitus shrugged. 'Not much, I suppose, but I didn't want to leave Jon thinking that the case was decided. We'll ride up there, look around and then head back to Halman's manor. Nobody saw anything, it's all just guesses and old rivalries. I doubt that either of them gave us the whole truth, and I expect this feud is the tail end of a grudge that won't settle, regardless of who owns a bit of grassland.'

'Maybe the shepherds really did steal Reeve Jon's flock?'

'Not if it meant their families getting turned out. And they'd have needed help to do it, someone to ship them far downriver. But there are any number of explanations. Maybe Jon got angry with them. Maybe they ran away together. Men who fall in love do that sometimes. Could be that Jon's made a complaint to try to salvage something from a bad situation.'

For once, I was impressed.

'You've a good mind for this,' I said. 'You should study the law.'

'I'm to be van,' Ovitus said glumly. 'I don't really have any choice.'

The directions we had been given were simple enough. We followed an overgrown path south for a way and then rode beside the stream until we reached the fallen tree that served as a bridge. Our next landmark was a fallon, alone in the meadow. Some ancient people, maybe the Faded, had thought it worth raising the tall pillar here. Now it stood alone, its importance lost through the ages, silently watching over the disputes of shepherds and thails.

'Something happened last night,' Ovitus told me. 'I've been wanting to tell you, but couldn't because that Ollan was with us.'

'Really?' I said, cocking an eyebrow. I had a sinking feeling.

'Yes,' he said, his face suddenly flushing crimson. 'Can you keep a secret?'

'Go on,' I said.

'A woman came to my bed last night,' he said. 'She wanted to—you know. She wanted to get in with me.'

'Really?' I said again.

'It's called the night-gift,' he said. 'I'd heard that it happens sometimes but I never thought it would happen to me. People try to sleep with Draoihn who pass through. And last night, it happened to me!'

I had expected as much. Ovitus's dreams of Liara were misguided, but there seemed something deeply wrong about accepting the night-gift. I'd had a lover, and he'd turned out cruel, and self-serving, but I'd chosen him because I liked him—liked what I knew of him, anyway. By the time I understood the kind of man he really was, I was already in too deep. I'd convinced myself that I loved him. I didn't believe you had to be in love to enjoy someone else's bed, but it seemed right that you shared it because you wanted to, not using it as a means to some other end, the act itself irrelevant. If I wanted to bed someone, I wanted them to want it too.

'I see,' I said.

'I know it wasn't about me,' Ovitus went on. 'It's just old superstition. They think that the trance-gift runs in bloodlines. It's why so many noblemen are Draoihn. If they have a child and that child is a Draoihn, then it's going to go to Redwinter. And that means their child will be powerful, and rich. Think about Adanost, Jathan and Gelis. When my uncle discovered their abilities, he paid their families a small fortune.'

Esher had told me about her mother, once a bartender in an Ashium den, now running a kitchen in the city. Ulovar's buyout. Building his little army.

'So how was it?' I asked through my teeth.

'I don't know,' Ovitus said. 'I turned her down.'

'You did?' And although he'd been bragging, I felt relieved.

'I'm saving myself,' he said, turning his face away to avoid any ridicule in my eyes. It was clear to me who he was saving himself for, and he was going to be waiting a long time. Maybe forever. I said nothing, letting the hoof-falls fill the silence. Ovitus kept glancing at me expectantly, waiting for me to talk.

'That's good,' I said at last.

'Have—I mean, you've—before, I mean?'

'Yes,' I said flatly.

'Who was . . . ?' Ovitus's voice trailed away. He realised as he spoke that any former lover of mine was most likely dead.

'It doesn't matter,' I said. 'He hurt me, in the end.' I felt that barren plain stretch out, spreading numbness within me, a cold, hard emptiness that filled me stronger than ever. Braithe was across that plain, with Lochlan, Sister Marthella, all of them. I wasn't stupid: I knew I'd only been a moment from kissing Esher in the kitchen. What would that have done to our friendship? I felt myself withdrawing from it, contracting like a caterpillar weaving its cocoon. Better to let those feelings lie safely across the scar. Better not to feel at all. Ovitus said no more about it, but his silence was just a mirror to the silence in my mind.

The meadows were peaceful in the dimming light of late afternoon. A man with a pair of shaggy dogs was visible in the distance, minding cattle. We passed by the fallon, the ancient obelisk thirty feet high, impenetrable yellow-grey not-stone. It stood sentinel over the dispute, a silent, impartial arbiter from the dawn of time. If it could talk, I thought, perhaps this would be easier to resolve. We sat in the lee of the pillar to take a little dried meat and small beer. The sky had held its load of rain so far, but now the lightest spots began to spit down onto my face.

'We should ride back,' I suggested.

'Wait,' Ovitus said quietly. 'Don't turn too fast. Someone's watching us.'

I remained still, though I wanted to turn.

'Where?'

'Over by those trees.'

A feeling similar to that I had experienced back in the tavern when the fight was about to start rose from the pit of my belly. I turned casually, thought I caught a glimpse of something moving in the distant woods. I couldn't be sure. A man who doesn't want to be seen is either embarrassed or dangerous. The wind blew cold, rustling the bare branches. I had a knife, and Ovitus wore his sword, but I didn't think anyone would trouble us here—not on LacNaithe land.

'If we're worth watching, then must be something here worth finding,' Ovitus said. His face had turned grave, more focused than I'd seen him before. 'I won't have the law broken on my land. Not right under my nose. These little lords will respect me.'

'Then what now?'

'Now we find out what they're hiding, and we make an example of them.'

'There are only a few hours of light left,' I said. 'Which way?'

'Let's split up,' Ovitus said, 'Ride around the tree line and see if there's anything amiss. I can't think there would be, but if that was Ollan, then perhaps Halman is nervous about something.'

'Or his daughter is. But what could there be? This is all just grass and woodland. Is there good hunting here?'

'Nothing out of the ordinary. Just deer, boar and the like, that I know of. We'll meet back here in an hour.'

I paid attention to the space around me as I rode, the insects, the mice in the grass and the wood pigeons calling from the trees. I had missed the wildness of the open country, and though the LacNaithe lands were crossed with fences, stone walls and hedges, something of the wild woods around Dunan resonated here. South splashed through a small stream, sending a pair of water voles scurrying for cover.

I was turning to ride back when I saw the ghosts. There were two of them, which was unusual in itself, especially out here in the country. Harranir was rife with ghosts, the people packed tight as cargo, but I'd seen none since we rode south. These two were wandering, adult, male, their forms tinged green and misty. One of them sat down on a stump at the edge of a copse of trees, holding its ghostly head in vaporous hands. I glanced around. Aside from the dead, I was all alone. I didn't fear them. They were just dead. But I had no doubt that these were Reeve Jon's shepherds. It was too great a coincidence otherwise, and the certainty of their deaths changed everything. Momentarily I thought of riding to find Ovitus, before sense and the harsh lesson that Veretaine had taught me quashed that idea. What would I say? If even Liara's father, a van of Clan LacShale, had been executed for the grave-sight, it was nothing that I could ever admit to. I needed evidence. And though I had never managed to learn much about why I saw the dead, I did know that ghosts first appeared where they died, tied to their bones. Only the Queen of Feathers had appeared to me in different places, and I couldn't say what she was at all.

They didn't see me, and nor had I expected them to. They stood blind and mute, wraiths among the trees. I approached, looking for some sign of them. Something that could help Ovitus.

'Where are your bones?' I muttered to myself. I didn't expect a reply. The dead couldn't hear the living. It had seemed like Lochlan had tried to speak to me, right after he died, but my mind had been reeling, caught up in the death throes of the Raine-that-was.

One of the ghosts raised its hand, as if it could grasp something falling from the sky. It looked so substantial to me. So real. Then it turned towards me, and its face changed. Its jaw distended, widened as it faced me directly and screamed, striding forwards with rapid, jerking steps. The shock of it brought out instinct.

'Back!'

I put my hand out before me as the screaming spirit stalked forwards. A shock of cold ran through my fingers, and I recoiled. But for a moment it was as though I'd touched something real. Not just vapour and imagination. Something true. The ghost had gone still, its unhappy, dead face looking down at the cold, winter-hard dirt. I kept my hand up between us. The ghost's fingers looked denser. More *there*, somehow. Slowly I reached out to it again, and the spur of cold wasn't so fierce this time. Something bled from me into the ghost-shepherd, flowing through his arm. The cold spread up, through my own. My lips turned cold; the back of my eyes seemed to chill.

'Here,' it said suddenly, looking me in the eye.

It saw me. It knew I was there.

This was wrong, all wrong. I had no reason to fear the dead. They were strange and often made no sense, but I'd grown up seeing them, and they had never been able to hurt me. Now I felt the grave's own cold in my fingers, my arm, inside my head. It was surely no coincidence that this ghost appeared to answer me, that its eyes stayed locked on me. There was so much grief there. I shook my hand, but the cold wasn't from lack of blood flow. I'd given this lost soul something of myself. Offered it a toehold in our world, and it had used it to speak that word: 'Here.'

'Show me,' I said. But whatever I'd done had already faded, and it returned to aimless wandering. I shivered. I wasn't going to inflict that painful cold on myself again. This was what awaited the unhappy dead, a void of scream-ing and invisible, lonely wandering. I scanned the grass again, but there was nothing here but sheep droppings and thistles. The nearby copse was grey and still smelled sweetly of decaying leaves, though winter had turned the ground hard. But there was evidence of old tracks here. Braithe had taught me to hunt, and now that I knew to look, I could see where the bodies had been dragged, could identify the disturbed earth. A hastily dug grave, marked only by some earth still heaped beside it, was obvious to my eyes now.

I found a flat stone to dig with, and it didn't take long to uncover mouldering cloth and rotten flesh a couple of inches beneath the surface. I didn't need to see any more. When I looked up, both of the ghosts were standing over me, looking sombrely at their final resting place. They faded, turning insubstantial, and then blew away on the wind. Perhaps they would be back later, or maybe seeing that someone knew what had happened to them was enough to send them on to the Afterworld. Good. I was glad they had gone. They had been murdered. The only questions now were by whom and why.

I rode back towards the obelisk as swiftly as I could and waited for Ovitus, flexing my fingers to shed the last of the deep cold. The lower the sun dipped, the more nervous I became. Ovitus wasn't one to want to ride in the dark, and it would take two hours to return to Halfera's hall. I shouldn't have left him alone. A putrid worm of discomfort began to uncurl in my belly. I waited as long as I could bear it, then scrawled a note for Ovitus, carved into a piece of rotting bark. It read 'Gone looking for you,' and I left it propped against the fallon before riding in the direction I'd seen him go.

Ovitus's horse was easy to follow. A big black mare called Guest, she left tracks driven deep into the mud. I followed the trail at a canter, hoping to find my friend riding towards me, but his path followed the tree line. Further hoof prints joined his, three pairs now crossing his and each other, all heading towards a log cabin standing close to a tree line. It was big, low, the lumber clean and newly cut, bark shingles across the roof. A new shelter for Halman's dead shepherds? There was no sign of Ovitus's horse beneath the lean-to stable. Horse tracks crossed the ground back and forth in a riot, and three large mounds of dark earth sat beside stacks of fresh cut wood.

I could no longer tell Guest's tracks easily from those of the other horses, and the paths around the cottage were well-trodden, but I knew he'd been here. No smoke rose from the chimney—in fact, there was no chimney, not even a smoke hole. My knock at the door was greeted with silence, and the windows were lightless behind the shutters. The door was locked. The belly-worm was growing larger by the minute, so I tried the shutters. They were latched from the inside, but one set was rattling and badly put together. Three hard blows with my palm smashed the light wooden latch away, and the shutter swung inwards.

I had anticipated a shepherd's hut, a simple one-room interior with a bed, table, chairs, maybe some shearing equipment. What I saw suddenly made sense of the mounds of spoil outside. There were no floorboards. Instead a deep hole led into the ground. I found a lantern, lit it and appraised the strange earthworks. The clutter of rural life lay haphazardly against the walls, a few piled blankets, an unstrung bow stave, a neat stack of halved log rounds beside a hatchet, an iron skillet. The room was dominated by that wide shaft right in the centre, its edges rough and shored up with planks. Shovels and picks, saws and an adze, tools for digging.

A tunnel into the dark.

I hated the grave-darkness, but there was no backtracking now. Not if I wanted to complete the task Van Ulovar had set us on. A wooden ladder led down into the darkness, but I thought that deep below I saw stone tiles. Stone? I clambered down the ladder, easy as a squirrel.

It was cold beneath the earth, different to the damp deadness of the crypts beneath Dalnesse. Clammy air whispered around my neck and muted sound as the ground swallowed me. Twelve feet down, and the floor was indeed stone—cut stone, carved with lettering that was nothing like the books I could read. I raised the lantern and looked down a tunnel, warm light cascading out. Planking had been erected along the walls; supports above me prevented the roof from collapsing, a sensible precaution even though the walls were dressed stone. Cavities lay along the length of the corridor, and within them—bones. Bones of chieftains, long since dead, some of them scattered across the floor as their treasures had been looted. It was an ancient barrow, freshly disturbed. Someone had begun digging down further at the far end. A mattock rested against the wall while a yellowed skull, ancient and uncaring, watched me from the shadows. A tomb, and a big one. It wasn't grazing land that had mattered here. The artefacts of bygone clan chiefs had been dug from beneath the earth. I somehow doubted that whatever had been found here had been declared.

I went very still.

Silence.

There were no ghosts: these bones had rested here for centuries, and for a moment in the damp, mouldering stillness of the pit I felt a deadly familiarity. I'd feared I'd walked into another undead thing's home. But no. This was a tomb in truth. Just the dead, and the smell of the earth above, and the lust for gold that will drive someone to murder.

There was no time to dwell on it. I knew I had to act. I had failed to find a way out of Dalnesse, and I had nearly died for it. Now another friend was in danger, and I had to move. I had to act. I had to do whatever was necessary.

I climbed back out. A creeping sensation tickled the back of my neck accompanied by a dirty, queasy feeling. I snuffed the lantern as I scanned the tree line. Nobody there. I stuck the wood axe through my belt, managed to find some strings near the bow. They were damp and poorly stored, and I was annoyed by the hunter's lack of care for his tools. The bow had an easy draw. I found four arrows, in as poor condition as the strings, but the binding on the heads was still strong. It would have to suffice.

I closed the shutters behind me as I clambered back through the window. Still alone. I had to find Ovitus, immediately. I circled the cabin and picked up his trail again, heading north away from the cabin, his horse's bigger shoes sunk deeper into the mud than those of the two horsemen who had joined him. The tracks passed straight into the forest, not following any trail, and I urged South after them. A half mile in, a pile of horse manure lay among the tracks. I jumped down, broke it apart and tested the warmth within. Horses are easy to follow; if they're well-fed, they shit all the time. This was recent. I urged South to a canter, ducking low-hanging branches. It had only been two hours since Ovitus and I had split up.

Moving silently came easily to me. Along the mountain trails, success depended upon it. It was a better way to hunt than the noisy chases the nobility enjoyed, with their yapping dogs and groundsmen flushing the beasts from their bushes. The mistcat and the fiahd know the way to hunt is stealth and silence. Most beasts are built for running, and if you aren't, then you have to take them unaware.

I was hunting now.

I saw them as I crested a bank and looked down across sloping ground. Three horses, two men riding and a third, larger shape slung over a saddle. They had stopped and appeared to be checking one of the horses' shoes. Ovitus was quite still. Maybe dead.

I felt the ridge of scar in my mind creaking, felt the heat rising in the crack, a fierce red glow in a bank of black. I gritted my teeth and drew the scar tissue back into place, buried the swell of feeling that threatened to emerge. It wasn't useful. I didn't need it. Didn't want it. It would not serve my purpose.

I recognised one of the men. Ollan, broad and gruff. The second was no less the warrior, his hair braided, a pair of swords at his belt, but it was the way he moved that confirmed his profession. Some men have an aura of violence around them. I had no doubt about this one.

I dismounted and tethered South out of sight along the ridge before I began to descend the slope. The trees were thick, but ground cover was light, and they didn't look back in my direction. Silent steps. Silent breaths. These were my prey.

I passed behind a tangle of bramble and branches surrounding a fallen tree, kept low. A wood pigeon called somewhere to the east. The forest was quiet as I rounded the trunk. I didn't plan, knew what had to be done instinctively.

I pressed up against a wide trunk, took two of the arrows in my bow hand and nocked the first. It was faster to keep them in the fist than a quiver, ready to launch, one in every heartbeat. I only had four arrows. They would have to be enough.

This was the hunt. This was *my* hunt.

Life had not been kind to me. It had made me hard, and it had made me something less than other people. I needed to be that lessened creature now. Needed the strength that rose from abandoning the morality of other people. I knew what I was about to do, that the invisible line I was about to cross would change me forever. I was about to commit murder. They hadn't seen me coming. It wasn't fair. Castus's words rose in my ears:

Only the weak insist that life be fair.

The man with the braids was furthest away and the harder target, but I chose him because I knew he was the most dangerous. I pulled the first arrow to full draw, aimed and loosed at him, then a second. The bowstring thrummed and arrows sailed, not perfectly straight because the arrows were warped, but straight enough. Broadheads. Hunting arrows, designed to wound and bleed an animal to exhaustion.

There was a moment, after I'd released the first arrow, when I knew the man would die but I hadn't killed him yet. He was both dead, and he was alive. A ghost in waiting.

The braided man didn't scream when the first struck him, but the second broke his silence. One in the chest, off-centre, one in the gut, and he went down. There was no surviving wounds like that, not without divine blessing and a dose of luck besides. He had neither.

I was already nocking my third arrow, but Ollan was fast. He was a battle-man, a clansman born to action. He saw his companion go down and threw himself behind a tree, guessing my position and blocking himself from sight. I'd been too slow. On the ground, the braided man was dying, his gurgles fading. Death can be a hard business. It takes time.

I was furious at my own failing. Castus LacClune would not have given him time to take cover. Ulovar LacNaithe would not have given him time. Vedira Robilar would not have given him time.

I moved swiftly to another tree. Two arrows left, none to waste, but Ollan didn't know that. He might even think I was two men, since my arrows had come fast. An eerie calm settled over the forest. I looked at Ovitus, slung and roped over his own saddle. It was impossible to tell whether he lived or not.

Ollan's head darted out, scanned for a moment and then hid again. He was a dangerous man. I'd seen that when I first met him, in the way he moved and the casual confidence with which he wore his sword. If I'd had to bet on who had done for those two shepherds, I knew where to put my money, and if he got close to me with that sword, then I didn't think the hatchet at my belt or a couple of lessons from Sanvaunt would do me much good. But he had to get to me first.

'Who's that? The retainer?' Ollan called. I didn't respond. 'You're making a mistake,' he shouted back to my silence. 'Your friend fell from his horse and hurt himself. We were taking him back to Halman's manor, you murdering bitch!'

I didn't believe him. I could have been wrong, but that was a concern for later. His claim didn't change my intentions. Ollan's life didn't matter to me at all, but Ovitus's did. I gained nothing by taking risks.

Ollan ducked out again for another look, and I made a mistake. I took the chance and loosed at him. My arrow was aimed well but the fletching was ragged, and I was too slow. The shaft whipped through the air and buried itself into the ground five paces past his hiding place. I winced, clenched my teeth in a grimace. One arrow left. At least he didn't know that.

'I see you found my arrows,' Ollan shouted. 'You only have one left. Let's parley?'

I ignored him. I'd been too hasty taking that shot, needed to stick to the plan. When he ran, I'd take him down. The forest was quiet. Branches creaked gently in the light breeze. A wood pigeon flapped away in a rustle of wings.

Patience.

Await the chance.

Ollan knew that too. He'd guessed my location, maybe from my arrows or maybe he'd seen me, and instead of fleeing, he ran to take cover behind another tree. I raised the bow too late, no time for a clear shot. He wasn't going to run. He was coming towards me.

I glanced from tree to tree, judging the distance. If he could cover the ground between two more trees he'd be just five large paces away, and then I had a problem. A single arrow would wound him badly, might make him falter, but people die hard and he might well reach me. Even with an arrow through him, a fighting man would probably be able to cut my head open. I once knew a man, side split open by an ox's horn, make it five miles through the forest. This had to be the last arrow, and it had to kill. A heart shot would stop him in his tracks, or a lucky artery would, but those were hard targets.

The best bet was the face or the leg, the face to take away his ability to fight me, the leg to cripple him. My jaw clenched tight. My eyes narrowed.

A draft horse walks on fallen leaves.

I brought everything into focus. Clear. Intense. I felt the rhythm of the world around me, *dhum-dhum-dhum, dhum-dhum-dhum,* as I awakened myself to awareness and understanding.

My mind melted into the trance, slowly, carefully. I sought around me, trying to focus on Ollan and the tree that defended him, and in the trance everything was clear. I couldn't see Ollan, but I knew where he was. I focused my mind, tried to keep my attention only on him. I breathed slow, drew the string, not to my eye where amateur archers take aim, but to my cheek so that the full draw of the bow was in the string. I wasn't sure how I knew, but I knew that Ollan was about to move. Sensed it in a push of the air. In footfall vibrations through the ground. He could be behind the next tree in a pair of seconds. My breath was immobile in my throat. Perhaps it was a whisper of wind that I sensed through the First Gate but didn't realise, maybe it was the tensing of unseen muscles bleeding into my mind, but whatever it was, I knew he was moving before I saw it. My fingers had released the string even before he emerged, and as he came around the trunk to look out, the arrow smashed into his chest below the collarbone. It was not a killing shot.

But it was good enough.

The impact knocked him over, and even better, he dropped his sword.

I ran at him, screaming, raised the hatchet and smacked it down. Ollan raised his hands to try to protect himself and things became messy. He lost fingers. I buried the thick axe head in his temple. He twitched a few times. The smell of blood was overpowering as the trance drummed in my head. I stared down at the body for a few moments longer before I realised that the other man was still whimpering. I walked over to him and saw he was delirious. He stared upwards with unknowing eyes and I finished him, worked with a hunter's professionalism. Just meat and bones.

I felt nothing.

I went to Ovitus. His face was warm. He was breathing. Good. That was good.

So it was done. I was a killer now.

I sat down beside Ovitus. Wondered at how I felt, which wasn't much, and how maybe I should have felt something more. But I didn't, so there wasn't much to ruminate on. I wondered what my friends would have thought if they could see me, all covered in blood. The colour of the Draoihn's coats—ah. Yes.

That made sense. They would have applauded me, maybe. The Crown matters: all else is dust. I had made dust of men.

A spirit stood watching me, quite intent with a look of quiet amusement on her face. She was lovely, in the way that a well-groomed dog is: beautiful, sleek, powerful. Her shimmering form was azure as a summer sky, the feathers above her ears sweeping back like wings, a bar of dark paint across her eyes.

She smiled, looking from me to the corpses and back.

'You've arrived,' the Queen of Feathers said. I didn't think she meant in the forest. 'Excellent.'

'Have I?' I asked.

'You're alive, and they're dead on the wind.'

'It would have been better to take them alive,' I said.

'Prisoners are a luxury,' she said. 'And one that our kind can seldom afford.'

I pushed myself up. I didn't know what she was, but she was no ordinary ghost. She had helped me before—had shown me magic, before. It would have been foolish not to feel a little fear, even as I wiped dead-men's blood on the forest floor.

'You told Veretaine and his friends about me.'

The Queen of Feathers appeared to sit down, though there was no chair beneath her. She crossed her long, slender legs, reclining as though supported by a divan.

'Everyone needs friends,' she said. 'Perhaps they will be yours.'

'You shared my secret,' I said, trying to hide my anger. 'You put me in danger. What are you?'

'Would a name help?' she asked. 'Would my name really make sense of the world for you?'

'Maybe,' I said. 'Are you Sarathi?'

She laughed.

'I am many things, Raine, just as you are, and have been, and will be,' she said. 'I warned you of the poison that Redwinter will pour into you, if you let them. The victors tell their own truth. Maldouen betrayed the Sarathi after the battle at Solemn Hill. Did you know the Sarathi turned on the Riven Queen and aided Maldouen in destroying him? They do not mention *that* in their histories.'

'I don't believe you.'

Her eyes glittered, dark and beautiful.

'Because they are fair? Because they would not do the same to you, if they knew what you are and what you see?'

I swallowed hard. Perhaps this was a road I did not wish to walk.

'Then what are you? How can you follow me? Are you one of the hidden folk?'

She laughed again. I suppose I had just insinuated that she was a fairy. I might have laughed too, but I was covered in blood.

'I am a friend. A lonely friend, who has few enough to speak with that I cannot afford to be picky about whose company I keep. Is that not enough?'

'No. You're something different. You're not human,' I said. It came out quickly, before I'd truly had a chance to think about what I was going to say, or how to say it. What it might mean to this blue-tinged spirit. But she just smiled, a long and lazy smile that didn't make me trust her any more than I already did.

She knew who I was. She'd told Veretaine and those others in Harranir about me. She'd helped me escape Ulovar with Hazia. That had hardly worked out well, but I had never been under any illusion that Ulovar would have killed me to get to Hazia that day. It would have been no different to what I had just done. A few moments before I'd felt proud of it. A task completed. A victory. *Excellent.* Not anymore. I shivered.

'Did you know what the girl who woke Ciuthach carried, that day on the bridge?' I said quickly. 'Did you know what she'd do?'

'That girl's mind was beyond help,' the Queen of Feathers said, 'and Ciuthach was a monster long before he was bound into that crypt.'

'Why didn't you stop her?' I asked. 'You could have thrown her into the river instead of Ulovar. If you had, people that mattered to me would not have died.'

'I am not so swift to kill as some. Ulovar survived the water. The girl might have too. But protecting her was not my task. I sought to protect you, nothing more or less.'

'Why? Why me?'

'Loneliness, perhaps?' But she didn't hide her ghostly smile well enough for me to believe it.

'You knew what was happening that day. You knew what she carried, didn't you?'

The Queen of Feathers sat forwards on her illusionary chair.

'So many questions,' she said. But a smile played around her pale blue lips. 'Why do you think I would know?'

'Because you were there, before it happened. You had to have been, even if I couldn't see you,' I said. 'You knew what she was going to do. So you must have known that Hazia had the page that could awaken Ciuthach. And you could have stopped her.'

'I have been very lucky with you, Raine,' the Queen of Feathers said. 'Most of those that can see me are dullards. Lacking brains, motivation, they herd geese or sheep or just sit there pushing brats from their wombs until they shrivel to nothing. But you're different. I can help you. The Draoihn do not see your worth, but it shines from you brighter than the sun. I wish us to be friends. I have been waiting for you for a very, very long time.'

'What if I don't want to be your friend?'

'I aided you, Raine, when you needed it the most. Am I not owed the benefit of your doubts?'

'I don't trust you. I'll never trust you. I reject your friendship.'

There is a time for being bullish, and a time for being firm in your convictions. When faced with a shimmering blue spirit, even when your hands are still wet with an enemy's blood, was perhaps neither of those times.

She changed.

The lightness in her eyes vanished, replaced by voids of dark and light that swirled together. She spoke words I had never heard before, sounds that clashed together like ships breaking beneath a hail of falling anvils. An unseen force gripped me, spun me around and slammed me into the trunk of the nearest tree, my arms spread wide around it.

'After all I have done for you, you speak to me this way? You owe me your *life*,' the Queen of Feathers hissed. 'Do not think that because you have suffered, or that because you have the grave-sight, you are so precious that you do not need to recall your manners. If you behave like a child, I shall treat you like a child.'

I struggled, but to no avail. My arms felt as though they were lashed around the trunk, but there was nothing there, not even air. For a moment there was nothing but silence, and then three sharp blows slashed across my backside as if from a switch, one, two, three. I gasped and whimpered in pain at each hot strike. Not hard enough to draw blood or break the skin, not even enough to tear my clothes.

Just enough to humiliate.

The force that held me disappeared. When I spun around, fists clenching in futile shame and fury, the Queen of Feathers was gone. I rubbed at my stinging posterior. Hardly a dignified way to end a battle. I'd killed two men. I'd have killed the Queen of Feathers as well, but—well. She was probably dead already. Whatever she was. Maybe I had just done something terribly, terribly foolish.

I needed to see to Ovitus.

The horses were skittish, on the edge of panic. Horses hate blood, and the stink of it was filling the air. My friend was slung over his own saddle, his legs and hands tied together with a rope beneath the horse's belly. The knot was so tight I had to saw through the ropes until I could heave Ovitus's impressive bulk down.

'You really need to start running with Jathan,' I muttered, angry at him even though he was unconscious. I felt around his scalp and found swelling at the crown of his head. Then I blew on his face to try to wake him, but that did no good. I took a flask of water and poured it over him. That had no effect either, and I began to think I ought to have left him roped up on the horse, but it was too late for that, and there was no way I could lift his dead weight alone. When he finally did come to, he looked around like a man interrupted from a deep sleep.

'Ow,' he said, putting a hand to the lump on the back of his head.

'Welcome back,' I said. If his head felt anything like my backside, then he was going to be rubbing it for a while.

To my relief, the next few minutes revealed that despite a resounding head-ache, there appeared to be no lasting damage. It took Ovitus some time to really understand where we were, what was going on and why his wrists and ankles were so painful, but eventually he caught sight of the bodies. He looked open-mouthed from them to me and back.

'What happened to you?' I asked.

'I'm not sure,' he said groggily, one hand gingerly testing the swelling on his crown. 'There was a house of some sorts. I was riding up to it and then—well, that's all I remember.'

I considered him carefully, seeing nothing but honesty in his doughy features.

'Looks to me like they hit you with a slingstone,' I said, though I was not convinced that was what had happened. I paused, took a breath. 'Is it possible that you fell from your horse and hurt yourself?'

'I suppose so,' Ovitus said. He winced as he prodded at his injury. 'My head hurts like a bastard.'

Whatever had happened to Ovitus earlier that day was a mystery we couldn't solve now. I wondered about Ollan's words. Perhaps they really had found him and taken him for help, or maybe Ovitus had stumbled onto their little exca-vation and they had been making him disappear as they had the shepherds. I had a lot of guesses, and not many facts.

'Do you want to talk about it?' Ovitus said. I'd been deep in thought.

'Talk about what?'

'About what happened? About what you did?'

'What of it?'

Ovitus was awkward, and his head was pounding, but he still found kind-ness. His concern went unhidden in his eyes.

'Killing those men can't have been easy.'

'The first one was. The second was hard,' I said.

'That's not what I meant,' he said, determined to discuss it.

'I know. But it was easy.'

'You don't feel . . . anything about it?' he asked. He looked disappointed.

I have heard old warriors talk about a time when they killed and felt repulsed and horrified by what they had done. Such men were built for a different world. I had been butchering animals for years, I had seen the ghosts of the dead, and I didn't regret what I'd done. Murder. I supposed that I was a murderer now. It didn't feel wrong, though. If I came on that scene again, I'd have done everything the same. Maybe it wasn't fair, but the world is not about fair. Castus LacClune would have understood, I thought.

'Why should I feel anything?' I asked.

Ovitus looked away uneasily. I think he wanted me to feel the way that he did, uncomfortable around the dead. Guilty, maybe. But I didn't feel guilty. I felt alive.

'I think it was Emocles who wrote that moral men are appalled by atrocities committed even in the name of good,' he said. 'I don't know. I just think that I would feel—I don't know. I just don't like that they're dead.'

'Do you wish I hadn't done it?' I asked.

'No, of course not. Thank you. I should have said that already. Thank you.'

'You're welcome,' I said. 'My lord.'

The warrior's ghost was rising. He stared around with greenish, hate-filled eyes. Ovitus pitied this dead man. If I were truthful, the one thing that I did feel was satisfaction. I had set myself to achieve something difficult, and I had met my goal. I'd been better than these two. Stronger. I stared back at the ghost, but it didn't say anything. I checked around for the Queen of Feathers again, just in case. She was nowhere to be seen.

'We need to get going,' Ovitus said.

'Just a moment.'

I groped through their pockets. Ollan had a purse of coins—a lot of coins, which I took, since he didn't need it anymore, but I stopped dead as I took a folded piece of paper from the warrior's pocket. Crudely written letters read:

Six feet tall. Fat. Apprentice. Brown hair. LacNaithe accent. Alive.

It was a description of Ovitus. It didn't make sense to me right away. Of course he was alive. Until I realised the final word wasn't part of the description. It was an instruction.

I folded the note and stashed it in my pocket before Ovitus could see it. He was woozy from the blow to the head, and I didn't want to distress him further. But I took one of the dead man's swords, and made sure we hit a hard pace.

Halfera's hall was hard to find in the night, but we managed it somehow. A half-drunk servant greeted us and bade us wait in the parlour for the mistress of the house. Halfera appeared in a pale blue gown. She was all smiles until she understood the damp, mud-coloured spray across my clothing and hands. Her face paled as her fingers clenched rigid around the arms of her chair.

'I hope no misfortune has befallen you,' she said, voice level but her words clipped.

'I am afraid we have awful news,' Ovitus said. I had determined the words we would use, but Ovitus was the one to say them. He was the ranked man, after all.

'Oh?' she said, an attempt at calmness, voice not quite breaking but not far off.

'It seems that some men of your employ were deceiving you,' Ovitus said, 'and had set up a, er, a secret excavation.'

'An excavation?' She swallowed hard, and I knew for certain that she knew everything. 'How strange.' She was already guessing the rest. Intelligent, controlled, deceitful, cunning. For some dreadful reason, it only made her shine. She pried her fingers from the arm of the chair and tightened the laces of her bodice. Not an accident on our first encounter after all.

'Your servant Ollan and another man have been digging out old barrows and selling relics illegally.'

'I cannot believe it,' she said, though she did, and her eyes went to the blood on my clothes. She met my eyes, knowing me for their killer, and there was fire there, fire and more hate than the ghost had mustered. She'd been closer to Ollan than perhaps we'd judged. She had the sense not to ask after him straightaway, maintaining the pretence that he was just her servant. 'You have proof?'

Ovitus floundered and glanced to me, in case we had some kind of evidence.

'Perhaps this discussion ought to be had in the morning,' I said. 'Thail Ovitus suffered a blow to the head and should retire for the night.'

Halfera's clever gaze moved from me to him. 'Yes,' she agreed, 'I too am tired. Should I send someone to tend to my thail Ovitus?'

He departed and we were left alone, and I watched the light in her half-lidded eyes.

'Speak plainly, Retainer,' Halfera said. Anger, maybe resignation or weariness, drove her words like a whip.

'Ovitus found your operation and your men attacked him,' I said. 'They were bringing him back here after they knocked him out. I don't know why.'

She sighed. Disappointment. Anger. Sorrow.

'I do not understand it,' she said. 'I gave Ollan orders that neither of you was to be harmed,' Halfera said. 'He was to guide you away.'

'You found an unlooted barrow on Reeve Jon's land.'

'The ground gave way and a man fell down there,' she said, looking out towards the dark window. 'We aren't wealthy, you know. It may seem like we are, but there are debts. Always debts to be paid, and my father has been diligent in supplying the soldiers Van Ulovar demands we send off for the Brannish king's army. Our van believes that it is the duty of all the nobility to be poor in order that they provide for the common people. Laudable aims, but not ones that let us live like the rest of Harran.' She fixed me with her eyes. 'You must be the one who killed them, even though you're just a slip of a girl. That fat lump has neither the guts nor the skill.'

'Ovitus is a gentle soul,' I said, surprised I was defending him. 'But yes. I killed them. You'll find the bodies out in the woods, if you look for them.'

'Who was the second man?'

I described him to her. She shook her head.

'I employ nobody of that description. We don't have fighting men here. What would we use them for?'

'He had this,' I said, holding the paper out to her. 'Makes me think that he wasn't interested in your digging operation. Makes me think he was after your thail. Why would Ollan help him?'

'I have no idea. And I'm far from stupid enough to try to engage in a plot against my own lord,' Halfera said. For all that she could have been born from a serpent's egg, I believed her on that front.

'And yet your man Ollan was riding with him.'

'Good deaths?' she asked, her eyes sparkling before she glanced up and blinked them dry. Lovers for sure.

'The stranger, no. Ollan? Yes, he fought well.' And he had, in a fashion, only it had been one-sided and I'd had too many advantages. *Only the weak insist that life be fair.*

'Good,' she said, slipping her hands into her sleeves. I sat across a table from her, wine untouched in cups before us. Everything was very still in the house. Maybe the servants were all pressed at the door listening.

'So you figured there was gold in the barrow, started having it dug out, and built the shack to cover the work. But it was risky to do all of that on Jon's land— maybe the shepherds found out, so you had them killed. Am I right so far?'

'I didn't order the shepherds killed, but men will be men,' Halfera said. 'We rely on people like you. Killers. People who don't care enough about what they've done to wash the blood off their hands afterwards.' She looked down at the dirty brown smears around my fingernails. The spatter across the backs of my hands. It hadn't even occurred to me. 'It's their nature to turn to violence. He never told me that he killed the shepherds.'

'But you guessed it.'

She said nothing.

'The shepherds' bodies are buried in shallow graves in the woods south of the excavation. They need to be buried properly.'

'So what now?' Halfera said. 'Will you march me before Van Ulovar so he can put out my eyes? Perhaps hobble me? That would be the punishment, I think.'

'It would be your father punished, not you, I suspect,' I said.

'My father has been bedridden for the last year, and has not spoken in three months. He is dying, and when he dies, I will inherit his debts and be forced to marry someone wealthy enough that I can keep my land. I had hoped the money we raised from the digging might buy me some measure of control. Or, it would have.' She fixed me with her glassy eyes, those life-filled, mesmerising eyes. 'You have not told the van's nephew everything.'

'I see no reason to change that,' I said. 'The men who did the killing are dead.'

'I will have to turn their families out,' she said. 'They were traitors.'

'Make no mention of the families and let them stay,' I said. 'Declare what you now discover on the land you bought from Reeve Jon, and then involve him in the business of digging it out. Give the appropriate cut of the profits to the van. The region stays stable. Nobody else has to be hurt. Those men acted alone. When you go to recover their bodies, find a note of purchase in Ollan's belongings, one that says he recently sold a flock of sheep. He was to blame for the deaths of the shepherds, for all of it. And you'll make no mention of the note that I just showed you. That is the price of my silence.'

Halfera walked to the fireplace, rested a hand on the mantelpiece and looked into the fire.

'You understand the game,' she said. 'It is a hard game to play. I would never have been so foolish as to allow my men to attack the kin of a van, let alone Draoihn. Can you imagine, if the van's nephew had vanished on my land? What were they thinking? I suppose that their foolishness has ended them.' She sighed, an echo of loss, then whispered, 'Ollan was a fool.'

'I suppose he was,' I said. I didn't mention that there was a remote possibility that Ovitus had simply fallen from his horse and I had mistakenly murdered them both. It wouldn't have changed anything.

'I knew you were dangerous the moment I set eyes upon you,' she said. 'I didn't know why, until I looked into your eyes. They're empty. I knew you for one of them. A killing-man. I suppose that's why Van Ulovar sent you.'

'I never killed a man before,' I said.

She looked me in the eye, saw the emptiness within me and gave a bitter laugh.

'But you have now. And you'll do it again. Not because you have to, but because you want to. You'll get a taste for it, and they'll say that it's in the name of the Crown and call you a hero. The Light Above made the world for people like you.'

We drank together, as enemies do when they are making friends, and it was a few hours before we retired to our beds. As she rang a bell for a servant to guide me to my chamber, she looked back at me.

'Do you feel anything? Anything for other people at all?'

I didn't answer her, and closed the door.

The question kept me unwanted company.

I felt some things. I felt fear, and I got angry and annoyed, and I'd definitely felt some things for people that I really didn't want to think about too hard. But when it came to what I had done, and the terrible things I had seen in the north—no. There was nothing there. A piece of me was missing. I had felt victorious before, glad of my accomplishment. The girl I had been before all this started wouldn't have felt that way.

Maybe she wouldn't have loosed that first arrow.

Maybe she'd have been dead.

27

The following day I threw up four times just from the headache. Ovitus talked with Halfera in the morning, and things began to settle out much as I'd asked. During the night a search of Ollan's rooms had turned up a crumpled, barely legible note of receipt for the sale of a flock of sheep. She didn't look at me as they spoke, not even once.

We returned to Uloss, where I hid in my room and vowed never to open that Gate again. Sanvaunt returned from his business at Valarane with a haunted look, eyes moving from face to face as though he didn't quite see us. I had expected him to ask how Ovitus had ended the dispute, but instead Sanvaunt disappeared into private chambers, Second Retainer Morag letting us know that he was not to be disturbed. He remained alone for several days. His letters were whisked away to Harranir. Ovitus kept to gentle pursuits, occasionally falling prey to dizzy spells. I passed the time shooting at targets in the castle grounds. There was one archer among the guardsmen who could give me a good competition, a Hyspian man in his forties. I made him shoot with me each time he finished his rounds, until Esher pointed out that he didn't compete with me because he wanted a daily archery contest but because he couldn't refuse a First Retainer when he was only Fourth.

'I must confess that tonight I would like to get home to see my wife, miss,' he said sheepishly when I mentioned it. I found that disappointing. Having someone to compete with had given me something to focus on.

'It didn't occur to you that he'd want to go home?' Esher asked.

'I didn't think about it,' I told her. 'How is it different to me having to wait on you all at table?'

'Because that's your job,' Esher said. 'It's not his job to shoot arrows.'

I didn't see how it was any different, and I doubted he did either. I didn't work an allotted number of hours. I just followed instructions whenever I was given them. It wasn't worth it in the end, though. It made things awkward between Esher and me, perhaps finally bringing it home that however much she attempted to include me, we were not the same.

We were different in more ways than one. I didn't want to sit around drinking the evenings into nothing. I wanted to go to Valarane. The monks there evidently had books, old books that even Redwinter lacked. Maybe in there I'd find something to explain the silver circles I'd seen in the sky, or find a reference to a Queen of Feathers. I had not forgotten the humiliation she had delivered, nor that she had shared my most dangerous secret with Veretaine and his friends. The first time I had met her, she had saved my life. She had been kind to me on the barge. Now I feared her. She had given me cause to, and I couldn't ask anybody about her or what she might be without further endangering myself—not unless I found mention of her somewhere else first. I knew this secret could cost me more than a thrashing.

When Sanvaunt finally summoned his cousin to attend him, Ovitus told him what had happened, give or take a truth or two. I had persuaded Ovitus that Halfera hadn't played any role in killing the shepherds, or concealing the excavation, and that she had proposed sharing the discovery with Reeve Jon. Had he known the truth, Ovitus would have felt obligated to tell his cousin so that justice could be served, but as Castus had said, fairness was not the stone the Light Above used as a foundation for the earth. There was something about Halfera that I liked, and seeing her harmed would have displeased me. Matters were resolved, order had been restored, and that was the important thing. It wasn't justice, but I'd seen how little justice there was in the world, from the children begging on Harranir's streets to my people, ridden down and strung up high in the north, and I felt no need to pursue it simply because I happened to be here.

I had determined that I would tell nobody but Ulovar about the note I had found. It would only have made Ovitus afraid, and he was still recovering, while Sanvaunt had that haunted look about him again. He was back on the rose-thistle, and there was always a light coming from beneath his door. Not that I was checking.

Why would somebody want Ovitus? I believed Halfera. It was possible that Ollan had tried to cover his murderous tracks by himself, but it was the written description that troubled me. Ollan had ridden with Ovitus, after all. There was some other agenda at work, but Ovitus wasn't anybody. Not yet. A van-in-waiting, and by anyone's judgement, he was unlikely to be a strong one. I was hardly adept in courtly politics, but even I could tell that when Ulovar died and Ovitus took the LacNaithe seat, Van LacAud and Van LacClune would see a new age of opportunity stretching before them rather than a threat. Who, then, had cause to wish him harm?

I didn't like the answer my reasoning threw back at me. There were no other legitimate heirs to the Clan LacNaithe lordship, but there was one wildrose. Sanvaunt took his service to the clan and Crown as seriously as Ulovar did.

A little lick of malice made me wonder whether Sanvaunt would be happy if some accident befell his inept cousin, off in the wilds. I tried to imagine how I would feel. I didn't like that answer either. I felt nothing for those poor dead fools in the north. Maybe I was incapable of grief? Maybe I'd never feel it again. But no. I'd felt it, when Nairna LacMuaid had felt the bite of stones. It hadn't just been fear for my own survival that had caused that sinking feeling within me—had it? I knew I was broken, but at least I'd managed one tear for her. Just one. But Sanvaunt was different. He was different because he cared so much, about everything. So much he left himself ragged and worn through.

I could not go to Valarane, but there was little constraint placed upon my activities at the castle, where there was already a full clanhold of staff. So when my fingers grew sore from drawing the bowstring, I found myself sitting alongside Ovitus in the clanhold library, although the books were nothing special, not the sort of thing I wanted. Before long, I grew tired of reading about former lords of the clan. LacNaithe was old, with many branches and sub-branches, and its scribes were proud of their accomplishments. I learned that there had been seven LacNaithe kings, though the clan hadn't held the throne for over one hundred years. When my eyes were sore from reading, I sat in a high tower, alone. Ovitus would hunt me down and disturb my solitude, sometimes to my annoyance, but sometimes as a relief. Since I had killed Ollan and the braided man, the corpse-faces of my loved ones had started to rise in my mind like a swell of vomit, but there was no accompanying pain. Most often it was Lochlan. He hadn't deserved what happened to him. It didn't hurt; it didn't make me happy. My scarred mind thought of him without request or remorse.

. . . . . .

A week after his return, Sanvaunt summoned me to his chambers. I was nervous. The cloud that had hovered over him since he returned from Valarane had hollowed his cheeks. His rooms were spotless, but that may have been the servants' doing more than his. A huge oil painting covered one entire wall, showing sombre, formally robed Draoihn around a crystal-shard-studded crown on a stone plinth. In their centre, a child with a wrap of cloth over his eyes raised his hands to the Light Above, streaming down to illuminate him. The artist had been a master. The legend below read: *Maldouen gifts Harranir the Crown.*

Sanvaunt looked like week-old shit. Shadows beneath his eyes, his hair unbrushed, unwashed, but there was so much anger clenched in his jaw that I stopped at the door. I didn't want to approach him.

'Get in here, Retainer. Now.'

He had never called me by my title before. I stared at him. I was lost for words.

'Get in here before I make you.'

I couldn't refuse. The air was thick and heavy with warmth from a fire burning too many logs. He closed his journal and placed several other large books atop it. Three times he'd hidden that book from me now, but by the hostility on his face, I didn't think asking about it would be a good idea. I took a seat across the table from him, where two plates of food sat uneaten. The bread had hardened, the meat and greens cold. I thought that I'd seen him angry with the apprentices on the day of the colour storm. I had been wrong. This anger was so strong it was pulsing from him in waves.

'I read Ovitus's judgement on the land dispute,' he said. His voice could have sliced through silk. 'I also know what happened.'

'Of course you did,' I said.

'Not the truth you fed to Ovitus,' Sanvaunt said with a raised eyebrow. 'The actual truth. I know about Halman's daughter's involvement, all of it.'

'I see,' I said. He may have been expecting some kind of reaction from me, but I sat as still as I could and looked straight back at him. Despite his rage, he looked exhausted, though he'd been in these rooms for nearly a week. Something rested heavily on his shoulders.

'So what do I do now, Raine?' he barked. 'Do I tell Ovitus that he was wrong? That he failed to dispense justice over a simple land dispute? Does he even know what happened?'

'He knows everything he needs to,' I said.

'We should not keep secrets from the future van.' Sanvaunt glowered at me. But his anger was already fading. He grabbed his flask, took a hit.

'And what about your secrets?'

'Don't start on at me about keeping secrets, Raine. I've heard enough from Ovitus about secrets you two have kept since the north.'

'You don't know anything about what happened to me there,' I snapped. 'Nothing at all.'

Sanvaunt's pupils widened as the rose-thistle took hold.

'It doesn't matter.' He rubbed his head with the heels of his hands. When he looked back at me, he was composed. 'You killed two men.'

'Yes.'

'How do you feel about it?' he said. I shrugged. Sanvaunt narrowed his eyes and spoke bluntly. 'Ovitus said there was a chance that he might have fallen from his horse, and that they were aiding him.' I shrugged again. 'The thought does not concern you?'

'I did what I thought was necessary at the time, to ensure Ovitus's safety. I may have been mistaken. I don't think I was, though.'

'But if you were?'

'Isn't this what Redwinter does? Kills people, on the off-chance they might be a problem? I played the odds. People die,' I said blankly. It was true. The sisters, the man Castus LacClune had killed, the shepherds, Ollan and the braided warrior. 'I've seen a lot of dead bodies this year. Not many of them deserved to die.'

'And that doesn't trouble you?'

'No.'

Sanvaunt's mouth was a hard line.

'You lied to Ovitus, to everyone about what happened. Maybe Ovitus can't spot a forged bill of sale, but I certainly can,' he said. I said nothing. It seemed pointless to either agree or disagree, given that he was right. 'Lying to me I can excuse. I'm just a wildrose whose uncle lets him play at taking charge from time to time. Would you have lied to Ulovar as well?'

I didn't like being called a liar. I didn't like being questioned about what had befallen me, and I'd long since decided not to let angry men vent their demons on me. My own anger sharpened my tongue.

'You're not Ulovar,' I said. 'So it doesn't matter. You're Draoihn, and I must defer to you. But you aren't the lord of Clan LacNaithe, even if you want to be.'

Sanvaunt stared at me with those dark, shadow-wreathed eyes.

'The clan has enough burdens without your lies.'

'It's a good outcome for everyone,' I said. 'Who knows what really happened?'

'You've lied to your future van,' Sanvaunt said grimly. 'You've let someone get away with orchestrating murder. I can't even tell Ovitus, because he'd feel obliged to fix it, and the error would undermine his authority.'

'I did what had to be done,' I said. 'Sometimes people need protecting from themselves. Maybe I shouldn't have shot those men, and maybe Ovitus would be dead for it. Maybe Halfera's land should be confiscated, and Reeve Jon should have nothing. Maybe Ovitus shouldn't believe what he's told, and everyone should end up the worse. Maybe my people shouldn't have been slaughtered as bystanders for the sake of somebody else's failings, but they were. I'm sorry if you thought I was somebody else, but this is what Ulovar would have wanted, and you know it.'

He breathed out slowly. I thought he was going to speak, to tell me I was wrong, but he remained silent.

'Is that all, Draoihn Sanvaunt?'

'No it is not.' He sat back in his chair, face set like stone. 'With the way events are progressing, I have no choice but to share something with you. Something that cannot go further than this room. Ulovar knows what I am about to tell you, and he is the only one who knows. Do you understand? Despite your lies, I have no choice but to trust you now. And not even Ovitus can know of this.'

I felt pressure shifting in the air around me and heard Sanvaunt fall into a trance. It was soft, rapid, like drips of water falling into a pool.

'What are you doing?' I asked, tensing.

'Listening,' he said. 'Ensuring that there's nobody behind the door.' His trance ended, the First Gate closing. 'Ovitus's parents were buried at Valarane,' he said. 'I say *were* because his mother isn't buried there anymore. When I went to lay flowers, I discovered the mausoleum door open. His mother's sarcophagus lid was cracked down the centre. Her remains were gone.'

'Gone?'

'Gone. None of the monks saw anything or know who did it. And Ovitus must not know.'

'Gone,' I said again. 'Why would anybody want to steal a body? It must be years old.'

'I can't answer that,' Sanvaunt said. 'But in the current climate, with Ulovar due to face trial, and after Hazia stole the relic, this has to be kept secret.'

'Why? How will you find the culprit if nobody talks?'

'Ulovar is not a popular van,' Sanvaunt said. 'He uses his parliamentary veto to block the other clans on many things, most notably reducing funding for Prince Caelan's forces with the Brannish. Keeping the Brannish king happy is an endless drain on everyone's coffers. Both LacClune and LacAud have a family member on the Council of Night and Day, who will stand in Ulovar's judgement and are already inclined to condemn him. We can give them nothing further to use against him.'

'But how would this possibly help them?' I said. 'It's a personal blow for Ulovar. His own sister.'

'I do not wish to speculate,' Sanvaunt said, but my mind was racing. They were just bones. 'And neither should you. I must have your silence, Raine. Will you promise me that? I don't ask it for myself, but for Ovitus. This would devastate him.'

'Then why tell me at all?'

'Because too many things are falling into place around us,' Sanvaunt said. His face was grim. How could he be only twenty-three, when his eyes looked like that? 'First one of Ulovar's apprentices goes mad, breaks into the Blackwell and steals an artefact. Then his sister's remains are stolen, and his nephew is ambushed. It reeks of a conspiracy against us. Against the clan.'

The figures on the painting gazed adoringly at the Crown before them. Their faces were serene. All of them but one, a woman in a blue hood who seemed to be weeping.

'Raine?'

I looked back to Sanvaunt.

'Maybe,' I said. 'But nobody knows why Hazia did what she did.'

'They don't,' Sanvaunt said. 'And probably never will.'

'Why trust me with this?' I challenged him. 'You don't even like me.'

Sanvaunt sat back. His expression slowly faded, muscle by muscle, as if each helped shift some kind of difficult thought into place. When it was done, he was blank as snow.

'Because of all the people that I can ask for help, you are the only one who was unconnected to any of this before it all began,' Sanvaunt said. 'Hazia cannot have entered the Blackwell alone. She was an apprentice, barely able to hold the First Gate. Ulovar is to be tried because he is responsible for his ward, and then for ignoring the grandmaster's command to remain in Redwinter. That he prevented the rise of Sarathi Ciuthach will count in his favour, but you are the sole evidence that he did so.'

'You don't trust anyone,' I said. 'So you're telling me?'

'I had to tell *someone*,' he said. 'I cannot bear all of this alone.'

His fist clenched, anger sweeping down his arm. This shadow that had been haunting him since he returned from Valarane was an ink-stain mass of roiling fury, one that he had absorbed into himself. He believed in duty above everything, but now somebody had made it personal. It wasn't just Ovitus's mother's grave that had been desecrated. It was his aunt's as well. And yet he'd never spoken of it in that way. The clan, LacNaithe, Ovitus, Ulovar: where was the time for his own pain?

'You've shown that you're resourceful and capable. It would diminish Ovitus's standing if he were assigned guards—he's to be Draoihn as well as van, and I can't protect him without his knowing the truth. He *must not* know the truth about his mother. He needs somebody to watch his back, to be ready to make the hard choices he can't.' He looked out of the window. 'He is not a strong man, we both know that, and I cannot be with him all the time. But he likes you, and you have protected him, and the two of you forged a connection in the north.'

'I understand,' I said. 'I'll be watchful.'

He nodded and looked out of the window, and I sensed that it was my time to leave. But as I did so, he called out to me.

'Raine,' he said. 'I know that I may not be as full of laughter as the apprentices. And I know that I may not always express myself as well as I would wish, and that I may not approve of all of your decisions. But—' For a moment he struggled with the words. 'I do not dislike you.'

I felt like a hand had reached into my chest to begin squeezing down on my lungs.

'You can trust me,' I said. 'I won't let you down.'

'I know.'

I nodded to him and closed the door quietly behind me.

28

Our return to Redwinter went nearly unnoticed, only a grey-robed gate servant greeting us. The grounds were silent, shadowed shapes moving through low, drifting fog. Even the four Draoihn practising their swordcraft made no sound, moving like spectres through guards and strikes. The red-and-white walls absorbed all sound as we climbed down from weary horses.

Tarquus met us at the door. The old servant had a clutch of papers in his hands, greeting us individually as we handed our reins to the groom and headed into the familiar scents of the greathouse, but he looked drawn, grey.

Something was wrong.

'Welcome home, such as it is,' he said. 'I will give you a few moments to ready yourselves, then there is someone to see you all in the parlour.'

We could all sense it. The quiet of the grounds, the stillness in the greathouse.

'Where's Ulovar?' Sanvaunt asked. His face had taken on a stony cast, fists clenched tight at his sides.

'All will be explained shortly,' Tarquus said, turning his face. 'You will not want to take too long.' The apprentices shuffled in, a flock of worried faces. Tarquus spoke quietly, a pleasant word issued to each apprentice in turn, some acknowledgement of how the journey had treated them or mention of things he'd arranged in their private rooms.

I went to wash the grime from my hands and found that new clothing had arrived during my absence. More shades of grey and blue, winter in silk and wool. I hurried downstairs, but I knew that nothing that was to be said would be good. The house felt dead, as though its heart had been cut out and all the blood stopped flowing.

Haronus LacClune awaited us in the parlour, the three, green-tinged furrows in his forehead gleaming metallically by the light of the cadanum lamps. He was dressed in the colours of his clan, blue roses on the white panels of his frock coat, white roses on the blue. He stood stiffly—I had put an arrow in his shoulder not all that long ago—and Sanvaunt and the apprentices filed in. He eyed them like a cat watching birds in a cage.

'To what do we owe this pleasure, Draoihn Haronus?' Sanvaunt said.

'Still speaking for the heir, eh Sanvaunt?' Haronus said. 'I am afraid that there's likely to be little pleasure here today, not for you at least. I always wondered how Ulovar would have furnished his greathouse. I see his tastes are as austere as his politics.'

'You did not come here to admire decorations,' Sanvaunt said. 'Where is Ulovar?' His fists were still clenched.

Haronus did not smile, but I could tell that he wanted to. He had a cruel face. I wasn't sorry I'd shot him.

'Your master is currently confined within a sigil-warded cell beneath Redwinter,' he said. Enjoyed the words, savouring them like fine wine. He reached out a long finger, pointing into an irrelevant distance like a schoolmaster finding some new revelation. 'New evidence came to light during your absence that casts an even more disturbing shadow on the events of the past few months. The grandmaster herself constructed the wards around him, such that not even a Draoihn of Ulovar's ability can break them. He is to remain there until Van Merovech LacClune arrives for the trial.'

The apprentices roared their questions, demanded to know why. Making declarations of outrage. Esher's eyes widened until they could have swallowed her whole face; Liara's eyes brimmed with tears. Ovitus's mouth fell open like a loose attic door. Haronus bore it all with seeming indifference. Only Sanvaunt remained calm, his dark eyes set on Clan LacClune's emissary.

'What evidence?'

'Evidence that points to Van Ulovar having accessed the Sixth Gate.'

The apprentices clamoured their outrage.

'Silence!' Haronus boomed, his voice amplified by the Second Gate, shaking a plate from a shelf to shatter on the tiles. 'Clan LacClune controls the excise duties on imports and exports moving in and out of Harranir,' he said. 'A sacred duty that the Crown bestows upon my clan.'

'And one through which you line your pockets, we know,' Jathan said.

Haronus gave him a cold look.

'Remember your place, Apprentice. You are speaking to a Draoihn of the Third Gate. I shall forgive one outburst. On the next I'll call you out for a duel.'

Jathan's eyes lowered instantly. He swallowed his defiance, buried his anger, and the other apprentices took his lead and fell silent. A far cry from the joyous faces drinking and shoving beans in each other's faces at Uloss.

'Go on, Draoihn,' Sanvaunt said.

'Our customs master discovered a wagon from LacNaithe purporting to be carrying a humble cargo of turnips through the south-eastern gate, three days ago. By chance, Apprentice Castus was overseeing another customs dispute. He sensed that something was wrong, and a little investigation proved they were carrying something far more sinister. Coffins. Bodies.'

I could feel alarm bells hammering in my skull. It's a trap, I thought, this is a trap and the walls are pressing in. And suddenly I knew. I glanced at Sanvaunt and then looked to Ovitus. His cheeks held bright spots of red; his skin was pasty. It wasn't fair. This wasn't fair.

'One was a young woman. Pretty, I thought, or she would have been in life. Have you ever seen somebody's flesh after it has been struck by lightning? The burn almost looks like a floral design. Beautiful in its way, though less so when it's spread across a corpse's chest.'

'That is a most serious discovery,' Ovitus said. His face was pale but gravely serious. He spoke like a lawyer. 'But there are fifty Draoihn of the Third Gate in this kingdom who could have done the same thing, so I do not see why my unc—'

'The second body was that of Actavia LacNaithe,' Haronus said abruptly. 'Your mother.'

His words finished like a book snapping closed, and the blood drained from Ovitus's cheeks.

'That's not possible,' he said by reflex. 'She's been dead for four years.'

'I confess I did not believe it myself until I saw her,' Haronus said. 'But Clan LacNaithe still practices embalming, and I knew her well when we were younger. To my grief, I recognised her. Quite the socialite, she was, before her marriage. And she wore this.'

He threw a medallion down onto the table. A stylised wyvern, looking back towards its own tail, embossed on a silver disc. Ovitus clutched at the pendant he wore around his own neck.

'It can't be,' he said. 'You're lying.'

Haronus LacClune raised an eyebrow.

'Under the circumstances, I will forgive you this outburst, Apprentice. Our Clans do not see eye to eye on many things, but grief will make a man forget himself. Her body was brought before your uncle, and he confirmed her identity. You may see her for yourself if you doubt me. Her remains are being held at the chapel.'

Ovitus's legs gave way. Jathan and Adanost caught him before he could hit the floor, wrestled his rag-doll body to a chair.

I looked to Sanvaunt, but he just stared straight ahead. Ovitus had not put it together yet. Hadn't realised that Sanvaunt must have known. But he would, and that betrayal would hurt almost as much. Ovitus began to weep, silent tears rolling over heavy cheeks.

Too many things are falling into place around us.

'This is a crime against all of LacNaithe,' Sanvaunt said, 'and still no reason to hold our van responsible. The grandmaster gave Ulovar the freedom of Redwinter's grounds. Why is he imprisoned?'

'His apprentice set about raising a force of the Night Below,' Haronus said. 'And now we find his sister's body in transit, with another fresh corpse alongside? He is entwined with the magic of death! What purpose is there in removing Actavia's remains other than to raise her from the Afterworld? Who else might wish to bring her back to life? And who else could possess the power to breach the Sixth Gate? Ulovar would not be the first Sarathi to hide within our midst.'

'Ulovar destroyed Ciuthach, one of the Riven Queen's own lieutenants!' I shouted. 'You only have to look at his eyes to see how he suffered for it. How can anyone believe that he seeks to harm—'

'Be silent, Retainer Raine,' Sanvaunt snapped. 'This is not the time.'

I bit down on my anger. Tried to swallow it, or at least hold it in check. I was only a retainer. I had no right to raise my voice to a Draoihn of the Third Gate, a man who could immolate me with a twist of his mind. But my blood was up. Ulovar had given so much of himself to get that damned page back to Redwinter. He had watched his own apprentice destroyed as Ciuthach took her. His eyes had never lost their bloody hue, and he had fought so hard, and endured the pain of carrying the cursed thing back to Redwinter. He had protected us—all of us—even those that refused to acknowledge it.

'I was there, Draoihn Haronus,' I said. 'I saw the rise of the Sarathi Ciuthach. It killed everybody I knew. Without Ulovar, that monstrosity would have escaped you all. He's not a villain. He's a *hero*.'

Haronus fluttered his hand at me as though shooing away an insect.

'I'm not here to debate with apprentices and servants,' he said. His words were not directed at me. I wasn't even worth challenging to a duel. 'My duty is to Redwinter and the Crown, as is all of yours. Ulovar will be tried for communing with the Night Below as soon as the council is ready to sit in judgement. But the grandmaster cannot take any further risks with Ulovar's apprentices. You too will be tested. She awaits you on the bridge to the Blackwell.'

Gasps of fear, widened eyes, mouths hung open, and Haronus LacClune led the way. Three more Draoihn, members of the Winterra in elaborately decorated armour, had been waiting outside, the steel wings on their helms wet with condensation.

'What does this mean?' I hissed at Esher as she passed. Her jaw was locked tight with abject terror, but I was not wanted. The Winterra led the apprentices away, and I remained in the greathouse, watching from the doorway, as they passed deeper into the fog.

'I never thought I would see such dark days for Clan LacNaithe, Miss Raine,' Tarquus said. 'Come in, out of the cold.'

'What will they do to them?'

'They will send them into the Blackwell,' Tarquus said.

'What will happen to them when they go in?'

'That is far beyond my powers to know,' Tarquus said. 'And beyond yours too. But I do not think that any that go down into the Blackwell return the same. They will need our help when they return. I know that you do not want to be here. That you did not choose this life. But we must do our jobs, to the best of our ability.'

'Our job is to stand by and do nothing,' I said.

'Or perhaps we are the oil that greases the wheel,' Tarquus said. 'There is no dishonour in a life of service, First Retainer Raine. I struggled hard to earn my position here. So I will serve, whatever those poor souls require, and I will try to bring them comfort from whatever nightmares they must endure.'

It didn't feel like enough. I couldn't argue with what he asked, though. Couldn't fight what seemed like the inexorable march of fate's drum. With every beat, that crack in the scar that lay across my mind seemed to flex, a glow forming along the seam that had torn in it the day Nairna LacMuaid died. There was magma behind that scar, the pressure building. It was contained there for now. I would not allow it to break free.

I polished the silverware. It was all I could do. I saw my face reflected in the back of a spoon. I wasn't so skinny anymore. My hair, white-blue and unnatural, brushed against my shoulders now. The scar that Hazia's knife had sliced across my face had healed into a ruler-straight line. Who was this girl staring back at me? Where had the old Raine gone when Ulovar broke my mind? Other faces floated in the silver, behind mine, as though they stood at my shoulder. Ovitus, his face streaked with tears. Esher, quivering with fear. Sanvaunt, mouth set, determination and honour holding back all else. I tried to find sympathy for them, tried to feel what they must be feeling now, marched towards that chasm and the narrow bridge of stone that spanned it.

I didn't want to feel any of it. I didn't want to have to think myself into their minds. I pressed back against my scar, seeing it for the gift Ulovar had intended it to be, and willed it to shut and never let me feel the pain of loss again.

The apprentices would not speak of what was asked of them, or done to them, but when they finally returned, none of them ate. Platters of baked fish and winter greens sat uneaten on the tabletop. They kept to themselves, secluded. I tried Esher's door, could hear her muffled sobbing within. She would not admit me. Not even Ovitus would talk about it. He sat and stared out from his window, as though the misty garden held something he desperately needed.

Ulovar was trapped beneath the earth, bound away in stone. I hadn't realised just how much space he'd filled in this vast, echoing house. He spent words sparingly, and the apprentices had always complained about his insistence on attending lessons and singing the hours in the church. They had behaved like his children, I thought, and he had accepted the role of parent. He had pushed them towards those things that would prepare them best for the hard world they had entered. In a single day, his removal had cast his apprentices into bleak despair. His presence was missed from the clan as though we had lost our heart. It was more than that, of course. The apprentices shivered at every quiet sound, and crept across the stairs as if hoping not to be noticed.

Perhaps Esher had been right, and I was fortunate that the grandmaster had turned me away. I had been spared whatever cruelty they had suffered at the Blackwell.

Winter cold settled upon us with all its callous bite, and a quiet evening several days later found me on the eastern side of the city, where the river flowed pure and clear before the city got her claws into it, the banks studded with landing points for the rod-and-line men.

'Have to wonder why they bother, don't you darlin'?' a familiar, unwanted voice said. Short-clipped hair, a scar twisting his upper lip, wearing a dull yellow surcoat over mail. Hess.

'I can understand it,' I said. I was afraid of this man and his friends. Afraid of what they knew about me, what they could reveal about me if they chose to. But I had barely spoken to anyone for days.

'The time they spend here, they might as well go buy a fish in the market from one of the sea trawlers. It ain't like fish is expensive.'

'They aren't here for the fish,' I said. Hess sat down beside me, his armour clinking.

'What are they here for, then?'

'They like the solitude,' I said. 'Busies their hands while they clear their thoughts. They think they need an excuse to sit and think. It's different for women. We talk to other women. Men find it hard to talk. So they fish.'

'And that's it? They just want to be alone?'

'Not just that,' I said. I tucked my knees up beneath my chin. 'Look at their clothes. They're labourers, builders, dock workers mostly. You ever do a job like that?'

'I've done my fair share of physical work, if that's what you mean,' he said. He had rough-skinned hands, a strong frame. I believed him.

'Back north, the merchants came up to the mining towns maybe four times a year. Those four nights, the villagers would go wild. They'd drink and celebrate like it was the solstice. Nothing else had changed, just some money turning over. The next day they'd need to be back down in the holes, doing the same work, chipping away in the dark. But on those nights, they got to *win* for once. And that's what the fishermen are doing. They're trying for little wins.'

'They want to beat the fish?'

'The fish, or chance, or just themselves, maybe,' I said. 'People wonder why the poor don't change. Why, if you're born with nothing, you don't spend your life striving for something else? All the beggars you see on the streets, the kids with filthy faces, the folk who whore for the price of a beer. They don't get to win at much. Can you imagine it? Every day, every single day, waking up to having nothing, to knowing that just to get that one beer, you're going to have to let some stranger touch you, or to get a day's work labouring, you need to beat ten other men who are all as desperate as you. The lords and the have-somethings look down on them. Sneer at them. But they'll never grasp what it's like, not just to lose, but to never win.' I gestured across the water, where a man drew a fish up on the end of his line. He unhooked it, called across to a friend nearby and held it up. It was small, just a silver flicker in his hand from this side of the bank. Then he threw it back into the water. 'Fishing is just a symbol. Like religion. Like being told that the Light Above loves you.'

'Bloody hell, darlin', you're as bleak as a cloud bank today,' he said. 'Come on. The boss wants to see you again.'

'I need to get back to Redwinter,' I said. I had my usual duties, waiting on the table and hot-pressing the apprentices' temple robes.

'Won't take so long,' he said. 'Besides. I got us a carriage.'

I looked around, and behind me was a plain, dark carriage with a pair of

dun horses in the traces. South had been tethered up behind them. I hated seeing they had touched my horse. I did not want to go with him. The hard-faced
woman, Najih, sat the driver's seat, watching with cold little eyes. I didn't have
a great deal of choice.

They were dangerous people. The Queen of Feathers had spilled my secret
to them, guided them to find me. I had not forgotten how her anger had risen,
how she had spanked me like a child. And yet, she had also saved me when
Ulovar had been intent on killing me to get to Hazia, and they were my only
link to finding out what she was. The only people I could ask.

Things couldn't get much worse. But I needed allies just then, allies with
whom I could speak freely.

'I'll go,' I agreed. 'But cross me and I'll kill you.' Hess grinned, his split lip
revealing his missing teeth.

'Wouldn't expect nothing less.'

Hess offered a hand to help me up, and I stepped inside. He drew the curtains, leaving us in darkness.

'Sorry about the gloom,' he said. 'Maybe it matches your mood, though,
eh? Where we're going, can't really let folks know where it is. What with us lot
having the spirit sense.'

'I'm not going to tell anyone,' I said.

'Not willingly,' he said. The carriage pulled away, bumping and jolting. Hess
lit a very small oil lamp that was attached to a wall mount, giving us a dim,
stinky light to see by, then produced a short-stemmed pipe. He puffed the bowl
to a glow, the thin, oily Ashium leaf smoke coiling into the air. Sighed as the
leaf's effect settled in his mind.

'I've said nothing, about what I saw at the stoning,' I said. The carriage felt
like a cage. 'I've seen the dead my whole life. I'm not going to start running my
mouth now.'

'You're a smart kid, Raine,' Hess said. 'How much do you know about your
van Ulovar?'

'I know enough.'

'You know what Fier is?' Hess asked. 'You know what it means?'

'It's the trance of the Fourth Gate,' I said.

'Right, darlin'. And the fourth trance is the trance of the mind. Doesn't
mean that they can read minds, least not as far as I know. Veretaine says that
ain't possible. But they can break you in other ways. If one of those Fourth
Gate Draoihn stripped away your ability to care about yourself, you think you
wouldn't talk? It ain't like you can do anything to stop it.'

I knew the truth of that better than anyone. Ulovar had sliced his mind across mine, back in Dalnesse when my mind was breaking and I'd been on the verge of sticking a knife in my own neck, and he'd left me changed. He had done it to help me—to protect me, from what I might do to myself, and now he languished in a cell.

The carriage journey took a long time, but in the gloom I had no way of telling how long, and the clatter of the carriage's wheels against the cobbled streets obscured most other sounds. Hess told me about his time as a soldier, hunting pirates along the west coast, all the way to the Glimmering Isles. He showed me a tattoo on his arm, mermaids singing to a ship.

'Saw plenty of those,' he said. 'Beautiful—that's what you think when you first see 'em. Tits like you wouldn't believe, hair all red and wet and salty as they swim alongside you. They don't have fish tails, though. That's just bollocks.'

'You're spinning me tales.'

'Out at sea we called 'em Drowners, on account that they only really want you to get in the water with 'em so they can pull you down and eat you. They drop the glamour when you're in with them. After that, you really don't want to know what they look like. Other lads couldn't see through it, not like I could. Maybe part of the grave-sight, I don't know.'

'So what did they look like?'

Hess grinned in the gloom. He'd obviously wanted me to ask.

'Imagine someone all carved out of old driftwood. Thin and bony, all knobs and lumps. Face almost like a skull, eyeless. Hair all tangled like fecked-up fishing line and weed all knotted together. That's what they really are. The sailors, they reckon they're spirits of the Faded that drowned.'

'I'd like to see them,' I said.

'Trust me, darlin', you really wouldn't.'

At length the carriage drew to a stop as the sound of a large, closing door banged shut behind us. Hess gestured me out, and I stepped down into a dim courtyard, walled by two-storey buildings on all sides, with an enclosed tunnel through which the carriage had driven. I felt very exposed, lost, and utterly unarmed save for the knife on my belt. Suddenly this all seemed like a very poor idea. Veretaine's people hadn't tried to harm me, hadn't done anything other than take me for a ride in a carriage, but they had shown me things. Dangerous things. Things that they had no true right to know about. Doors and windows looked down over the courtyard, but they were boarded, or empty, and the buildings looked unoccupied.

It was precisely the kind of place you'd bring a man to kill him. A man, or a girl.

'I don't want to be here,' I said. My hand rested on my belt knife.

'None of us want to be here, darlin',' Hess said. 'But that's just the hand the Light Above dealt us, her and her bloody Lords and Ladies and all their nonsense. But you've nothing to fear from us. Like I said. Your master has ways of pulling information out of people that make a hot knife look like a child's toy. You want to know more about that, you ask Najih up there. She'll tell you a thing or two about what a Draoihn can compel you to do.'

The woman, all thick wrists, broad, dark face and heavy legs, jumped down from the footplate. She landed like a long-cat, heavy bodied but somehow light and silent on her feet.

'You're too inquisitive by far, kid,' she said in a dockside accent. 'If the Light Above loved the curious, there'd be fewer penalties for being that way. Let's move. Don't want to keep the boss waiting.'

They left the team in its traces, moved a rotting crate out the way of one of the doors and, with a tug, pulled it open. Beyond the walled enclave I could hear dogs barking. Lots of dogs, like a pack was roaming the streets, all yelping and barking as one. What use anybody could have to keep so many dogs in a city I could only guess at, and the answers weren't especially pleasant. This was a bad place. I'd been treated gently, with kindness even, but I'd have to be a first-rate idiot to think that meant I was safe. I realised as I was led beyond the door that I'd allowed myself to be taken to a place I didn't know, and where nobody who knew me could guess I'd gone.

They said that they didn't want to harm me. I'd lost any control over the matter.

The building's interior was bare and dirty, signs of rough-sleeping and the smell of urine oozing from the walls. Hess and Najih led me along, until we came to a closed cellar door. When they prompted me to descend the creaking wooden stairs, I hadn't any choice about that either.

What I found below was not what I expected at all. This wasn't a cellar. It almost looked like a street. A paved floor, old buildings to either side, decayed and forgotten. Like someone had bricked it up and carried on building a city over the top.

'There was a city here, before Harranir,' Hess said. 'The Age of Strife, back before the war between Hallenae and Maldouen, covered it in ash and fire. Harranir was built on top of it, but the old places are still here. Buried deep.'

Najih lit a lamp, leading the way deeper into the dark. Hess motioned that I should follow. I was tensed, ready to run, but if Hess or Najih meant to kill me, they'd had more than enough opportunity already. I kept my guard up, but they didn't want blood. The floor was wet and slick with grime and algae beneath my boots.

'Mind your footing,' Hess said. 'The path can be treacherous. It dries out as we go deeper.'

'How did you find this place?'

'It's no great secret,' he said. 'There are a bunch of entrances to the under-city. Not many want to come down here. People fear the dark, and rightly so. The things that live in it. The roof's not always stable. The warrens are huge and rambling. Some who get lost down here never find their way back.'

'But you can?'

Najih held her lamp up to the wall. A thick line of white chalk ran along it with chevrons pointing the way back towards the entrance.

'Some of it's mapped. Don't leave the paths marked with the arrows, and don't go wandering off into the dark. There's no daylight down here, not ever.'

I stuck closer to her after that, the tunnel too reminiscent of the crypt beneath Dalnesse that had led Hazia to Ciuthach. It felt wrong down here. Dead buildings stood to either side. Some of them seemed filled with stone; others had hollow windows with dark spaces behind them. Above, the street was roofed with cut stone.

'This place was already dark before they built Harranir on top of it,' I said. My voice was hard, tinny in the enclosed space.

'Very observant of you,' Hess said. 'This was Delatmar. They were skilled builders until the Age of Strife saw an end to them. It was demons, you see? Nine devastations were visited on us, including a poison rain that swept the world. The people covered their cities with stone and lived without light. The fires below the mountains kept them warm back then. Hot air still blows down here, sometimes. But it was their undoing as well.'

I heard motion from within one of the building shells. A small fire burned within, and two dark little creatures, dirty and fearful, camped around it. They had a fish on a stick over the fire but scuttled away from the lamplight.

'Beggars,' Hess said. 'You'll find more than a few down here.'

'They looked strange.'

'The darkness does that to everyone, after a while,' he said. 'Everything seems strange in the dark.' There was truth to that.

Najih turned down another street and eventually brought us to a door that seemed to be cut into the rock itself. It was new—thick, heavy wood. Unreadable sigils and glyphs formed a circle across it. She fished a key from her pocket and set it to the lock, took two attempts to get it to turn. Gestured me inside.

It was like a bathhouse inside, a large room flanked with rows of columns holding bright lamps. Tiered steps led down on each side of a rectangular depression in the floor, twenty feet wide and more than forty feet long. The ceiling rose higher, balconies looking down on what I guessed must once have been a bathing pool but was now a dusty, dry pit. At the far end of the room, hooded old Veretaine awaited us in a throne-like chair, swamped by the number of cushions around him.

He was not alone. Other, younger, men and women were waiting for us too. They were robed like priests. They watched.

'Young Miss Raine,' Veretaine said, his ruined voice catching on every stone surface. 'You are welcome here. My thanks for coming. It is not easy for me to go up into the city, and these cold days are the worst.'

Hess and Najih took me across to him. There were other chairs to sit in. Bowls of dates and nuts sat on a small table beside Veretaine's chair.

'Why am I here?' I asked. My voice was harder than I intended, flinty, but part of that was from my jaw wanting to lock up. It was cold down there, bitterly so, and almost lightless. I wondered what they did down here, not just Hess and Najih and Veretaine, but the other men and women who stood around, apparently without purpose or activity to occupy them.

The answer was obvious, really. They were waiting for me.

'Words reach me, even down here. Big words and small, important and meaningless. They all come down to one who listens enough,' Veretaine said. His voice was a rustle of funeral shrouds. 'My feet are twisted. My hands are broken. Even my sight is gone. But I listen. I listen very, very carefully, and I hear things.'

'What am I doing here?' I asked again. I didn't like his riddling. I wanted to ask what I needed and be gone.

'You are learning,' Veretaine snapped. Quite at odds with the quiet-voiced man who'd drawn me to watch an execution. But he soothed himself, twisted fingers clicking as he laid them against the arms of his chair. 'Do you remember what I told you before?' he went on. 'We are Those Who See. All of us here, we see. As you do. Some of us have had the spirit-sight all our lives. Some have come to it more recently.'

'You all see the dead?' I asked.

'They tried stoning me,' Hess said. He gestured to his scarred lip, the teeth missing behind it. 'They got in one good rock and a few shitty ones before I got away. I was only thirteen.'

'I didn't see them until I lost a child,' Najih said. 'Lost the baby before it were born. Husband punched me in the gut. Killed the babe. And that's when the sight came to me.'

They all had a story. Some had seen ghosts since they were young. One man claimed to have been struck by lightning while trying to secure a weather vane to a church roof.

'We died, Raine,' Veretaine said grimly. 'Or some part of us did. We died and were remade. That's when the spirit sense begins. We cross over and are brought back.'

'I drowned once!' I said. The words leapt out of me. It was such a relief. Such enormous relief to be able to tell someone. To let the words out after all this time, to people who wouldn't fear and kill me, just for being what I was. 'When I was born, I didn't breathe. The birth-cord was wrapped around my neck. Is that why I see the ghosts?'

'We have each had to walk our own path through the veil,' Veretaine said. 'Some, more painfully than others. But none of us asked for this. None of us chose it. Imagine if there was a choice. Or a way to make others see what we see? Perhaps then they would not persecute us. Hurt us. Kill us, because of the vagaries of fate.'

Veretaine reached up slowly and began to push back his hood. His brittle, twisted fingers couldn't grip the edges properly, couldn't curl to make a fist. The undead thing, Ciuthach, had been horrible, but he had been long in the earth. It was worse seeing this on a living, breathing man. I swallowed. Hard.

Veretaine's eyes had been put out. Not just ruined, but gouged from his head. Empty sockets of twisted scar tissue stared at me from within. He was old, but not as old as I had imagined. Maybe fifty. Fifty-five. Sprouts of wispy hair protruded from his scalp, as though most of it had ceased growing and only shreds remained. He would not have frightened children: he would have terrified them.

'We each,' Veretaine rasped again, 'have walked our own path. But we did not bring you here to compare the cruelties of other men.'

'Then why?'

'We have need of you, child of the north,' he said. 'The tide of the world is beginning to turn. The Queen of Feathers walks among us, and change is afoot. We will not be cowering in the dark forever. And there is but one true strength: friendship. I need to ask it of you.'

I had been feeling uneasy. That feeling only grew stronger. I found myself glancing around the room, looking for exits. But I was down in their darkness, and I had never been a runner. Trapped in this dead city, with people who saw the ghosts just as I did, who knew too much about me. I kept my mouth shut. Veretaine couldn't see me, not without eyes. But somehow he was looking right at me.

'I had not intended to put such pressure upon you so soon,' he said. 'But I had not expected the van of one of the great clans to bring you so tightly into his inner circle either. Or to make you kill for him. Yes, we know what you did. Better than anybody. The spirit who dresses in feathers came to me. She told me of your deeds in the forest.'

Chills ran up my spine, along my arms, hairs rising.

'Who is she?' I said. 'What is she?'

'Old,' Veretaine said. 'Very old, and very powerful.'

'Is she dead?'

'I do not think mortal terms such as alive and dead can be applied to her. She has never offered me a name. But she has aided us, when we have need.'

'What is this friendship you want from me?' I asked.

'Forces move against the clan that shelters you,' Veretaine said. 'You have seen it yourself. The clan of LacNaithe cannot be allowed to fall. Even if they bring down Van LacNaithe, his nephew must be protected.'

'I don't understand. Why do you care what happens to Ovitus?'

'If they move against the van, they will strike against his family next,' Veretaine said. 'We have no other ally of your standing within Redwinter. If you sense that the heir is under threat, he must be saved.'

'I'm just his servant,' I said.

'But you and he are close. Closer than a master would be with one who serves him for nothing but pay. One day, Ovitus of LacNaithe may become van. And where better to change the future, to create a better future, than to position one of our own at his side? Would you not council him to lenience? Council him to more just decisions? Might you not guide him to the truth?'

The truth. I had not done well feeding that to him of late. It was for his own good, wasn't it? Or maybe it was for mine.

This was not what I had expected. I thought of that scrap of paper, hidden away in my room, that held Ovitus's description. Somebody had wanted him taken alive. But why?

'Ovitus will never be a strong van,' I said. 'Not strong enough to stand against the likes of Merovech LacClune or Van LacAud.'

'And yet, is LacNaithe not the closest ally of Clan LacDaine, the king's own clan? Will Prince Caelan LacDaine not become heir? If Prince Caelan is successful and takes the Crown after his father's death, he must court LacNaithe for its assistance and influence. And there, perhaps, we might also make some small difference.'

I stood in silence for some moments. I felt no kinship towards these people. They had suffered, but many people suffered. The vagrants on the streets, those who took sick and wasted to nothing, those who followed sooth-sisters for a fragment of joy and been murdered for it. They had all suffered misfortune, just as I had. I didn't want to be like them, though. I didn't want to bind my-self to a group who led people through the shadow, with talk of plotting and political gain.

'Was Ovitus LacNaithe attacked at your order?' I asked.

'Of course not. Ovitus LacNaithe can be moulded into an ally. The boy has a good heart. Ask yourself. Who would benefit from Ovitus LacNaithe's de-mise? The removal of a weak, lack-spirit heir?'

I still hated the answer I found. I hated what it said about me, how I felt about a young man who had offered me nothing but friendship.

'The clan,' I said.

'And who cares more for the clan above all else?'

No, no, no, no, no, no, no. I didn't want to have to say it. I didn't want to think these things, not when I had felt something for him, not when I was about to betray him with a word. I wanted none of it to be true.

'Sanvaunt LacNaithe,' I said quietly. 'If Ulovar is destroyed, and Ovitus gone, then even a wildrose would inherit the seat. There are no other children. And if he controlled LacNaithe, he would have power to serve his precious Crown.'

The last words left my lips like bloody spittle.

'Yes,' Veretaine said. 'Sanvaunt LacNaithe has much to gain if Ulovar and Ovitus fall.'

A floor had dropped away from me, and I was spinning, fluttering through the dark. How could Sanvaunt want that? How could he be so cold as to un-make his own uncle, his own cousin. How could duty come first?

But he had been the one to go to Valarane, to discover his aunt's missing bones. He had entrusted his cousin's safety to me alone, in place of a ring of clan guards. I was nothing to him but a girl he could barely look at, not even an apprentice. Had I allowed my pride and whatever confusion Sanvaunt stirred up in me make me accept something that was so obviously foolish?

I stood there in silence and confusion and eventually said the only thing that made sense to me.

'I will think on what you've said.'

'Ulovar LacNaithe is beyond our ability to help, and the hour grows late,' Veretaine said. He groped beside him with broken, warped-bone fingers, and raised a small talisman in front of me. A simple bone-carved charm, a bird, suspended on a bark-string thong. 'This is a sign of friendship, known to none but us here. Whilst you wear it, you shall have our friendship.' He held the charm out to me, and I couldn't refuse him. Hess had a similar bone-cut charm around his own neck, and I noted that the others wore them too.

'Thank you,' I said. 'The world is a dark place without friends.'

'For now, your friendship is all I can ask,' Veretaine said. 'But one day I may be forced to ask for your help, Raine. And when I do, remember that it could be you sitting here with shattered fingers and ankles that cannot bear your own weight. I am told that it is dark here, beneath the world. My darkness will last forever. But my people will guide you back up to the light.'

I rode slowly back to Redwinter. My mind was a pit. The faces of people that I'd met, that I knew, tumbled into it like discarded carnival masks.

Could I truly believe that Sanvaunt was behind this? There was much for him to gain—but he cared for his uncle and for Ovitus. Didn't he?

Alive.

I knew he thought Ovitus was unfit to lead. Saw a naïve, indolent man wishing his life away on dreams that would never come to pass. Did he plan to deposit his cousin in some quiet absolution house, far from the politics and danger that Ovitus hated so much?

Would Ovitus even oppose it? And if I forced my hand down into my chest and groped for the truth that lay there, could I really say that Sanvaunt was wrong?

The lands and power that LacNaithe controlled were vast. Ovitus was kind; his nature was so sweet he could sicken himself on it. How could he possibly match the likes of Haronus LacClune? Haronus was only the spokesman for the clan. Their van, by all accounts, was ten times worse. Merovech LacClune, father of Castus LacClune. Castus LacClune who'd put a knife into a man's throat and had barely blinked as the blood spattered his face.

Who would I want leading the clan I was sworn to?

But motive did not equate to guilt. Sanvaunt would have needed to persuade, or trick, Hazia into entering the Blackwell. He had been tested by Grandmaster Robilar, along with Ulovar's apprentices, and whatever ordeal he had endured, his innocence had been proved. If he was behind Hazia's theft, he had another ally, someone much more powerful than he was. If he was somehow behind the charges brought against Ulovar, then he had also exhumed his aunt's body and sent it to the city, and that was a greater mystery still. It brought dishonour upon his own clan. That wasn't necessary, if Ulovar and Ovitus were gone and he was set to inherit anyway.

It seemed impossible. Sanvaunt was duty-bound to the Crown as strongly as Ulovar. He would never have unleashed Ciuthach for personal ambition.

I thought of that book he had. The one he was always writing in, the one he tucked out of sight whenever I entered. I had to get my hands on it. Maybe he was stupid or arrogant enough to leave a trail in the paper. Without evidence, all I had was supposition and assumption.

My shoulders felt like I'd been yoked to anvils. I'd found something here, here in Redwinter of all the places on the face of the earth. I'd seen it forming around me, felt it gathering me into its embrace. A place in the world. It wasn't fair. And Sanvaunt LacNaithe was part of its core.

No. What did it matter? He'd been good to me. Then cold to me. Good to me. Cold to me. Ulovar must have told him what I'd witnessed, and once he knew, he'd turned against me, the moment he'd understood my testimony could exonerate his uncle. The uncle who had given him responsibility, and position, and then demanded that for all his work, his accomplishments, his duty, that he would serve his younger cousin. A young man who couldn't even muster the nerve to tell a girl how he felt about her.

But he'd also helped me out.

He was so formidable, as much a pillar of LacNaithe as Ulovar.

He made my head spin. I couldn't bear it.

The wind among the trees was making my eyes water. I wiped treacherous definitely-not-tears from my eyes. The snatterkin were grumbling, deep in the shadows, but I bared my teeth at them, and for once they quieted.

Nobody admitted me into the LacNaithe greathouse, so I let myself in. It was quiet. No patter of servants' feet, tapping down the corridor. No smell of cooking. I slung my riding half cloak onto a peg and trudged slowly up the stairs. When had my feet become so heavy? All of me had grown heavy. Heavy and useless and pointless.

I joined Ovitus in his chambers. Sanvaunt had asked me to protect him. Veretaine had asked me to protect him against Sanvaunt. Everyone was so concerned with his wellbeing, except maybe Ovitus himself. A jar of cider rested beside him, as it often did in the days since the grandmaster had tested him in the Blackwell. His eyes weren't on the open book in his lap. He stared into the fire, one eye twitching in thought.

'The winds of time scour all men clean, and leave nought but bones behind,' he said.

'I'd rather have a bath,' I said. This was the wrong way around. I was supposed to be the grim one. But his experience in the Blackwell had cracked something inside him. 'You're feeling melodramatic, then.'

'Not my words,' he said. 'Eudiricles. The king, remember?'

'I remember.'

I stared at my feet for a little while. Ovitus was content to sit quietly. Winds of time, I supposed. I didn't know how to begin. How to start talking without revealing what I was, and what I knew, and what I feared.

I took a breath. Held it. Steeled it.

'Something has to be done.'

'Something,' Ovitus said. 'I know.'

'We can't just sit here. Merovech LacClune's entourage is approaching the city. We're running out of time.'

'It's being worked on,' Ovitus said. He took a long drink of cider. The room was stiflingly hot, the fire over-banked. Ovitus reached out and tossed on another log. I took off my coat, hung it on a peg by the door and took a seat away from the flames.

'Did Sanvaunt find anything useful in the book that he retrieved from Valarane?'

'Nothing,' he said. 'Another dead end. As for Hazia—she couldn't have entered the Blackwell alone.' He shivered despite the heat. 'The forces that guard it—I could feel the evil, Raine. I could feel it along my bones, under the flesh. Pulling at the roots of my hair, getting beneath my teeth. Only a Draoihn of the Fourth could shield themselves against it. And Hazia never walked beyond the First.'

He drank again. He looked as though every part of him was slumping, collapsing downwards, melting like a candle. The bags beneath his eyes were the same colour as the bruise on his temple.

'I'm sorry, Ovitus.'

'I went to see my mother today,' he said. 'They decided to keep her remains here, for now. She's here with us, Raine. Unburied. *Disturbed*. Do you think that the dead stay linked to their bodies, after they die?'

I knew they didn't. Most of them didn't, anyway. Most ghosts simply rose, then drifted away to nothing. Maybe it would have given him comfort to know, but I could never tell Ovitus that.

'Bodies are just flesh and bone,' I said. 'They aren't us. Not our essence. Cut off an arm and you're still the same person. Wherever your mother is, they're just bones. Winds of time, you know?'

'I want to hurt them,' Ovitus said quietly. 'Whoever did this. I've never wanted to hurt anybody before. But when I find them, I—I'll—' His words dissolved into humourless laughter, thick with self-mockery. 'Who am I trying to kid? I'm not built to hurt people. Look at me. The only thing I could do damage to is a tavern's supply cupboard.' He grabbed a roll of his belly in one hand.

He hated himself just then. Maybe it was the powerlessness. Or maybe the attack, the pressures, and the knowledge of the responsibility that could be thrust upon him were all building to a weight he was no longer able to bear. I reached out and put a hand on his sleeve.

'I'm going to help you,' I said. 'Do you trust me?'

'Oh, don't worry, Raine,' he said. Hardness that I'd never heard in his voice before rose out of the self-pity. A hardness that caused me to draw my hand back, suddenly unsure whose arm filled the sleeve. 'I've taken action. We'll have answers soon enough.'

I felt the grinding of ancient cogs beginning to turn, rust flaking away.

'Ovitus—what have you done?' The greathouse was so silent. 'Where are the others?'

'I've done what nobody else was prepared to do,' he said. When he looked to me, his green eyes were either drunk or desperate or deranged, or maybe all three. 'They'll be back soon. We should prepare.'

He rose without another word and left the room. I followed. I had never thought of Ovitus as a dangerous man. But there was something to fear in the swift-taken actions of a man who has been bent too far. He led me down into the wine cellar.

'Howen won't be pleased if you mess up his system,' I warned.

'Who's Howen?' Ovitus asked.

I frowned. 'Second Retainer Howen. Brown hair. Nice man.'

'Oh. He's gone home,' he said. 'The retainers who live here are confined to their rooms.'

'Why?'

'I'm the lord of the greathouse in my uncle's absence,' Ovitus said. 'They have to do what I say.' It wasn't what I'd asked, even if it was true.

Arched buttresses supported a vaulted ceiling, the walls lined with rows of bottles, vintages from across the kingdom and beyond.

'What now?'

'We wait.'

We waited. It was cold down there. Ovitus muttered to himself, reciting lines of poetic philosophy back to himself. Words of strength, encouragement. He didn't answer any more of my questions. Sounds of a struggle came from above. I looked to my friend, but he just stared towards the stair. He picked up a cloak, embroidered with the wyvern of Clan LacNaithe, and swung it around his shoulders. In that moment, he cut a regal figure. A future leader.

A man.

Jathan and Adanost staggered down the stairs, a struggling figure between them, a bag over his head. His hands were tied behind his back. Esher followed, a wild look in her eyes, then Colban and Gelis. Liara came last, and she at least looked mortified. The young man that Jathan and Adanost shoved forwards was finely dressed. A white rose on blue, a blue rose on white on his panelled coat.

Clan LacClune.

'What have you done?' I hissed.

Jathan and Adanost forced the young man to his knees, each holding a shoulder. I heard the captive's panting breaths, damp through the hood.

'He struggled a bit,' Jathan said. He had a swollen lip and a smear of blood across one cheek. Adanost just grunted. His knuckles were scraped, bloody. He reached forwards and stripped the bag away, and I found myself looking into the simmering fury of Castus LacClune's eyes. His cheek was swollen, his lip split.

'In the name of the Light Above and all her Lords and Ladies, you're as stupid as you are fat, LacNaithe,' he growled.

Liara flinched.

'We'll do the talking here,' Esher yelled. Her hands trembled at her sides in hard-balled fists.

Castus had eyes only for Ovitus, standing over him. Nowhere near as afraid as I thought he should be.

'Ovitus,' I hissed. 'This is wrong. You can't do this.'

'Be quiet, Raine,' he said. He drew himself up. He was tall, and suddenly all that weight looked like strength rather than encumbrance. 'LacClune.'

'You've got some fecking nerve, LacNaithe,' Castus said. He spat bloody spittle at Ovitus's feet. 'Do you have any idea what you've started?'

'Started?' Ovitus said grimly. 'I haven't started anything. But I'll finish it. I know you were close to Hazia. How did you persuade her to break the vault?'

Castus looked from Ovitus to the apprentices that held him. And then he began to laugh. He threw his head back, the sound bouncing from the ceiling vaults.

'What's so funny?' Ovitus demanded. 'Tell me. Tell me or I'll hurt you. Don't think I won't.'

I tensed. Castus had been good to me, hadn't he? For all they said about Clan LacClune, he'd sat with me, spoken with me like an equal when we were anything but.

'Esher,' I said imploringly. 'Please, you have to stop this.'

'It has to be done, Raine,' she said. 'We have to do something. To find the truth.'

Her passion was so misdirected. It seemed screamingly obvious to me, but the apprentices wore the haunting of the Blackwell like shadowed wings on their backs.

'Something isn't this!' I said.

'At least one of you has brains,' Castus said.

'Silence, Raine,' Ovitus snapped. And there it was. Ovitus as van. Ovitus as our commander and master. It felt cold and hard and alien. 'LacClune here preyed on Hazia. He made her do it.'

'You dumb waste of flesh,' Castus snapped back, his laughter vanished and mocking anger on his face. 'Is that what this is about? About Hazia? Because you wanted to feck her and she chose me instead?'

Ovitus raised his fist then. He'd put on gloves, and it was a big fist. I reached out and took hold of his arm.

'No,' I said. 'Don't do this.'

'Control yourself, Retainer!' Adanost barked at me. 'This is Draoihn business. LacClune have been working against us from the beginning. It's their fault Ulovar is in a dungeon right now.' He jerked his head towards the door. 'Get out of here.'

But Ovitus hadn't moved, hadn't strained against my grip. He didn't want to hit Castus. This wasn't him. This was desperation, frustration and terror doing their work. Anyone could break under those pressures.

'You can't do this,' I said. I addressed them all. 'What are you thinking? You *idiots*. You want to start a clan war, now of all times? You want blood sprayed across Redwinter? What do you think Merovech LacClune will do to you if you beat the shit out of his son?'

'You should listen to her, LacNaithe,' Castus said. 'Your woman seems to be keeping your brains for you.'

'I'm not his woman,' I said. The words flashed out of me, hardly the most important thing just then, but I felt a bite of indignity at the assumption. I was a retainer, and Ovitus was a thail. I wasn't some richly kept mistress.

'Tell me,' Ovitus repeated. 'Why you dug up my mother.' The last word choked him.

Castus leaned back, earning himself a shove from Jathan.

'Are you mad?' he said. 'What possible business could I have with your mother? And you think that Hazia and I were lovers? You honestly think that's true?'

Ovitus's face was red with heat. His raised fist trembled.

'Hazia was my friend. Not my lover. She used to come to our greathouse to escape your endless pining after her, back before someone else caught your eye.' He thrust his head back towards Liara. 'You were her friend too. Tell them.'

'I—I don't know what you mean,' Liara said.

'Yes, you do,' Castus drawled, as though this was intensely wearying, rather than dangerous. 'You just don't want to say it in front of your future lord. But I'll say it. She—'

Ovitus had a lot more mass than I did. He was taller, stronger, and when he swung at Castus, I couldn't hold him back. But I slowed his arm just enough that Castus managed to sway from the blow, and it caught him on the top of the head, instead of right in the face. Ovitus hopped back, shaking his hand. Bad idea, punching skulls. Castus was laughing.

'Support me, or get out!' Ovitus told me angrily.

'You know this isn't the way,' I said. I tried to put it all into my face. All my imploring, desperate wish that he wouldn't be this man. Wouldn't become Braithe, striking out to punish me because I'd made him feel small. Ovitus—my friend Ovitus—had to be in there still, beneath the drink and the pain. He had to be.

'I'll tell you two things for free,' Castus said. 'First is something that you should know to your core, since you're going to run a great clan one day. Lac-Clune and LacNaithe have never been friends. But if we take you down, it will be because you've failed the Crown. You think that LacClune would release something like Ciuthach on the world? Are you as utterly delusional as you seem?'

Ovitus thrust his fists down at his sides. He wanted to glower, or he wanted to cry, or maybe both. His teeth were locked tight.

'And here's the second,' Castus said. 'You lot are fecking terrible. As servants of the clan, and the Crown, and as Draoihn. You think you're learning, but you don't even know what Eio is capable of. You're weak on the practice court. Your trances sound like a herd of rhinar trampling through a glassworks. And you have no idea how a master can put it to use.'

On the other side of the room, I saw Liara's eyes go wide.

'His ropes!' she said, and that was all the warning they had.

Castus's hands were free, and he slammed an elbow into Jathan's groin, sending the apprentice reeling back in pain. He was already springing up, knocking Adanost's fist aside as though it were nothing, and I heard his trance whispering through my mind, a horse galloping across fine sand, so soft but so deep. He struck at Adanost, ripped two of the gold rings from his ear and then knocked him down with a palm to the face. Esher came at him launching punches, but Castus flowed like water, like he knew exactly where each attack was coming from, shadowing in to stop her arm and then hammering a downward blow to her gut. She heaved for a moment, and then fell backwards.

Ovitus just stood there, shock written across his face. The other apprentices backed away to the edges of the room. Tears gleamed on Liara's cheeks.

'Not so easy when you don't jump me coming out of the shitter, is it?' Castus said. He spat on the floor. 'Pathetic.' Adanost made to rise, but Castus sank a kick into his gut, sending him rolling over.

I hadn't moved. There was nothing I could have done against Castus. And I didn't think that I wanted to. The young LacClune heir looked around at the apprentices who remained upright.

'I think we're about done here,' he said. 'I'll see you all at the trial.' He stalked towards the stair, and the apprentices scurried out of his way. His boots tapped briefly on the steps, and then, gone.

I ran to crouch over Esher. She was turning purple, her white eye shining. And then something inside her released, and she sucked in a terrible, pained breath.

'Are you all right?'

She stared up at me and Liara, her disappointment in herself bright in the tears that welled around her eyes. Angrily she dashed them aside.

'I proved them all right,' she said bitterly. 'Damn it all.'

I didn't understand, but it wasn't the time.

Ovitus crouched down, then unceremoniously deposited himself on his backside on the dusty cellar floor. He looked as dazed as the apprentices on the floor. Half of Adanost's ear was missing, and Jathan didn't look like he'd be impressing the quartermaster again anytime soon.

'I—I don't know,' Ovitus said, his last attempt at holding on to some semblance of pride in the midst of a plan that had gone terribly, horribly wrong. 'Can we trust him? He was sleeping with Hazia, I'm sure of it . . .'

'Castus doesn't even turn his sheets that way,' I said angrily. 'And that's hardly the important thing right now, is it?' I glared at the apprentices. 'Didn't Ulovar tell you to search the archives for something that might explain how Hazia got into the Blackwell? Shouldn't you be doing something useful? Something that uses those vaunted Draoihn brains of yours? Why in the name of the Light Above did you think that this would work?'

'You can't speak to us that way,' Adanost said, one hand pressed against his torn ear, blood dripping down his cheek. 'We could have you flogged.'

'You could try,' I said. 'But you won't manage it before I go to Sanvaunt, and the Light Above help you if he finds out about this. You won't manage it before I go to Haronus LacClune, and tell him what you tried to do to his kin. I doubt he'd let you off with a sore cock and a ripped ear. You're lucky that Castus thinks the lot of you are so far beneath him that I doubt he'll even demean himself by reporting this. Now get out of here. All of you. Out!'

It was the most that I'd ever shouted at anyone in my life. It all just rose out of me and boiled through. *These* were the best of us? The ones destined to wield magic, to be above the law? I recalled Ulovar, knee bent in a lunge, eyes bulging and bleeding as he took Ciuthach's head off. That was the strength needed to turn back the Night Below. These pitiful little wretches were idle, spoiled and careless. They didn't deserve the power bestowed on them.

That power should have been mine.

They obeyed me. Esher couldn't meet my eye. Even Ovitus tried to get up, but I put my hand on his forehead and pushed him back down.

'As for you,' I said. 'You're better than this. I *know* you're better than this.'

'I don't know what else to do!' he roared, and I heard his clumsy, careering trance blossom within him, thudding, discordant blows of a mallet. We stared at each other for several moments.

'You don't have to be cruel to be strong,' I said. 'Remember Eudocles.'

'Eudiricles,' he corrected me in a mutter.

'Whoever. Strength doesn't come from being more brutal than the other side. And there's strength inside you. I know there is. Maybe not with weapons and fists, but you believe in people. You want to help people. So do it. Help Ulovar.'

'How?'

'What's the huge question we've been unable to answer all this time?' I said. 'Hazia was just a pawn. Whose pawn? Who benefited from freeing Ciuthach?'

Ovitus wiped his eyes.

'Nobody,' he said.

'No,' I said. 'Someone must. She didn't go into the Blackwell by chance. We've obsessed over *how* Hazia managed it. What we need to ask is *why*.'

31

'I hope you're proud of yourself,' I said. 'You bloody fool.'

Ovitus didn't look at me. He hung his head, hands clasped before him.

'I had to do something,' he said hoarsely.

'So you attacked another apprentice? The LacClune heir? That was going to get you what you wanted? What were you thinking?'

'I had to do something!' he repeated. He fell backwards onto his bed to stare up at the ceiling. I was too angry to sit down. I'd spent the night awake, waiting for the greathouse to be roused, for men in blue-and-white LacClune roses to come and take the whole idiot gaggle of them into custody. An assault, on the future van of Clan LacClune, within Redwinter's own grounds. It had been an act of monumental stupidity.

'You will do something,' I said. 'You'll get back to those books. You'll find out the truth. What did you want? You wanted to be the big man of action?'

'I just want it to end,' Ovitus said. 'I'm not like you, Raine. I'm not made for this.'

'I wasn't made for this either. Life just crushed me into this shape.'

'We're finished, Raine. They don't need to have definitive evidence against my uncle. They only need half the council to believe that he's even toyed with Skal. The Sixth Gate is forbidden. There is only one punishment.'

'It won't come to that,' I said. 'Now get off your ass and let's do something about it.'

I put the apprentices to work. There were many books in the greathouse, and though every illuminated line had been trawled during the days after the colour storm, there had to be something. Some way to learn how Hazia had bypassed Redwinter's most powerful wards and raised Ciuthach from beyond the grave. I hoped that we would find a new truth within those tomes, would learn how she had been drawn down to the madness that torn page had contained.

They sat in sullen silence, reluctant to leave one another's company, subdued in the weak winter light. Nobody moved to light more lamps. The gloom suited them. Sanvaunt had been gone all night, and when he returned in the midmorning, he went to his chambers without speaking a word to anybody. Nobody told him what had happened.

I had to do *something*. Ovitus had been misguided, but at least he'd tried to act. It was down to us now. Me, just a retainer, and a few apprentices.

'It's useless,' he said. 'We've been over these a thousand times and more. Not even Ulovar understands why Hazia did it. Or how she got in there. The only person who knows that is Hazia, and she took that secret with her into death.'

Into death.

He was right, I supposed. My memories of Hazia were vague, brief images in the dark. I'd been bleeding, in pain, but I remembered her confusion. She was only half-aware of what she was doing. She had been broken. The page was to blame for that. Ciuthach's influence had reached out of that cursed thing and drawn her to him. But Hazia was gone.

The Queen of Feathers must have known. *Very old, and very powerful*, Veretaine had told me. Beyond death. Not a ghost, not like the ordinary, mundane spirits of the dead—if any such thing can be mundane. But something else. She had knowledge that she shouldn't. She may have humiliated me, but desperation was setting in. If she'd just come to me again, maybe she could tell me what I so desperately needed to know. I would take any ally I could get.

The day dragged on, meals were picked at, and as evening descended, the apprentices disappeared to bed, one by one. Ovitus drank too much, his bruised fist resting on a prime cut of steak that might have fed a poor family for a day. Maybe a servant would take it home when he was done with it, but I didn't think it looked very appetising, greying in the warmth. Liara was the only one still reading. Her soft, round face was shadowed deep in the lamplight.

'Can I ask you something?' I said. She placed a finger on the line that she'd been reading, pushed her eyeglasses away from strained, reddish eyes. She seemed a far cry from the girl who'd made a kitchen full of servants fall around laughing. We didn't have much to laugh about just then.

'Of course,' she said. Ovitus gave a deep, low snore.

'It's about your father.'

'Oh,' she said. Looked away. 'I don't like to talk about that.'

'I understand,' I said. But this was too important. I had to speak of it. 'Did he ever—did he ever mention a woman? One who wore a crown of raven feathers.'

'I don't understand.'

'A Queen of Feathers. You know. A spirit of some kind. Maybe like the moon horses, or maybe just dead.'

'He never spoke of that,' Liara said quietly. 'He kept it all secret. From everybody. For a long time, I think.'

'Do you know why he could— I'm sorry. I know this is hard. Do you know why he could see the dead?'

'What has this to do with anything?'

'Maybe something to do with Hazia,' I said. I blanked my face. 'Maybe something to do with why she did what she did. They're the enemy, aren't they? The Sarathi.'

I could see the pain that every mention of him brought to Liara's eyes, as though I were ice expanding within a mountainside crack, inexorably splitting the stone apart. But I had to ask. If we were to save Ulovar, I had to ask.

'My father never said anything about it. Not even at his trial. But I think—it started when he was poisoned. There was a clan feud. Between LacShale and Kallion. He suffered—don't think he didn't. For three days he was fading, yellowing like old butter. Then a healer managed to get an antidote into him. After that he wasn't the same. A brush with death, I suppose. It wasn't his fault.'

'Then you don't think that he deserved what happened to him?'

'I didn't say that,' Liara said quickly.

'You don't have to agree with the law,' I said. 'It's made by men, not the Light Above.'

'He had to be punished for what he'd done,' she said sadly. 'The nature of the punishment was cruel. Sometimes, though—sometimes they ask us for cruelty. It's the nature of the Draoihn. The Crown is too precious to risk to those that can't turn their hearts into islands. That's what they tell us.'

'But he never mentioned a Queen of Feathers?' I said.

'No,' Liara said. 'What does this have to do with anything?'

'Just something I read,' I said. 'Trying to find links. I'm sorry. I shouldn't have asked.'

'It's nothing that people don't already know,' she said sadly. She looked across at Ovitus. 'I feel sorry for him, you know? He just isn't made of the right clay for all this. But there's a good heart in there somewhere. He didn't want to hurt Castus. He's just desperate.'

'I know,' I said. I pushed my chair back. 'Good night, Apprentice Liara.'

'Good night, Miss Raine.'

I left them there together, slipping quietly from the room.

I didn't know where I had to go. Not clearly. Veretaine and his people had been careful to hide their location from me, but I had one idea. One final, probably absurd idea. Based on something that Hess had said.

I knew nearly nothing about Veretaine's group, other than they had the ability to do what I needed them to do, and that they had seen the Queen of Feathers. I needed her help. But to find them, in a city the size of Harranir? They were somewhere in the undercity. That was all I could say. But a hunter has to think like their quarry. Find the places that they will go, understand them. Most animals are simple. They need food, water, sex and sleep. People are only slightly more complicated, markers of their passage left scraped through the world.

But I couldn't do it alone. I took a deep breath. I had crossed a line in Halfera's lands, had taken lives. Made my choice. But I needed help, and to ask for it—to endanger myself this way—made my skin crawl.

I knocked on Esher's door. There was no response. I entered anyway.

'I don't want to be disturbed,' she said. Esher sat in front of the mirror at her dressing table, a brush forgotten in her hand.

'Too bad,' I said. The words I had to summon were down at the bottom of the bog, tangled with swamp weed, buried beneath rotting branches. I reached down into that quagmire murk inside me and dredged. 'I need you. Are you my friend, Esher?'

She turned to me.

'Yes. I've wanted to be your friend since I met you on the tor. But I'm no use to anybody.'

'That's nonsense,' I said. 'I need your help, but more than that, I need your friendship. I think I can trust you.'

'You shouldn't trust me with anything,' she said. Her eyes had not moved from her reflection in the mirror before her. 'I don't know anything. I can't do anything. I'm just a half-blind girl who can't control herself. That's what they say about me. That I'm erratic. That I don't think before I act.' She lowered her eyes from the mirror. 'And I've proved them right.'

'Esher,' I said. 'I don't have time for this. I might have to kill someone tonight, and I need you. Are you with me?'

'Kill someone?'

'Yes.'

'You're serious, aren't you?'

'As a blade,' I said. 'I have to find someone.'

'Raine, if I've learned anything from what Ovitus told us to do, it's that violence isn't the answer.'

'This is Redwinter,' I said harshly. 'Violence is always the answer. It just needs to be pointed in the right direction. You said your mother worked in an Ashium den, before they got closed. If I wanted to find a man who smoked it night and day, where would I go looking?'

Esher seemed disappointed.

'You want Ashium? It's bad stuff. Rots your brain.'

'I know that,' I said. 'I need to find a man with tattoos on his neck who stinks of it. Where would an old soldier go to get his fix?'

Esher pursed her lips.

'You really are serious.' She stood, and some of the dark malaise left her eye. 'There's a place, if it's still there. I can tell you where it is.'

'No,' I said. 'I don't have time to wander the streets looking for a hidden leaf-den. I need you to show me, and then never speak of this again. I wish I didn't have to ask this of you, but it might be the difference between Ulovar living and dying. I don't have time to slow down, and I can never explain it. But I need you to be my friend and show me. Please.'

Esher stood a little taller.

'Get the horses and I'll meet you downstairs in ten minutes.'

When she descended, Esher had wiped the defeat from her face. She had hardened, reforged herself, rising from the ashes like a glorious phoenix. Her golden hair was braided, and she wore Draoihn oxblood, sword and dirk at her belt. She held another sword out to me.

'If we're going to do this, take this.'

It was a beautiful weapon, a single-handed sword with a curved, one-edged blade. I had no real training with a blade, but I'd had no training with a hatchet, and that hadn't saved Ollan.

Horses, saddles, the smell of well-worn leather, and out into the night. We descended the mountain slope, past the grumbling snatterkin, onto the foggy moors, Harranir's lights a haze below.

'You really can't tell me why we're doing this?'

'Would it change anything if I did?' I said.

'No,' she admitted. She smiled at me. Shy, like an animal snuffling its nose towards an offered hand. 'Thank you for trusting me.'

'Of course I trust you,' I said. I wanted to say more. Wanted to say that I felt like I could trust her with everything I'd ever felt. That I wanted to take her to the bath and step down into the water with her, and kiss her cheek, and her forehead, and her mouth. That I was terrified about what that meant, and that I couldn't afford to risk myself that way again. That it had mattered more to me than I realised that she would do this for me. That there was a part of me that burned for it.

Ulovar had cut through my mind, and for that I was thankful. I only re-alised then, riding through the low-hanging fog with Esher, that he hadn't broken me. I hadn't been whole. I had been broken before Niven LacCulloch had penned us in, and it hadn't been Ciuthach's raging eyes, or my mother's selfishness. Braithe had been the false-light along the shore, a wrecker, and I had broken myself in trying to reach something that wasn't even there. I had drowned in the freezing waters of his disdain. I had been flotsam before I even knew where the shore truly lay.

I was Raine, of the north. Raine, of Redwinter. I was Raine, the wildrose daughter of a High Pastures clerk. I was Raine, retainer of LacNaithe. I was just Raine, and all that encompassed.

I was Raine the hunter.

I was hunting again now.

Esher and I kept cowled and hooded along Harranir's roads. The fog had kept people indoors, which suited me well enough. She led the way down towards the docks. She was good as her word, and didn't ask why we were out, late in the night.

'That's it,' she said, indicating a tannery. A good choice, if you wanted to hide another unpleasant smell. We tethered our horses in a silent alley, and watched from the shadows, fog and night turning us invisible to distant eyes. 'There's a hatch around the back. The soldiers smoke down in the cellar. They might not let you in, and it will be a bad crowd inside. I'll come with you.'

'No,' I said. 'I don't need to go inside anyway. Just have to wait for him to come out.'

'Who are you looking for?'

'A man who used to be a soldier, with a torn lip and swords and roses on his neck.'

'Swords and roses is Clan LacShale's crest,' Esher said. 'Liara's clan.' She wanted to ask more, of course she did, but I stared straight ahead.

'I know. You should go now.'

'I can't leave you here alone. Not like this.'

My heart twinged as though a violin player had just plucked a pure and beautiful note. We watched as men and women emerged, or headed towards the hatch that led down beneath the ground, but none of them had Hess's build. No use going in there. I couldn't know if Hess came here, and even if he did, would he be there tonight? Maybe he was off doing Veretaine's secret work, hunting down more people like me on the road. But I didn't think so. The smell was always so powerful on him, that skin-deep smell earned by soaking in other men's smoke. If he wasn't here now, he'd come. Two days was all I had.

Esher's hand was cold when she put it in mine. My hand was cold too. I should have worn gloves, but I was glad I hadn't.

The night was deep when people began to clear out. We lurked in the shadows, but there were too many people to pick anyone out easily. They didn't carry lanterns, knowing their way in the dark. If Hess had been in there, then he had to be leaving now.

'I need you to use the First Gate,' I said. 'Look for him for me. I can't see well enough in the dark. Everyone looks the same.'

'You can use it too,' she said.

'I'm no Draoihn,' I said.

'Aren't you?' Esher gave my hand a squeeze.

'It just happens to me,' I said. 'I do it when I don't realise, and then my head hurts.'

'You can do it with me,' Esher said. I felt the rise of her rhythm, *dum-dom, dum-dom, dum-dom*, a dancer hopping from drum to drum. I tried to push myself into it too, but my mind twisted and squirmed away from me, coiling inwards like a snake.

'Your mind doesn't want to join the rest of the world,' Esher said. 'You have to expand yourself outwards. Let all of you become part of everything else. You can do it, Raine. I know you can do it.'

I tried, but nothing came to me. Trying to force it out of me was like trying to wrestle an angry eel through a tiny hole.

'He's there,' Esher said. 'Your man. Broken lip, LacShale tattoo on his neck, finishing his pipe off. Leaning against that beam, see him? That's your man. Light Above, the reek of Ashium on these people.'

I couldn't pick Hess out, or smell them at this distance. That was Eio, though, the First Gate.

'Thank you,' I said. I squeezed Esher's hand, a warm, sweaty paw clasped in mine now. I looked at her beautiful face. 'I have to go now. You can't come with me for this part.'

'Why not?'

'I can't tell you. Will you trust me?'

'I'd rather go with you,' Esher said. She reached up and put her warm hand on the cold of my face. For a moment I entirely forgot what I was supposed to be doing and closed my eyes. Just breathed in the lightness of her scent, sandalwood and dried wildflowers.

'I know,' I said. 'But you can't.'

'You need to get after him if you want to catch up to him,' she said. 'Be careful, Raine.'

I wanted her to come with me. Of course I did. But the things I had to ask Hess—nobody else could hear them. I couldn't explain it to her, and she didn't ask. She just trusted me. That scar in my mind trembled. It creaked against this new feeling, this feeling that was so new and full and bigger than the open mountain sky.

'I'll be careful.'

'I'll wait for you at the southern gate.'

A final squeeze of my hand, a smile, and I headed off towards the dispersing crowd. I was about to put a sword to a man's throat, but my footfalls seemed lighter than misting breath.

Harranir was never truly asleep, despite the cold and the dark. I was just another traveller on foot, small and unthreatening in the night. Hess didn't even look back over his shoulder as he turned down streets that grew darker and narrower still, his gait unstable. He turned down along a narrow alley, a row of poor tenements. I could smell the Ashium odour he left in his wake, floral, bitter, nauseating. Eventually he reached a doorway, fumbled for a ring of keys in his pocket, and let himself in.

I didn't wait. Didn't want to give him time to settle in and fall asleep. I was after him and banging on his door moments after it had shut.

He blinked when he saw me. Couldn't quite grasp what was happening or why I was there. I shoved towards him, and Esher's sword was in my hand. Hess saw the blade, fell back away from it, but I had a hand on his shirt and the point ready.

'Just stay there!' I said. My voice sounded high. 'Is there anyone else here? In the house? Anyone at all?'

'No,' he said. His hands were out to the sides, open, like he was trying to calm a skittish horse. 'Just me. Put the sword down—'

'Sit. Sit and be quiet. Sit there.'

I shoved him towards an old armchair before an unlit hearth. The whole place had a hard-lived look. The furnishings were worn, tattered. Old bowls of pottage mouldered on surfaces, unwashed clothes lay piled against a wall. A real addict's home. He sunk into the armchair, a cloud of Ashium stink in his wake. The same I'd smelled on him each time I'd met him. Understand the prey. Know what they want, where they'll go. Hardly surprising that a soldier with the spirit-sight would want to numb his mind every night.

'What are you doing here?' he asked.

'As a man who shows up out of nowhere and seems to know all about me, you should hardly be surprised that I can find you when I want to,' I said. 'You're certain we're alone? Because if anyone comes down those stairs, I'm going to stab the shit out of you first and worry about them later. Understand?'

'It's just me,' he said. Sounded tired.

'I need some answers, Hess,' I said. 'Who is the Sarathi in Redwinter?'

He stared at me, eyes narrowing.

'There are no Sarathi,' he said. 'Redwinter destroyed them all. Just as they want to destroy you, and me, and everyone like them.'

'There has to be a Sarathi in Redwinter,' I said. I didn't threaten him with the sword, but I hadn't stopped pointing it at him either. 'It's the only thing that makes sense. Nobody else has cause to try to raise the Night Below's servants. I need to know. And you people know. The Queen of Feathers knows.'

'The Queen of Feathers knows everything,' Hess said. 'But she doesn't serve us.'

'What is she?'

'I don't know.'

I believed him, damn it. He was growing calm. Understood that I wasn't about to shank him. And the truth was, it might be harder than it sounded, even if he was fugged with leaf. He'd left his sword belt by the door, but he was still twice my weight.

'I have to speak with her.'

'You can't just demand to speak with her,' Hess said with a laugh. 'Not even the boss can do that. I've never even seen her.'

I believed him again. Damn it twice. He rubbed at dry eyes, and I wasn't sure what to say anymore. My plan was unravelling fast.

'We tried to warn you,' he said eventually.

'You told me that Sanvaunt LacNaithe is the one who benefits,' I said.

'But you don't believe us,' Hess said.

It had all sounded so believable, down in the dark, surrounded by others like me. I'd felt them welcoming me in. Felt them confiding in me, offering me something true. Why had I found it so hard to believe? Why had I taken no action against him? I didn't like the answer that I was drawn to him. I didn't want to be weak. Didn't want to be made a fool of. But it just didn't fit what I knew of him.

'Sanvaunt LacNaithe is obsessive in his duty,' I said. 'But I don't think he's evil.'

'Evil?' Hess grunted. His voice was thick, tongue swollen. 'What does that even mean? Your precious friends in Redwinter would condemn me for my evil. The same evil you carry inside yourself. Isn't that right? We're just afflicted—or blessed, depending on your point of view. Look what it brings us all to, Raine. You're standing over me with a sword in your hand, defending the very people who tear us apart, who would tear you apart, given the chance. And why? Because they gave you a position? Because they gave you money? How can you be so easily bought?'

'They are not bad people,' I said. I felt the weakness in my own words. 'They just don't understand. They think those with the spirit-sight are all Sarathi in the making. And I've seen one. I saw Ciuthach. You cannot imagine what he was. What he could do. I understand their perspective. And you have no evidence to support Sanvaunt LacNaithe being behind any of this.'

Hess went quiet, breathed deeply for a moment. He closed his eyes. Thinking.

'I have something that might persuade you,' he said. He raised the stone-bird charm that hung around his neck, a mirror to the one Veretaine had given me. 'Even if our offers of friendship are not enough.'

'Friendship is easy to claim and dangerous to test,' I said. 'What else do you have?"

'A message,' he said. 'One that I intercepted. A long time ago. One that pertained to the apprentice, Hazia. Before she did—whatever it was that she did. I can show you. But I'll need you to lower that blade.'

I breathed in, breathed out slowly. One. Two. With a sigh, I sheathed it, but put myself between him and his own sword belt. Hess got up slowly. No threat, nothing sudden. He crossed the cluttered room to a shelf that held only half the books that it could have. He leafed through one until he drew out a folded piece of paper, a broken wax seal across it.

'Here,' he said. 'It didn't make much sense to me at first. But what you suggested—that there might be a Sarathi in Redwinter? Well. Read it for yourself.'

He passed it to me. The seal was a layer of black wax, a second circle of green over it. A stylised wyvern looked back over its shoulder. Clan LacNaithe.

'Where did you get this?'

'It doesn't matter. Just read it.'

I flipped it open. The edge was stained, dark brown spots. Along the top were an evenly spaced series of symbols that I didn't understand. Magical symbols? Runes or sigils. Some kind of code, maybe. But I could read the words beneath them.

> Ulovar's girl is stronger than any of them realise. She can do what they cannot. I would have her trained in the skills that only you can provide, as you once trained me. It is essential that we have her on our side for the fight that is to come.
>
> Forever your disciple,
> Sanvaunt LacNaithe

More strange symbols below.

I stared at it.

The words clamoured like bells of black ink. They seemed to stare back at me from the page, boring into me. *Forever your disciple.*

Sanvaunt served some other master. Not his uncle. Not Redwinter. There was no address, no name.

'Where did you get this?'

'I killed a man, and took it from him,' Hess said. 'Is that what you want to hear? He wasn't the first man I killed, Raine. Probably won't be the last, before all this is done. We are not Sarathi. We do not want the dead to rise, and we do not want the Night Below to regain a foothold in this world. We just want peace, and to be left to live our lives as we see fit. So we watch for those that fall towards the dark. Veretaine is our protector. Your Sanvaunt LacNaithe is handsome and courageous, proud, and wears duty like a cloak. But the words there are plain enough.'

'Whose disciple is he?'

'We have never learned that,' Hess said.

'I'm keeping this,' I said. 'I need to take it to Redwinter. To the grandmaster. Now.'

'Wait,' he said as I turned for the door. 'Whoever he wrote to—he is not the king. Somebody has trained him. Another who is more powerful than he is. How many can enter the Blackwell? Ulovar. Merovech. Onostus. Hanaqin. Lassaine. Kelsen. And Grandmaster Robilar. You cannot go to any of them. Not alone.'

'Then what do I do?' I demanded.

'You wait,' he said. 'You wait for all of them to gather together. The trial. Show them at the trial. Expose Sanvaunt there.'

32

Esher threw herself into me so hard that we fell down on the ground together, much to the amusement of the people doing late-night duty on the southern gate.

'You're all right,' she breathed into my ear. 'Thank the stars, Raine. Thank the moon horses.'

'Not sure they had anything to do with it. But thank you for waiting.'

We dusted ourselves off and untangled knees and elbows.

'Did you—'

'It didn't come to that,' I said. 'It was useful anyway.'

'I wish you could tell me what it was.'

'I know,' I said. 'Me too. I have something. We may save Ulovar yet.'

'Can you tell me what it is?'

I shook my head.

'That's all right,' she said. 'That you have it is enough.'

I could have cried all over her just then.

We rode hard, back to Redwinter. My skin was crawling, my eyes stung and winter cold snatched at my hood. The snatterkin seemed to hiss, whispers and promises fluttering past my ears at the edge of hearing.

Even now, I couldn't share what I had learned with Esher. She and Sanvaunt were friends—even if she believed me, I would put her in an impossible situation. She might go to him, demand an answer, and I couldn't tell her where I'd obtained the evidence. I kept a hand pressed against my breast, the letter Hess had given me tucked safely away, but I couldn't bear to release it, lest somehow it fluttered away into the night. Our lives, all of our lives, were caught up with that piece of paper. Ulovar, Ovitus, the idiot apprentices, and maybe all the people of Harranir too. Sanvaunt was in league with a Sarathi—a true Sarathi, who had helped Hazia into the Blackwell. One who had corrupted her, led her to steal that page. To bring Ciuthach back into the world.

Sanvaunt. In our midst the whole time.

I held Clan LacNaithe's throat in my fist. Even if I revealed Sanvaunt's treachery, would that turn the council's decision in Ulovar's favour? Unless I could unmask the true power behind Sanvaunt's betrayal, they could simply declare him to be the Sarathi. Maybe if I could get to Ulovar, I could tell him. But would he even believe me? Sanvaunt was his nephew, and he'd never seemed to care if Sanvaunt was a wildrose or not. There was nobody he trusted more. That guise of duty and honour had worked so well. But it seemed so obvious now. I'd even seen Sanvaunt participate in Ulovar's arrest. How in all the rivers of Skuttis had we been so blind?

We passed the horses' reins off to a groom who looked startled to see horses ridden so hard through the clouded dark. It seemed so natural to me now, even after just a few months, to expect others to do the work for me. I had been seduced by it all. Nobody looks beyond their own horizons. I had allowed my eyes to be sewn shut with threads of comfort, promises of a future I had never before expected or considered. My life had been so small.

I needed more. More than just a single letter. I couldn't name the hand I'd taken it from. If I was going to do this, going to bring Sanvaunt to justice, I had to be careful. I had to go armed with everything, everything that I could bring to the fight. There was nobody who would be glad to hear what I'd learned. Nobody who would be pleased by this.

'What can I do to help?' Esher asked.

'Nothing,' I said. 'Just say nothing. The fewer people who know what I'm doing the better. But be safe. There's more going on than anyone knows. But I can help Ulovar. I know I can.'

'I believe you.' She smiled at me. 'Thank you for trusting me. Even after I was so stupid.'

We hugged. Parted.

The greathouse slumbered in the dark, mouse-step hours of the night. I padded up stairs that no longer welcomed me, slipped inside my bedchamber, an oversized room that had belonged to a dead girl. I had to act.

Instead I sat on the bed, rested my face in my hands and began to cry. I couldn't have said why I wept. Didn't understand it. I just felt that something bright, and good, and magical in the world had turned to dry ashes and bitterness. My heart felt like it had been struck through by a sliver of steel, pinned like an insect on a board. And the anger. So much anger, hot and deep and raging along the edges of the scar that ran across my mind. How could someone be so cruel? So deceitful?

Hess was wrong about one thing only. Men will wax philosophical about whether good and evil truly exist. But I had looked upon Ciuthach, and the magic of the Night Below, and I knew in my heart that evil did exist. Evil was the complete absence of empathy, of care for any other living thing. The will to exploit, to own, to dominate, and to take whatever was desired, for whatever price needed to be paid.

And that, I supposed, was Sanvaunt. Hungry for power. Hungry for authority. Using people. Digging up his own aunt's bones for some dark, deathly purpose. Sending men to attack his own cousin. I didn't understand all of it. But even knowing some of it was enough.

And dear Light Above, was that what I had become too? I had killed two men and felt nothing for it. I had been ready to kill Hess. The scar had been protecting me from my own torment, but what had it cost me? I had become something less than human. But maybe that made me the one person who could solve this nightmare. Ulovar did not deserve to be broken, blinded and left to sink into the river. He was a good man. If I was not good, could not be good, then I would serve someone who was.

'Raine?'

I heard the tap on my door. Ovitus.

'What is it?' I asked.

'I—I thought I heard you crying,' he said.

I snarled at myself. Wiped my eyes off on a pillow. Stomped to the door.

'What?' I demanded, pulling it open. Ovitus had a pallid cast to his skin, drained and clammy. Dressed in a long white nightgown, a pale monk in the dark, he looked embarrassed to see me. A lonely candle shed weak light along the corridor.

'Are you all right?'

'Why shouldn't I cry? When everything is going to shit? Why aren't you crying?' I was ashamed to be caught out. Being so weak. 'What are you doing? Listening at doors?'

'No,' he said. 'I was coming to see you. About something important. That I only just discovered, tonight.'

I glanced up and down the corridor.

'Get in here.' I pulled Ovitus inside, stalked over to the dresser, reversed the chair as I'd seen the Draoihn often do and sat down with my arms resting on the back. I gestured that he could sit on the bed if he wanted. 'What did you find?' I prompted. Heard the urgency in my own voice. 'Something from the books? Do you know—have you found out how Hazia got into the Blackwell?'

'Er, no,' Ovitus said. 'It's not that.'

'Then what?'

He looked abashed, rose tinting his cheeks.

'I was down in the kitchen,' Ovitus said. 'I was just making myself something to eat. And I could hear Sanvaunt and Liara talking in the next room. San was about to go out about some business or other, and Liara was asking him about his responsibilities . . . and . . . I shouldn't have listened. I know it was wrong.'

'What did you hear?' I said, my breath catching. If someone else understood. If Ovitus was the one who could bring to light what I'd learned—

'And I heard Liara say that she thought I'd make a really good van. That I had the right *qualities*.'

I waited. I looked at him. Ovitus was smiling. Smiling like a dog that brings in a dead rat, even as he blushed harder. I shook my head, shrugged at him.

'So?'

'Don't you see?'

'See what?'

'I think she likes me,' he said, reverently, almost a whisper. 'I think she really does like me. You know. In *that* way.'

I stared at him, my mouth ajar. I felt my lip lowering, my eyes getting wider and wider as I tried to take in exactly what it was that he was telling me. I had to force out three long, slow blinks as Ovitus gazed back at me like some kind of hound. I rose from the chair, walked slowly across the room, and sat down beside him on the bed. Placed my hands on top of his.

'Are you saying,' I said, in the voice that only alley cats and the furious can truly produce, 'that with the council sitting tomorrow, where your uncle, the van of your clan, is to be tried for treason and worse, that you came to my room, in the middle of the night, to try to tell me that a girl who clearly has no interest in you whatsoever might *like* you?'

I smiled at him. My cruellest, most furious, red smile.

'Well, that's not fair,' he said, pulling his hands back. 'She *does* have interest in me, didn't you hear what I said? She said—'

I interrupted him in the same quiet, lethal tone.

'I do not give any number of pig-shitting fecks what she did, or did not say, about what she thinks about you. I will tell you for a fact, plain and simple, that she does not want you. She is not interested in you. As a man. As a partner. This little dreamscape you've created where maybe she likes you, maybe she doesn't like you, maybe it's difficult, maybe the positions make it awkward— it's all just shit swilling around in your delusion. In the pit of your wasted, pointless mind. We're sitting on the brink of disaster. Lives are at stake. Yours. Mine. All of ours. Yesterday you were having your people beat another clan heir in front of you. Today you're creeping around at night, believing that the aching in your poor little heart somehow matters? Light Above, Ovitus! You are the stupidest, most tragic man I have ever met.'

'How dare you?' Ovitus said. His eyes shot black with fury. 'You just don't understand.'

'Oh, I understand,' I said. Forge heat curled from my tongue. I had all the anger I needed to match him. 'Let me tell you how it works. If she liked you? You'd know it. It'd be obvious. It'd be blindingly obvious. We aren't some mystical species of nymph, unsure of what we want. She knows you want her. She obviously knows. And if she wants you, she knows she can have you.'

'I'm not—I don't just go with—I'm—You can't speak to me like that!'

'Oh, I can't? Why not, Ovitus? Aren't we friends?' I growled. 'Isn't that what you claim? Or are we master and servant? Because if we're friends, then I can tell you the sorry truth that I should have told you a long time ago.'

'Maybe we aren't friends,' Ovitus said. His spluttering was over. His eyes had narrowed. His fists had clenched. 'Perhaps I have been living under a delusion. About you.'

'Fine,' I said. 'In that case, I'm going to start screaming that the master of the house has come to my fecking bedroom in his nightgown.'

Ovitus stood before me, shaking with anger. My words had found their targets, sure as any arrows I'd ever loosed. Hadn't they? Ovitus's armour of delusion was stronger than most breastplates.

'Fuck you, Raine,' he said. 'You're meant to care about me. But you don't care about anyone but yourself. And you're wrong about Liara.'

He turned and stormed out, slamming the door.

I sat there for few moments, the argument's heat and my rash words warming the air around me. Played it back through my mind. My temper had really got the better of me. But while I'd been riding through the dark, hunting dangerous men, demanding answers—he'd been eavesdropping, hoping to hear something nice about himself.

I sat bolt upright. He'd told me one thing, and one thing only, that mattered.

Sanvaunt had been on his way out.

Ovitus's aching heart be damned. This might be the only chance I would get.

I changed my boots for slippers, soft and quiet. Cold filled the corridor as I padded through, along the hall, around the corner and then up another flight of stairs. The greathouse was huge—ridiculous that it was called a house at all, frankly—but I knew Sanvaunt's suite of rooms, in the eastern wing. I needed to get there quietly. Couldn't let them hear me. Nobody could know what I was about.

Sanvaunt had praised me for standing against the two men who'd taken Ovitus. Had admired my grit. That grit was going to bite him hard in the ass now.

The door to his rooms was locked. Of course it would be, especially if he had anything in there that he wanted to keep from prying eyes. What was he even doing tonight, out in the world? Following him would have been even better than snooping through his things, if only I'd known he was leaving. But he was a Draoihn of the First Gate, and I'd seen his caution before—entering Eio to ensure that nobody was listening at the door before he spoke to me. He was nobody's fool. But there had to be another way in.

I had an idea, and it was probably stupid. Stupid, or brave, or maybe inspired. I moved to the end of the corridor, where a large window looked out over the greathouse's private gardens, towards Redwinter's perimeter wall. I unlatched it, felt a freezing gust of night wind swoop in along the corridor. I could do this. I had to do this. Slowly I climbed out onto the window ledge.

A lip of stone ran around the edge of the buildings, six inches wide. The ivy grew thickly here, and it would have to do for handholds. I wasn't afraid of heights, but I had a healthy respect for the thirty-foot drop beneath me. Better not to look at it. Better to focus on the task at hand. I filled my hands with the ivy's thick stems and slowly manoeuvred myself out onto the stone lip. It wasn't so bad. Keep three points of contact at all times: either two feet and a hand or two hands and a foot. One point to move, three to keep me stable. Come on, Raine. You can do this.

It was slow going, and the night was freezing around me, and the corner of the building was hard to navigate. I clung to the ivy, bunched it in my fingers, flinching every time a little more tore from the wall, but then I'd done it, made it around the corner. Occasionally the ivy would groan and begin to tear away. But I slowly made my way along, inch by inch, past Jathan's rooms, the windows quiet and dark, the curtains thankfully drawn. I tried to be silent. I counted the windows, and eventually came to what I thought had to be Sanvaunt's. His curtains were drawn too, but there was light behind them, warm and golden. No locks on the windows, but latches on the inside. A fistful of ivy in one hand, I slid the thin blade of my knife between the shutters, brought it up quickly and the latch fell loose. Swinging inside was the easiest part.

The room smelled of the whale oil in a lamp that had been left burning unattended. The fire had been banked before he left, two large logs glowing, half-burned. I closed the shutters, latched the window again. Looked around.

Sanvaunt's bedroom was not what I had expected. Not at all. I had imagined it to be ordered with military precision, everything in its proper place, the bed smoothly made, books in neat alphabetical order on the shelves. I had to ask myself whether maybe I was in the wrong room after all. This was a mess. The bed was unmade, a pillow lay slumped on the floor. An old bowl with a small puddle of forgotten soup vied for space on a campaign desk with stacks of paper, polished stones, a glove missing two fingers. Not the orderly little place that I'd imagined at all. The only things that seemed to be set in order were a suit of polished iron mail hanging on a wooden mannequin and a set of equally well-oiled weapons hanging from a rack alongside it.

I had to stop myself gawking. That wasn't why I was here. I'd come to find something to incriminate him. I didn't know what. I only knew that no matter how carefully it moves, everything leaves a trail in its wake, and a skilled hunter can always find it. But where, in all this mess, would I start? At least if I tore the place apart it would be difficult for him to tell.

I started with the desk. The soup bowl was just old soup; the rocks were just old rocks. I looked through the books. Nothing interesting, some of them copies he'd made himself, judging by the handwriting. Some of them I recognised; a couple I'd read myself. *Lessons on the Spirit War*, by Autolocus. Those damned Haddat-Nir kings. Texts we'd been searching through after the colour storm, or as we sought any information about the Blackwell. But they were just books.

The desk had drawers, but none of them were locked. Letters, or copies of letters, contracts that had been written on two halves of a page and then zig-zag cut down the centre so that each party would be able to present a uniquely matching half if a dispute arose. They covered armament supplies heading out to the Cold Plains, purchases of horse-breeding stock, instructions to those that held his thaildom for him.

But of course. He wasn't going to leave the good stuff in an unlocked drawer. Where, then? Tucked inside a book? Beneath a loose floorboard? A crack in the wall? I began to feel a growing sense of fear, urgency rising like bile. I didn't have all night, and it's harder to search through disorder. I began to pull books from his shelves, leafing through them for anything loose. Sometimes I found flowers, dried and pressed between the pages, or a note tucked there—but they were his personal commentaries on the text, notes he'd made during his studies. My frustration mounted, necessity rising. I had to find something. There *had* to be something here.

And there it was. On a bottom shelf, buried beneath three other books. There was a book in a language that I didn't understand, and as I stared at it, I knew that these symbols I was looking at were similar to the ones on the note Hess had given me. Yes. This was something. I couldn't understand a word of it—if they were even words. Maybe they were secret Sarathi codes. Maybe they were ritual spells, the kind that Ulovar had used to bring down Dalnesse Monastery. But they were something I could use. Maybe. Ovitus would surely have some idea of what it meant. I was still angry with him, but maybe he could redeem himself.

I was about to head out when I saw something, peeking out at me from beneath one of the pillows. The battered leather cover of a book. A book I'd seen Sanvaunt writing in, the one he tried to keep hidden, that he tucked away whenever I caught him with it. My heart was in my throat as I crept over and pulled it out. A simple clasp held it closed. Now that I was here, holding it in my hands, I feared what I was about to find. This was what I'd come for.

Line after line of Sanvaunt's neat, elegant script filled the pages. I stared at the words. Tried to grasp what I was seeing. It—it didn't make sense. What was this?

> *Dylaine crossed the room and put his arms around Roanna. He held her tightly to him, whispering into her ear that she was safe. But he was the one who found safety there, within her embrace, safe at last from the perils of the heart.*

I wrinkled my nose. Who was Dylaine? And who in all the freezing rapids of Skuttis was Roanna? I skimmed another page.

> *'You'll not have me defeated yet, sir,' Dylaine declared mightily, closing the visor of his gleaming helmet. 'And nor will you mistreat this fair lady! Even if she be born to the lowliest farmstead in my lands, I love her, I do, I love her with all of my heart.'*

It was like an invented history, or a play. A play set out on a page. But instead of actors doing the parts, he was just . . . describing what happened. Was that it? Or was it some kind of code? Some way of passing information? What possible use could Sanvaunt have for this?

> *Roanna's hands fumbled at the strings that bound her bodice closed.*
> *'I didn't save you from a witch just so you could ignore me, my lord. I'll have you as I want you,' she said as her dress dropped to the floor.*

Oh my.

I stopped reading and clapped it shut. My heart was beating drums in my ears as heat flushed my face.

'Found something interesting?'

I turned on my heel, reaching for Esher's sword at my belt, but Sanvaunt flowed across the space like a ribbon of fire. He caught my hand, bent my wrist away, and I heard the flare of his trance spilling from him. I tried to swing my free fist but he thrust two fingers into the muscle of my arm and the whole of it went limp before my blow could connect. His fingers dashed out again, so fast that I didn't feel the impacts until I was already falling, a pair of fingers striking into my sternum, then again just above my collarbone.

Falling . . .

All of the fight, the strength, everything went out of me. I collapsed like a pile of stones. I couldn't move. I couldn't do anything except blink and wag my chin. I felt nothing below the neck, my arms and legs paralysed by whatever Sarathi sorcery he'd called forth.

Sanvaunt stared down at me, a slick of perspiration across his brow, his hair hanging loose and free around his face. There was pain written there.

'I suspected that someone would come for me,' he said. 'It had to happen, eventually. But I didn't think it would be you, Raine. I never thought they could break your spirit.'

I was tearing myself apart, silently, internally. My mind crashed around inside my skull, begging my limbs to move, to move, to do anything. To let me know they were still there. I could just about acknowledge them. Like when you sit on your hand by mistake and then you can't bend the fingers. There, but not there.

Ciuthach's eyes had terrified me, but Sanvaunt's were somehow worse.

He lifted me. I'd thumped my head against the floor when I fell, and there was a sharp pain stabbing into my brain. Sanvaunt checked my scalp with quick, deft fingers. He pressed against my cheek, turning my face, looking into my eyes, pulling the lids down. His trance ran through him, infusing every part of him, all the way to the tips of his fingers. Then he propped me against the board at the foot of his bed like a doll. Wiped away a trickle of drool that leaked from my mouth, took my sword and knife from my belt and tossed them away to clatter against the wall.

'I'm going to have to release you,' he said. 'Else you'll not be able to talk. And you're going to answer my questions. But, Raine, if you try to so much as flick a hair on my head, then the next blow will leave you choking on your own tongue. Do you understand me?'

He spoke in a hard, base growl. I had never heard such deadly cold in a man's voice before.

I made a noise that sounded like *nnnnnghhhhh*, which he took, fortunately, to mean yes. Sanvaunt placed a knuckle where he'd struck my collarbone, forced it in, and then gently began to exert pressure against the opposite side of my neck. Something popped inside me, and the feeling returned in a rush, a river of self flowing through me. I gasped, bashed my head against the footboard as I swung my head back to suck in warm air. But Sanvaunt's strong hand was around my throat.

'What was your price, Miss Raine? What did it take for them to buy you? Or were you one of them from the start?'

'One of whom?' I said. He exerted enough pressure that I felt it, but he wasn't crushing down. Wasn't throttling me. Not yet.

'Who's leading this conspiracy?' he said. His fingers hardened. 'You're going to tell me, or may the Light Above help me. I don't want to hurt you, but I will if I have to. Who sent you to kill me?'

'To kill you?' I struggled the words out. 'I'm not here to kill you. You're a traitor. You cold bloody bastard. You've betrayed your own cousin, your whole family. And for what? To be van?'

I saw the change in his eyes, the blackness within them fading. Something else appeared there. I didn't understand it. But there was a shift within the way he held me. The way he looked at me.

'If you're not here to kill me, then what are you doing?'

Didn't seem much point lying now. The anger spurred the words out of me on jets of heat. Anger, and sadness, and oh Light Above, was this grief raising its head again? He could kill me here and now, and Ulovar would die, and Esher and even stupid Ovitus would go on living side by side with this bastard. I stood no chance against Sanvaunt. If he crushed my throat, nobody would find my body until the trial was done. So to the Afterworld with all of it. There was no point in holding back now. I'd found his secret book of Sarathi magic. He would never let me leave this room alive.

'I know what you've done! I know everything!'

'What do you know?'

'I know that you dug up your own aunt. I know you tried to have Ovitus abducted. And I know you serve some other master. You're his *disciple*. But I'll tell the Council of Night and Day all of it. You're not going to get away with this.' I glanced to the book, fallen open on the floor.

Roanna's hands fumbled at the strings . . .

Sanvaunt followed my eyes.

'I thought I was wrong. Hoped I was, anyway,' he said. Weariness seemed to absorb all his rage. 'But if you were willing to use Ovitus that way, I should have been stronger. I should have had you sent away. If you were willing to toy with him like that, why wouldn't someone else find a way to use you?'

The anger was gone, and his hand had grown unsteady. A slight tremble in his grip. And pain. Not what I'd expected from the man who was planning to kill his own cousin, to falsify charges against his own uncle. It was the pain that made me speak.

'Your cousin? What are you talking about? I never hurt him.'

'He doesn't even see it,' Sanvaunt growled. 'You saw his weakness and took advantage. Saw a lonely, rich man and knew you could use him. I know you seduced him on the journey south, just as my feckless father did my mother. It must have been easy. Ovitus will trust any woman who shows him a kind word. He's so desperate to be valued, and you're so beautiful and so sure of yourself. You used him, to climb the ladder for your own gain. But I'm not blind, the way he is. I see your game. You didn't need to involve him. There was a place for you here regardless. Such a damn waste.'

An incredulous laugh forced itself up, past those strong fingers on my neck.

'What are you talking about? I never *seduced* Ovitus. Have you lost your mind?'

Sanvaunt's grip didn't slacken.

'I had it from his own lips.'

'What?'

I felt cold. Cold all over. No. No, he wouldn't have done that. Wouldn't have said that. No.

'Ovitus told me what happened between you on the road. That you were lovers. That you wanted it to be a secret. But I grew up in disgrace because my mother had been seduced into a social-climber's bed. I didn't want to believe it of you. I tried not to believe it. And now you've found someone else willing to buy you, and sent you against me.' His fingers gripped tighter. 'Who is it? Who is behind this?'

A sweeping wave of nausea overtook me. The floorboards spun and I began to choke. Sanvaunt eased up, let me go.

I still felt as though I were choking. Betrayed. An absolute, utter betrayal of trust and the sudden understanding. The way that Sanvaunt had changed towards me. Ovitus had lied. He'd lied and cast me as his woman. As his secret fuck in the night.

And Sanvaunt had believed it. He thought I'd got here by whoring myself to that nasty, lying, deceiving little—

I fell to my left and vomited. My breath wouldn't come. Tears blinded me. I'd trusted him. I'd called him my friend. I'd listened to him rave about Liara, and I'd tried to care for him.

'That lying sack of shit!' I yelled through the taste of bile. 'That fecking piece of pigshit filth. I'll tear his lying fecking tongue out of his mouth!'

It took me a moment to get myself back together. I felt like a wound had been opened right down my centre, a red and weeping crack into my very being. All this time in Redwinter, the lie had been swarming around me like noxious smoke, poisoning the way everyone viewed me. A fecking lie. I remembered Ovitus leaving Sanvaunt's room, all flustered before I made Sanvaunt spill his ink. He'd seen us in the church. He'd been *jealous*. I glared up at Sanvaunt.

'How could you have been stupid enough to believe it? Ovitus's head is full of his own bullshit. He lives in a fecking fantasy world. And you just accepted it?'

The realisation hit Sanvaunt like a battering ram to the forehead. I saw it in the change in his posture, in the open fall of his mouth.

'No,' he said.

'No!' I said. 'No, fecking no!' I wiped my mouth on my sleeve. 'That's what you thought about me? All this time? I came here as Ulovar's *witness*. And why, by the Light Above, would I try to attack you in your own room with a sword I hadn't even drawn?'

Sanvaunt's rage, his fight, was all gone. He slumped down onto the floor beside me.

'If you weren't here to kill me, what are you doing here?'

'I'm proving that you're trying to take over the clan.'

'You don't trust me?'

'No!'

He sighed. Shook his head.

'Well, I trust you. I'm no enemy of the clan, Raine. Whatever evidence you think you have against me, you should take it to whomever you wish. Take it to Merovech LacClune. He'd never miss a chance to attack us. Take it to the grandmaster. Have it delivered to Ulovar, in his cell.' He turned back to me as I stood, took me in. 'I have nothing to hide. Nothing to fear. I'm no traitor.' He stood back, offering me the door.

We had been horribly, terribly wrong. A tight-clenched fist uncurled in my chest, and for the first time in days, my heart felt as though it could beat to its natural rhythm again.

'But then—what's this? What does it mean?' I pulled Hess's missive from the inside pocket of my coat. Thrust it towards him.

'How did you get this?' he said. But he didn't move to take it. Didn't try to stop me leaving. Instead he moved across the room, reversed the desk chair and sat.

'That doesn't matter.'

I killed a man. He wasn't the first man I killed, Raine. Probably won't be the last.

'I trusted that note to a man who disappeared from our service one week ago,' he said. 'If you have noticed, I have been absent most nights—I have been trying to locate him. So forgive me, but it matters a great deal.'

'A week ago? But—but Hazia died months ago. Why would you send this about her when she's already dead? And the spell you put on it . . .'

'Raine,' Sanvaunt said. 'Someone has been filling your head with lies. That much is obvious. That letter was written to Lady Datsuun. She's Dharithian, with a clanhold in the city because she's an exile from her homeland. I am assuming that you do not understand Dharithian. I have a poor hand for it, so I wrote only her name, and the date it was sent, in her tongue. She always chastised me for being miserable at it, and her tongue is just as sharp as it was when I trained under her.'

'She trained you?'

'She and her son.' He took a deep breath. 'Have it translated, if you need to. But Miss Raine, I was not writing about Hazia.'

Ulovar's girl is stronger than any of them realise. She can do what they cannot.

'Then who?' I said.

'Who do you think?' he said, sadness, weariness hanging on his words. He was always so strong. Always so straight-backed. He looked as if the world were hooked around his shoulders, and he were the one bearing its whole weight.

He'd believed in me. Despite Ovitus's lies. Still, he'd believed in me.

She can do what they cannot.

He wasn't talking about the Sixth Gate. He was talking about the men I'd killed near Uloss. He'd wanted me to be trained. Trained to be deadly. Trained to hold power. And that I knew it now had left him looking like he'd been washed down a river in flood. I had made a fool of him. I had accused him of being a traitor to his own clan. I had thought him a servant of the Sarathi, the worst crime any person could commit.

'Oh, I don't know,' I said. 'Maybe it's about Roanna.'

He cringed.

'That . . . is not for other people to read.'

'What is it?'

'It's nothing,' he said. 'They sell them in the city. They call them romances.'

'Can I read it?'

'No! I think we have more pressing business to attend to.' For the first time, a wry smile curled his lip. 'And even if we had nothing more to worry about than warm sun and a gentle breeze, I would not let anybody read that in a thousand years.'

I smiled back. It felt good to smile. There had been too few smiles of late.

'Fine,' I said. 'I'll keep your secret.'

'You know my truths,' he said. 'And now, Miss Raine, you must tell me yours.'

From below, outside, a bell rang softly.

33

It was far too late for visitors.

Sanvaunt picked up one of the swords from his collection. He had quite a lot of swords. More than was necessary for one young man to own, certainly. I picked up Esher's.

'I don't really know how to use it,' I said.

'It's not complicated,' he said. 'And if our enemies sense that something is amiss, you might be glad to have it.'

I was all too aware that my breath smelled of bile. Sanvaunt smelled of warm leather, a workman's sweat. He smelled like strength, and I liked it. Probably some effect of bashing my head.

We met Tarquus in the hallway, roused by the outdoor bell, but Sanvaunt sent him back to bed. The hairless servant-head cast us a suspicious look, perhaps wondering what we were doing about so late at night. A grim feeling filled my stomach. Who else had Ovitus lied about me to? The thought sickened me.

Sanvaunt cast me a wary look, then proceeded to open the door a fraction, one hand on his sword hilt.

'Courier brought this message to the gates,' a voice beyond the door said.

'Who's it for?'

'Addressed to a First Retainer Raine of Clan LacNaithe, figured she must be someone here,' the man said. Sanvaunt took it, thanked him, passed him a coin. Closed the door.

'Who was that?'

'The night porter.' He held it out to me, but I shook my head.

'You read it,' I told him. He broke a plain brown seal, and his dark eyes skimmed the words quickly.

'It says that Ovitus is in danger. It asks you to bring him to a safe place. "The house where truths were spoken." So your friends can watch over him.' He turned those eyes up at me. 'What is this, Raine? Who are these people?'

I shook my head. There was something that I had to do.

'I can't tell you that.'

'The time for secrets has long passed,' Sanvaunt said. 'I need to know, Raine. This may be the proof we need to save my uncle. The council will adjudicate tomorrow. Unless we bring them something, you know the penalty Ulovar will face. I love my uncle, Raine. But this goes beyond one life. If Ulovar falls, Ovitus and I will be honour-bound to raise banners against those who damned us. And we cannot prevail against LacClune, LacAud and LacDaine. Clan Lac-Naithe will die. So I must have the truth from you. Now.'

Feck it all.

'They're some kind of cult,' I said. It was the easiest thing I could think of. I couldn't tell him the truth. Not the real truth.

'And they want you to bring Ovitus to them.'

'I have a theory,' I said. 'I think I know how Hazia got into the Blackwell.' I shook my head. 'No. I *know* how she got in.'

'Are you going to share that with me?' Sanvaunt asked.

'I can't,' I said. 'But I have to test it.'

'You haven't really told me where that letter came from,' Sanvaunt said. 'Or why there's blood on it. Why it was never delivered.'

'I can't tell you that either,' I said. And I couldn't. Because if I told him what I knew, it would mean my death. Death at the hands of those I called my friends. 'I have to ask you to trust me. I can make this right. I know that I can. But I'm the only one who can prove Ulovar is innocent. And until then, I need you to trust me. Please.'

Sanvaunt pushed the long, polished black scabbard through his belt. He cut an imposing figure in that oxblood coat. Tall. Sharp jawed, a swordsman's build.

'I trust you. What do we do?'

'I have a task to perform,' I said. 'If I'm right, then having done it, I can prove Ulovar should go free.' Although what would it mean for me, when it came time to tell the truth?

How was I ever going to explain any of it? Even if I didn't explain it all, how hard would it be for them to put two and two together?

Blinded, broken and thrown into the harbour, to sink and rot with the rubbish.

'You think it was the same people who attacked Ovitus in the forest?'

I nodded.

'What do they want with him?'

'They need him alive,' I said, remembering the note. 'I understand it now. It's not a political game. It's not the Sarathi or the Night Below. It's revenge, pure and simple.'

'Revenge for whom?'

'For Van Kaldhoone LacShale,' I said.

'Kaldhoone LacShale was . . .'

'I know what you all think,' I said. 'He was blinded, hobbled and thrown into the harbour. Only, either he managed to get out of the harbour or someone dragged him out. He commanded four Gates, didn't he? Maybe he prepared himself somehow. With some kind of spell. Or maybe he used his trances, or someone caught him in a net, I don't know. But he's alive. I've seen him.'

'That's not possible.'

'It is. I've spoken with him.'

'Van Kaldhoone certainly has reason to seek vengeance on Ulovar. If you're right.'

'I am right. He got to Hazia somehow. He made her enter the Blackwell. It didn't even matter what she took, I think. What mattered was that she was exposed for what she was: Hazia was like Van Kaldhoone. She had the grave-sight.'

Sanvaunt stared at me.

'Yes she did,' he said quietly.

'You knew?'

He nodded silently.

'How?'

'Hazia was fostered with us, at Uloss, when she was small. She was too little to understand that revealing what she saw would cost her life.' He shook his head. 'And my uncle knew too. But he used the Fourth Gate to tie her mind. To cloud what she saw.'

I stared at him aghast.

'He protected her? But what about—what about what he did to Kaldhoone LacShale?'

Sanvaunt shook his head. Old pain.

'LacShale had lost his mind. He was consumed with rage, Raine. He murdered a man in broad daylight, and he went to war against the grandmaster. LacShale thought his position as Draoihn placed him beyond the law. But it doesn't—if such a blatant display went unpunished, what would that mean? The law against the grave-sight is supposed to prevent the Sarathi from ever rising again. But what good are we to anybody if we abandon the laws of the land?'

Ulovar had tried to protect Hazia from herself. Just as he'd tried to protect me from the grief that lurked beyond the scar in my mind.

'Raine,' Sanvaunt said quietly. 'I understand what this means too.'

'Just don't say anything,' I snapped. I couldn't face the look in his eyes. I needed to move fast, now. Before what I knew became public knowledge. Ulovar and Sanvaunt might show me mercy. But I had no certainty where anybody

else was concerned. I had to give them my proof, and once that was done, I had
to go. I had to be gone before they read it, saw it, understood it. Long gone. A
hard day's ride gone. My time at Redwinter had to end. Not because I wanted
to go, but because to prove Ulovar's innocence, I had to expose my own truth.
And that truth meant my doom.

'We have to take this to the grandmaster,' Sanvaunt said. 'If you're right. If
Kaldhoone LacShale is alive, then he's a true threat to Redwinter. He has to be
stopped.'

My guts were doing flips at what that meant.

I was kicking the doors off, now. Shining light onto the dark and secret part
of me that I'd kept hidden all these years. There was a price for doing it. But it
was a price that I had no choice but to bear. I just hoped that I could retain my
freedom for long enough to make a quiet departure, before everything went
off. That stash under my bed was going to pay off after all.

'Someone needs to stay here to look after that lying, piece of shit cousin of
yours. I don't know what it is they want with him. But they want something.
That note they sent is intended to get him into their hands, tonight. It's no coincidence that it's the night before Ulovar's trial. Maybe they just want to get
rid of him so he can't stand witness.'

'Maybe they want to get rid of you both.'

Yes. There was that.

He wasn't the first man that I've killed.

'I can't delay. We have to go to the grandmaster now. I have to tell her what
I know.'

Sanvaunt's brows arched.

'Raine,' he said. The word hung between us like the tolling of a bell. 'This
could end badly for you.'

'I know,' I said. 'But I owe Ulovar too much to back down now. He saved
me. He defeated Ciuthach, and he saved me from madness and death. It'd be a
poor show if I didn't try to repay him. I'll go to her alone if I have to.'

'No. I'm coming with you,' Sanvaunt said. 'Wait here. I'm going to tell Ovitus
that he's not to leave the greathouse. He's safe enough whilst he's in Redwinter.'

Sanvaunt disappeared upstairs. It was better for him to give that message
than me, that was for sure. I felt oddly guilty about having shouted at Ovitus,
despite what he'd done. It played through my mind as I waited at the foot of
the stairs. I wondered if Ulovar had heard the same rumour. I hoped not. He
wasn't the type people went to with gossip, and he'd been with us on the road.
Light Above, but I hoped that he hadn't heard it. Somehow I felt like I was the
one that should be ashamed. Me, when it was Ovitus's doing entirely. It prob-

ably hadn't seemed like so very much to him. Just a little fib. He couldn't have sullied Liara's good name, and it wouldn't have played into his fantasies about her to remove her from that pedestal. He didn't even see her for who she was. Didn't see the bright, funny girl who could set a room to laughter. But me? I was a poor girl from the north, secretly desiring him, a secret, steamy fuck as his spoils of battle. I could have puked if Sanvaunt hadn't knocked everything out of me already. Ovitus had dirtied my name with his own selfish imagination. I took my shame, balled it up and buried it beneath my anger. I didn't think that we were friends anymore.

The night was quiet. The grounds were vast and black. The few lights of the other greathouses were small in the distance. My breath plumed in the air, white spirits on the night. We crossed a lawn that could have been a park in some other place, cutting a route directly towards the grandmaster's residence. It was late, and she would have to be roused. But who would we meet tonight, the young, mesmerizingly beautiful woman, or the broken crone with bands of iron holding her head together? I feared them both equally.

'Do you feel that?' Sanvaunt said. He held out an arm to stop me.

'Just the cold,' I said.

'Something isn't right.'

There was nothing around us save a few artfully grown trees, their trunks twisting like sinew. But there was something in the air. I felt Sanvaunt's trance reaching out, brushing past me, a beat so quiet, so solid that it could have been the beating of my own heart. Slowly he reached down, grasping the hilt of his sword.

'What is it?' I asked. But I heard, as if it rose up from the bones in my feet, a slow, breathy whisper passing through me.

Raine, the voice sighed. *Raine, you are our friend, did we not agree on that?*

I'd stopped dead. I could feel it now too. A prickling in the air. Something I hadn't felt since I was back in Dalnesse. An emptiness in the spaces between breaths, cutting between thoughts, a colour in the blackness.

Bring the heir to me, Raine, the voice whispered through me. *Who are your true family? Who are your kin?*

'I have no kin,' I breathed, my breath a white cloud in the night.

'Raine,' Sanvaunt warned, drawing his sword.

This is not the hour to raise walls before us, the voice whispered into my marrow. Veretaine's voice. Kaldhoone LacShale's voice. I reached beneath my shirt, drew out the bone amulet. *And those that stand—*

I tore the amulet from its thong, and the voice cut out, dead. A mark of friendship? No. Not friendship. I dropped it.

I tried to drop it.

I couldn't drop it.

'What in Skuttis?' I muttered, shaking my hand, trying to unstick the shard of bird-shaped bone. I could transfer it between my hands, move it around my palm, even loop it around a wrist—but the moment I tried to end all contact between me and the little talisman, it simply wouldn't go.

'Where did you get that?' Sanvaunt whispered. He was scanning the dark, tugging me along by the arm, beating a retreat across the magpie lawn.

'Kaldhoone LacShale is not happy with me,' I said quietly. 'I fear he may have put in a contingency in case I didn't follow the plan.'

Sanvaunt's eyes were on point like a setter's, scanning the darkness. His fingers were clenched hard as irons around my arm. 'Raine,' he said quietly. 'I think you're going to need to run.'

There was a hiss, a buzzing in the air, and then an insect fluttered in front of my face. I swatted at it, caught it. Like a huge grasshopper, but winged. I tossed it away. Another appeared, then another.

'What in Skuttis are these?'

Sanvaunt's teeth were bared white in the night.

'They're locusts.' When he looked at me, his eyes had turned hard. 'It's that charm. Its binding you to a demon.'

Something moved in the darkness. A tall, famine-thin figure crossing the lawn with an awkward, jarring gait. A ragged white dress clung in shreds to her shoulders, falling to scraped and bloodied knees, corpse-grey flesh and staring, blinkless yellow eyes. Insects whirled in a storm around her, a mist of legs and wings, but through the haze I saw broken shards of yellowed teeth, a black flint axe in one hand, a rusted sickle in the other.

My jaw froze in place. My limbs began to shake. Light Above. This was more than one of the hidden folk. A true demon.

Sanvaunt drew his sword. Another pair of locusts landed on me.

'What the feck is that thing?'

'A Mawleth,' he breathed. 'A creature of the Night Below.' He took a fighting stance, his sword bare before him, both hands on the hilt. 'Run to the grand-master. Find the council. Only they have the power to stop it.'

It staggered, but crossing the ground too quickly for its ragged pace. Her expression was the absence of hope, her mouth spilling chittering locusts, her eyes fixed on me and the bone charm in my hand. The locusts were flying into my face, around my eyes, but I felt her deathless malice. I couldn't face that. Nobody could.

'Run!' I said. The locusts flocked towards me, trying to land on me, a chittering cloud that grew thicker even as I swiped my hands through it.

The Mawleth's growl rose like distant thunder, a toad-croak of hunger, and hatred, and the darkness below. And then it sped for us, weapons cutting the night.

It moved too fast. Its gait had been lumbering, uncertain. Now it lashed forwards with the precision of a striking mistcat. And it came for me. Sanvaunt parried the slice of the rusted sickle, then released his hilt with his left hand, raised his forearm to parry the descending haft of the hatchet. He kicked out, knocking the thing back, but it was on him again in moments. He slashed out, a broad defensive stroke that hacked through half the Mawleth's neck. For a moment I scented victory as bright yellow ichor gushed from the wound, but the damage was healing even as the Mawleth fixed its eyes back on me. It turned its assault on Sanvaunt, sickle hewing, axe hacking, and now he fought only to parry and draw back. A rip of the sickle scored down his coat, tearing the dark leather open to reveal brighter red beneath.

'I'll hold it off,' Sanvaunt said, his voice breaking like a ship against hidden rocks. 'It's you it wants. Run, Raine. Run. Go!'

Locusts filled the air, a storm so thick I could hardly see ten feet ahead. Their bodies battered into me, itching and scratching. I could do nothing here.

'I can't leave you!'

'Raine, go!'

To my shame, I did.

I fled from the Mawleth as its broken toes clawed across the manicured lawn. I heard Sanvaunt issue a challenge in a language I didn't comprehend, sank into a stance that would have terrified a trained fighter, and then I lost them to the plague of wings and legs surrounding me.

I had to reach Grandmaster Robilar. She was the most powerful of the Draoihn, if anyone could combat a demon of the Night Below, it was her. But I was running half blinded by the cloud, charging through the dark. I staggered as I ran right into a low hedge, hard little branches tearing at my shins. I hurdled it, and ran on, white plumes of breath spilling into the air. I ran towards lights. Anyone who could help me.

And then I saw them ahead of me. Yellow eyes through the insect haze. I heard fetid, wet breath, smelled carrion stench rising around me. She could have been sister to the first, butcher's hooks in knuckles skinned to white bone. A second Mawleth right ahead of me. My feet skidded on the damp grass. Its mouth opened wide, a split tongue lolling, madness and hunger sending her bony legs skittering across the ground. Terror ripped right through me, and a jet of piss came out. I backed away. It had cut me off from the grandmaster. I couldn't go forward. Couldn't go back.

Distantly I heard a man cry out. Sanvaunt! But I couldn't help him. I couldn't help anybody. The locusts were growing thicker, like hunting dogs set to flush out prey.

I had to lose them. Had to go somewhere that they couldn't follow.

I put all my strength into my legs and I ran. My mind had opened into a trance of its own volition, the beat of it flooding out into the world. I was shouting, yelling for help, but in the huge grounds, nobody was going to hear me. I ran on through the madness.

Before me, a bridge spanned out into a greater darkness below. A bridge over nothing. The Blackwell lay ahead. I sprinted for the bridge, but even now my speed flagged. The slathering of the creature's dangling tongues, the ring of hooks clashed together and the gliding drag of its feet rose behind me. Closer. Closer! I ran onto the bridge. It was narrow, only four feet wide, and the drop to either side was a plummet down into the canyon below, but I couldn't slow.

Eio, the trance of the First Gate, radiated out. I felt it all. Felt the buzz of the locusts' wings all around me, sensed the paths and patterns of their flight. I sensed the stone beneath me, and my own feet, each brief connection propelling me on. I crossed the bridge with the surety of a mountain goat.

Come on Raine. You've faced nightmares before. You can do it again.

I sped over the last of the bridge and spared a glance back. There was the Mawleth, blurred by the rush of millions of tiny wings, but its eyes glowed through the swarm. It stopped at the edge of the bridge, staring across the expanse, hissing. For a moment I hoped it was going to throw itself blindly forwards, fall crashing down into the abyss. What did I know about fighting demons? What could Sanvaunt's sword do against it? A hot well of pain and rage held itself silent in my chest at the thought of him trying to fight one of those things. I'd run. I'd left him to death.

The Mawleth hissed as it stepped onto the bridge. The air seemed charged around it as it sank to all fours and began to prowl, cat-like towards me.

It locked eyes with me.

There was nothing there. So much nothing. As if it wasn't truly a piece of our world at all. It didn't belong here. There was nothing, and from whence comes evil but from the absence of good? That must be some shitty philosophy Ovitus had shared with me.

The Blackwell lay behind me. Just an archway framing a stair that led down into the pillar of rock. No other choices, now. It was down into the darkness, and possible safety, or wait for that thing to draw its awkward, gaunt body across to me. No choice at all.

As I started down the stairs, the locusts fell away. Abandoned me completely. Those that were clinging to me dropped like stones, falling, dead on the floor. Magic. Protection. I'd made the right choice. This was the Draoihn's vault, and we had spent months trying to work out how a simple apprentice like Hazia could have bypassed the wards and spells that awaited me below. I only had a theory. She wasn't the clue. The clue was Kaldhoone LacShale, and his followers. They all possessed the grave-sight. The Draoihn of the Fourth Gate could shield their minds against the magic beneath. That was why so few of them could enter here. But what if there was another way to avoid those magics?

Hazia had been an apprentice, trained only in the first trance. But if she, like me, had been lured in by Van Kaldhoone LacShale, or Veretaine as he gave his name, then maybe she had found a way through. If I was wrong, then there was no way back, so I'd better be spirit-damned right.

Ulovar, bent kneed, his sword outstretched as Ciuthach's head fell from his shoulders.

Ulovar, collapsing to the ground, his eyes ruined and bloody.

Sanvaunt, standing his ground to protect me.

Esher, putting her trust in me without question.

These people of pride and duty. There was good in them. I had to try.

I wiped tears from my eyes. I hadn't been able to help Lochlan or Kella or the sooth-sisters. Maybe these people weren't my family. But they had shown me kindness, taken me into their home. They deserved whatever I could give them.

The stairway was nothing like I had imagined. Crudely cut, narrow, no carvings or friezes. Veins of cadanum ran a foot from the ground, a foot from the ceiling, lighting my way as I spiralled down into the darkness. It was colder here than it had been out in the night.

It came to an end, and before me a corridor stretched out. At least a hundred feet long. A path ran down the centre, set with red and white tiles, the same stone that formed the vast walls around Redwinter. To either side, every ten paces, a pair of statues faced one another. They looked like huge toads, caught in time, polished marble. I had no idea what their relevance was, but at the end of the tunnel, an archway called me on, lit with a pale, waxy light. Not cadanum or lamp oil. Not fire. Something else.

Eio still beat soft and heavy within me. There was an unease written into the stones themselves. Etched into the air. It wanted me to turn back. Warned me that this was not for me. But I couldn't stop. Not now. I took my first step forwards.

A spirit appeared between two of the toads. It didn't seem to see me, drifting slightly off the ground. It was not human, had never been human. Its fingers were too long, distended; its jaw hung slack and harboured too many teeth. Whatever it was, or had been, it appeared in long robes, eyeless, wrinkled. A shadow man, a thing of another realm, its spirit bound to these stones. I stepped back from it, and it drifted past me, disappearing into the rock.

I'd seen worse things than spirits already that night. I began to walk forwards, and as I did, another spirit drifted into my path, appearing from between the toads again. Similar to the first, but a different individual. Its head swung left and right as if it searched invisibly for something. I swallowed hard. The corridor beyond had filled with drifting spectres, greenish-white, blind, lost and bound to a world that did not belong to them.

None of the others could see them. Not even the Lord Draoihn, not even those that commanded four or five Gates, not even the mighty Grandmaster Vedira Robilar understood what guarded the Blackwell. The spirits were incorporeal, but to step into one of them would bring about a clash of worlds. It would bring madness, would tear a mind apart. These wraiths hated me, us, all of life. No living thing should share its space in existence and time with these things.

Robilar, Ulovar, they had to shield their minds because they couldn't avoid these invisible guardians. But Hazia had not had to defend herself, or shield herself as the council did. She only had to dodge them. Like me.

They moved slowly, drifting, gliding. I stepped past the second, waited as a third went by, then forwards again. Surrounded by the dead, surrounded by ghosts of things that wanted to tear me apart no less for their state of undeath, I moved forwards in swift, carefully placed steps. Once, a spirit surprised me, appearing from the stone to my left, and I had to step back quickly. I didn't touch it, but I felt the brush of its will alongside my own. A flickering sense of utter terror, utter powerlessness, rippled through me. But it lasted only a moment, and I managed to calm my pounding heart. To walk right into one of those things without protection would likely have caused it to burst. Little wonder the others hadn't spoken of this. I had to be careful. But I had to be fast.

I dodged around a few more. And then I was at the arch. The portal that led into the Blackwell. The soft, dry white light filled the archway. I stepped through.

Not even the grandmaster knew what the magic that protected the Blackwell was. They simply couldn't see it. But I could. And I had beaten it.

Pushing through that light felt like forcing myself through a film of warm butter. A little strange, but not unpleasant. When I opened my eyes again, it was not at all what I had expected. It felt like the nave of a vast cathedral, only it was a single room, roughly circular but in truth having about twenty-four straight walls. I had no idea what that shape was called. But it was as though I stood at the base of a tower. Impossibly tall, the walls rose skyward, on and on, until I could no longer see how far they stretched above me. And every wall was windows, windows of stained glass in beautiful, bright colours. The light shone evenly through all of them, as if the sun were at their backs, focusing two dozen times into the room.

The coloured glass depicted men, women, and other things that were both like them and not. They wore oxblood-red, some in robes, some in coats. Names, if that's what they were, were written as though on glass scrolls beneath them, but I didn't recognise any of them. One depicted a child, a wrap of cloth across his eyes. Another, a woman shining with holy fire and light. A bent-backed old man in a cloak of crow's feathers. Heroes and holy martyrs of another time, perhaps.

It was beautiful. Impossible and beautiful. And not what I was here for.

A series of plinths, stands and racks held the wealth of the Blackwell.

On the nearest, to my right, I saw the page I had once shown to Lochlan, the page that had ushered Ciuthach back from undeath. Placed here by Ulovar.

Something fell into place in my mind, like a wooden ball rolling down a hole in a carnival game, fitting so obviously, so precisely. Echoing in its certainty. Hazia had not come here looking for something in particular. She'd been sent here to take something. *Anything.* Van Kaldhoone LacShale didn't know what lay down here. He'd just wanted one of Ulovar's apprentices to take something. So she'd taken the first thing she could lay her hands on, and the page had done the rest, taking her mind, demanding her obedience, her wild charge into the north to reunite it with the book. Nobody—not even Kaldhoone LacShale, maddened by vengeance as he was—had intended to unleash Ciuthach.

My whole world had been destroyed by *mistake.*

The Draoihn who could enter this place knew better than to meddle with what they found here. These were the relics and artefacts of a bygone age. They were not made for us.

A suit of armour, a thousand years old or more, made from polished blue lapis lazuli and bronze. The statue of a cowering warrior, one hand raised as if to shield his eyes. A rusted dagger, the blade somehow still wet with ruddy oil. One pedestal held nothing but a pile of grey dust. A stack of sharpened bones.

A pair of clocks, their hands suspended in time. A staff with a serpent's head. What, horribly, appeared to be the grey-skinned head of a child, scarred and scaled. All of it strange, all of it deadly. I kept my hands to myself.

In the centre of the room was a clear circle, devoid of the clutter of plinths and racks containing the Draoihn's relics. The floor was mostly pale marble, but here, both jade and cadanum had been set into the stone in patterns. Six circles, each within the next, overlaid with six circles, each overlapping two others. Runes and sigils.

I had seen this before. I'd seen it in Grandmaster Robilar's office, spread across the wall. I had seen it again, in the sky over Harranir, the day the colour had fled the world. Six circles within six circles. Six trances, six Gates for mortal men to pass. Eio for the self. Sei for the other. Taine for the energy of the world, Fier for the realm of the mind. Vie for life. Skal for death. And when all of those forces were understood and joined together, they made Gei: creation. Everything. Six parts of a whole. None more important than the other. All of them essential.

Which meant that they knew. Grandmaster Robilar, Ulovar, all of the council members who had walked here. They knew that the Sarathi, the Draoihn who had passed the Sixth Gate, the Gate of Death, were as key a part of this world as they were. And yet, through fear that they would serve the Night Below, they were destroyed wherever they were found.

My whole life I had shied away from my gift, for that was what it was. Had feared it, avoided company for fear of discovery. But it had been more than that. I'd feared myself.

I gasped, something heavy and consuming falling from me, a boulder I'd carried for too long. I hadn't known how great a weight that had brought down on me. How heavy a burden that had always been. I felt it melting away from my chest. From my heart. I wasn't poison. I wasn't twisted, and I did not deserve to die.

Sanvaunt. I thought of Sanvaunt. He was probably dead now.

A circle that encompassed all of creation. Me, the things around me. Warmth and cold, the thoughts that happened beyond the confines of my own body. Life. Death. I stepped into it. Everything was one. Everything was together, unseparated, part of a vast cosmic whole. I needed help. I needed an ally. And I was going to call one to me now.

I sat down cross-legged. I placed my hands against the floor, surprisingly warm to the touch. Closed my eyes and tried to settle my Eio. Felt along my skin, my nails, the brush of white hair against my neck. I knew where it all was. Everything. Even against the rapid pulsing of blood through my veins, I could sense the wrongness around that rusted dagger, and the void of emptiness in the pile of dust. All of it in relation to me, the tiny, imperceptible signals that everything in existence gave off. It was all one. That was the trick. Everything was one thing. The tiny gaps that separate us from the things that we touch, the space between grains of air. They weren't real. They weren't any bigger or smaller than any other thing. Just gaps. And a gap is nothing. When you discount the nothing, there is only the something, all squashed up together, a single piece. Just one piece of everything.

When we died, some intrinsic part of us—the soul—went away. It left the oneness, venturing down into Skuttis, or up into Anavia, to the Night Below or the Light Above. But when they remained—when they stayed with us—they were still part of the grand mosaic that formed the world.

The world was interlocked. Everything was one. And if everything was one, then I could breach the distance.

'Queen of Feathers,' I said, drifting on waves of existence that I barely understood how to perceive. 'Be here now.'

I felt the tug against my mind. The circle around me began to hum, began to glow with fierce, binding energy. A spirit-circle. A summoning circle. A circle that was both life and death and everything else all at once. Ancient magic, the kind that no living Draoihn could command, reached up to wrap me, vines of coursing light binding around my limbs, threads of darkness reaching up through bone and vein.

A howling mind-wind assailed me. I opened my eyes. Nothing else in the room moved, nor did the wind lift a hair on my head. But I felt it nonetheless. I felt the drag through the aether, the circle doing the work for me. Cadanum shards glowed within its boundaries, casting their light upwards, but in colours so pure and blue and clean, like none I'd ever seen before.

And then she stood before me. And I knew that I had made a colossal mistake.

The Queen of Feathers. My guardian. My guide. And at one time, a source of humiliation. Ally of my enemy. She rose dark and terrible before me now, at the edge of my circle, and blistering fury coursed across her lovely features. Her soft, night-dark hair flowed around her like serpents, festival streamers caught in a gale. Black wings unfurled behind her, blotting out the windows, but her eyes glowed with an unholy, shadow-edged light.

'How dare you command me?' she roared. She bared her teeth, and I saw them grow sharp, a predator's bite.

Too late to back down now.

'I command you to assist me,' I said. 'Queen of Feathers. Help me escape this place. Help me against the demons that pursue me.'

The Queen of Feathers looked to her left, then her right, then up towards the endless void above.

'Ugh,' she said. 'This place. A tragic memorial to self-aggrandisement. Whatever has brought you here, little Raine? You understood the soul-guard placed here, I see. But what do you hope to accomplish?'

'I was chased here by a Mawleth,' I said. 'It's a kind of demon.'

'I know what a Mawleth is,' the Queen of Feathers snapped. 'I was riding the currents that wash between the stars a thousand years before your grandmother was born. But it's no easy thing. There's a great price to be paid for that. And why would they set something so vast upon someone as . . . incomplete . . . as you?'

Her eyes were a swirl of stars and the passages of dust and time that flowed between them. And she was furious. I should not have done this. I had no idea what I was dealing with.

'Then I command you to send them back from whence they came!' I declared. It sounded good to me.

'Do you indeed?'

The Queen of Feathers began to walk around the edge of the circle. She reached towards it, but recoiled as sparks lit her fingers, running beneath her ghostly blue-tinged skin. Her eyes narrowed.

'What a joy it must be to meddle with things so far beyond your understanding. Command me, you say? You've no power to do that, little Raine. I heard your call, and you gave me a thread on which I could ride. The circle is good for that, it's true. But a thousand years and more have given me little cause to listen to the whims of children. I should flay the skin from your face and use it to gag any more of these absurd demands.' She tapped at the circle again, but blue-white sparks spat again.

'Not while I'm here you can't,' I said.

'And when you leave?'

'You helped me before,' I said. 'You saved me from Ciuthach. Why save me then, if you're only going to leave me to die now?'

'You sit within the seventh circle, that which contains the six Gates. You should comprehend everything. And yet your understanding is like that of a flea, compared to mine. Why should I reveal my thoughts to you?' She shook her head slightly as if something about that annoyed her.

'I need your help,' I begged. My bargaining position was getting weaker by the moment. 'Please help me.'

'You need to help yourself, little flea,' she said. 'That is what we always do. We help ourselves.'

'What can I do against one of those things?' I asked. 'I don't know how to fight demons. Tell me how I can beat them.'

'What do I gain in return for helping you here?' She spoke the question aloud, but somehow it didn't seem directed towards me. For a moment I almost felt that I'd been forgotten.

'Whatever you want.'

Feathered wings beat the air behind her.

'Yes. That was it. A bargain, now, that is something that perhaps can be worked with.' She smiled. It was frostbitten and somehow echoed the emptiness of the Mawleth. 'You will owe me a favour. A single favour, no matter how large or small. That I shall demand of you at a time of my choosing. And you will not resist. You will swear it upon your true name, and the bond will be forged. Do we have a deal?'

It sounded like a very bad deal. It certainly wasn't what I had intended. But I thought of Sanvaunt. I thought of Ulovar. I couldn't stay down here. I had to escape before anyone knew what I'd done, or I'd be interrogated, maybe even tortured. Nobody was permitted to enter the Blackwell.

'Yes,' I said. 'I swear it.'

'And your true name?'

'I swear it on my true name,' I said.

The circle flickered around me. Light and sparks danced around the golden circles set into the floor. I felt a wave of something pass through me. A shadow, a lifting. A breeze, a stone.

'And what is that name?'

'The bond has been made,' I said. 'I can feel it. You don't need my true name, even if I did know what it is.' And I didn't. My name was Raine. But a true name, somehow that was something deeper. Something more unequivocal. The Queen of Feathers smiled.

'Very well. Look around you, little flea. You sit among the armaments of Draoihn who were making war when even the world was young. Arm yourself and deal with the demons that hunt you.'

'That's not helping me!' I cried. But the Queen of Feathers only smiled, a lazy, wolfish smile.

'Be careful of the bargains you make, little flea. I've told you how to destroy that which hunts you. Whether you take the advice or not, my part of the deal is fulfilled.'

'That's not fair!' I cried.

'I'll give you one last piece of advice for free,' the Queen of Feathers said. 'Call me in this way again and I will find you, and I will make you beg for the

Mawleth's hunger before I'm done with you.' She tossed her lovely hair back behind her shoulders. 'And remember, always, that you owe me.'

And she was gone. I felt the power in the circle around me dying away. The room was no less brightly lit, so many sunrays bearing down on me, but I felt the darkness that had been here moments before. Maybe she had saved me once. But the bargain I had made sat foul and black on my mind.

I had to get out of here. I had to help Sanvaunt. Use the weapons? Hardly a good choice. Old swords, spears, a rusting knife, a pair of gauntlets that should have been too big for any man. Rods and staves with various ornate heads. What use was any of it?

And then I saw a familiar shape. The midnight-blue bow stave I'd taken from Ciuthach's barrow. Ulovar had taken it from me—and he'd stowed it down here. I picked it up, turned it in my hands, saw the gleaming threads of silver running through the polished wood. The string shimmered into life at my touch, the wood creaking as it bent itself to take its shape. It felt right in my hand, thrumming as though eager to fight for me again. But on its own it wouldn't be enough. The bow had done *something* against Ciuthach. It had stopped him for long enough to break his mental hold on Ulovar, allowed him to behead it. Now I needed arrows. And in this place, there had to be some. It did not take me long. A quiver of seven arrows, white shafts with blood-red runes carved in spirals around them. The fletching was a mixture of gold and pale blue; the heads seemed to be chipped from stone. But if they were down here, they had to be worth something. I slung the quiver over my shoulder. The arrows were longer than I usually shot, just over three feet long. It felt good to be armed again. Armed, and ready.

Who was I kidding? I would never be ready to fight those things. Not even if I was armed with a thousand arrows.

Sanvaunt. Esher. Ulovar. The scar in my mind was pulsing. I felt the crack that ran along it baying, the well of magma-hot fire behind it. I wasn't doing this for myself.

Time to fight for the people I loved, or time to die for them. There was no choice to make at all.

34

I bypassed the ghosts. All of this strife and trouble. Just because of some Light-damned ghosts.

I kept an arrow nocked as I ascended the stair. I'd been down in the Black-well for half a candle's length. I didn't know what to expect when I emerged. Maybe I'd find that the Draoihn had been roused, had taken the fight to the Mawleth. If that was the case, I had to slip out without being seen. But the night was still deep. And as I approached the top of the stairs, I could hear the chirping of the locusts. They filled the world outside, a swarm whirring through the air, but fewer than there had been when it chased me. The Mawleth had not gone far.

I risked a peek around the spiral staircase. No sign of it at the entrance. My fingers rested on the end of the arrow shaft, and I felt something through them. That blue-and-gold-fletched arrow felt almost alert. Almost alive in my hand. The bow's midnight-blue wood offered back warmth to my hand. It had served me well before. It had to do so again.

No sign of the Mawleth on the promontory of rock that led down into the Blackwell. No sign of it on that narrow bridge. I was trying to hold the first trance, but my head had begun to pound on all sides. I couldn't focus on it. I had to let it go. The world reverted into the simple and mundane, and the drop to either side of the bridge somehow looked deeper and blacker as a result.

The night was quiet. Nobody had raised the hue and cry here, it seemed. Which meant Redwinter slept. Which meant that Sanvaunt was dead. Brave, foolish Sanvaunt. He should have run with me. A swell of something vast hammered against the ridge of scar that Ulovar had driven through my mind. No time for it. No time for anything except escape.

Since the locusts were fewer, the Mawleth was probably further away. Maybe both of them were. I stepped out onto the bridge, unsteady this time. My heart hammered harder than the trance I'd just dropped. I stepped carefully, knees bent. Creeping forwards, horribly exposed. I was halfway when I heard it.

The Mawleth had indeed been waiting for me.

It hung from the rock face beneath the Blackwell's promontory, clawlike nails thrust into the stone. And now it began to draw itself upwards. Split tongue lolling, the white-clad corpse woman dragged herself up the rock. Up and onto the side of the bridge.

I knelt. The locusts swarmed from the tattered robes across her back, chirping their song as they filled the bridge's expanse, moving into my eyes, blinding me, filling the world with their tiny bodies.

I drew back on the bowstring, gleaming moonlight, back to my ear, felt the full flexing power of the bow. The Mawleth was a narrow target, but the insects flurried and whirled around me. The stave creaked; the fletching seemed to hum into my ear.

'Back to Skuttis,' I whispered. 'You're done.'

I released the string.

The arrow sped through the cloud of locusts, forging a tunnel through the air, a clear cylinder through which I could see into the mad, empty voids of the Mawleth's eyes. The arrow sang, punched hard into the Mawleth's body and disappeared. The demon reeled back as glowing yellow ichor burst from the wound, spraying in jets, incinerating locusts. It roared, a vast sound that crashed over the whole of Redwinter as the liquid fire in its blood cast the night in bright shades of gold and red. Its jagged, cracked nails dug into the narrow bridge as it clawed at the wound.

I nocked a second arrow. Drew back and loosed again. The second punched into the clavicle below her neck. The demon howled again, and this time cracks of bright fire ran right through it, spreading, tearing through its form and blazing with a red-white luminosity, lighting the bridge's underside.

'Come on,' I whispered through rapid breaths. 'Come on, die, you fecker.'

Every instinct demanded I run, but I rose. Slowly I paced along the stone, reached the end and looked back. The demon was tearing at its own flesh, ripping away white-leather skin as its own life fire poured out as if from a liquid centre. I held an arrow ready. But I wouldn't need it. The Mawleth folded in on itself, then dissolved into a cloud of ash and molten fire, spilling from the bridge, until nothing remained but embers in the dark.

Insects were falling dead from the air around me. I brushed them from my shoulders, ripped them from my hair. One down. Still one left.

I was running again, the hunt upon me. I hunched low as though that could hide me. Kaldhoone LacShale wanted me dead. I could expose him now. I could expose him and bring the full wrath of Redwinter down upon him and his acolytes.

They'd made me believe they aspired to peace. To be protected. Maybe for some of them it was true. But they were being used by a man who cared only for vengeance. Only to make others suffer. And he would use every means at his disposal to do so.

I ran for the lawn on which I'd abandoned Sanvaunt. The ground was churned to mud. No sign of the Mawleth, no insects in the air. And then I saw the shape. Lying face-first, down on the ground. Face-first. Down. On the ground. Just like I'd seen them all in Dalnesse. Sprawled. Broken. Dead.

I felt the crack. The splintering of that ridge of scar in my mind. Felt something slicing into it, cutting it hard and clean.

'No,' I said as I ran to him. I rolled him over to see his face. Brave, foolish, duty-bound Sanvaunt. He hadn't deserved this. He deserved to be a stupid knight in one of his stupid romances. I'd brought him to this. If I hadn't told him, if he hadn't stepped out with me into the dark, he wouldn't be here. He wouldn't be dead right now. He'd fought, and died with a sword in his hand.

Only he didn't have a sword. I looked around for it. It lay nearby, a twisted steel ruin. Melted, warped into something else entirely.

Wait.

He killed it?

I put my ear over his mouth. Breathing. Faint, but oh Light Above, he was still alive and I wanted him to be all right with such force it rose like fire through me and set the whole world alight. The scar in my mind shuddered and reeled, and then it was falling away, tatters of unneeded tissue flaking off, revealing the hard and broken landscape beneath.

I felt it all then. I felt love and I felt tearing, agonising grief all at once. They blossomed and flared, and they filled me with so much fury that I would have raised all the spirits of all the dead and cast them at my enemy if only I had the power. But against that tidal wave of violent anger, something soft but so, so strong surrounded me like gentle, determined hands, cupping me and holding me steady. I didn't know what it was. But it was what I needed.

There was blood around his lips; his breathing was shallow, his pulse barely there. Hurt on the inside? A punctured lung maybe. Injuries that I couldn't help. But I knew someone who could.

'Stay there,' I said, pointlessly. And then I ran for the LacNaithe greathouse.

I sounded the bell, clanging it hard enough to wake the servants, but Esher flung the door open wide-eyed, armed. She hadn't slept.

'What's going on?'

'Go to the grandmaster. Sanvaunt is bleeding to death in the magpie garden. If she doesn't heal him, he'll die. Get the grandmaster to help him, now!' I was screaming at her by the time I finished.

She didn't question me. Didn't doubt me for a moment, even as the blood drained from her face.

'Come with me,' she said.

'I have to check on Ovitus,' I snarled. 'He's the target. I have to guard him.'

Esher nodded and was out the door. I stormed up the stairs.

I looked down at my wrist: the bird charm was gone, maybe lost somewhere in the flurry of locust wings. The Mawleths were a backup plan, only intended to scrub out a misplaced flick of the quill. Kaldhoone had tried to have me bring Ovitus to him, and they intended to kill me if I did anything else. That much was clear. Trying to have me bring Ovitus to them had been a big move—a gamble. It wouldn't be their only attempt to take hold of him, not now we were forewarned. But was it worth this? Why did he matter so much? Kaldhoone LacShale already had Ulovar where he wanted him.

I hammered on the door to Ovitus's bedchamber, no longer caring about stealth, no longer caring who I woke. There was no response. I flung the door open. Sanvaunt had told him not to go anywhere, but his room was empty. The covers were rumpled, his nightgown in a pile on the floor. Where had he gone? Maybe down to the kitchen for some kind of late-night snack? I stormed through the greathouse, calling his name. Servants, Howen, Ehma, Bossal and Patalia appeared, bleary-eyed; Jathan and Adanost emerged from their rooms asking what in all the freezing rivers of Skuttis was going on, but I had no answer for them. He wasn't in the greathouse.

I had to find him.

Maybe Van Kaldhoone had him already.

As I passed my room, I realised I was still carrying the bow and the arrows I'd taken from the Blackwell. I couldn't carry any of that around. If anyone realised what I'd done, stopping me would become their priority, not finding him. I'd have to get them back in there, or bury them, but for now I'd stow them under my bed. I stepped into my room and saw lying on my unslept bed a piece of parchment. An opened letter, waiting for me.

My darling Ovitus,

I know that the feelings that I have for you are returned. I have tried to wait, but I can wait no longer. Would you meet me tonight? I will be waiting for you at the fountain in the greatmarket. I must speak my love to you tonight.

Yours eternally,
Liara LacShale

It made no sense. What was this doing here?

It made absolutely no sense whatsoever.

Except, horribly, it did.

A wash of coarse white misery swarmed over me. I was still angry at him. So, so angry. But the friendship we'd shared wasn't gone. It was changed, maybe even sullied, but I couldn't let it all go. And he was angry too, angry because of the way that I'd spoken to him, and so I knew precisely why this was here. It had been delivered to the greathouse after we left. And Ovitus had read it, and left it here for me to find. His proof that I'd been wrong. He wanted me to read it and see what a fool I'd been for doubting him. For shouting at him, calling him stupid and tragic, for saying he was dreaming.

I was running around killing demons, his uncle was to be tried for treason, and still, in his utter self-absorption, this was what drove him. He was broken in some way that I didn't understand. Maybe would never understand. I crushed the letter in my fist and screamed.

The apprentices were clustering around my door.

'Where is she?' I yelled. I knew I sounded half-hysterical. 'Where is Liara LacShale?'

'I'm here.'

Liara looked like she'd been roused alongside the others, her hair netted for sleep, a robe over her nightgown. I thrust the letter towards her.

'Who's waiting for him? How many? What are they going to do with him?'

'Calm down,' Jathan said, but I could see that they were all wary of me. 'What's happening?'

'Who is waiting for him?' I demanded.

Liara read the letter. A look of such blank consternation had crossed her face that it seemed so believable. So utterly, incredibly believable.

'You didn't write it?'

'No, I—I don't understand. This is my writing. It's my seal. But I don't—I don't remember writing it. I would *never* say this to Ovitus. Not like this. And—why would I send him . . . ? I don't know what's happening.'

'You need to calm down,' Jathan was saying.

I knocked his arm away. 'Sanvaunt is lying half-dead in the magpie garden. Go to him. Look after him. Keep him alive until Grandmaster Robilar can help him. I'm going after Ovitus.'

They looked shocked. Of course they did. But for Draoihn apprentices, they were a weak-willed bunch, and the rage flowing through me caused them to step back.

'What do you mean?' Adanost started, but I shut him down.

'Just go!' For once they obeyed, all except Liara, who stood holding the letter in her hands. Staring at it like she was going mad. It must have felt that way.

'Someone made you write this,' I said. 'And I know who, and I know how they did it. But they had to get to you. Had to get a hand on you. That's how the Fourth Gate works, isn't it? They can't control you, but they can make you forget. That's what was done to me. Ulovar made me forget how to feel grief. But it only works as long as they can touch you.'

'I— Yes, that's true. But nobody would—'

'Somebody has. You've been used, and you haven't even been aware of it,' I said. 'I'll explain it all later. But for now, you have to help me. I need to know what holdings Clan LacShale has that have entrances to the undercity. Some kind of run-down place.' I tried to summon back everything that I could recall, the day Hess had driven me in the blacked-out carriage. 'It's somewhere where you can hear a lot of dogs barking. That's where they've taken him.'

'Do you think someone has hurt him?' Liara asked. There was genuine concern in her voice.

'I don't know. They wanted him alive before. But whatever it is, it coincides with Ulovar's trial tomorrow. And if I don't get to him before they do whatever they've planned, then they win. And they do not get to win. A run-down place. An entrance to the undercity. Lots of dogs nearby. Where?'

Liara blinked back tears.

'There was a place, years ago. Just tenements, on Smallacre Street. I've not been there since I was a girl, but—there was a dog farm one street away. For packs of hunting dogs. I used to be allowed to pet them sometimes.'

'Then that's where they're taking him,' I said.

'Should I come with you?' Liara asked. She seemed earnest.

'No,' I said. I shouldered the bow. 'The bastards tried to play me. But I don't have to play by their rules anymore.'

35

Grooms do not get enough credit. You go into a stable, ask for a groom and they have your horse saddled and ready to carry you in an astonishingly small amount of time. Horses, well, horses can be temperamental, and maybe they don't want to carry you as fast as you want to go, but you have to hand it to the grooms.

South wasn't happy at being brought out of her stall so late at night, but she didn't really have any choice, and I was off towards Harranir. Could have waited for actual Draoihn to come help me. Could have gone and explained everything I knew, although that would likely have gone very badly for me. But every minute that I spent trying to make somebody else understand was another minute closer to Kaldhoone's plan coming to fruition—whatever it was.

I had rough directions towards Smallacre Street. I could find it. I'd only paused to grab what I needed. My leather wrist guard, enough of my own arrows to hide the ones that I'd stolen from the Blackwell, a lantern and a hood. Not much of an arsenal, but it would have to do.

By the time I was down the mountain path and into Harranir, dawn could only have been an hour away, two at the very most. The sleepy guards at the gates noted the direction I'd travelled from, saw the Clan LacNaithe insignia on my hood and waved me through.

I found Smallacre Street. The dogs must have been sleeping. Everything was quiet. I rode past once, glancing up and down for anyone standing outside, but it all seemed pretty calm. I had no choice about leaving my horse. I hitched South to a post on the next street, hoping that her Redwinter brand would be enough to keep late-night passersby from deciding to try their luck, but truth be told, the penalty for horse theft was a swift hanging, and no horse trader would risk that for a profit. But it didn't matter. There was no time to worry about it.

I slunk in the shadows, the night black and solid beneath a high, open moon. Moved swiftly from darkness to darkness. I was angry. So, so angry. The way that I'd felt when I saw Sanvaunt's body, sprawled facedown in the mud. I'd thought he was gone. I'd thought I'd lost out on chances I'd never thought to take. And I wouldn't allow that to happen to me again. My life was my own.

I found it. I knew it by the closed double doors, a tunnel big enough for a carriage to pass through. A smaller door was set into them. I dismissed the idea of giving it a kick. This needed to be done slowly. Carefully. But Light Above, I needed to move now.

I pressed a hand against the smaller door's hinges, pushed it open a crack and peeked inside. The courtyard I'd seen before lay beyond, and the building to the left held the entrance down into the undercity. A lone figure sat on watch. A man I didn't recognise, biting his fingernails, bored, sat atop a wooden crate. He looked so ordinary. So plain and uninteresting. Nothing about him to say that he was the lookout for dark work. Maybe he was just some local man, hired in to stand watch. He had a sheathed sword on the crate beside him, but he didn't look like a warrior.

I would never find out who, or what, he was. There was no time for that. I pushed the door open with my foot, my arrow already drawn. He fell backwards over the crate as the force of the midnight-bow punched into him. Just an ordinary arrow, a bodkin head. He didn't make a sound. An easy shot at this range. An arrow through the heart, or close enough. I ran to him quickly, quietly, and drew Esher's short, curved sword. Easier to use than the hatchet had been back in the woods. I came away sticky. Red.

I breathed a gasp of relief. I thought it would feel different this time. Thought that since the scar had cracked and shredded away from my mind that I would be struck with the thoughts of the girl who had wept and screamed in Dalnesse Monastery. But she was gone. The scarred girl was gone too, and I was something new, and different. I was the sum of the experiences, and all that grief was down within me somewhere, but there was so much anger flowing through me, determination like I had never known. I was not Raine from Dalnesse, or Raine beneath the scar; I had shed my old skin and become something else. Not broken by Braithe, not the Raine who could end a life without a thought. I was stronger. Powerful. If Kaldhoone LacShale did not fear me, then he ought to.

There had only been one sentry. I took back my arrow, saw I'd lost the tip inside his chest somewhere and tossed the useless shaft away. It didn't matter. He had a key to the old tenement, and I took his knife as well, tucked it into my boot. The building had that same, wall-piss stink, and I descended down into the darkness beneath the world. I'd brought a lantern, but hadn't checked it for fuel. Only one-third full. It would have to do. I didn't plan on being here long anyway.

I would like to say that my plan was to rescue Ovitus, to force them to release him at arrow-point. But I already knew that wasn't likely. There were people down here who had tried to kill me. People who had tried to kill people I had come to care about. People who had summoned demons from the Night Below. And people who needed to be silenced.

I couldn't keep my bow drawn with the lantern in hand, so I slung it over my shoulder and carried the sword. The lines of chalk, marked with chevrons, still showed me the way. I heard scuttling in the dark. Pale faces, maybe not quite as human as they should have been, appeared now and again, squirming away from the light that invaded the under-streets of once-mighty Delatmar. I wondered if this great city had ever seen the likes of the Mawleth that I'd destroyed back in Redwinter. This part ought to be easy. Raine, demon slayer. Write me a fecking song.

The chalk led me to the door I needed. I dimmed the lantern until it was barely a glow, sorted through the guard's ring of keys. Found one that worked on the second try. I raised the hood over my hair. No point giving them a bright white target. Nocked an arrow, held two others in my bow hand. This had to be over quickly. I could hear voices beyond the door, muffled. They had the numbers. I only had surprise.

I eased into the room. I had once thought it a bathhouse of some kind. Somehow I'd known that this was where they would bring Ovitus. It was so throne-like. Too much a seat of a darkling king's power. Kaldhoone LacShale saw himself as an avenger. Thought himself righteous, both when he'd murdered his consort's husband, and again now as he sought to avenge himself on Ulovar. Starting with his nephew. Passing through the doorway, I came out behind one of the pillars and slipped up behind it. Risked a look across the room.

Like some kind of grandiose, barbarian playhouse show, the conspirators had lit pitch torches in sconces around the room. Light cast back from blackly gleaming water in the central depression. It wasn't just for drama. For them, this was some kind of ritual. The man who had called himself Veretaine sat in his shadowed throne in the centre. He was flanked by four people on either side, his followers, dressed in long, formal robes like holy absolution brothers. Five men, three women. Hess was among them, and Najih, the thick-wristed woman. Just in front of them all, two of the men held Ovitus by the shoulders. He was on his knees, his heavy shape slumped, head hanging, but he was alive. Which was something. I wasn't too late.

'My only regret in all this is that I will not get to see your uncle's face as he realises the truth,' Kaldhoone LacShale said. His hood had been cast back to reveal the empty pits where his eyes had been torn from his tormented face. 'But I will feel it.'

'I have done nothing,' Ovitus protested.

'You never do,' Kaldhoone said. He leaned forwards, wincing as his bony, twisted fingers pressed against his knees. 'None of you ever stop and think. I took my vengeance against a man who killed an innocent woman. And behold. See what your uncle did to me.'

'You spoke with the dead,' Ovitus whimpered. 'It was the law. He had to do it. It was his duty.'

'Duty. Is that what this was?' Kaldhoone said. 'Do you think your uncle's sense of justice extends to all?'

'Of course,' Ovitus said.

'Good. I am counting on it. You see, young heir to Clan LacNaithe, he is going to have to do it again. He is going to have to follow his precious law. Do his precious duty. And he is going to do it to you. Justice will be served.'

'Justice will be served,' Those Who See intoned in unison.

'I'm no nightcrafter,' Ovitus said. And for a moment I found a touch of warmth in my heart for his defiance. 'You commune with the dead. You see the unliving. Whereas, I am a true servant of Clan LacNaithe and Redwinter. If I have to die for it, then so be it.'

Kaldhoone didn't laugh. He was too torn, too broken for that. But his lip quirked in a grisly sneer.

'Oh, you will die, Ovitus of Clan LacNaithe. And once you have died, we shall pump the water from your lungs and force breath between your lips. And you shall live again, and you will be cast back into the midst of your uncle's own trial. Revealed for what you are. You see, young man, I am not going to leave you dead. I am going to change you. You will be as you term us, a nightcrafter. When we die and come back, that knowledge of the dead returns with us, you see. And no, no, it won't be your fault. Just as it wasn't my fault.'

'Or mine,' Hess said.

'Or mine,' Najih joined in.

Kaldhoone reached forwards to stroke Ovitus's sweat-soaked hair. 'I will make you one of us. And then, to prove his innocence, your uncle will have no choice. He will have to order you blinded. To order your limbs smashed by hammers. To have your broken, shattered carcass dragged through the streets. And he will watch you hurled into the harbour. Do you think that the likes of Van LacClune and Van LacAud would accept anything less? Would Grandmaster Robilar allow you to walk free? I think not. I could have killed your uncle. I could have burned the air around him as he walked by me unsuspecting. But his life will be nothing once this is done. I will rip his mind apart with grief. And then, and only then, will I have inflicted on him a fate worse than what he has done to me.'

'Please,' Ovitus said. 'Please. I'm innocent.'

'We were all innocent,' Kaldhoone hissed. 'Justice will be served.'

'Justice will be served,' his followers chanted.

'Oh, I don't know about that,' I said as I stepped around the pillar, my arrow levelled towards the throne. 'It's the weak who waste their breath insisting that life be fair. Get your hands off him right now, or you're all going to die for a second time. Me, I've died twice already, so that would only make us even. But I'll make damn sure you don't get up again this time.'

Dark eyes turned on me, half-shadowed at the far end of the pool. Nobody made to move.

'Ah,' Kaldhoone said. 'Our little sister. I had thought it strange that the Mawleths disappeared. Am I to assume that you managed to dispose of them?'

'They weren't so tough,' I said.

Sanvaunt, facedown in the mud.

'I had thought to bring you into our midst,' Kaldhoone said. Hess and Najih began to split away from the onlookers.

'Any of you move and I'm letting this fly,' I said. 'Don't think I give two shits about any of you. Let the boy go. Send him over here.'

'How quaint,' Kaldhoone said. 'But you have very little idea of what you're dealing with.'

I knew enough to track him down here to his secret lair, and still men were underestimating me.

Ridiculous.

'I know what you are,' I said. The holes in Kaldhoone's face narrowed, an old reflex for empty, ire-filled sockets. His lip quirked.

'Then you know that you cannot contend with the Gates that I command. I am not like you, little sister. Arrows have no power over me.' He flicked an impatient claw. 'Drown the boy.'

There is a point in every conversation where there's nothing left that's worth saying. A point where the argument can go on, where words can be traded, ideas thrust and parried, and everybody knows that nothing is going to change. Few people's minds are ever changed by talk. It is much easier to change them with an arrow.

I loosed three in succession, snatching them from my bow hand as quickly as I loosed them. The two men holding Ovitus pitched backwards screaming. The third arrow I sent towards Kaldhoone.

It shattered in the air before him, wood, metal and fletching flying apart as I felt his trance flare to life. Taine, the Third Gate, the mastery of the energies of the world. It roared like a rolling avalanche of snow as it obliterated trees and clans. He thrust a hand towards me, and I saw the momentary build-up of light around his hand, just in time to hurl myself back behind the pillar. A bolt of blue-white lightning ripped across the room, missing my hiding place by inches, blasting stones from the back wall, filling the air with the smell of scorched metal.

A pretty good shot for a man who didn't have any eyes. He wasn't just in Taine, he was in Eio, probably Sei as well. Three trances blazing together at once, *DHUMDHUM DHUMDHUM* thundering through my mind, but they were wild, undisciplined, filled with raw power but lacking all finesse. However powerful he was, Kaldhoone LacShale was still human. People have their limits, and working three trances at once couldn't be easy.

'Kill her!' Kaldhoone barked.

Well, shit.

There were still six of them, and perhaps he was right. In my anger, I'd ignored the fact that the man who had led this plot from the beginning, eyeless or not, commanded four Gates. Even blind, he could sense me with Eio. His hands may have been shattered, but he could harden his skin to stone with Sei. He may have been crippled, but he could draw on Taine to throw fire and lightning. And while I knew he was prepared to manipulate the minds of his subjects with Fier, he did not control them. People made all kinds of bad decisions. Out of fear, out of misplaced hope, out of desperation. But nobody was making them drown Ovitus, and that made them fair targets.

Hess and Najih ducked left, while the other four acolytes ran right for the cover of the row of pillars that lined the room. Ovitus staggered backwards, tripped over his own cloak and splashed into the pool that they'd intended to drown him in. He looked around in terrified panic, splashing and falling, thrashing and falling again in the chest-deep water.

I drew one of the Blackwell arrows. There was no point holding back now. I saw the larger group, drawing weapons from beneath their robes, swords and hatchets. Plenty of them to do the job on me. It would only take one of them to get close. I drew and then let fly at the nearest. Not a hard shot, but it wouldn't have mattered if it had been.

The arrow evaporated as it left the bow. A ribbon of blazing white light arced across the room and detonated among them in a flaring burst of energy. The acolytes screamed, their bodies cast into incandescent profile as the light hurled them across the room, smashing into the walls, knocking a torch from its sconce to sputter and die in the water. These were really good arrows.

Choking dust billowed across the room, the air filled with debris.

'What's happening?' Kaldhoone cried. 'What was that? Kill her. Kill her now!' His head switched side to side as though if he only strained enough, he might grow new eyes and be able to see me. I reached for another arrow.

Hess and Najih charged towards me down the row of columns, swords drawn and raised, ready to cut me through. I ran for the far side of the room, towards the other row of pillars. Kaldhoone sensed it, the beat of his trance thundering around us, so loud and chaotic in my head that it would have burst my eardrums if it was any true sound. He lashed out, and the fire from the torches flowed together into a ball and then spat across the room. I threw myself forwards just as a hand snatched for the back of my cloak, and a scream rang out behind me. I rolled across the ground, looked back to see Najih writhing against the wall, her whole body engulfed in bright fire, her skin melted and sizzling against the wall. Hess staggered back behind her. The torchlight was gone. Only the firelight of Najih's shaking body lit the room. Her eyes melted from her sockets, her tongue blackened, shrivelling. Hess screamed a furious battle cry and ran past her.

From the floor, I drew an arrow and loosed it into him. He reeled, white fletching in his shoulder. I had new cover from behind the pillar. I grabbed the next arrow from my quiver and sent another one into him, taking him high in the gut. He staggered, still not quite done, but his legs were starting to deny him as he closed. I dropped my bow, drew Esher's sword and met his downward swipe with a clang. Had the former Clan LacShale soldier been on his best form, I doubt that I could have matched him, but he had two arrows in him, and dying was slowing him down. He swung again; I made an easy parry to the side and hacked back at him. My sword hewed through his face, finishing the work on his lips that a rock had done years before, and he fell away.

Najih's whimpers faded slowly. Her vocal cords had burned away. And hopefully her mind. She may have followed Kaldhoone's deranged plan, may have plotted murder with him, but that was a horrible way to go. A way I might easily go. I lay panting, my back up against a pillar. The sizzling flames across her body were the only light left to us. I couldn't hear Ovitus splashing around in the pool any longer. The only thing I could hear was the raggedness of my breathing.

'I know where you are, girl,' Kaldhoone said. 'You think I cannot sense you? Your arrows cannot hurt me, child. It is only a matter of time before you die here.'

'I'm trying not to think about that,' I shouted back. Sweat ran in rivulets down my face. I tried to push my mind back through the First Gate, but as I did, my head shrieked in pain. I wasn't trained. I didn't know how to access the Path of Self or the Path of Awareness. I only ever fell into it by accident. And soon I was going to be blind here. 'I tell you what, though,' I called into the dark at the far end of the hall. 'You're going to have a hard time getting out of here, aren't you? I'm guessing that was all your people. Maybe you can crawl. Maybe you can find a way out of here. But I doubt it.'

A blast of force smashed into the pillar, obliterating stone and sending shards of broken masonry spinning through the air. Something sharp lashed across my face, a ricochet. Blood ran beneath my eye, but I barely felt the sting of the laceration.

'Yes, keep talking child,' Kaldhoone said. 'Keep talking and you'll have your second death soon enough.'

'I told you earlier,' I called back as I fished in my quiver for one of the Blackwell arrows. 'My birth-cord strangled me once, and then I fell into a lake.' The Blackwell arrows were four inches longer than the rest. It wasn't hard. I still had four. 'Maybe if you'd died more often, you wouldn't be so mad about it.' Four arrows. If more of them would turn into lightning, I might just still pull this off. But the truth was, I had no idea why that one had worked when the others had simply buried themselves into the Mawleth. They might explode in my face, for all I knew. That's the chance you take when you steal from the Draoihn's holy vault.

'You really think you have the strength to beat me, child?' Kaldhoone croaked.

'I'm not sure. I'm learning a lot about myself today.'

Okay. Time to do this.

I pushed myself to my feet, wincing as something sharp cut into my thigh. A chunk of masonry, dagger-shaped, dagger-sharp, had buried itself in me. I hadn't noticed it before, too full up on battle-rush and the prospect of impending death. But I felt it now. I screamed and slid back down onto my arse. Felt the blood running across my thigh. I didn't need the pain. I needed it to go away. Not now. Not now. I had to be fast. Had to move like shadows and wind. But I couldn't even see him anymore, we were both too far from the feeble light emanating from Najih's burning remains. The stink of hot bacon grease permeated the air.

'Don't want to come out anymore, is that it?' Kaldhoone said. 'You think I pity myself? I should have died in that harbour. It was only my hold on these people that had me fished from the water. I've faced death in a way that you can only dream of.'

'It's not a fecking competition!'

Another blast of concussive force hammered into the pillar, chips of deadly stone flurrying past me, bouncing from the walls. I heard the crack run through the pillar's core, old and deep, and even as the agony coursed through my leg, I made myself stand. Flakes of stone began to fall away. I braced my wounded leg. And then I hurled myself towards the next pillar in line.

Kaldhoone had been driven to cruelty in his thirst for revenge. Beyond cruelty, deep into a mad, sick place in which nothing mattered but his own need for revenge. But he still commanded Gates, and they weren't slowed by his crippling. Another blast ripped past me, missing me by a hair's breadth, but this time it tore my cloak and the quiver of arrows from my back, scattering them against the back wall.

No!

They were my chance. My only remaining weapon against him. I still had my sword, but what good was that going to do against power of that kind? The last light from the burning woman's body was fading, the intense heat consuming the last of her, leaving us in total blackness. Me, at least. For Kaldhoone, everything had been dark to begin with.

A great cracking sound ran through the ceiling above us. The remains of the broken pillar collapsed into rubble, and a great groaning began in the blackness. A key part of the structure had been brought down. The whole place might come down with it. I hoped that Ovitus was swimming quietly away; he'd gone quiet. I didn't think that even he could manage to drown if he could put his feet to the bottom.

The spirits of the men and women that I'd killed were beginning to rise around the room. They looked around in horror, staring at ghostly hands, shaking their ghostly heads. I lay against the pillar and let the breath flow in, flow out. I could hear Kaldhoone wheezing. His power was not unlimited. He had to draw it from somewhere. But I suspected that he still had enough to break me, limping as I was.

I saw Hess's spirit. He stared at Najih, charred and melted to the wall. Her own spirit had emerged too. She looked to Hess, an aching depth of sadness cast through her features.

'We never wanted this,' she said as she reached out to touch his face, but her ghost hand passed through him as she faded away into nothing. Hess remained. He looked from me, then to Kaldhoone. He threw his head back and howled, a scream of pain and grief.

'I served you,' he roared. 'I saved you. And you did this to us? You used us. You took my mind!'

The ghost stormed across the room. Where he moved, a dim light moved with him as he stalked ghost-steps over the water, and I saw Ovitus beneath him, cowering in the pool, unaware of the shade that passed over him.

'Oh, enough, Hessen,' Kaldhoone growled. 'You were a sworn-sword. You served me in any way I saw fit.'

I winced as I shifted, and another well of blood spilled down my leg.

'There was no new, fairer world,' Hess said. 'You just wanted to use the old one.' He stood impotently before his former master, just an angry ghost on the wind. Powerless.

Or was he? I'd helped a spirit before, the shade of a dead shepherd.

'Hessen,' I called out. 'Take it. Take what you need.'

I reached out to him. Not with a hand or leg, but with whatever it is that connects us beyond the physical. Eio shows us that we are all one thing, all merely different parts of a whole, only separated by gaps of nothing, and nothing is nothing, so we are all one. But the spirit-sight showed me that there was more to this world. That there was something of us that goes on beyond the darkness, that lives another life when we are gone. I reached for him, across the gulf of space, the nothing that connected us, and I began to feed myself into him.

The wispy light that surrounded him began to intensify. Solidified. Hess's ghost began to strengthen, his wisp-shrouded form hardening, curling vapours becoming solid lines. Cold stole through my body, from my feet and hands, and then from my very core. I gasped as it began to leave me. Gasped as I felt a chill behind my eyes, as my lips began to numb. My jaw locked tight, and I screamed.

'What are you—no—' Kaldhoone said. Ghostly hands reached out and took hold of him beneath the arms. 'No—it's not possible. It's not possible!'

He lashed out with the fury, the force he had left. Blasts of force, of fire, sparks of lightning and beams of darkness flashed out across the room, smashing into pillars, crumbling stone, hissing as they met the water. But Hess's ghostly hands continued to lift him up. Kaldhoone tried to bat at him, swinging his ruined limbs, but there was nothing there to connect to.

My legs were numb. My head was speared with damning cold; my face had locked rigid as I continued to reach out, to pour my vitality into the dead man. And then there was a splash as Hess tossed Kaldhoone into the pool. Not much force behind it. Not much of anything.

'That's enough, darlin',' Hess's ghost said. He folded his arms. He'd been handsome once. There was no split in his lip in the realm of the dead, no missing teeth. I sagged, the last strength I possessed failing me. I was cold. So cold. There was splashing coming from the pool. Gasps and choking sounds. Kaldhoone couldn't stand. Couldn't pull himself out. I would have liked to have seen his ghost. But there was nothing left in me, not heat, not blood, and besides, I could hear that the roof was starting to come down.

36

The trial of Ulovar LacNaithe, son of Ulovaine LacNaithe, van of his clan, and Lord Draoihn of Redwinter, began on a day when the mist lay low and thick upon the ground. Rumours leapt like wildfire that morning. Some were claiming that demonic forces had appeared within Redwinter itself. Others said that the van's nephew had absconded with his commoner lover during the night. The Council of Night and Day came together, and they sat and listened to the accounts of what was known. The account that Van Ulovar could give of himself, and how his apprentice Hazia, once fostered at his home, could have come to breach the Blackwell, to try to unleash the dead back on the world. Sanvaunt LacNaithe, shadow-eyed and leaning on a crutch, tried to make some fanciful claims, that somehow a dead man was behind it all, but the councillors were not impressed. A last desperate attempt to keep his kin alive. His words were met with derision.

I missed all of that. I limped into the great Round Chamber sometime after midday, leaning on the shoulder of the young man who had dragged and carried me out of the darkness. I had been unable to stand. Barely able to speak, even when he took wrong turns. We ended up emerging from the ancient undercity of Delatmar in some other part of the city, maybe a sewer, but that memory, like all of that journey, was hazy. I clutched our prize beneath my arm the whole way. With what little strength remained to me, I had held on and wouldn't let it go.

Ulovar was thinner than last I'd seen him. Frayed at the edges, just as I was. But his bloody eyes took on a new light as he looked at us. I tried to smile, but my face wouldn't move.

The grandmaster was lush and beautiful at her gilded lectern. She stared down at the two newcomers in this place of law and ruling with hard, dangerous eyes. We were filthy from crawling through dust-filled passages, and I could see the assembly looking down on us. My eyes were sunken, my skin as pale as snow, my lips nearly blue. I leaned on a straight midnight-blue stick threaded with veins of silver.

'Apprentice LacNaithe, you appear with exceptional tardiness,' Grandmaster Vedira Robilar called down as we interrupted the councillors' deliberations. I didn't listen to what they were saying. None of that mattered now.

'Pardon my lateness, Grandmaster,' Ovitus said. He propped me up carefully and then stepped aside to bow. It was all I could do to remain upright against what I was hoping nobody would realise was the bow I'd stolen from the Blackwell.

'I assume you are here to plead your uncle's innocence?' Robilar said, her voice ringing out, louder than it had any right to.

'No, Grandmaster,' Ovitus said. 'I will speak if I must. But it is not for me to tell you. I present to you First Retainer Raine, of the mountains.'

The council's eyes switched to me, the pale, white-haired girl barely able to stand before them. I reached into the sack I had beneath my arm. It seemed to take everything I had to hook my fingers into the eye sockets. But I dragged out my prize and tossed it into the centre of the room.

'The head of Kaldhoone LacShale,' I said. 'Whom you believe suffered your justice, four years ago. Who plotted against the man who stands accused today. Who abducted Ovitus LacNaithe, to try to turn him into a nightcrafter.'

'You expect us to believe this girl? Some servant?' a hard-faced man on the councillor's bench said derisively. He had a resemblance to Castus LacClune. His father, I supposed.

'I had to kill a lot of people to get this head,' I said. 'And you all should have done a better job of killing him the first time.'

The chamber erupted. I staggered, but strong hands caught me. Not Ovitus. Dragging me around had tested his limits as well. Even though I wanted to be furious at him, technically he had dragged me out of there and saved my life. He still had a lot of grovelling to do. But an arm scooped in beneath my shoulders, holding me up. I could hear the voices behind me as I was led from the hall.

'This trial is over,' Robilar called out. 'We have proof before us that Sanvaunt LacNaithe's testimony is true. I see no further case to answer. Ulovar LacNaithe is to go free, to continue his work as a loyal servant of the Crown.'

'But, Grandmaster,' LacClune said savagely. 'We cannot just take her word. She is just a commoner. She has no clan. She's not even Draoihn.'

'No, Merovech,' Robilar's voice echoed over him, magnified, bouncing from the wall. 'But she will be.' I looked back at her over my shoulder. A dangerous smile played across her lips. 'Go and rest, Apprentice Raine. I am sure you have a story to tell me in time. But for now, you look like the dead.'

Well. There was probably more truth to that than she realised.

· · · · · ·

I lay on my back, staring up into a winter sky that was empty of everything, and so open to possibilities that it had never seemed more foreign, or more welcoming. Esher lay at an angle to me, the tops of our heads nearly touching, hair fanning out in the grass. It felt good to be out in the light. I'd been abed for six days. I couldn't face being spoon-fed anymore, or any more staring at the ceiling. The occasional battle shout or clash of swords rang from a practice field not far away.

'Do you think you should get a special title for being a hero?' Esher asked. 'Something special we should call you?'

'I liked it when you called me Fiahd,' I said.

'Wildcats are only small,' she said.

'What exactly are you suggesting?'

'You took down some pretty big game.'

I propped myself up on one elbow so I could look her in the eye.

'Do you ever feel like you're falling? Like there's just so much world, and you don't know where you're going to land in it?'

'Maybe after a lot of whisky.'

'We should get moon horses. One each. See where they take us.'

I lay down again. Such an empty expanse of sky over the mountains. The first clear sky we'd seen in a while. The mountain breeze was brisk, but I liked it that way. Cold on the skin. Bright, somehow.

'How are you feeling?' Esher asked. We hadn't had much opportunity to talk. Redwinter had been a throng of activity as they scoured the city, and undercity, to make sure that the threat was over, that the Crown was secure. Even Clan LacClune put all their weight behind it. Ulovar had put his apprentices straight back to their training.

'I feel like I died a while ago and got replaced. And then someone took the dead girl and the new girl and mixed them up together, and now I'm whatever came out the other end of a sausage mincer. There was a time when I couldn't feel anything. And then I think that maybe there was a time when I chose not to. But it's good. I think I'm me. Really me. Maybe. Is it all right not to know?'

'I meant your leg,' Esher said. 'But yes. We're only seventeen. We're learning. I think it's all right not to know how you feel about some things.'

There was a lot more I could have said about that, but not to Esher. Perhaps not to anybody. And I thought maybe that wasn't so bad a thing. I'd hidden who and what I was for so long. At times I'd hated myself. I hadn't chosen my grave-sight, but even if I had, what did it matter? I was a good person, I thought. Not the arm-flower that Braithe had wanted me to be. Not the underfoot pest my mother blamed her condition on. Not a nightcrafter, twisting and plotting in the dark. I was Raine, once of the High Pastures, now of Redwinter. I didn't know all that much about her. She got to be whatever she wanted to be.

A wide, hunched figure made his way along a gravel path, heading towards the greathouse. He glanced in our direction, then averted his eyes. Wise decision. Ovitus had kept himself cloistered whenever he wasn't forced down to a lesson. It was the fastest I'd seen him move within the grounds.

'Have you spoken to him yet?' Esher asked.

'No,' I said. 'Despite what he told Sanvaunt, I can't help but feel sorry for him. He was nearly murdered. And he did drag me out of there when the roof was coming down.'

'But his lies are not so easy to forgive.'

'I don't know what choice we have. We're allied with LacNaithe, aren't we? He did a stupid, jealous thing, but it's not like he set demons on me or tried to burn me alive. I'm waiting for him to apologise. And when he does, I'll give him a piece of my mind, and he'll sulk a bit, and then maybe we'll be friends again.'

'But he'll be van one day,' Esher said. 'We're supposed to be able to trust him. How do you trust a man who'll do that to you? How can you follow his orders, after what he did?'

'Maybe this was the lesson he needed to be taught,' I said, dismissing the uncomfortable thought. The truth was, I did worry that if I continued down this path, one day it would be Ovitus who gave the orders, Ovitus's house that I lived in, Ovitus who controlled my life. But I'd changed these past months, and maybe so could he. I told myself that when I needed to.

Ovitus disappeared into the greathouse. Esher rolled over and kissed me on the forehead.

'Fiahd,' she said. 'Maybe that is your hero name.' She pushed up on her elbows. 'I should go and see Liara. She's not been doing so well.'

'You think I should see her too?'

'No. Not yet. You killed her father. That takes some time to work through. Besides. I think Ulovar wants you.'

We hugged a goodbye, and she went off on her way. I picked up the blanket we'd lain on and joined Ulovar, who sat on a wall watching the Draoihn at their sword practice. He looked better, but his eyes were still red as sunset. We both carried scars from that day beneath Dalnesse, and we always would. I sat beside him.

'There are a great many things that don't make sense in the story you told Grandmaster Robilar,' Ulovar said.

I watched the Draoihn at their practice, swords flowing in whirls and arcs in a display of perfect unison.

'A lot of them don't make sense to me either,' I said.

'Like how you escaped from a Mawleth,' Ulovar said.

'Sanvaunt killed it,' I said.

'Mawleths always come in pairs, Raine,' he told me. 'And the grandmaster knows that. Sanvaunt achieved something unbelievable by killing even one. He claims not to recall how he did it, but no Draoihn of the First Gate should have been capable of it. The grandmaster sees the loose threads as easily as I. She's pondering the same questions I am.'

'I know,' I said. 'Would you believe me if I said that I don't remember?'

'No.'

'What if I said I killed it myself?'

'Also, no.'

I shrugged.

'Not many more options, are there? But I'm still alive, and even if the winter isn't done yet, it feels good to be outside. Sun on my face. That's all I ever really wanted from life, I think. Just some sun. Not a great deal to ask, is it?'

Ulovar smiled at me. It was such a rare thing to see. Although, I wondered, perhaps he'd be able to smile more now. He was a man of duty and honour. To be cast down and challenged on it must have broken his heart. He'd borne it better than I could have.

Ulovar stood, put his hands around his mouth and shouted.

'Sanvaunt, for the sake of the Light Above, get your posture right. I've never seen you so bloody distracted.'

On the training lawn, Sanvaunt paused for a moment, nodded and shook himself out. He rejoined the flow of the drill smoothly. But I was sure he flicked his eyes towards me just briefly. Maybe things were different now. Maybe he could allow himself to be a little bit distracted. It was, of course, absolutely not my fault. I ran a hand through the back of my hair, looked up at the sky.

'What now?' I asked. 'Now that you're free and it's all over. What happens next?'

'Well, for one thing, you have to learn the actual words for dawnsong, noon-song and evensong,' Ulovar grunted. 'No more mouthing them and pretending. And once you're strong enough, you'll be meeting under Master Hylan with the rest of the apprentices. I'll be training you to reach the First Gate properly. And after that? Who knows. There's always something needs doing.'

'Or something that needs killing,' I said.

'Well, yes. Unfortunately, there's that too.'

I pulled the blanket closer around myself and nestled against him. Rested my head on his shoulder, like he was my uncle too. Like he was family.

And for a little while, I was content to pretend that maybe he was.

Dramatis Personae

Dalnesse Monastery

Raine (clanless)—A girl who abandoned her mother to follow the sooth-sisters

Braithe of Sealand—Raine's lover, in assumed command of Dalnesse's defence, formerly a sailor

Sister Marthella—One of the sooth-sisters, accused of terrible crimes

Sister Anthra—One of the sooth-sisters

Lochlan—A farmer who joined the sooth-sisters

Kella—One of the sisters' followers, formerly a court musician

Farlan—One of the sisters' followers, formerly fought in the Kwendish civil wars

Fergus—One of the sisters' followers, a brawler

Niven LacCulloch—A lord, holding the rank of thail

LacNaithe Household in Redwinter

Ulovar LacNaithe—Van of the clan, Draoihn of the Fourth Gate, holds one of the seats on the Council of Night and Day

Ovitus LacNaithe—Heir to the LacNaithe clanhold, nephew to Ulovar, cousin to Sanvaunt, holds the rank of thail as well as being an apprentice

Sanvaunt LacNaithe—Draoihn of the First Gate, nephew of Ulovar, cousin to Ovitus

Esher of Harranir—An apprentice sponsored by Ulovar

Jathan of Kwend—An apprentice sponsored by Ulovar

Adanost of Murr—An apprentice sponsored by Ulovar

Colban Giln—An apprentice sponsored by Ulovar

Gelis LacAud—An apprentice sponsored by Ulovar

Liara LacShale—An apprentice sponsored by Ulovar, youngest daughter of Kaldhoone LacShale

Hazia LacFroome—An apprentice sponsored by Ulovar, fostered at Valarane with Sanvaunt and Ovitus

Tarquus of Redwinter—First Retainer, servant

Ehma of Harranir—Second Retainer, servant

Howen of Harranir—Second Retainer, servant

Bossal of Harranir—Fifth Retainer, servant
Patalia of Harranir—Fifth Retainer, servant

LacClune Clanhold

Merovech LacClune—Van of the clan, Draoihn of the Fourth Gate, holds one of the seats on the Council of Night and Day, father of Castus
Haronus LacClune—Draoihn of the Third Gate
Castus LacClune—An apprentice living at Redwinter, son of Merovech

The Council of Night and Day

Grandmaster Vedira Robilar—Leader of the Draoihn order, head of the council, Draoihn of the Fifth Gate
Kelsen of Harranir—The king's personal healer, Draoihn of the Fifth Gate
Ulovar LacNaithe—Van of Clan LacNaithe, Draoihn of the Fourth Gate, usually at Redwinter, uncle of Ovitus and Sanvaunt
Onostus LacAud—Draoihn of the Fourth Gate
Hanaqin (clanless)—Draoihn of the Fourth Gate
Lassaine LacDaine—Draoihn of the Second Gate, great-niece to King Quinlan LacDaine, commander of the Winterra
Merovech LacClune—Van of Clan LacClune, Draoihn of the Fourth Gate, father of Castus
Kyrand of Murr—Draoihn of the Third Gate
Suanach LacNaruun—Draoihn of the Second Gate, master of artifice

Rulers

King Quinlan LacDaine—King of Harran, bearer of the Crown, father of Caelan LacDaine
Prince Caelan LacDaine—Prince of Harran, son of Quinlan LacDaine, with the Winterra, fighting wars for the king of Brannlant
Henrith II—King of Brannlant

Those Who See

Veretaine
Hess
Najih

Legendary Figures

Hallenae the Riven Queen—Made war against the world, defeated at Solemn Hill by Maldouen and the last surviving generals. Hallenae was imbued with the power of the Night Below, which was bound and stored in five Crowns. Slain over seven hundred years ago. The year is counted from the date of her defeat.

The Faded—The lords of the hidden folk, long since banished from the world

The Mystic World

The Draoihn

The Draoihn enter a series of existentialist trances that allow them to expand their consciousness into the world around it, become one with it and then affect it. To do so, they open a Gate in their mind.

EIO: The First Gate—the Gate of Self. Allows exceptional sensory perception by expanding the essence of one's self into the connected world around. There are about one thousand Draoihn of the First Gate, most of whom are sent to serve the Winterra, supporting the king of Brannlant's territorial expansion.

SEI: The Second Gate—the Gate of Other. Allows the expansion of consciousness into nonliving matter in the physical world around the trance holder, and the manipulation of the Other. There are only one hundred Draoihn of the Second Gate, around half of whom serve under Suanach LacNaruun working on artifice at Redwinter.

TAINE: The Third Gate—the Gate of Energy. Allows the expansion of consciousness through energy, the transmission of that energy and its redirection. As every scientist knows, energy cannot be created or destroyed. There are only thirty Draoihn of the Third Gate.

FIER: The Fourth Gate—the Gate of Mind. Allows the expansion of consciousness into the minds of living creatures the trancing Draoihn touches, enabling them to impact the thought processes of that creature's mind. There are only four Draoihn of the Fourth Gate—Ulovar, Merovech, Hanaqin and Onostus.

VIE: The Fifth Gate—the Gate of Life. Allows the expansion of consciousness into the physical forms of oneself as well as other living matter. This is mostly used for healing. There are only two Draoihn of the Fifth Gate, Grandmaster Vedira Robilar and Kelsen of Harranir, who acts as the king's personal healer.

SKAL: The Sixth Gate—the Gate of Death. The old power of the Sarathi. Modern Draoihn are forbidden to even attempt to access it. There are no Draoihn of the Sixth Gate.

GEI: The Seventh Gate—the Gate of Creation. The Seventh Gate is purely theoretical, a concept used to understand how the Faded changed the world as they did thousands of years ago.

The Sarathi

Former Draoihn of the Sixth Gate, they sided with Hallenae the Riven Queen and enemies of the world.

The Hexen

Destroyed by the Draoihn during the Betrayal War, they burned the Glass Library of Redwinter.

The Knights of Tharada Taan

The knights drew their power from the Everstorm around Tharada Mountain, until the Draoihn destroyed it and ended their power.

Acknowledgements

For their assistance in bringing this story onto these pages, I would like to thank:

My agent, Ian Drury, who finds homes for the stories I've always wanted to tell.

My editor Claire Eddy, who saw Raine's potential and took her forward.

My editor Gillian Redfearn, who helped Raine to grow and champions her still.

Sanaa Ali-Virani and the team at Tor, whose tireless work keeps the cogs turning.

The team at Gollancz, whose labours never go unappreciated.

Gaia Banks, Alba Arnau and all of the team at Sheil Land Associates who have sent my words around the world.

And finally, this book would never have got here without the assistance, suggestions, and ongoing support of my first reader and editor, my inspiration, my companion and my love Catriona Ward, who is all the colours of my heart.

About the Author

ED MCDONALD is the author of the Raven's Mark and Redwinter Chronicles series of novels. He studied ancient history and archaeology at the University of Birmingham, and medieval history at Birkbeck, University of London. McDonald is passionate about fantasy tabletop role-play games and has studied medieval swordsmanship since 2013. He currently lives with his partner, author Catriona Ward, in London, England.